LEBENSBORN: Spawne... [illegible] world conquest, it was ... [illegible] swell the ranks of the master race—a dread arm of the SS that stormed across Europe killing, raping, destroying . . . stealing the children.

VICTORY: A small, surprisingly wealthy organization of simple, hard-working Americans. A sudden rash of deaths—all suspiciously linked to Victory—forces the issue. Where does the money come from? Where does it go?

Behind the grass-roots patriotism of Victory, does the evil of Lebensborn live on? Is there a link between Victory and the mysterious Odessa fortune, the largest private source of wealth —and most lethal economic weapon—the world has ever known?

THE AXMANN AGENDA
It may be unstoppable!

THE
AXMANN AGENDA

Mike Pettit

A DELL BOOK

Published by
Dell Publishing Co., Inc.
1 Dag Hammarskjold Plaza
New York, New York 10017

Dell ® TM 681510, Dell Publishing Co., Inc.

ISBN: 0-440-10152-2

Printed in the United States of America
First printing—February 1980

To Marilyn, Aubrey, and Lucille

ACKNOWLEDGMENTS

It is difficult to thank everyone who helped and inspired me in the writing of this book, but a few deserve special mention: My great friend Joe Armstrong; my agent, the incomparable Gloria Safier; and my editor, Linda Grey, whose patience and dedication will always be appreciated.

I would also like to thank Marcella Arnow, Barbara Moss, Terry Clark, Alice L. Smith, Mary Puspurica, Ellie Citrone, Arthur B. Calcagnini, Leslaw Jurewicz, John Verdier, Richard Beene, and Joy Cook.

THE
AXMANN AGENDA

PROLOGUE

Poland: June 1943.

It was the end of spring, and fear and panic ruled the land. Each day new rumors of terror and wholesale death spread from village to village, told in whispers behind closed doors.

The tide had turned against the Germans. In the middle of the deadliest winter of the war, they had been defeated at Stalingrad and were in retreat. The Allies had marched through northern Africa and were driving on to Sicily. The Jews had risen up in Warsaw and held the SS at bay for thirty-three days with nothing more than bricks and sticks and a few guns.

With each defeat, each humiliation, the Nazis redeemed themselves with new horrors against the weak, trampled people of occupied Europe.

In the concentration camps, the gas chambers and crematoria worked into the night. Whole villages were razed. *Einsatzkommandos* roamed the countryside killing suspected partisans on the spot. Slave labor poured into the great factories of the Ruhr and the Rhine, to send the *Wehrmacht* back to the field with new bullets and tanks and fresh uniforms.

In Poland spring came as always, strong and warm after a hard winter, completely indifferent in its beauty. The meadows grew sweet and green again. The flat brown fields were turned and planted with rye. Streams of blue forget-me-nots ran along the edges of winding country roads. In the sky, larks threaded between columns of black smoke rising from the chimneys of Auschwitz, Treblinka, and

Maidanek. The gardens of the death camps flourished in soil fertilized by ashes from the giant ovens. The oaks sprouted new leaves, and the men, women, and children of Poland marched to their graves.

In Europe they called it *Schwarzfrühling*, The Black Spring. By the end of summer, those who remained in the little village of Rydz outside Krakow called it *Śmierć przyszła wiosna,* the Spring of the Dead.

The day started early for the men of Rydz. The first light of morning came at three, a thin strip of gray at the edge of the horizon. By four a red sun was rising over the plains. By six the men, dressed in old shapeless caps and loose gray shirts, were in the fields, working under the eyes of the *Volksdeutsche,* ethnic Germans who lived in Poland and ruled the countryside as petty lords. The villagers sweated to produce the contribution demanded by the Nazis, for which they would be paid in bad vodka.

By noon the white sun was straight overhead.

Anya Masiewicz walked to the field where her husband was working, bringing him an extra piece of harsh bread for lunch. She was dressed plainly in a rough white cotton blouse and black skirt. Around her neck she wore a medallion with the imprint of the Holy Mary, a wedding gift from her husband in the days before the Germans. She brought her two small daughters with her—Margosha, three, and Ela, who was barely one. The older child clutched her mother's hand. Anya carried the little one in one arm with some difficulty, for she was late in her seventh month.

When Henryk saw his family coming toward the field, his face brightened. Margosha broke free and ran toward him. He bent down to lift her up and toss her gently in the air. The little girl cried out with joy, threw her arms around her father's neck, and held on tight. Anya followed close behind with Ela. Henryk stopped and kissed them both.

"I brought you another piece of bread, with butter," Anya said. "You will need it."

Henryk's face wrinkled into a frown. "You should save it for the children. There is not enough as it is."

"We have enough."

"It is too far for you to walk . . . with the children. You know better," he began, but Anya shushed him, with a sidelong glance toward Margosha, the three-year-old.

"I am strong enough," she said, and softened her rebuke with a smile.

"Tak," he said with affection. "That you are."

He looked with admiration at her protruding belly. She was a tall, sturdy woman, with thick blond hair and rounded hips, perhaps the descendant of the Teutonic knights who had conquered Poland in the twelfth century and left their seed in the countryside.

Margosha led Ela away.

When the children were out of hearing, Anya said: "Henryk . . . there is talk. About the Nazis."

The two little girls laughed in play in the distance.

Henryk wiped his forehead wearily. "What do they say?" he asked.

"They say they are taking the children. The Nazis are taking the children."

"Who says?"

"Old Tymoteusz, that's who. Old Tymoteusz says it."

Henryk frowned. Tymoteusz had been the chief of the village of Rydz for longer than Henryk had been alive. Tymoteusz was not given to idle talk. "It is the Jews, Anya. They are taking the Jews. The Hitlerites will not come here. All the Jews are gone. We have no more."

Henryk thought of his friend Moishe, the tailor, roused from his sleep in the middle of the night and taken away, never to be heard from again.

"That is not what they say," Anya insisted. "They are taking all the children, Polish children. Tymoteusz says they gather them in the school yard and take the pretty ones."

Henryk glanced at his two daughters playing in the shade of a linden. He always enjoyed parading them through the village. They were his two little beauties, blond and blue-eyed like their mother.

"They say the women in brown grab the children from their mothers. Sometimes they come in the night. They gather the children up and put them on trains. The same trains used for the Jews."

"There, you see. I told you so," Henryk said. "They are taking the Jews. They would not use the same train for Jews and Poles. That is the way they are, the Nazis."

But he did not believe it. He spat on the ground in disgust. *Przekleci Hitlerowcy*. Damned Germans. He hated them. They had turned his beloved Poland into a slaughterhouse.

"No, Henryk." Anya was trembling. The blood had left her face. "This time it is not the Jews. The women in brown were in the village today, with the SS. Tymoteusz said they were looking for children."

The women in brown. The Brown Sisters of the SS. Henryk had heard of them. Matronly, middle-aged women devoted to Hitler, who regarded all but Germans and Nordics as subhumans. Their brutality was becoming legend. They would tear a baby from the breast of its mother if it would serve the Führer.

"Did they see you?" he asked.

"No . . . I don't think so."

"The children?"

"I don't know."

"Go back to the village, Anya, and keep the children inside. Stay away from the road. If they do not see them, they will not take them. There is no reason for the Germans to know of us and our children. We have done nothing."

"Do you think that matters? You don't have to be a Jew or a partisan. That was in the beginning. Now it is enough to be a Pole."

Henryk put his hand on her shoulder. In the days before the Germans, that would have been enough to quiet her fears. Just his hand, large and rough, full of authority and love.

"What would the Germans do with a three-year-old girl?" he asked. "A little one who can barely walk? They want children to work in the fields, sew uniforms. Can our pretty ones do that? Eleven, twelve, yes, but not the babies."

For the first time Anya smiled. Yes, of course; they needed strong hands, not babies.

"As long as we give them potatoes, milk, their damned *kontyngent*, so their soldiers won't starve, the Germans need us. They are not stupid, Anya. If they take my children, I will burn down the fields."

Anya nodded. She felt the old will and determination

of her husband, the way it had been before the Nazis reduced strong men to slaves.

"Now go home," Henryk said, and patted her stomach
stirring with child. "Our new son will be born soon. You
must rest."

Anya left the field with her children, but she did not
go home. She went instead to the medieval monastery on
the hill overlooking the village and brown fields, to pray
to the Blessed Virgin, for three hundred years the Queen
of Poland.

"Blessed Mother, save my children," she beseeched the
white stone face of the Madonna. "Save them from the
Hitlerowcy."

When Henryk came home from the fields, to his wooden
house with a high-pitched thatched roof at the edge of the
village, the evening meal was warming in the oven. Little
Margosha ran to him. *Tatuś, Tatuś!* He gathered her up
in his thick laborer's arms, closed his eyes, and pulled her
soft little body tight against his chest, hoping she could not
feel the falling in his heart.

"See?" he said to Anya, with relief. "No Germans. Nobody."

After dinner, they dressed the two girls for bed, tucked
them in, and kissed them good night.

Henryk stopped at the foot of his daughters' bed. He
watched their small, tender faces compose into sleep. They
were fair and beautiful, just the kind of children old
Tymoteusz had said the Germans wanted. But what could
he do? Nothing. Kiss them good night; keep the rumors,
the whispers, from their ears. That was all. This is what
the Nazis had done to him. This is what had become of
Henryk, the man.

When they were alone, Anya said: "Henryk, hide them.
Hide the children."

Henryk looked around the small room in despair.
Where would we hide them? Remember the Bastockis?
They hid in the cellar. The SS broke through the
floor."

"Then take them away. We can go away."

"Where would we go, Anya? To Poznan? To Berlin?
The world is all the same to us now. If the SS bastards

catch us on the road, they will shoot us. The children too."

Anya's face broke, tears ran down her cheeks. Henryk put his arms around her.

"Blow out the candles," he said. "We will wait in the dark. If someone comes, we will run. That is the best we can do. Pray to the Blessed Virgin, Anya. Pray hard."

They waited in the darkness, cold and tense, speaking only in whispers. Occasionally Henryk smoked his pipe, but not for long. They jumped at every small noise outside.

At midnight, Henryk rose from his chair.

"You see," he said. "Nobody. Come, let us go to bed. The fields are still there tomorrow, no matter what."

At three o'clock, fists pounded on their door.

Henryk jumped up, sharply awake, his heart beating fast and hard.

Silence.

The fists pounded again.

"Open up!"

Henryk ran to grab his knife. Where was it? It had been on the table, but in the darkness . . .

The SS men burst through the door. There were four of them, with two snarling Alsatians. Two of the men seized Henryk before he could find his knife and pinned back his arms.

Anya screamed. Her face was white with fear.

The SS *Hauptsturmführer*, the captain in charge, spoke with great authority. "There is no need to worry," he said. "We have come for your children. Both of them. It is for health reasons, nothing more. They will be returned to you later, after they are well."

"They are not sick," Anya said. She was standing in front of the door to the children's room. The filthy Hitlerites would have to walk over her to get them. "They are little, small. . . . Please . . . not sick."

"They are babies," Henryk pleaded. "You don't need our children."

"Stand aside," the SS captain ordered.

"No," Anya cried, "they are babies. On the Blessed Mother—"

The short, thick Nazi slammed his fist into Anya's

face. She fell across the doorway, blood pouring from her mouth and nose.

The captain was furious. The woman was still blocking the door.

"Stupid cow!" he shouted and kicked her hard in the belly with his boot, then again, harder. She gagged and retched.

Henryk struggled to break free.

"No, not the babies. Please, God, I beg you," he pleaded at the top of his voice. "Not my little ones. Take me. Please! Take *me!*"

The SS men laughed. "We can do both," they said.

The captain flung open the door to the children's room.

Margosha, the three-year-old, was awake, sitting up in bed, rigid with fear, her eyes wide with terror. Little Ela had stirred at the noise.

"Take them!" the captain ordered the *Obersturmführer,* his first lieutenant.

The young, blond lieutenant went to Margosha.

"Up," he ordered.

Margosha screamed, and recoiled in horror.

The lieutenant grabbed her by the arm and jerked her out of bed. She started to cry. The SS man pulled her toward the door, barefoot, still in her nightshirt, clutching a cornhusk doll.

"Mama! Mama!" Margosha screamed. "Don't leave me! No! No!"

Anya came to her knees and reached for Margosha, but the SS lieutenant pushed her away.

The captain grabbed Ela from the bed. She was still half asleep, bewildered. "Let's go," he ordered. "These are the last."

"No!" Margosha screamed and stretched her arms out to Anya.

Anya's hand went to her throat. She felt the medallion of the Blessed Mother. She ripped the thin silver chain from her neck and pressed the medallion into Margosha's hand just as the lieutenant wrenched the child away.

Anya rose to her feet, her belly splitting with pain.

The children were being herded to a van waiting by the road, already packed with other children from the village.

The young ones cried and begged for their mothers. The older ones were mute, stiff with terror.

Anya stumbled to the door. Blood trickled down her leg.

"No," Henryk ordered, pulling her back. "There is nothing we—"

But Anya had spotted Margosha, crushed against the rails of the open van. She lunged out the door and staggered toward it.

Margosha saw her mother and cried out: "Mama! Mama!"

The SS captain standing at the rear of the van with his men, laughing, lighting a cigarette, saw the pale, bloodied Anya stumbling toward him.

"Przekleci Hitlerowcy!" Anya screamed. "Give me my children."

Annoyed, the captain pulled his Luger, aimed for the belly, and fired. The force of the bullet threw Anya backward, to the ground.

"Good shot, Herr Axmann," the blond lieutenant told the captain. "Damn good shot."

The van pulled away in the direction of the train station.

Henryk ran to his wife, pulled her into his arms, and touched her face. Blood soaked her coarse white nightgown. Tears ran down Henryk's blunt, weathered face.

Anya looked up at him, her bright blue eyes, the eyes he had always loved to look at, clouding over.

She struggled to speak.

"Do not cry for me, Henryk. I am glad to die. I will give no more children to the Germans."

"Anya . . ."

She looked up at him one more time. "You always had such big ears," Anya said, and smiled.

She gasped and closed her eyes and let go. Henryk picked her up, heavy and limp, and carried her back to the house, back to their marriage bed, out of the sight of the Nazis. There was nothing more the Hitlerites could do to her now.

Henryk sat down in the crude wooden chair in the kitchen and put his face in his hands. Each breath was an effort. His hard peasant's body shook violently. His head was jammed with the cries of his wife and children.

Then he saw it. The knife. He sat up straight. Yes, the knife his father had given him. The one with the pearl handle. Sharp, deadly, made for a man.

He picked it up and ran the sharp edge over the back of his hand, drawing blood. "A damned fine knife."

It was not hard to find the SS men. The cries of the women at the train station could be heard far into the night. The SS ignored the women, and pushed the children into the boxcars. When a mother reached out for her child, well-trained Alsatians growled and snapped and drove her back.

Henryk searched the faces above the black uniforms, looking for the short, thick SS *Hauptsturmführer* who had knocked at his door. He was standing at ease, watching his men pack the children into the boxcars. The silver death's-head on his black cap glittered in the moonlight.

Henryk stalked him, slowly, silently. When he was ten yards away, he clenched the pearl handle tight in his fist, raised the long knife above his head, and broke into a run.

The SS *Obersturmführer* looked up to see a figure charging his commander.

"Axmann! Watch out!" he shouted.

Axmann turned, and the knife missed its deadly mark. The sharp blade sliced the SS captain's left cheek. Axmann brought his hand to his face with a cry of pain. Blood wet his fingers.

The SS men surrounded Henryk and wrestled him to the ground. They pinned him down and held his face in the dirt, while the lieutenant pressed his heel into Henryk's wrist until he released the knife. Then he handed it to Axmann.

Henryk struggled to get up.

"Let me stand! Let me stand!" he shouted.

He did not want to die like a mongrel dog, with his face in the dirt. He wanted to die standing, defiant. Like a man.

The SS men pushed his face harder to the ground. His mouth pressed into the earth, muffling his pleas.

Axmann plunged the long knife into Henryk's back, all the way to the pearl handle.

"Stupid Pole," Axmann said, and spat on the corpse.

The young blond lieutenant held a handkerchief to his captain's face.

"That will leave a nasty scar," he said.

Suddenly there was shouting in front of the train. The women of Rydz had thrown themselves across the tracks.

"To hell with them. Tell the engineer to move out," Axmann said.

The train started up. All but one woman left the tracks. The train pulled out for Kalisz and crushed her to death.

"Stupid Poles," Axmann told his lieutenant. "Stupid fucking Poles. We are going to come back and burn this place to the ground."

CHAPTER 1

Saturday, November 30, 1974

Henry Stramm kept his eyes closed, pretending to be asleep. He was sore and bruised, but he felt more disgust than pain.

For the past twelve hours he had been a captive. Twelve damned hours, and no end in sight.

His prison was a small, low-slung fishing shack at the far end of Island Beach State Park, in Seaside, New Jersey. The cabin, made of driftwood, aluminum, and scrap lumber, had been only half-heartedly insulated against the winter. It had two rooms. The front room served as the common room, where the fishermen ate breakfast around a hand-painted wooden table discarded from some wife's kitchen years ago, hung their slickers on rough pegs, and stored their rods in a handmade rack. In one corner there was a bare sink, its enamel dull and discolored, and a two-burner stove fueled by liquid gas. Flies and fishing hooks lined one wall. The back room was paneled in rough, unfinished plywood, and was cluttered with an odd mix of six beds and two cots.

Stramm was lying on one of the high, lumpy beds, his face to the wall, keeping perfectly still and breathing quietly, as if in deep sleep.

Considering the circumstances, he thought his act was pretty damn convincing. A gun was pointed at his head, ready to scramble his brains at a wrong move, and the short stump of a man who was doing the pointing looked as though he could slit his mother's throat on Mother's Day, then go out for a steak.

But this was hardly the time for self-pity. This was the time to think fast, which was why Stramm was playing possum. He had to figure some way out. Slowly, methodically, he rolled the whole chain of events over in his mind for some clue, some reason he had ended up like this— tied up and half naked in a drafty fishing shack at the end of nowhere, with no one to come to his aid but two ospreys and a herring gull.

And to think he wasn't even getting paid for participating in this freak show. Not one damn penny. In fact, he'd volunteered. Almost, anyway. Henry Stramm was one of the elite corps of men and women who worked without pay for the Civilian Investigations Unit, the most secret and clandestine arm of the Federal government's family of intelligence and security services.

Henry Stramm had been asked to join the CIU in 1968. It hadn't taken all that much to recruit him. He had always loved puzzles and secrets, something the CIU had already known when they approached him. And it wasn't going to be all that dangerous, they said. Just enough to make it interesting.

Not dangerous, hell! Somebody ought to have his dick chopped off for that one.

But Stramm had to admit, even now, that never in his wildest imagination had he believed that his current investigation would end like this. In 1970 he had been asked to investigate Victory, a right-wing organization headquartered in Philadelphia. At first, he had hoped to nail Victory on tax evasion. After four years of intense investigation, he had traced the roots of the organization to Seaside, New Jersey. There, the case had broadened far beyond the simple matter of unpaid taxes. Stramm had been convinced for some time that he wasn't dealing with a gang of petty thieves who buried dollars in the sand, but he was never exactly sure of the beast he was tracking. He had tracked blind, and was therefore prepared for anything. Anything, that is, but the one thing that had happened.

He was not prepared to get caught.

It never entered his mind.

Now, lying on a bed in a fishing shack with goose bumps

on his butt, looking like an advertisement for an S&M magazine, he had to deal with realities.

It was certainly not that Stramm had conducted the investigation with wild abandon. He was, after all, an accountant, a profession more notable for breeding Talleyrands than Scarlet Pimpernels. It was just that Friday had been a long day. He had left Manhattan after seven and hadn't checked into the oceanfront motel until after nine thirty. He had gone for a walk along the beach before turning in for the night. The waves were breaking fast, crashing to the shore in a thin, cold spray. There was a boat anchored in the distance, its lights bobbing in the choppy waters. He felt free, exhilarated. There was a strange kind of peace standing at the foot of the rough sea, its violent strength barely harnessed, the water rushing to the edge of the beach, then receding, to regroup and throw itself at the land again.

He hadn't even noticed the two men coming up behind him.

The men—one short, squat, and dark, the other tall and lean—had grabbed him from behind, planted a gun in his ribs, and brought him to the fishing shack.

The short squat one ran the inquisition. Who was he? Why was he here? Stramm had told the ugly little fart that since they were the ones who had driven him to the other side of God's country, they knew damn well why he was there. The answer had set off a string of reprisals that Stramm would just as soon have forgotten.

The tall, lean sidekick had left to make a telephone call. When he returned, the perverted games ended and Stramm was told to go to sleep, that they'd have more to say to him tomorrow.

It occurred to Stramm that his kidnaping had been accomplished with a fair amount of ease. They had known where he was, where to find him. How the hell? The identities of the Unit's civilian investigators were under closer wraps than the Manhattan Project had ever been. No lists were kept which could be stolen or leaked. Not even Washington had a central file.

An informer!

The Unit had a goddamn informer! Somebody on the take.

Of course. It had to. He had checked into the motel, called—

Stramm jerked, shivering at the realization, and opened his eyes.

The short, squat man who had devised the questioning the previous night waved at Stramm with his gun.

"You awake?"

Stramm just stared at the man. "No," he said. "I am not awake."

"You want your head bashed in?"

"Leave him alone, Spade," the tall, lean one said.

Spade was indignant. "He's just fuckin' around."

"No, he's not. He's hurt. You hurt him . . . last night."

"You got a pussy for a heart," Spade said, spitting in disgust.

The tall, slender young man would not be deterred. "The man is hurt. Anybody would be."

"You see something wrong with my methods, Robinson?" Spade asked.

"Sick," Robinson said, and walked to the window overlooking Barnegat Bay.

"You don't complain none."

Stramm watched the two men. His captors were an odd pair. Spade looked as if he had been born six feet tall, then compressed to five feet seven. There was a slight hunch to his shoulders; his neck was too short and his arms too long. Robinson, on the other hand, might have just come in from the beach. He was six two and blond and had the energetic, uncorrupted look of a summer surfer.

Spade walked over to Robinson. "Go up to the big house and see what we're supposed to do with this dude."

Robinson zipped up his parka.

"You have to ask?"

"Don't get smart."

Robinson left silently, without a retort, and Spade settled back into his chair, keeping his eyes on Henry Stramm.

The wind came off the bay in gusts, rattling through the walls of the cabin. Spade tapped his foot to pass the time. After an hour he began to pace the room.

Stramm sat up and looked out the back window of the

cabin to the bay. Whitecaps ripped the cold blue water. "Even the fish are cold in that water," he said.

"Forget it," Spade said, flatly.

"What?"

"I said forget it. You ain't pulling me off my guard."

"I wasn't trying."

"The hell you weren't. I know them kind of tricks. Forget it."

A chill ran through Stramm. He had wanted to divert Spade's attention so he could start working at the knots binding his hands. Time was running out.

A car came to an abrupt stop by the side of the cabin. Doors opened and closed, and feet shuffled in the front room. "You stay here," a man with a heavy accent said. "I will tell you when we are ready."

Robinson and a short, thick-necked man entered the back room. The man, in his late fifties, was dressed too formally for early morning in a blue pinstripe suit and wing-tip shoes. His hair was thin, faded blond. He kept his head tilted to the left and looked at Stramm out of the corner of his eye. "Is this our guest?" he asked.

"That's him," Spade said. Then, turning to Robinson. "What took you so fuckin' long?"

"It was my decision," the man said, firmly. "Last night when Robinson called, I began to think. Perhaps our visitor may be able to help us with a little problem."

"How?" Spade asked.

"I will tell you later," the man said, dismissing Spade. "Right now, I must make an examination." The man turned to Stramm. "You are very tall, sir. May I ask if you are German?"

"No," Stramm answered, puzzled.

"Norwegian, perhaps?"

"My mother was. Is that all right?"

"Oh, perfectly so. Would you stand up, please?"

It was a command, not a question. Stramm rose awkwardly from the bed, still stiff from the night before.

"Very slim hips," the man said. "That is good. Are you in athletics?"

"I ran track. Years ago."

"Good. Very good."

"Anything else?"

"No. My eyes tell me what I need to know."

The man turned to Robinson. "He has a nice long face, don't you think? And see the bridge of his nose? Absolutely perfect. You shall be well rewarded for this, I promise you."

"What for?" Spade asked. "I caught him."

"Indeed, Spade, but that is your job. However, it is Robinson who told me that our guest could be of use to us."

"What'd he say?" Spade asked.

"He said our visitor would make a perfect German."

"I'm not responsible for a thing, Mr. Schaeffer," Robinson said. "You and Spade can take all the credit."

Schaeffer ignored him and turned to Stramm.

"Now, my friend, I have a request to make of you. If you do exactly as I say, you will be free to go."

"Let's hear it," Stramm said.

"We have a young girl," Schaeffer said, "who would very much like to have a child. But, as you may have gathered, not just any father will do. He must have certain qualities. These qualities, I am happy to say, you have in abundance. What is more, you have a good spirit. You are adventuresome, if lacking in caution."

Schaeffer folded his arms and waited for a reply.

"I don't think I understand," Stramm said.

"It is not so difficult," Schaeffer said. "We are going to exchange something. Your freedom for your body. That is not so unusual. Women do it all the time, although for smaller stakes, I think. Now, do you understand?"

"No."

"Come now, my friend," Schaeffer said impatiently. "We are grown men. You are going to have intercourse with the young girl in the next room. Is that so bad?"

Stramm shrugged his shoulders. "I'm not exactly in top condition this morning. I hope you understand."

"Yes, I am truly sorry about that. But I am also sure you will overcome it."

Schaeffer turned to Spade. "Take his clothes and then we will proceed."

Schaeffer started to leave the room, but Robinson reached out and stopped him.

"Mr. Schaeffer . . . don't you think . . . she and me . . ."

Indignant, Schaeffer loosened Robinson's grip on his arm. "Absolutely not," he said. "Now get on with it. I do not have all day."

Schaeffer left the room. Robinson cut the rope binding Stramm's wrists and hurled it to the floor.

"Gimme your clothes," Spade ordered Stramm.

"I quit performing when I left the circus," Stramm said.

Spade moved in, the gun in his fist. "Look, mister, you're gonna do as I say or you're gonna get your head bashed in. Understand?"

"You're very persuasive," Stramm said. He took off his shorts and handed them to Spade. "Mind if I keep my socks on?"

"Suit yourself," Spade said. "Go get the girl," he ordered Robinson.

"Wait a damn minute," Stramm said. "You're not going to stay in here with us."

Robinson laughed bitterly. "I don't think you get the picture, mister. Spade wouldn't miss it for the world."

Spade turned red. "Shut your mouth!"

"No dice," Stramm said. "This isn't Times Square."

"Shut up!" Spade shouted, shaking with anger. He pointed the gun at Stramm's heart.

Stramm smiled. He knew he could win this hand.

"Have it your way, Spade, but I'm warning you. I can't do it with a crowd." Stramm held up his right hand. "Raised a Presbyterian."

Robinson cut in. "I'll guard the back. You wait in the front room. He won't try anything."

"I don't—" Spade started.

"You'll just make him nervous."

"All right. Go get the girl." Spade turned to Stramm. "Don't try anything smart."

"Speak to the girl," Stramm said dryly.

Stramm watched from the back window as Robinson walked past the cabin. He stooped to pick up a rock, then continued on to the water and sat down on the edge of the wooden pier that extended unevenly into the bay. Robinson turned briefly toward the cabin. Suddenly, he threw the rock across the water with all the strength in his arm. Then, as if the will to care had left him, he bowed his head and fixed his gaze on his feet hanging over the edge of the shaky pier.

Stramm returned to the bed and sat down. The door to the room opened and a girl entered and began to undress, without saying a word.

Stramm stared at her. She was more woman than girl, blond, a slender body with firm curves. She was at that indeterminate age between twenty-five and thirty-five, but definitely a woman; a woman you would look at twice.

He almost felt he knew her. Yes—he had seen her before, at the maternity home in Toms River. It was her eyes; they were different then. When he had seen her at the home, they were wild. She had begged to hold her child, but it was a child that would never be. It had been born dead.

Now she stood naked before Stramm, unashamed but silent. The eyes that had once grieved for a child that was not were now steady with purpose.

"Under other circumstances," Stramm said, "this would be a pleasure." He looked down between his legs. "I don't think it's going to work."

"It has to," she said.

She pushed him back with her hands and started caressing him. She worked her way down to his groin. Stramm's body awoke at the pleasure and she mounted him.

When they were finished, she got up quickly and began to dress. Stramm sighed. It was the worst lay he had ever had. He hadn't enjoyed it. She hadn't enjoyed it. Maybe Spade should have watched. Then at least somebody would have enjoyed it.

"I know this sounds a little silly, but I'm Henry Stramm."

She nodded.

"Got a name?" he asked.

"Ellen."

Same name, thought Stramm, as the ghost in the maternity home.

"Some people around here have first names. Some have last names. But nobody seems to have a first and a last name."

She shrugged, but didn't answer.

"Well, have it your way. Everybody else does."

The girl finished putting on her stockings and shoes and started to leave.

"Is that all?" Stramm asked, feeling almost indignant.

"I'm sorry," she said seriously. "Thank you."

She left. Spade and Robinson entered the room. Spade was still clutching the gun.

"May I have my clothes now? Please?" Stramm asked, in mock politeness.

Spade did not answer. He turned to Robinson and said: "Take the girl and Mr. Schaeffer back to town. Then come back and get me."

"Why don't we just wait?"

"Because you'll vomit, that's why."

The blood left Robinson's face. "Spade . . ."

"Go on," Spade said, irritated. "And don't waste any time. It's getting cold in here."

Stramm's shoulders tightened. He knew that if he was ever to leave the cabin alive, he had to be ready to act fast. He waited until he heard the car pull away from the driveway, then rushed Spade, aiming for the squat man's eyes.

Spade pulled the trigger. The bullet ripped through Stramm's gut and slammed him against the wall. Blood poured out of Stramm's belly. His bowels emptied onto the floor.

Spade crunched his heel into Stramm's face to be certain all the life was gone. It was.

He got a handful of paper towels and started to clean up the cabin. If Robinson saw all the blood and shit, he'd puke.

Charles Winston, the Eastern Director of the Civilian Investigations Unit, ran his fingers through his thinning gray hair and checked his watch. It was ten P.M. He had expected Stramm's call by five.

Something was wrong, damn it. He could feel it.

He had given Henry Stramm the Victory investigation because Stramm was an accountant. A very good accountant, as a matter of fact.

When the Eastern Region had been assigned the task of investigating Victory, the main concern of the Unit Steering Committee had been whether Victory was taking unfair advantage of its tax exemption. A good accountant seemed just what the case needed. But the investigation had gone on for so long and had taken so many odd turns.

Henry Stramm was the most punctual man in the CIU; when he said he would call by five, you could depend on it. But five o'clock had come and gone, and as the passing minutes lapsed into hours, the Director's concern had begun to deepen. He was now at fever pitch, but there was absolutely nothing to be done. The Director wasn't even certain exactly where Stramm was. All he knew was that Stramm was somewhere near Seaside, New Jersey, tracking down the elusive Executive Secretary of Victory.

He looked at the white telephone in the bay window of his library, the CIU hot line. The telephone that would ring if Stramm called.

If!

This was not the time to be thinking like that.

Winston picked up *The New York Times*. He had already read it from front to back this morning.

The FBI and CIA were at each other's throats again, and this time, they had made the headlines. It was a tiresome but common problem in most intelligence services. Russia's KGB would almost rather have tea with the British MI 6 than work with the GRU, and the British Secret Service had infinitely more respect for the KGB than for Scotland Yard's Security Branch. The FBI and CIA were no different, at war this time, as usual, over jurisdiction.

The Federal Bureau of Investigation had a monopoly over all counterintelligence operations in the United States. The Central Intelligence Agency was responsible for all foreign intelligence operations. Unfortunately, an eclectic group of saboteurs, spies, foreign agents, and garden variety criminals plied their trades without regard to that neat division of authority and responsibility. There were occasional cease-fires in the long war, but no real peace, and by the late fifties, the two agencies had escalated their jurisdictional disputes into a new art form.

The CIU was itself the child of one of their more passionate feuds.

In 1960 a high-level Czechoslovakian Party official defected to the West. He was given a new identity and resettled in Boulder, Colorado. The FBI kept the defector under close watch, but not close enough, for the CIA managed to contact him without informing the FBI. Hoover was incensed. The CIA had violated its charter by operating within the boundaries of the continental United States. But even more important, it had violated an interagency agreement with the FBI which required the CIA to notify the Bureau before contacting an alien living in the United States. Hoover broke off all liaison relations with the CIA.

The young new President, barely settled in the White House, was outraged. He was interested in results, not intragovernmental rivalries. He ordered his brother, the Attorney General, to solve the problem.

After all attempts at mediation had failed, the CIU was created in 1961 by the unwritten executive order of President John F. Kennedy to act as a buffer, to take up the slack in the gray area where the authority of the FBI and CIA seemed to overlap. Created without the burden of codified rules and regulations, the CIU was not encumbered with territorial restrictions.

The original name of the CIU was the Current Investigations Unit. It was set up with a Central Director in Washington and divided into four regions: East, West, Midwest and South. Each region had a local Director, two full-time investigators, and a limited secretarial staff. The main policy body was the Unit Steering Committee, composed of the Attorney General, the Secretary of Defense, four Senators, and four members of the House of Representatives, and was chaired by the Vice President. The reports and recommendations of the USC bypassed the National Security Council and went straight to the desk of the President.

It was firmly believed that the overhanging threat of the CIU would eventually force the FBI and CIA to end their rivalry—a belief which only proved that even at the highest levels of government, men can be naive. The only thing the CIU produced between the FBI and CIA was a mutual antipathy to the CIU.

When the Kennedy administration was abruptly and tragically ended on November 22, 1963, in Dallas, Texas, J. Edgar Hoover thought he saw his chance to rid himself of the CIU. He had always viewed its creation as a personal reproach and, more important, as a threat to his absolute eminence in domestic investigations.

The FBI Director, in his expert way, courted the new President with stories of the Bureau and spiced them with revelations about the private lives of the titans of Washington. To all of this, Lyndon Johnson, an earthy man who enjoyed a good story, turned an eager ear.

Then Hoover made his play. The CIU, he complained, was a ragtag collection of meddling incompetents whose biggest accomplishment to date had been to break down morale in the FBI and CIA. He asked the President to dismantle it. Lyndon Johnson had virtually invented the art of flattery, but he could not be flattered—or intimidated. A perceptive and creative man, Johnson understood the value of a thorn in the flesh of J. Edgar Hoover, and like most highly creative men he loved the dark. He loved secrets and intrigues. He loved the CIU. He guided it, nourished it, and protected it. In 1966 he changed its name to the Civilian Investigations Unit and converted its investigative staff from professionals to civilians who worked part time without pay. As it turned out, the crusty Texan's application of populism to Potomac bureaucracy was a stroke of genius.

The CIU became the most trusted and effective organization in the Federal intelligence network, its men the most disciplined and dedicated. The civilian investigators were anything but amateurs. They were bright and highly skilled, and they were considered the most ingenious, resourceful, unorthodox, and ruthless of all the government's intelligence and security personnel. They took charge of investigations that threatened to provoke a bloodletting between the crew cuts in the Bureau and the Ivy Leaguers in the Company, and covered cases that seemed ill suited to the FBI or the CIA, or which neither the FBI nor CIA could be trusted to conduct without prejudice—often because of their own involvement. Cases like Victory.

Charles Winston folded his paper and put out his pipe. It was midnight and still he had heard nothing. In eleven years as Eastern Director, he had never lost touch with an investigator like this. He looked at the white telephone by the bay window. It became a rebuke, a symbol of despair.

The Director picked up the telephone and called his assistant, Robert Davison.

"Robbie? Charles here. Did I wake you?"

"No, not at all."

Winston was not surprised. He knew his aide was a night owl. "I haven't heard from Henry," he said. "He was supposed to check in by five."

Winston preferred to use only first names over the telephone, even though the CIU hot line was, theoretically, untapped and bug free.

"Not like Henry," Davison said. "You worried?"

"Worried as hell."

Davison took note. Winston was an old-fashioned man who almost never swore unless he was in distress. "What do you want me to do, Director?" he asked.

"Put out some feelers. I know he was going to Seaside, New Jersey, but I don't know where he was staying, or what name he was using. For all I know, he slept on the boardwalk."

"Not likely."

"No, but not like him to leave much of a trail, either. He's a very thorough man."

"One of the best," Davison agreed. "I'll get to work on it."

"Sorry to keep you away from a good night's sleep . . ."

"That's what you pay me for," Davison said with patent loyalty. "Don't worry about it."

"We'll talk tomorrow," Winston said. He was satisfied. Davison would check his contacts in the police department and his network of shadowy figures who lived at the edge of the law. Davison, perhaps because he was young, had a flair for the unsavory, which was invaluable at times. And, to the Director's constant amazement, Davison could not only communicate with these people, he could abide them.

Winston sighed and slumped in his chair. It was a bad turn of events, and just when he had decided that it was time to take his leave of government service.

Charles Winston had been appointed Director of the Eastern Region of the CIU in 1953 when his predecessor decided to return to a less Spartan life as the president of a Fortune 500 company. Winston had been an Assistant Attorney General for the Southern District of New York and would have continued his career with the Justice Department had he not been asked to take the Directorship.

Now Winston had just about decided to retire, despite the camaraderie of his colleagues and the pride he felt in his work. He knew he was too old to start over, but he was lonely. Part of him was gone. His wife, Bea, had died in October 1973, after losing a three-year fight with breast cancer. It had been a difficult time—the money, the strain, the shattered dreams, the agony of seeing Bea slowly slip away. It did things to a man.

At one o'clock, Winston gave up his vigil and went to bed. There was nothing else he could do.

CHAPTER 2

Sunday, December 1, 1974

Winston awoke at six o'clock Sunday morning from a fitful sleep. The town house on Cranberry Street in Brooklyn Heights was strangely quiet, much as it had been in the first months after Bea Winston died. Death was in the air. There was a chill in the house that even a roaring fire in the hearth would not warm.

If only the white telephone would ring, with Henry Stramm at the other end. But it didn't.

Just before noon, Robbie Davison called.

"Henry's been found in a garbage dump," Davison said. Davison had acquired Winston's habit of using only first names.

A wave of nausea passed over Winston. "Where?" he asked quietly.

"Queens."

"Dead?"

"Yes. I'm sorry, I assumed . . ."

"I know," Winston said. He had assumed, too, but he thought he might as well ask the question.

"What's our source?"

"Police Department. It will be in the *Daily News* tomorrow."

"First page?"

"No, buried. It's speculated that it's another gangland killing. There's been a rash lately."

"Yes, there has," Winston said. "I don't suppose the *Times* will carry it at all."

"No."

"Any pictures?"

"In the *News*? No. I don't think anybody had the time or the interest to take them. A cop found him about eight o'clock this morning."

"Then there's nothing we need do about the newspapers," the Director said solemnly. "Well, at least there are some small favors. Meet me about six at the office. We have to make arrangements to clean out his files. Can you get any help from the police?"

"It'll be risky," Davison said. Then, reproached by Winston's silence: "Okay, okay. I'll see what I can do."

"I'm sure you'll succeed. I'll see you at six."

Charles Winston had spoken without emotion to his young aide, but it was a flimsy coverup for the sadness he felt. As he replaced the receiver, his shoulders sagged and his arms hung heavy at his sides. It took a great effort to prop himself up, to pull his shoulders square and prepare to go to the office. Henry Stramm was the first agent Winston had ever lost except through retirement and he felt the loss personally. The CIU was an investigative unit. CIU investigators were supposed to compile facts, write reports, and make recommendations. They were not supposed to get killed.

Winston shook his head. He should have kept a closer watch over this investigation. This one had been different from the others.

In 1969, an organization known as Victory had come to the attention of the Unit Steering Committee, after being virtually ignored by everyone since its foundation in the early fifties. There really wasn't any reason to pay much attention to Victory during the fifties and sixties. It was only half as large and far less vociferous than most of the other superpatriot organizations. Unlike its sister, the John Birch Society, Victory preferred to concentrate its efforts in the local community, and therefore rarely caught the eye of the national press.

Victory believed that Communism would be stopped at the neighborhood street corner, at that idyllic intersection of Elm and Main where shady oaks and front-porch swings stood for the best this country had been and to which it must return. Victory believed the fight would be won in the church pews, not the seats of Congress; in the libraries and classrooms, and the hearts and minds of the gentle people who lived in their hometowns.

Membership in Victory was not exclusive. You could be a dockworker or an oil millionaire; a schoolteacher or an heiress. It was unlikely, however, that you would be a college professor, a Wall Street banker, an Episcopal minister, an Oriental, a black, or a Jew. And, notwithstanding that Victory wanted everyone to be a true-blooded American, it was almost certain that you were not a Cherokee, a Mohawk, or an Iroquois.

Nevertheless, its members, as a whole, had incomes miles above the national average, and were not niggardly with their passion or their pocketbooks. The coffers of Victory never knew hard times.

It was the generosity of one of its members that finally brought Victory to the attention of the CIU. In 1969 Cassie Roberts, the widow of a wealthy oil man in Port Arthur, Texas, had died peacefully in her sleep at seventy-three, leaving Victory the bulk of her 15-million-dollar estate so that its torch of vigilance would never burn dim from lack of fuel. The estate included several insurance policies made over to Victory, royalty rights in oil wells still pumping mightily in the Spindletop Field, blue-chip stocks, bonds, and convertible debentures.

The main problem for both Victory and the estate of Cassie Roberts was that she also left a son and a daughter. It was not that her children didn't share some of Cassie's views. They had no objection to patriotism, but Cassie Roberts had driven it into the ground. Declaring their new-found belief that nothing was good that was carried to the extreme, they contested the will. Their arguments were two-fold: (1) Victory had taken unfair advantage of a sick, old woman; (2) Cassie Roberts was a nut. The battle raged in south Texas with neither party budging a penny, until finally, in May, just before the Dogwood Festival, a settlement was reached out of court. It worked out fine: Everyone got something and no one liked what he got.

The contest to break Cassie Roberts's will had been so heated, and, in typical Texas fashion, so public, that it attracted the attention of the Unit Steering Committee, who decided that an investigation was in order. The investigation was divided between the Eastern and Southern Regions, since the organization was based in Philadelphia, Pennsylvania, and Cassie Roberts had been a Texan. Winston had assigned one of his most capable men, Henry Stramm. Peter Fleming, a tall, robust Texan known for his relentless pursuit, had been delegated the responsibility of the Southern Region.

Taxiing to his office on West 20th Street, Winston thought about whom he would ask to take over now that Henry Stramm was dead. He had to be careful. The investigation had taken on special risks. By the time he arrived at headquarters, Winston had decided on a replacement. He lit his pipe and waited patiently for his assistant to join him.

Davison was always fifteen to thirty minutes late, but in his consistent tardiness he had created his own punctuality. He arrived at the brownstone office at six twenty, slightly out of breath and red in the face from the chill wind and his own exertion. Darting his eyes around the room to satisfy himself that he and the Director were alone, he said: "I have the files."

"Any trouble?" the Director asked, taking the folder from Davison.

Davison shrugged. "No more trouble than you would expect."

"Good." The Director took a moment to thumb through the folder. "I'll read this tonight," he said finally.

Davison nodded.

"I have decided on a replacement for Henry."

Davison waited to be informed. He did not ask who it was; a certain protocol had developed between them.

"I have decided to ask John Parks." The Director took a long drag on his pipe, then continued: "You don't know him. Not yet anyway. He last handled an assignment for the Unit in nineteen seventy, two years before you arrived. He is a good, solid man . . . a puzzle solver. He had this fascinating little habit. He used to diagram murder mysteries as he read them and try to guess the ending. He'd put each character on a separate page and jot down little notes under their names. He figured out the ending to *Murder in the Calais Coach* that way. Really a very remarkable mind."

"What'd he do with *Ten Little Indians*?" Davison asked. Then: "Are you sure he'll take the assignment?"

The Director shrugged. "No."

"Four years is a long time to drop out of sight. He may not be the man you remember."

"A man doesn't change much past thirty," Winston observed. "He'll be a little rusty, but he won't have lost his talents."

"Why'd he drop out for so long?" Davison asked.

"He's on Wall Street. When the recession hit in seventy, he had to turn his attention to his business."

"Lost him to the dollar, is that what you mean?" Davison said, unimpressed.

"Not exactly," Winston said. "We lost him to survival. Those were rough times. But he ought to be all right now. I'll know better after I meet with him." Winston drummed his fingers on the desk. Finally, he said: "This is a hell of a note."

"You mean Henry?"

"Yes."

"You wouldn't think Victory would be the kind of assignment that would take you on a one-way trip to the garbage dump," Davison said.

"No, you wouldn't."

"I'll tell you what I think," Davison said. "I think something stinks, and it's not just Victory. Henry was too smart to get killed."

Winston frowned. "Unfortunately, no one's that smart."

Davison was unconvinced. "We guard our investigators like the keys to the kingdom. No one could have found out about Henry and what he was doing unless there's a leak."

"A leak?"

"Yes, goddamn it. A leak. An informer. Somebody in the Unit."

Winston sighed. "It's a possibility," he said after a long silence. "But your conclusion is based on an assumption, not facts."

"The hell!"

"No, now think a minute," the Director said patiently. "Henry has been murdered. That we know for sure. It's a fact. You assume, however, that Victory did it, and therefore that the Unit has an informer. If Victory is responsible for Stramm's death, you are probably right. If not, you're wrong on two counts."

Davison took a seat in front of Winston's large oak desk. "What do you think?"

"Me? I think we should proceed with the investigation. If Victory is responsible, that will turn up, as well as the informer, if there is one." Winston picked up the phone. The Southern Director had half of the Victory investigation. He had the right to know—but not too much. The conversation was brief.

"You didn't tell the Southern Director very much," Davison said when Winston had replaced the receiver.

"Didn't I?"

"You know you didn't. You didn't tell him that Henry was dead. You said he had dropped out of the investigation because of a hardship."

"Since when is death not a hardship?" Winston asked, without smiling. Then: "I don't want anyone but you and me to know about Henry right now. First, we have to replace him. We're not certain that John Parks will take over." The Director took a long drag on his pipe. "How about dinner?" he asked.

"No, I think I'll go home. I'm dead tired."

Winston scrutinized his young aide. "You look tired," he said. "You've also lost weight."

Davison shrugged it off.

"Something the matter?" Winston inquired.

"Too much work."

"You keep your mind on it too much," Winston reprimanded him. "You're too young for that. Go home and get some sleep."

Suddenly, Davison was weary. He wanted the conversation to end.

"Better yet," Winston said, "take some girl to dinner."

"Sounds great," Davison said automatically. "See you tomorrow."

"Just a minute."

Davison waited as Winston went to the office safe and extracted a printed bill from Sears showing a balance due of $22.65. It was a CIU code letter which meant that the investigator should contact the Unit immediately if he had time for an assignment. In this discreet way, no CIU investigator was ever pressured to take an assignment. All he had to do was neglect to answer the code.

Winston made out the bill to John Parks, and looked up the address of his firm in the Manhattan directory.

"Mail this at the main post office on Eighth Avenue," the Director said. "It'll be delivered tomorrow morning."

Outside, in the crisp night air, revulsion gripped Davison. The last thing he wanted to do was to go home. Kate would be there, high as a kite, plundering him with her sickness. He mailed the bill, then took a cab to Lexington Avenue across from Grand Central Station, where the hookers were hiding in the shadows of the buildings. He picked out a tall, black girl with long thick legs who promised to go around the world and more for twenty bucks plus room charges. What the hell, Davison thought as he followed her over to Third Avenue. At least she looked clean. Not that he really cared.

CHAPTER 3

Monday, December 2, 1974

John Stuart Parks was a tall, handsome man, almost as fit at forty-one as he had been at twenty when he threw the discus for Yale. His face was striking from any angle; almost too much so for the Eastern Director, who preferred forgettable features.

Parks's eyes were a cool, firm blue and set wide apart, and his nose was straight and thin. A few strands of light-brown hair always seemed to be falling across his forehead. It was a fresh face and there was an air of devilment about it, but it was also lined and a little rough.

John Parks had joined the CIU in 1967. He was almost the perfect Unit man. He was wealthy; his time was his own and he could underwrite his own expenses. He was quick and easy to train. He was skeptical of power and didn't believe in the divine right of Western nations, which made him a pariah to the CIA. He would never follow an order unless he believed in it, and he was a dues-paying member of the American Civil Liberties Union, which put a whole world between him and the FBI. The CIU didn't want spooks. It wanted independent, ethical men who were slow to condemn and quick to question. Resourceful men, not hollow men filled with straw. They would be the most ruthless, if the need arose, because when they agreed to undertake an investigation they did so because they agreed it needed to be done.

John Parks had made the bulk of his personal fortune in the hot issues market of the 1960's. When the recession of 1970 hit and the Dow-Jones took a sustained nosedive for the first time in years, Parks suspended active service with the CIU and turned his energy to reorganizing his business. He was founder and President of American Investing Corporation, now the umbrella for a financial conglomerate that conducted money management services, a business advisory service, a brisk brokerage trade in securities and commodities, and other related economic ventures. Parks's specialty was the business advisory service, which brought willing corporate sellers together with willing corporate buyers, and vice versa.

The lessons of 1970–72 were not lost on Parks. He had learned to diversify and delegate. He had hired experts who had proven wise in the understanding of the economy and its surpluses, shortages, weaknesses, and strengths; men who could negotiate business deals, put together companies, and advise businesses as well as he could. American Investing Corporation just about ran itself.

By late 1974, Parks had also learned that his life had become beset with patterns.

In the morning he would arise at six forty-five, make toast and coffee, then eat the toast and drink the coffee along with a glass of orange juice. He had a set routine of bathing and dressing which ended with a quick buffing of the shoes. Upon leaving his apartment, he bought *The New York Times* and read half of it on the Lexington Avenue Subway to 1 Chase Manhattan Plaza. At the office *The Wall Street Journal* awaited him, neatly folded on his desk.

His workday was well ordered. At the close of the day, the secretaries set their watches by the time he walked out the door. He timed his exit from the office to avoid crowds. He knew when they accumulated and when they dispersed. He took the shortest route to the subway and could tell you the exact time it took to reach the particular spot on the platform where he always waited for the train.

On Monday, December 2, Parks rose from an uneasy sleep. The day before he had felt the full impact of the routine that controlled his life when he had actually caught himself counting his steps home from the subway. He knew it had taken discipline, which in and of itself had dictated routine, to accomplish in business what his competitive nature had compelled him to do. But now the pattern was beginning to gnaw at him.

He was in a sour mood. He dressed quickly, ate breakfast at a small Greek restaurant a few blocks from his apartment, and arrived at his office thirty minutes late.

Miss Jones, his enormous secretary who subscribed to the blood-and-iron philosophy of Bismarck, met him at the door, her arms folded in rebuke. He ignored her and ordered coffee.

"You have your coffee at ten thirty," she told him.

Park thrust his hands into his pockets. "I want it now," he said sharply. He realized that he shouldn't be surprised that everyone else had become accustomed to his routines.

Miss Jones brought black coffee.

"You have an invitation from your friends the Stanleys," she said. "For a cocktail party. It's tonight. Remember? You've yet to respond. It's still on your desk."

Parks shuffled the papers on his desk. "They are not my friends and you know it. They are merely social contacts."

"Shall I telephone your regrets or shall you?"

"Why would I do that?" he said, without thinking.

"Because you don't accept invitations on week nights."

"Oh?" Parks said. Another routine had emerged. "Don't I?"

"No. Never. Not even for Catherine Deneuve."

"Well, never mind that. Anything else?"

"Your mail," Miss Jones said, drawing in her breath with a heave of her massive chest. "A reminder from your tailor to pick up your suit, two bills, and an advertisement for a new Washington newletter called *Corporate Reports*. Do you want it?"

"No."

"I didn't think so. It's in the trash."

Parks frowned. "What if I had said I wanted it?"

"You didn't and you don't," Miss Jones said with authority. "A man who won't read *The Kiplinger Washington Letter* won't read *Corporate Reports*. Too shallow."

That had been Parks's exact reaction. Miss Jones knew him too well.

"You're also ten minutes late for your nine-thirty meeting. Mr. Jorge Del Campo from Madrid."

Parks snapped his fingers. "Damn it! How long has he been here?"

"Ten minutes. They were exactly on time," Miss Jones

said with admiration. "Not a minute early, not a minute late."

Miss Jones believed that punctuality was next to godliness, and therefore never lived in peace with the rest of the world except for one week a year when she made her annual trip to London and stood before Big Ben.

"They?" Parks asked, gathering his papers and searching for his Mark Cross pen.

"He has his son with him."

"Son?" Parks was only half listening, still searching for his pen.

"So I assume. A boy, anyway. About twelve or thirteen. A very nice young man, I might add, dressed just like his father in a blue suit and red tie. Very cute. Your pen is in the top left-hand drawer."

Parks opened the drawer and found the pen. Miss Jones looked at him with concern. She had rarely known him to be late for an appointment. He was the closest thing she had found to Big Ben in corporate America, but right now his timing seemed to be off.

"Are you all right?" she asked.

"Fine, just fine," Parks said, finally pulled together. "Where are they?"

"In the conference room. Michael DeFalco is with them. He has been alone with them for the last five minutes. Ten more and he will drive them back to Spain."

Michael DeFalco was a far cry from Big Ben. In 1970 he had turned in his hippie beads for a Texas Instruments calculator, and condescended to apply his degrees from Harvard and the London School of Economics to the commodities market, where he managed to combine the disdain of a Marxist and the avarice of a capitalist with sufficient ruthlessness to acquire a reputation among commodity analysts as a man to watch. Parks had had to double his salary to hire him away from Macro International. DeFalco was still a raw talent when he came to American Investing Corporation, but under Parks's guidance he had matured into a perceptive, articulate expert in a field of hip shooters and high flyers—all without sacrificing his rhetoric or his disdain for the Establishment. Miss Jones had never been concerned about Michael DeFalco's talent. She only wanted him to wear his coat and tie over matching slacks, not blue jeans. When she won that battle, she tried to convince him to restrict his unmatched ties and shirts to four or less colors of the rainbow. She lost.

As Parks reached the conference room, DeFalco was holding forth on the virtues of Amnesty International, and the Spanish businessman and his son were staring blankly past him at the view of the Statue of Liberty and the deteriorating Brooklyn waterfront. DeFalco was dressed for the occasion in a black shirt with white collar and a purple, white, and orange tie.

Señor Del Campo and his son, Luis, rose when Parks entered the room, and exchanged formal greetings. Del Campo was dressed elegantly in a blue serge suit. He was trim and tanned, making it difficult to judge his age. There was a confidence to the move of his shoulders, as if he were accustomed to command. He spoke flawless English, with a slight, undefinable accent. His young son was fair, blond, and solemn.

Del Campo shook Parks's hand and sat back down, pulling his chair up to the long mahogany conference table. The businessman was anxious to get on with the meeting. He had no time for pleasantries or small talk. He spoke first, going to the heart of the matter.

"As I stated in my letter, Mr. Parks, I am interested in the commodities market, and therefore have requested a meeting with you and your leading expert in the field."

He looked sideways at DeFalco, who had slumped down in the chair and was staring at the ceiling.

"You've got him," Parks said, nodding toward DeFalco. "The best on the Street, his abuse of haute couture notwithstanding."

DeFalco sat up straight and smiled coldly, showing long, white teeth. He looked like a baby sand shark. "They say Einstein dressed in a sweat shirt to meet the Queen of England," he said.

Señor Del Campo bowed his head in respect. He understood sand sharks. "I am sure he did."

The Spaniard put his hands on the table and leaned forward. The preliminaries had ended.

"You will perhaps think that the request I am about to make is unusual, something which you are not accustomed to doing. Therefore let me first give you some background. Spain, as I am sure you know, is still a very poor country. We are not well organized in the ways of commerce. That is not to say that we do not have universities, economists, industrialists. We do, but we need more. We need . . . no, we must develop a strong new business class. A body of men who have the knowledge, expertise, and dedication such as you have concentrated here on Wall Street. Men who can master the instruments of business, who do not have the old families' disdain for hard work.

"That is not to say that we do not want theory," he said, continuing. "We do. There is one theoretical exercise that we want you to explain in detail. We want you to explain how to corner the market, as you say, in a commodity. Preferably something like wheat or potatoes or corn."

DeFalco whistled in surprise, and Parks studied the Spaniard for a clue to his purpose. The meeting had taken an unusual turn.

"It is only a teaching exercise, Mr. DeFalco, but we believe it is both a practical and important one."

"And illegal," Parks said, "under most circumstances."

"To do it, yes," Del Campo said. "To teach it, no. Are you telling me it has never been tried?"

"Sure," DeFalco said, and shrugged. "It's been tried. So has jumping off the Brooklyn Bridge, but damn few ever swam to shore."

"Then it has never been done?" Del Campo asked.

"Yes," DeFalco answered. "A few times. Once in the early sixties in black pepper. There have been a number of squeezes, which is sometimes as good as a corner. Take sugar—it just happened. The price went from ten cents a pound to sixty-six cents a pound, and the cost to the consumer was an extra ten billion dollars. Most often, however, it fails, but not before it disrupts the whole damn market. People have gone to jail over these kinds of games."

"I take it that if the corner is effective or the squeeze, as you say, large enough, the consequences are terrible."

"In more ways than one," Parks said. "You're playing with the food supply. Farmers would go bust, banks would go under, prices would go out of sight. It's like a house of cards."

"That, Mr. Parks is why we have come to you. A group of businessmen, of whom I am one, have decided to dedicate part of their wealth to founding a school which will help create and train this body of men."

"It may not be the blessing you think," DeFalco said.

"That is easy for you to say—you are already there," Del Campo said coolly. "We judge otherwise. It is our belief that a strong, skillful business class is essential to Spain's future development. We will worry about handling the problems of prosperity when we get there."

"Touché," DeFalco said.

The Spaniard's son looked at DeFalco with hard blue eyes. Del Campo, too, stared at DeFalco strangely.

Parks interceded. "We are not here to place a value judgment on your motives, Señor Del Campo, or your goals. People come to us every day with far baser motives and much less altruistic goals. But they are generally more specific."

"Yes, certainly. Let me, too, be more specific. We would like your company to prepare a detailed, readable explanation of the commodities market. One that can be understood by students as well as scholars. We have found most available material unacceptable from the standpoint of actually dealing in commodities."

"I know what you mean," DeFalco agreed.

Del Campo smiled. The two men, the businessman and the ex-flower child, had reached an accord.

"What would happen if you cornered the market and then refused to sell?" Del Campo asked.

DeFalco rolled his eyes. "Whistle Dixie on the way down the tube."

Del Campo stared at him, puzzled.

"Whole economies could collapse," DeFalco explained. "Governments could fall. There'd be panic. Maybe a worldwide depression before it was over. That's why no government would let it happen. They couldn't afford to."

"I understand," Del Campo said earnestly, "and for that we can all be thankful. But for this exercise, I want your imagination to run free. You may make any assumptions you want. Unlimited money, hundreds of interlocking corporations, adverse weather conditions. Construct the perfect model, no matter how fantastic.

"Then, of course, we want you to tell us why it will fail, and why virtually all others have failed. There are more lessons to be learned in defeat than in an uncertain victory."

"It's an interesting assignment," Parks interjected. "More like a work of fiction."

"In a way," Del Campo said.

"But I'm not sure we can do it," Parks said.

"You have the expertise, and we are willing to pay handsomely. Is there some other obstacle?" Del Campo asked, concerned.

"Laws, maybe," Parks said. "And our reputation."

"I doubt if the written word is illegal," Del Campo said, "and you have my pledge that it will be kept confidential. We would prefer it that way for our own purposes as well as yours."

Parks turned to DeFalco. "Can you do it?"

"Sure, but not overnight."

"How long?"

"Two months, maybe three."

Parks turned to Del Campo.

"Tentatively, I'd say we could do it, but it is not exactly an inexpensive undertaking."

"We never thought it would be. Do you have an estimate?"

"At least a hundred thousand. We wouldn't touch it for less."

"We wouldn't expect you to. All we ask is our money's worth. We are also willing to pay Mr. DeFalco a handsome bonus if the report is timely and as good as we expect it to be."

Parks rose to terminate the conference. "If we decide to do it, you will get full value for your dollar."

Del Campo nodded in a stiff military fashion. "Such is your company's reputation, Mr. Parks," he said, extending his hand.

"I hope we haven't bored your son," DeFalco said.

The boy looked at DeFalco coolly, with the contempt of one who has been underestimated, but did not speak.

"He has not been bored," Del Campo said. "That I can promise."

"He didn't seem to miss much," Parks said.

Del Campo spoke for his son. "No, he did not."

"Will you be in New York long?" Parks asked, feeling the conversation had grown awkward for Del Campo, although he didn't know why.

"Unfortunately, my son and I leave for Madrid tomorrow, but you may call or telex me at your convenience. I am hoping that your answer will be yes. If it is, I shall return personally to receive the report."

Parks and DeFalco reassembled in DeFalco's office for coffee and a postmortem. DeFalco's office was a large, plush corner room, with deep blue carpet and a Queen Anne mahogany desk. Floor-to-ceiling windows on two sides provided a robust view of Manhattan. The walls were covered with posters from DeFalco's days in Haight-Ashbury, now framed in gold leaf. Adjoining the office was the company's commodities trading room, where men sat by their telephones and stared at a large black trading board that mechanically posted changes in bids for each commodity over a twelve-month period.

DeFalco's secretary brought coffee.

"Well, what do you think?" Parks asked.

"Weird."

"I don't mean Del Campo, I mean the job."

"Double weird."

"Can you do it?"

"With midnight oil and Herculean discipline, it's a piece of cake."

"Didn't you do your master's thesis on something similar?"

"Yes, that's right. I did. On the corn blight. We thought the world's corn supply was going kaputt. NASA was monitoring the crops from the air, the CIA was sneaking off grain in suitcases to Hawaii for safekeeping. Now that's a story for you."

"You seem surprised that I remembered," Parks said.

"To tell you the truth, I am."

"Del Campo knew it too," Parks said.

"Think so?"

"Of course. A man like Del Campo doesn't agree to spend a hundred thousand dollars unless he knows what he's getting." Parks finished his coffee. "Did you buy his story?" he asked.

"No. Did you?"

"No, I didn't. I'm not even sure he's Spanish. What do you think's behind it?"

"I think he wants to try it."

"So do I, which is why I haven't decided whether we'll do it. We have enough profiteers in this business without some rich egomaniac fucking around with the world's food supply. I have to check with our attorneys."

"He'll lose his shirt if he tries," DeFalco said.

"Maybe," Parks said. "And maybe that's why we'll decide to do it. What'd you think of the boy?"

DeFalco shook his head. "Was that a boy or a skin graft off an iceberg?"

"Good question. But I'll tell you one thing, he didn't miss a word."

"Sucked it up like a vacuum cleaner."

"Don't you think Del Campo seemed a little old to have a son that young?" Parks asked.

"Give him credit," DeFalco said. "He kept the Roto-Rooter running when the rest of us would have hung up the jock strap."

Parks stood and walked to the door.

"Are you going to take his bonus if he offers it?" Parks asked, grinning.

"You're damn right."

"And get corrupted by the system?"

DeFalco laughed. "Listen, if there's one thing I've learned on Wall Street, it's that not all the whores work in Times Square."

"There is, of course, a difference between learning the facts of life and actually spreading your legs."

DeFalco shrugged. "What the hell. We've all got to go down some time. Anyway, I need a new car."

Miss Jones had organized the papers on Parks's desk into small piles, separated into telephone messages, office memoranda, and personal bills and letters.

Parks picked up the stack of bills and letters. Attached to the letter from his tailor was a crisp note from Miss

Jones stating that if he did not care to have a final fitting, she would send a messenger for the suit and have it delivered to his apartment. Parks scribbled "do just that" on the note. There was a statement from Paul Stuart showing a credit balance and a bill from Sears for $22.65. He tossed the bill from Sears aside. An error. He didn't have an account there.

He turned and walked toward the window, then stopped. There was a jolt in his head, like the clang of a ship's bell in a fog.

Slowly, he returned to his desk and picked up the bill from Sears.

He read it again. "Balance due: $22.65."

For more than four years, the business had been so much his life that the Civilian Investigations Unit had been almost erased from his mind. His shoulders shook with the chill of excitement. It was like a sweet voice from the past calling at his back.

Parks breathed deeply. A pay phone. Yes. That was the rule. It all started to come back.

He put on his coat and told Miss Jones he would be out of the office for a while. In the elevator, descending from the fifty-second floor, his hands were clenched into fists inside his gray wool topcoat. He walked a controlled, moderate pace to the telephone booth at the corner of William and Pine and dialed. An hour ago, if you had asked him cold, he might not have remembered the number, but now he remembered the number, the code, the whole procedure as if it had just been taught to him.

"Yes," a flat voice answered. It was Miriam Messinger, the Eastern Director's secretary, who, Parks knew, would reveal nothing until the caller revealed much more. It was prescribed Unit procedure and Miss Messinger had never varied in all the years that Parks had known her.

"Are my trousers ready?" Parks asked, the CIU code indicating he was alone and wished to talk.

"They certainly are!" Miss Messinger said. She had a sharp ear for voices and remembered each investigator even if she had never met him. "The Director would like to see you. Is tomorrow evening convenient?"

"Anytime you like," Parks said.

"Good. Can you be contacted tonight?"

Parks thought for a moment. "I'm going to a cocktail party at eight and will be home by twelve. Why?"

"One moment, please." Miss Messinger left the phone. In less than a minute, she returned. "Exactly where is your party?"

"Bedford Street. In the Village. Why?"

"The Director asked. It's quite routine."

"Certainly."

"And you still live at the same address? Mitchell Place?"

"Still," Parks said. He wondered if she recalled from memory or was looking at a file. In point of fact, it was sheer memory.

"That will be all," Miss Messinger said, terminating the conversation.

Parks took a taxi home that evening and did not buy the *New York Post*. He showered and shaved and went out to eat before going to the party. As he left the apartment he was certain he saw someone watching him from across the street. He dug his hands into his trousers and bent his head against the wind. He didn't want the thrill of getting back into Unit work to cause his imagination to run away with him.

The thought of the party was beginning to annoy Parks. He was restless and did not particularly feel like standing around making small talk with people with artificial smiles. The Stanleys made bad drinks because they bought cheap liquor, and they gave terrible parties because they invited boring guests.

When he arrived in front of the Stanleys' Village brownstone, the thick curtains were open and he could see expensively coiffured women and their escorts milling around. Parks resisted the temptation to hail a cab and go home. He knocked on the door.

The usual Stanley collection had assembled. Polite, proper, influential, dull people. Fortunately, they would become a little more interesting as the night wore on because they couldn't hold their liquor.

Parks spied someone new in the Stanley crowd, a tall, slender blonde standing against a wall sipping a drink. He thought she looked bored. Great. They had something in common. He fixed his own drink, a bourbon on the rocks, and greeted the hostess. She had, of course, worried that he would not make it and did so want to see him and had missed him so much, etc. Then she fluttered away to her other guests. The act, Parks decided, was overdone and overpriced.

He edged toward the blonde.

"We haven't met before," he said by way of introduction.

"No," she replied, and smiled. "We haven't."

"I'm John Parks."

"Let me guess—American Investing Corporation."

"You've been well primed."

"Not at all. I overheard someone talking about you. You were late."

"So I was. Let's play the other half of the game. What's your name?"

"Louise." She stared into the center of the room at one of the other guests. Parks looked at her half smile and studied her thoughtfully. He found her sexually appealing, interesting—and cold.

"The drinks they make here are terrible. I'm glad I don't pay for them," Parks said.

"If my mother hadn't taught me to be polite, I would agree with you."

"I know a place where they make better drinks. That is, unless your mother also taught you not to take advice from strangers."

"She only taught me not to take candy."

"My place," Parks said.

"You just got here."

He looked her in the eye. "Get your coat."

The blonde with the half smile got her coat and came back. She looked at him. "If it matters, I prefer Manhattans."

As he hailed a cab, Parks felt certain that the man standing near the corner opposite the Stanleys' town house was the same man he had seen earlier that evening. Parks nodded to him but the man did not respond.

Parks instructed the driver to Mitchell Place, a short, sloping sliver of a street opposite the UN Towers.

The taxi driver, a chunky man in his sixties from the Bronx, was irritated at the instructions. "Around the corner from Beekman Place. Right?" he said.

"Yes."

Parks had no intention of hassling with a cabbie.

During the jerky ride up First Avenue, Parks was plagued by thoughts of the man on the corner of Bedford. Upon catching Parks's eye, he had turned his face away into the wind. Then, with the same sudden rush and blink of awareness that occurs when the unconscious coughs up a word or a name that two days ago you tried to remember and couldn't, an image of the Director at his white telephone with the Manet print at his back flashed before him and he laughed out loud. Everything fell neatly together. Clever man, the Director. "Exactly where is your party?" Miss Messinger had asked. "It's routine." Routine, hell.

It bothered Parks that his reaction had been so slow.

The yellow cab pulled up in front of a fourteen-story coop whose red brick had been darkened with age and Con Edison soot. Parks gave the cab driver a generous tip to compensate the man for the insult to his knowledge of the streets of New York. John Parks had sympathy for the small irritations of life.

Inside the apartment, he took the woman's beige wool coat and escorted her to a long, chocolate-brown velvet couch facing the wide-hearthed fireplace in the living room.

"Manhattan, right?"

"Yes. Dry."

Parks put on a Janis Joplin record and went to the pantry, which he had converted into a bar, and prepared the drinks. Louise made herself comfortable on the couch. She was wearing a black dress with a deep neckline that exposed her white breasts, which were not so large as to overcome the dress, but large enough to catch the eye.

Parks returned with two full glasses.

"This one for you," he said, handing her the Manhattan.

He sat down close to her and kissed her on the ear. She moved away. Parks smiled. He knew this woman, and why she was in his apartment, and they were both going to have some fun out of it.

He took her drink away and set it on the clear Lucite Parsons table by the couch. He lowered a strap of her dress and a white pear-shaped breast fell forward.

"I think we better talk," Louise said.

Parks placed a warm hand on her breast.

"I have a message for you," she said.

"I know." Parks lowered the other strap.

"You do?"

He unzipped her dress. "Yes. Where do I meet him?"

Louise was distracted. "Who?"

He kissed her. "The Director."

He lowered his lips to her nipples.

"Take the five fifty-nine from Grand Central to Harrison. He'll be waiting in the park."

"Good. Now let's stop the small talk."

"Okay," she said softly. "Just remember."

"How could I forget?"

CHAPTER 4

Tuesday, December 3, 1974

Grand Central Station is a massive structure of marble and stone, crowned by the heroic figures of Mercury, Hercules, and Minerva. The heart of the station is a great center hall, 385 feet long, covered by a vaulted blue-green ceiling supported by stone columns 125 feet high. The constellations are spread out in all their glory across the ceiling, like the sky itself, and like the sky itself are ignored by the tumultuous thousands who walk under it each day.

Grand Central was built in 1913 by the hands and hearts of men who would live to hate the Hun, fight a war to make the world safe for Democracy, enter into the Noble Experiment, reach heights of new prosperity in the Roaring Twenties, and lose it all in the Great Depression. Now it is the home of trains that overheat and run late. Its great center hall is littered with ticket stubs, newspapers, candy wrappers, and all the other kinds of life's debris that can be used up and thrown away, including wrinkled, dirty, ragged old men and women who sleep on its wooden benches. Grand Central Station speaks no more of Mercury, Hercules, and Minerva.

The five fifty-nine express left Grand Central on December 3rd at six thirteen under the cover of night, arriving in Harrison at six fifty-five. A thin slab of cloud hung low overhead and the smell of rain was in the air. At Harrison, the gray and blue pinstripe suits and five-o'clock shadows poured off the train. Numbed by the hot, crowded train, or a little scotch, the commuters hurried to waiting cars filled with children.

Harrison, New York, once the home of Amelia Earhart, the great adventuress of the air, is now a bedroom community of New York City, where lawyers, bankers, brokers, and business executives repair each evening to sleep their dreams and dream their sleep.

Charles Winston was already sitting in the small park by the tracks when Parks arrived. The park was empty and covered in shadows.

Parks recognized him from a distance but did not speak until he was beside him. "Good evening, Director," Parks said warmly.

"Good evening, John. It's good to see you. I'm glad you could come."

Parks took a seat next to Winston on one of the metal cup-shaped seats that were joined together, four in a row. "You certainly pick appropriate places for reunions."

"Like it?"

"Perfect. Aren't you afraid of the mummies?"

Winston laughed and looked to his left at the parking lot, where the cars were beginning to pull out. "They do look kind of dazed, don't they? The last thing they'll worry about is us."

"It's that damned train," Parks said. "It's so hot, it makes your crotch sweat."

"Well," the Director said, as if he had some sympathy for Parks's plight, "going back will be more comfortable. How have you been?"

"Fine. Just fine."

"How's business?"

"Couldn't be better. Why? Want some stock tips?"

Winston dragged on his pipe. "No. Just interested. Does it still take most of your time?"

"For my officers, yes. For me, no."

"Then perhaps you'll have some time for the Unit again," the Director asked.

Parks smiled. "I thought you'd never ask. Got anything in mind?"

Winston turned to face Parks squarely. The night was heavy. A mist hung in the air.

"Yes. Something very specific," he began. "A while back we were asked to investigate an organization known as Victory, a little group of superpatriots that didn't catch anyone's eye until the late sixties. The Steering Committee got concerned because of some of its activities. Particularly fund raising."

"Why the Unit?" Parks asked. "Why not the FBI or the Treasury Department?"

Winston frowned. "Why do we get most things? It either didn't fit or they couldn't be trusted," he said. "The Treasury Department is capable enough, especially since Victory's tax exempt status is in question, but the investigation was thought to be broader than that. The CIA was out of the question because it was domestic. And the FBI was a little tainted."

"Tainted?" Parks asked, amused.

"Yes, tainted. You may remember, some time back, a story about a right-wing paramilitary group in northern Illinois that gassed and terrorized the American Friends Service Committee and other groups opposed to the war in Vietnam." Winston did not wait for an answer. The question had been rhetorical. "Fortunately, the group is now defunct, but ninety percent of its members came from Victory, as well as some of its money. Guess where the rest of its money came from."

"The FBI?"

"Yes, and the Army's intelligence unit headquartered in Evanston."

"Good God," Parks said in disgust.

"The Chicago police also had a hand in it."

Parks whistled low. "Where does the corruption end? That's always the final question."

The Director paused for a moment, then continued. "The request from the Steering Committee was simple enough—find out as much about Victory as possible, including its power structure, the magnitude of its fund raising, and the breadth of its activities."

"How far have you gotten?" Parks asked.

"We were fairly well down the road, I'd say, when we hit a snag."

"What was it?"

"The Eastern Region investigator working on the Victory assignment was found dead in a garbage dump in Queens."

Parks grimaced. "That's a snag all right."

The roar of the train passing through the station on its way to Stamford filled the evening, and forced a silence between them.

After the train had passed, Winston continued. "He was found Sunday morning. His name was Henry Stramm. Do you remember him?"

"Quite well," Parks said. "He was in my training class. Are you sure it was Victory that killed him?"

"No. I have no evidence. People meet their ends for personal reasons too."

"Sometimes," Parks said. "But is it likely?"

"No."

"I didn't think so. Now what?"

"We finish the investigation. If someone in Victory killed Stramm, it will turn up. Of course, we can never bring him to trial. We'll have to take care of that ourselves."

Parks shrugged his large shoulders. "Let's cross that bridge when we come to it. Tell me more about Victory."

Winston ran his fingers through his thin hair. "Yes, of course," he said. He repacked his pipe and lit it. The mist began to thicken. It would rain soon.

"Victory was started in Cambridge, Massachusetts, in nineteen fifty-three. At least that's as far back as anybody can trace it. It's composed of little groups scattered all over the place. Cells, if you will, although I'm sure Victory would take umbrage at that description. By nineteen sixty it had over one million card-carrying members, with heavy concentrations in Dallas and Orange County, suburban Chicago, and to some extent Scottsdale, Arizona, and Cape May, New Jersey. However, by the end of the sixties its numbers had decreased considerably, by at least half, I'd say."

"Where does its name come from?" Parks asked.

"From its motto: 'Victory over Communism requires the ceaseless vigil of every true American.' "

"And extremism in the pursuit of liberty is no vice. Right?" Parks said. "They must have loved Goldwater."

"They did," Winston agreed. "It was their second greatest disappointment."

"What was their first?"

"Richard Nixon."

"Watergate?"

"Oh, good Lord no. They thought that was a con job by *The Washington Post* and *The New York Times*. Not that they really cared by then. It was Kissinger, and the trip to China. They felt betrayed. But they aren't really all that involved in national politics."

"No?"

"No, not really. They have their opinions, of course, but they prefer to spend their energies in the community, fighting fluoride in the drinking water, keeping sex education out of the schools, banning textbooks that say too much about the United Nations. They did that in Houston once."

Parks sat up straight and stretched. "I know the type," he said. "Grannies in tennis shoes wearing their DAR pins on the Fourth of July. No cause for alarm. Certainly no cause for a Unit investigation."

"Certainly not, if that were all of it. The little Victory groups are harmless enough. Each goes its own way. Local stuff. The problem is not the groups, it's who actually runs Victory."

"What do you mean?" Parks asked.

"We can't find out," Winston said. "Victory is sitting on millions of dollars, and we can't tell you who runs it, who gets the money, who writes the checks."

Parks took a Marlboro from his pocket, lit it, and waited for Winston to continue.

"After an old woman down in Texas died and left Victory about fifteen million dollars, the *National Enquirer* ran a story claiming that Victory was the richest of all the superpatriot organizations. Apparently, this old woman in Port Arthur wasn't the first to leave her estate to Victory, lock, stock, bonds, and barrels, shall we say. Victory had been encouraging this for some time. The *Enquirer* claimed that some of Victory's members had died rather suddenly after making Victory the sole beneficiary of their life insurance policies."

"Interesting," Parks said, stubbing out his cigarette. "What became of it?"

"Nothing. Victory used the old tactic, 'Never complain, never explain.' The matter was forgotten. At least by the *Enquirer*."

"But not by the Steering Committee."

"No. There was just too much money, too many unanswered questions. The possibilities for abuse were just too great to let the matter rest. Think of what organized crime could do with a thing like Victory."

"It's not hard to think of some interesting possibilities," Parks said.

"Now, in all fairness," Winston went on, "Victory does support some worthy, if peculiar, causes."

"For example?"

"For example, the Manhattan Medical Services Corporation, which is a euphemism for a sperm bank. They also support a home for unwed mothers down in New Jersey."

"You must be kidding."

"No. I don't know why they do. Particularly the sperm bank. It must tie in with their antiabortion crusade."

"It still doesn't sound like anything an investigator would be killed for."

"I know," the Director said. "I have the diary Stramm kept on the investigation. Perhaps you'll get more out of it." He turned to face Parks. "Tell me, do you still read mysteries with the book in one hand and a pencil and sketch pad in the other?"

"I have refined it to a stenographer's notebook and a felt-tip pen," Parks said. "You amaze me."

"That I remembered? I've indulged in your game ever since you told me about it. Fascinating little pastime. I often do the same with investigations."

"Did you do it with this one?" Parks asked.

Winston shook his head. "No, and I should have. I didn't keep a careful eye on this one." He was visibly disturbed at his failure.

"Why not?" Parks asked, without malice.

Winston sighed. "Because it went on for so long."

"It probably wouldn't have made any difference."

Winston tapped out his pipe. "My assistant, Robbie Davison, thinks there is an informer in the Unit."

"On what grounds?" Parks asked.

"On the simple grounds that Stramm is dead."

Parks shrugged. "What do you think?"

"I don't know. It's hard to believe."

"If you were forced to believe, who would you pick?"

"I couldn't," Winston said.

"All right, then name everyone who had any knowledge about Stramm and the investigation."

"There were three," Winston said. "My assistant, Robbie Davison; Miss Messinger; and the Southern Director."

"What about your assistant?"

"Well, since he thought of the idea, I hardly suspect him. And I certainly don't suspect the Southern Director. The Southern Region has part of the investigation."

"What about Miss Messinger?"

A light rain began to fall. The station area was deserted, as well as the streets. The commuters had all gone home and were sitting down to dinner.

"She knows everything, of course, and has access to everything."

Winston hesitated.

"Does she know Stramm is dead?" Parks asked.

"If she reads the *Daily News,* she does. But typically, she has said nothing."

"Does any one of them have a grievance against the Unit?"

"Not really. Miss Messinger might, if it were in her, but it's not."

"What is it?"

"I tried to promote her to Assistant Director status, but the Central Director turned it down."

"Why?"

"Because she is a woman. That was the real reason, if you ask me. Thirteen good, solid years with the Unit, and . . . Well, it's done, I suppose. But Miss Messinger doesn't seem to mind as much as I do."

"You're really fond of her, aren't you?" Parks asked softly.

"Yes. Yes, I am."

Winston seemed to meditate for a moment. The aroma of John Rolfe tobacco sweetened the night air. It was seven forty. The streetlights, the headlights and tail-lights of cars, and the green and red fluorescent glow from the diner across the street pierced the night. Winston wondered whether he should reveal one indiscretion. Last December the pain of approaching Christmas without Bea had overwhelmed him. From the first week, when the firs and blue spruces were going on sale, Winston had been wracked with loneliness. His house was barren of tinsel and wreaths and the sounds of Christmas. When Bea had been alive, the brownstone was always redolent with the odors of plum pudding and evergreen. So, two days before Christmas, he had invited Miriam Messinger to dinner and they had eaten too much and drunk too much and forgotten themselves too much, as can be expected from two people alone and lonely in New York two days before Christmas. But they had both put it behind them the next day. It had never been mentioned. No, Winston decided, there was no need to talk about a few hours, a few minutes, from the past when it shed no light on the investigation and might make two people who had other-wise aged rather gracefully look a little silly.

"She is really a very lovely person," he said finally. "So, as you can see, none of the three people who could be the informer has a reason to be."

"There is always one reason," Parks said tightly.

"What is that?"

"Money. It's like the flu. It can touch anybody. Any one of them short of cash?"

"We are all short of cash at one time or another."

"I mean a lot of cash," Parks interrupted.

"Not that I know of," Winston said. "But then, I wouldn't really know."

The Director rose. The rain was light but steady. His hair was wet and beads of water ran down his forehead. "No sense getting soaked," he said. "We can continue this tomorrow."

He handed Parks a black plastic folder. "These are the notes we took from Stramm's office. I've already read them. His notes on the investigation are, of course, written in code. It may take you a while to translate them, to get the hang of it again, but you'll manage."

"I'm sure," Parks said, taking the folder.

"You go on and catch the next train," Winston said. "I'll have coffee across the street and catch the ten-seventeen."

"By the way," Parks said, "I like the way you send your messages."

Winston frowned. "Next time I'll do it by a more conventional method."

"Oh, no," Parks said with a laugh. "Please don't. I also spotted the tail you put on me. Did she tell you that?"

"Yes. She reported fully."

"That's one report I'd like to read. What was the tail for?"

"To check your reflexes. They could have gone rusty, you know. Anyway, you passed."

Parks extended his hand and Winston shook it firmly, warmly. "I'll call you tomorrow," Parks said.

The eight forty-seven train to New York arrived on time and Parks settled himself in the half-empty rear car. He stowed his wet raincoat in the overhead rack, settled himself comfortably in a seat meant for three commuters, lit a cigarette, took out a stenographer's pad and felt-tip pen from his briefcase, and began to write.

The Director, after finishing pancakes, bacon, and two cups of coffee at Cappy's Diner, caught the ten seventeen to Grand Central.

Brooklyn Heights has been the home of poets and writers and dreamers for more than one hundred years. The poet Anne Sexton said that a girl could suffer two horrors by dying too soon: She could die with her seed unplucked, and she could die without seeing Brooklyn. Anne Sexton had seen the Promenade in the spring rain, that graceful walk along the edge of the East River that overlooks Wall Street and the Brooklyn Bridge. Thomas Wolfe once lived on Montague Terrace, one block from the river, but he had another view. He said that only the dead knew Brooklyn. Perhaps he had seen the coming of the single-room-occupancy hotels that sprang up in the

Heights in the late sixties and early seventies—tabernacles
of decay to which only the dead and dying repaired. The
Pierrepont Hotel on the corner of Hicks and Pierrepont
was just such a hotel. By 1972 the Pierrepont was the
home of desolate welfare families, pensioners reduced to
eating dog food, pimps, prostitutes, addicts, and thin-boned
women with clouded minds. In this hotel, which once
housed the Brooklyn Dodgers and Edna Ferber, eighty-
year-old women were raped and old men were gagged and
beaten and left for dead. In 1973 two respectable Heights
businessmen were knifed by addicts living in the hotel, and
an aroused community closed it down.

The hotel was dark now, bereft of even the half life
which once stirred within it, much as rats crawl in cellars.
Soon it would be renovated and turned into low-cost apart-
ments for senior citizens.

Miriam Messinger lived directly across from the old
hotel, and she was more than happy to have it boarded up.
Now she could come home at seven thirty or eight o'clock
and not hold her breath until she had safely locked her
door.

Miriam Messinger had rented her three-room apartment
on Pierrepont in 1971 and had decided to spend a little
extra for a wood-burning fireplace. It was at times like
these that she knew her extravagance had been justified.
The fine mist that had turned to rain in Westchester had
spread to the city and was coming down in heavy, cold
sheets. It was nine o'clock and she had built a fire and was
enjoying a glass of red wine before she unwrapped her
real extravagance.

There was not much ceremony in Miriam Messinger's
life, as she had lived it mostly alone for the last thirty
years, and what little there was she had to create for
herself. She intended to introduce herself to her new ac-
quisition with a certain amount of pomp. So, after finishing her wine, she combed her hair, carefully repaired her
makeup, and straightened her skirt. Then, satisfied, she
went to her bedroom and slowly unwrapped the long box
just out of cold storage from Abraham and Straus.

She refused to rush it.

She looked admiringly at the black ranch mink coat
neatly folded in the box, stroking the soft fur occasionally

as if to assure herself it was real. After savoring the coat in the box as long as she could bear it, she took it out and put it on, parading back and forth in a grand manner in front of the floor-length mirror on the back of her bedroom door.

She had gotten it on sale in April. "A perfect steal," she said out loud.

She definitely would have paid five thousand for it on Fifth Avenue at Saks or Bonwit Teller or, God forbid, Bergdorf Goodman. Imagine, saving at least two thousand.

Of course, everyone would wonder where she got the money, how she could have possibly saved it up on her small salary. Even Charles Winston would wonder. But, paragon of discretion that he was, he'd never ask. Even if he asked, he'd never know the true answer. He'd never know how much he had helped her get the money.

Oh, well, it was no use thinking about that. It was better to think about the mink coat.

CHAPTER 5

Wednesday, December 4, 1974

The fireplace was smoldering with a large pile of white ash. It was nearly five A.M. John Parks closed Henry Stramm's diary and drank the last of his coffee, his tenth cup of the long night. He had been reading, decoding, and transcribing the diary of his fellow investigator since ten thirty the night before, breaking his concentration only long enough to refill his cup, empty the ashtray, and put a new log on the fire.

Parks rubbed his eyes, opened a fresh pack of Marlboros, and began to reread his notes. The diary was meticulously detailed, including dates, places, and times. Stramm's remarkable memory was evident on every page. He had recorded whole conversations verbatim. Parks was able to relive Stramm's four-year investigation from day to day, almost as if he'd been there.

The tale recorded in the diary was complex.

When the investigation was handed over to Stramm in January 1970, he decided the easiest way to conduct it was from the inside, so he set out to find a Victory discussion group to join. He learned about one that met on Staten Island on Tuesday nights, and contacted its group leader. After several telephone conversations Herbert Norton, the group leader, agreed to meet Stramm for lunch to talk things over. He explained that not everyone could join a Victory discussion group. That was a rule. Norton invited Stramm to Zito's (Dutch treat, Stramm had carefully recorded), an Italian cafeteria buried in a basement on John

Street that served cheap, heavy pasta with a watery tomato sauce. Norton explained that his job allowed only forty-five minutes for lunch, but that it would be enough time for them to get acquainted. Norton, Stramm later learned, was a back-office employee for one of Wall Street's second-tier investment banking houses.

Herbert Norton was prompt, arriving exactly at noon. Stramm had arrived ten minutes earlier and was waiting for him. Norton was a squatty man. His hair was short and neatly clipped, with a pompadour in front. He wore a plain brown suit, a green wash-and-wear shirt, and a narrow tie stained from other lunches at Zito's. As he talked, he stuffed large wads of spaghetti into his mouth. The thin tomato sauce ran down his chin onto the napkin tucked in at his collar.

Stramm couldn't eat.

"What's the matter? Ain't you hungry?" Norton asked.

"I have a little indigestion," Stramm said. "It comes and goes. I'm sorry."

"Listen pal, you don't have to apologize. I get it all the time. It's something they put in the food."

"I never thought of that."

"Well, you have to watch out for them, that's all. That's what we're all about. Victory, I mean. But we'll teach you. Don't you worry."

"Does it mean I can come?" Stramm pretended excitement.

"It sure does."

"I'm very grateful. Are you going to put in a good word for me?"

Norton continued to stuff spaghetti into his mouth. "Don't have to. I'm the one who decides," he said proudly. "It's all up to me."

Stramm bowed his head in a nod of appreciation. "Then, thank you."

"Think nothing of it." Norton wiped his mouth and threw the soiled paper napkin onto the floor. "I just have to personally meet anybody who wants to join our group, that's all. I can size a man up. I can tell where his heart is."

Norton leaned over the narrow table and beckoned Stramm into confidence. "You can't be too careful. You

just can't tell much in a name these days. It ain't like
it used to be when every nigger was named Roosevelt.
Why, Stramm could have been anything. You know what
I mean? We believe in law and order, but there ain't no
law that says we can't associate with who we want to on
our own free time."

"And a good thing, too," Stramm said for effect. "It
would be downright un-American."

"That's right, pal. That's what it's all about. America.
What do you do for a living?"

"I'm a CPA."

"A what?"

"An accountant."

Norton tried to make a joke. "Oh, boy, you had me
worried with all those initials. Sounded like some radical
group."

"It stands for Certified Public Accountant." Stramm
saw no reason why duty required him to go so far as to
laugh at Norton's jokes.

"Well, we can certainly use a man who's good with
figures," Norton said, somewhat offended at the rebuff.
"How's business, anyway?"

"As good as can be expected with all the lefties running
amok with private enterprise."

Norton was mollified. "Know what you mean. We'll
see you next Tuesday, will we?"

"With bells on."

Norton wrote out the address for him on a paper napkin,
using a felt-tip pen that smeared on his hands. Meetings
began promptly at seven thirty, he said.

The following Tuesday Stramm arrived at Norton's
house on Staten Island at seven twenty-five, which pleased
Norton no end. The meeting began at seven thirty sharp
with a recitation of the Pledge of Allegiance. Then the
group sang "America the Beautiful" *a cappella*. There
wasn't a voice on key except for a tall, stringy young man
with a red-and-purple, pimple-marred face.

Norton then introduced Stramm to the rest of the group.
He was a different man altogether from the pig at Zito's—
jovial, effervescent, self-confident. You would never have
believed how adroitly the man could run tomato sauce
down his chin.

There were five other members of the group. Addie May Vernon was a widowed schoolteacher whose speaking voice wandered two octaves above Joan Sutherland's high C. She wore her hair in a bun and white gloves on her hands.

John Deever, an undertaker from Brooklyn, was in his fifties. His eyes were dirty gray, like frozen ditchwater, and were wrinkled at the corners from squinting in constant bereavement. He spoke in a monotone, as if at any minute he would announce the procession to view the deceased. Then there were Anthony and Mary Oliver, seventy if they were a day. They ran a mail-order business, and it must have been successful. Mr. Oliver hadn't skipped a meal in fifty years and Mrs. Oliver wore a mink, which she kept on throughout the meeting. Mark Altman, the pimply-faced kid who could sing on key, sat at the back of the room and rubbed his hands together the entire time. A regular Lady Macbeth in tennis shoes, Stramm noted.

Herbert Norton gave a short lecture on the virtues of private medicine and how Social Security, Medicare, and Teddy Kennedy were leading the nation down the primrose path to Communism. Stramm thought about sending Norton a copy of *The Road to Wigan Pier* in a plain brown wrapper.

The meeting was opened up to general discussion at eight thirty-two, and Addie May Vernon demanded that something be done about the hippies.

"Cut their ba . . ." Mr. Oliver started to say.

"Anthony!" Mrs. Oliver said, heading him off. "They should either go to work or go to jail. That's what we mean," she said.

"I agree," said Addie May, her voice absolutely reaching for the Little Dipper.

"We all know they're living on welfare," Mr. Deever said.

"Well, something has to be done about these peace marches. Peace, peace, peace. That's all you ever hear," said Addie May.

Mr. Oliver snickered and Mrs. Oliver gave him a look that would have cut Lizzie Borden dead.

"Well, you can laugh and carry on," Addie May reprimanded them, "but there aren't many men around to defend a woman anymore. My late husband would have knocked their brains out. And those Communists, too. I'm glad he's not alive to see it. It would have killed him."

The undertaker nodded his head in sympathy.

"Why," Addie May continued, "any fool can see the Reds are going to walk straight through Vietnam to Australia to the United States of America. And where will the men be? In a peace march in Washington. I tell you, it would have killed him. I'm just glad we never had any children."

"Maybe we could have a countermarch someday," Mark Altman offered. "An America Day parade to show people what it really means to be an American."

Stramm decided he'd better offer something since everyone was getting in on the action. "Why don't we just join one of those peace parades and bust some heads, like Mrs. Vernon's husband would have done."

Addie May fluttered. "Well, that's for you men. I wouldn't be much help there." But she didn't say they shouldn't do it.

Norton had a sick grin on his face. "We men can talk about that later, but it certainly is not without merit, Mr. Stramm. Certainly not. Well, folks, it's nine o'clock. Time to go home to the little ones, or whatever."

"To my cat," Addie May said to Stramm in a half giggle.

"Mr. Stramm, would you lead us in the Lord's Prayer?" Norton asked. "They can keep it out of the schools, but they can't keep it out of my living room."

Stramm led off, and the group followed, each in his own cadence, finishing in a ragged chorus of "amens."

Norton took Stramm's arm as he started to leave and shook his hand firmly. "I like the way you think, Stramm," he said, winking. "You've got the stuff."

He spent the next three months attending the Staten Island meetings, trying to learn as much as he could about the Victory organization. But real knowledge was virtually impossible to come by. Stramm was forced to conclude that Norton knew almost nothing about the superstructure of the organization except the names of the men immediately above him, Albert Kline, a Philadelphian, and Adrian

Reese, the national head, who also lived in Philadelphia.

In late April 1970, Norton asked Stramm to stay after the meeting. Mr. and Mrs. Oliver roared away in their Eldorado and Mr. Deever and Addie May and the pimply-faced kid took off, in high spirits, in one of Mr. Deever's hearses. When they were alone, Norton told Stramm that they had been invited to join some construction workers and others in busting up a peace rally that was going to be held on Wall Street.

"We'll get a chance to really kick some ass," Norton said. "The cops are in on it with us."

Stramm was trapped. He couldn't get out of it and maintain his credibility with Norton. It was either beat up the kids or stop the investigation.

Norton grinned maliciously. "I can't wait," he said. "Can you?"

"No," Stramm said. "I can hardly wait."

At noon on Friday, May 8, 1970, hundreds of youths from sixteen to twenty, wearing peace symbols and long hair, gathered in front of the old Treasury Building at Wall Street and Broad, under the shadow of the statue of George Washington, to protest the killing of students by the Ohio National Guard at Kent State University. At exactly the same time, hundreds of construction workers, off-duty policemen, and other workingmen, wearing hard hats and American flags on their lapels and chanting "All the way, USA," began their march down Broadway.

Henry Stramm and Herbert Norton joined the long column of red and yellow hard hats as they turned the corner of Broadway and Wall Street and, marching behind a cluster of American flags, swept past the thin police line. The workers poured down Wall Street, a tidal wave of raging bodies. The students scattered, seeking refuge in the lunchtime crowd, but it was no use. The workers sought them out. Hysteria erupted.

The workers chanted, "Love it or leave it," and stalked their prey. The demonstrators were easy marks for the big-armed, thick-chested workers, who were greater in strength and brutality and purpose.

Henry Stramm took refuge behind the columns of the New York Stock Exchange building and watched in disgust. As the slaughter abated, he slipped away and headed home, ashamed, for the first time, of the business he was in.

By the end of 1972, the Staten Island group had disintegrated. The decline started with the sudden death of Mark Altman in September. Norton reported it at the following Tuesday night meeting, but Addie May Vernon already knew. Norton, unmoved, gave no details except for the date of death, then he asked for a moment of silent prayer for the departed. Addie May cried all the way through the silent prayer, and was comforted, almost professionally, by Deever, who stopped just short of telling her that Altman was better off. Addie May couldn't control herself and Norton had to stop the meeting. Deever offered her a ride in his hearse and she accepted. Stramm asked to join them.

On the ferry to Manhattan, Addie May broke the silence in the car. "It doesn't seem right taking the ride home without him. He was so quiet, so sweet. It's so scary, the way it happened. It just goes to show you that when the Lord calls—"

"How did it happen?" Stramm asked her. "Do you know?"

"It happened in his bathtub. In his very own bathtub, if you can imagine that."

"I can't," Stramm said.

"Well," Deever said, "a lot of people die from household accidents. More than you know."

"Is that so?" Addie May said, in distress.

"On my word."

"Do you know how he died in his bathtub?" Stramm asked. His curiosity was growing.

"They say he was taking a shower and slipped on the soap and hit his head."

"And *that* killed him?"

"Oh, no," Addie May said, as if she were instructing her seventh-grade English class. "He drowned." She stopped to shudder. "The water overflowed and came down into the lady's apartment below and she called the police. But they were too late, of course."

Stramm shook his head.

"That's what I mean by being scary. It could happen

to any one of us." Addie May paused to contemplate. "I suppose a bath would be safer."

"You can never tell," the undertaker said. "Household accidents."

"Well, just as my mother used to say, even some good will come from bad. The dear, sweet thing took care of us all."

"Oh?" Stramm said. "How?"

"In his insurance policy. We are his true beneficiaries."

"You mean each of us?" Stramm was not sure he understood. "You and me and Mr. Deever?"

"No, silly, of course not. I mean Victory. Our dear group. We are all his beneficiaries. He had a fifty-thousand-dollar life insurance policy, and he told me that he named Victory as his beneficiary."

"He was a real American," Deever said. "I wonder if it was double indemnity."

"Yes, I wonder," said Stramm.

"Well, I don't know," said Addie May, "but it so inspired me that I changed my will and did the same thing."

The ferry was docking and the car vibrated from the powerful rumble of the motor underneath.

"It was the least I could do," Addie May said, her voice falling. "After all, I have no children."

"Have you told anyone about this?" asked Stramm.

"Oh, yes. I told Mr. Norton over a month ago. I told him about Mr. Altman. Mr. Altman—Mark—was too shy."

It wasn't too long after that that Addie May decided to retire and move to Savannah, where she thought she could make her pension stretch further. Anyway, she told the undertaker, during her last ride across the East River in the black hearse, it just didn't seem the same coming and going to meetings without Mark Altman. The Olivers were the next to go. Mrs. Oliver decided that the long drive from Riverdale was getting to be too much for her husband, whose eyes were beginning to fail. Stramm thought it was as much a frailty of the spirit as of the body, for each time the couple came to a meeting, Altman's empty chair must have reminded them of their pressing mortality. At last the undertaker also lost heart.

And so the group faded away, one by one, led by the death of the quiet young man who always sang on key.

Norton was crushed. He lived in a secondhand house, had a secondhand job, and except for Tuesday nights lived a secondhand life. Now, even his small moments of glory were gone.

It seemed the end of the road for Stramm, too. He approached Norton with the suggestion that they form another group, but Norton was downhearted. It wasn't as easy as you might think, Norton informed him. In the fifties and sixties, yes. But by now the war and fuzzy politicians had dulled the people and distracted them.

"People just don't care anymore," Norton told him, defeated.

But Stramm was not willing to give up. He suggested that if they couldn't form their own group, they join another. Norton wavered. The only other group he knew about for certain was in Philadelphia, which was attended by Main Liners, including Adrian Reese, the President of Victory.

"Then let's go to Philadelphia," Stramm prodded him. Stramm needed Norton's former status as a Victory group leader as an introduction to the Philadelphia meeting.

"All right," Norton said, reluctantly. "If they'll have us."

In March 1973 Norton and Stramm attended their first Philadelphia meeting, held in the parlor of a beautifully renovated row house in Society Hill. Norton sat near the door, silent, his slick, greased hair shining under the pale light of a brass wall sconce. It was Norton's one and only trip to Philadelphia.

For Henry Stramm the story was different. By the end of the summer he was made assistant group leader. His subtle lectures on Communism, the environmentalists, and détente were tailor-made for the Main Line crowd. In Philadelphia, unlike in Staten Island, you spoke in innuendos, not accusations. Even the President, Adrian Reese, eyed him with interest.

In September Reese asked Stramm to join him, after the regular Tuesday-night meeting, for a late dinner at Bookbinders. Bookbinders, an unpretentious restaurant in Society Hill with rich desserts and high prices, was still doing a brisk trade when they arrived at nine thirty. The maitre d' welcomed Reese by name and escorted them across the wide-planked floor to a corner table.

After they had placed their orders, the aging, gracious Reese turned to the subject of Victory. Reese told Stramm that Victory funded local efforts in a number of ways, but two that he had direct contact with, and of which he was particularly proud, were the Valley Forge Maternal Care Home in Toms River, New Jersey, and the Manhattan Medical Services Corporation in New York City.

The Valley Forge Maternal Care Home was a home for unwed mothers.

"They are a community burden," Reese explained. "Our opportunity to serve—so long as the Federal Government is kept out. We accept no Federal funds, and turn no one away. Victory pays almost everything. Then, of course, we are able to place the young ones with families that will raise them in the right way. This is our only benefit, but you must admit that it is a great one."

The Manhattan Medical Services Corporation was, in simpler terms, a sperm bank.

"It is one of the few in the country," he informed Stramm. "Of course, we have to subsidize it heavily." Then Reese turned to Stramm in great confidence. "It is late in the day of our purpose for delicacy, so let me speak plainly. I ask some of our members to avail themselves of the clinic. You can never tell what life will bring. You may marry and be childless or . . ." Adrian Reese was too genteel a man to continue with the obvious. "We cannot allow simple fate to determine whether the best of our race will endure. Besides, it is good insurance."

"Do I need permission or anything in writing?" asked Stramm.

"Oh, no," Reese said. "It is available to the public. Otherwise we would lose our tax exemption."

Stramm promised to go.

Then Reese approached the real point of the meeting. "We are all grateful to have a young man such as you join our organization. We do not often attract such quality these days, although the dangers are no less great. More often we get oafs like Norton. You are much appreciated and—" Reese paused, to give impact to his next words.

"We would like to have you work more closely with the national organization. Much of it is done here in Philadelphia, so it would not be as much trouble as you might at first think."

"I am honored," Stramm said.

"Then you accept?"

"It's a privilege."

"Good!" Reese said. "Then let us drink to it."

Stramm's work with Adrian Reese concerned fund raising. Victory increased its monthly pleas for money. Some months, pamphlets were mailed out which suggested ways to enrich Victory—making over your life insurance policy to it, remembering it in your will, making a gift of a few shares of dividend-paying stock. Reese expressed suspicion of direct fund raisers (Victory had always done very well without them) and, he confided, he himself was personally responsible for raising more than five million dollars during his association with the organization. Even if Reese did not care for a particular fund-raising idea, he always made it clear that his discontent was in no way a criticism of the Executive Secretary.

In time it became clear to Stramm that the real power, indeed the absolute power, within Victory was in the hands of the Executive Secretary, who was never identified by name or address. Adrian Reese, the President, had no authority to initiate or command, except in small, meaningless ways. The will of the Executive Secretary was the will of Adrian Reese.

To be sure, Reese did not consider his job unimportant, though it became apparent that he was nothing more than a glorified bookkeeper. All monies raised and collected went to the Executive Secretary. All lists of new members, the roster of wealthy contributors, and the names of the Victory legion who had made over their insurance policies or had remembered Victory in their wills were handed over to the Executive Secretary. Reese did not really know the purpose of the lists, but his faith was absolute: The Executive Secretary would use them for the ultimate good of Victory and the country. Stramm was not so sure. But he kept his thoughts to himself, and waited.

Over the next few months, Stramm drew close to Reese and gained his confidence. Dinner became a ritual, as

Reese, a good if misdirected man, had no family of his own, and came to cherish the companionship of Henry Stramm.

In December 1973, as they were celebrating the holiday season in a grand fashion at Bookbinders, Stramm approached the subject of the Executive Secretary.

"He's a bit of a mystery," Stramm said. He knew he had to walk lightly. One wrong word, one question too sharp, too probing, would destroy four years of hard, tedious work.

But the wine had mellowed Adrian Reese. "No, not really," he said. "It is just that he prefers to work alone, without publicity. The Executive Secretary is a great man, Henry. He has devoted most of his life to our country, to fighting the Communists."

"I would think he would want to be out front, leading the fight."

"Oh, no," Reese said. "I don't think that would suit him very well at all. That is for us to do. You and me and others like us. The Executive Secretary's genius is organization, not people.

"Besides," he went on, "there are so many fools in the world. One time—" Reese paused, and an instant of terror struck Stramm, making him hold his breath. Had his face betrayed too much curiosity? Had he asked the wrong question?

Reese leaned forward. "One time we had an incident."

Stramm took a long drink of coffee before replying. "When?"

"Some years back. In the sixties. The Executive Secretary was assaulted, hit in the head." Reese reflected on the incident. "It was frightening."

Stramm showed concern. "That's terrible," he said.

"Yes, it was terrible, but it was a terrible time. The early sixties were the days of our greatest triumphs and our most vicious vilifications.

"When Kennedy was assassinated, they blamed us. A man in Arizona went and emptied his shotgun into the front window of the Birch Society's office outside Tucson. In 1964 they made poor Barry Goldwater look like a fool.

"It was not too long after that that the Executive Secretary and I were waiting for a taxi in front of the Plaza, in

New York. That's when it happened. The Executive Secretary was hit in the head by a rock. We were just standing there, doing no harm, when this old woman threw a rock at him. She screamed something like, 'axe man, axe man! Nazi Nazi!' then ran into the crowd and disappeared.

"I have never seen anything like it." Reese's thin patrician face twisted into a look of horror as he remembered the incident. "You should have seen that woman, Henry. She was dirty, filthy. She was crazy."

"Was the Executive Secretary badly hurt?"

"As it turned out, no. It looked worse than it was. There was blood all down his face. It was just a flesh wound, but it really frightened him. It frightened all of us. You see, this is what they have done to us. Called us Nazis, blamed us for the death of a President."

Reese leaned forward in his chair. "Since that time, I have insisted that the Executive Secretary go out in public as little as possible. We have to protect him with everything we have. He must be able to continue his work!"

The opening Stramm had been waiting for had appeared. He clenched his hands into fists under the table to steady himself.

"Do you think I will ever get to meet him?" he asked, calmly.

Reese reached out and touched Stramm's shoulder with affection.

"Someday, perhaps," Reese said. "I don't know. You are like a son to me, Henry, and still I cannot tell you any more than I already have, so great is my commitment to this wonderful man. But if times change, someday, perhaps you can."

Stramm never broached the subject of the Executive Secretary with Reese again. Reese had said all he would ever say on the matter.

Stramm, discouraged, continued to pursue other roads to the Executive Secretary. Reese allowed him to take over much of the paperwork, including his expense reports. Stramm examined each of Reese's gasoline receipts and marked the location of the station on a map. By April 1974 a pattern finally established itself, and Stramm knew the general location of the Executive Secretary: Seaside,

New Jersey, a small resort town that lay on a thin island across the bay from Toms River.

In May, Stramm offered to make a thousand-dollar contribution to the Valley Forge Home in Toms River. Reese was delighted, and arranged for Stramm to make the contribution to the Home in person.

The Valley Forge Maternal Care Home was on Blackmoor Road, a narrow back road in Toms River. The Home was 500 yards from the road, hidden from view by tall pines and spreading oaks. The entrance wove in and out among the trees, until at last it ended in a clearing, revealing a stark, two-story stucco building, rectangular and blocky, rather like a small hospital.

Percy Davis, the director of the Home, came to the reception area to greet Stramm and usher him to his office personally. The two men settled in the comfortable corner office. Tall windows let sunlight wash the room while allowing the eyes to feast on a garden of red, yellow, pink, and white flowers that ran from below the windows to the edge of a curtain of green oaks. Stramm declined an offer of coffee.

"Mr. Reese has informed us of your gracious intentions," Davis said, continuing the formalities. "Needless to say, we are most grateful. Grateful for your contribution and for your interest. Not many people think of us or our work as very important anymore. Florence Crittenden may be forgotten, but we still have our blossoms in the dust."

"I'm sure," Stramm said with sympathy.

"Right you are," Davis said, as enthusiastic as if Stramm had made the short speech instead of he. "Every girl doesn't take the pill. Or they forget. An abortion is not an option open to everyone. The new morality is not one hundred percent upon us, Mr. Stramm."

"That's fortunate."

"I agree wholeheartedly. But our numbers are small and shrinking." Davis paused. "I would very much like to show you around. Of course, our tour must be somewhat limited. There are certain . . . delicacies. Nevertheless, we can see some of the empty quarters, the recreation area, certain of the maternity facilities. And, last but not least, our garden. The peonies—"

Davis was stopped in midsentence by a high, forceful scream from the corridor outside his office. It was the kind of tortured scream that would shatter the tranquility of a thousand peonies. Davis, after the initial shock, jumped to his feet and headed for the door. The screams kept coming. Angry voices shouted. Stramm followed Davis to the door.

Two men and a woman struggled with a pale blond young woman with ravaged eyes.

"You stole my baby!" she screamed. "You stole it! You killed it!"

"Get her back to her room," Davis ordered.

The two men tried to restrain her, but she was wild and strong.

"Ellen! Ellen, listen to me," the other woman pleaded. "Please stop this. Please!"

Ellen stared at her with red, dilated eyes. Then she spat at Davis and threw out her accusations. "Murderer! Thief!" she screamed. "I want my baby! I want my baby!"

Davis stepped between her and the orderlies. "Ellen! Get back to your room! We're not taking any more of this!" Davis's tall, angular body was as rigid and unbending as tempered steel. He swelled with fury, but contained it in every way except for his hands, which were trembling. "Mary," he said to the woman who had been pleading with the raging patient, "she's your sister. Make her get hold of herself, or else get her out of here."

It was Mary's turn to become enraged, except that she found no need to suppress it. She took two quick steps forward and gave Davis the back of her hand.

Davis's head snapped to one side.

"Just remember who you're talking to," she said to Davis under her breath. Then she turned to her sister. "Come with me, Ellen."

The two men who had been so ineffectual in either calming the wild Ellen or protecting their stunned director grabbed Ellen's arms.

"Take your hands off her," Mary ordered.

The men complied. Mary took the haggard young woman's arm and gently led her away. The hysteria had wilted to tears.

Percy Davis, his left cheek still cherry red, returned to

his office without speaking. Stramm followed him, but could think of nothing to ease his embarrassment.

Davis looked out the tall windows. Finally, his field of peonies, tulips, and irises composed him.

"I'm sorry," he said. "That was most unusual. She should be in a hospital."

"You don't have the facilities?"

"Not for the mentally ill."

"Is she?"

"What do you think?"

"I'm not a doctor. I don't make those kinds of judgments."

"Didn't you hear what she said?"

"I could have heard it standing in the middle of the Verrazano Bridge, but I'm still not a doctor. Please understand, I don't believe you stole her child or killed it."

For a moment, Davis looked as though fury were about to overtake him again. Then his business sense took hold of him. He was speaking to a contributor.

"I can certainly appreciate your position," he said, with great understanding. "Ellen Rider's child was born dead. Her nerves—if that's what you call it—were shattered by the time she came here. Her confinement was most difficult. The great complication was that she wanted to keep her child, which the Home frowns upon. When she delivered, we were still trying to convince her to do the right thing for her child and put it up for adoption. Her child was stillborn. It was more than she could handle."

"Do you call that mental illness? I call it grief."

"Perhaps I spoke too hastily. Nevertheless, we are not equipped to—"

"I understand," Stramm said, not having the stomach for more. He rose. "I hope you won't take offense, Mr. Davis, but I would rather take a tour another day. Somehow it—"

"Oh, I understand," Davis said, with relief. "If it wouldn't cause too much trouble, I'd prefer it, too."

"No trouble," Stramm said.

Stramm wrote out his personal check for one thousand dollars and left.

Outside the Home, the woman named Mary was sitting

on a bench smoking a cigarette. Her body was limp and
her fine, brown hair hung in strings around her face. It
was as if she had summoned up all the fire within her to
fight for her sister against Davis, and now had no more fire
for her own use. She looked up at Stramm as he passed
by, but without interest.

Henry Stramm's diary recorded that he continued to
work in Victory's national headquarters in Philadelphia,
doggedly pursuing the identity of the Executive Secretary.
One of his methods of detection was to sift the contents of
the trash baskets, looking for bits of information carelessly
thrown away. The day before he left on his expedition to
Seaside, he found a number scribbled on a piece of paper.
He thought the number might be a bank account or post
office box, and duly recorded it in his diary. It was the last
line of the last entry in the diary.

Parks wrote the numbers down on the back of one of
his business cards, then added two more logs to the
dwindling fire, and, as the wood crackled, threw the book
on the fire and watched the red and yellow flames consume
it, as the sun rose over Manhattan to wake eight million
people.

John Parks read the sign on the door. "Manhattan
Medical Services Corporation." He pressed the buzzer and
was let into the reception area, which, like its receptionist,
was white, spare, and antiseptic.

He introduced himself with the pseudonym he had used
on the telephone earlier that morning when making the appointment. "Henry Wallace. I have an eleven-o'clock
appointment."

The receptionist barely looked up from her papers.

"How do you do," she said, and handed him a questionnaire. "Have a seat and fill this out. The doctor will be
with you shortly."

Parks took a seat on a black-and-white plastic chair and
filled out the medical questionnaire. One other man was in
the reception room, calmly reading *The Wall Street Journal*. Handsome, in his mid-thirties, he wore a blue pinstripe suit, a Phi Beta Kappa key, and a Morgan Guaranty
Trust stone face. Parks almost laughed out loud. If he un-

derstood the procedure correctly, this tall, elegant product of Park Avenue wealth sitting across from him would soon go into a side room, hang his Brooks Brothers suit on a peg, pull down his jockey shorts, and jerk off.

Just after the business executive was asked to proceed past the reception area to the doctor's office, a fair-haired, athletic young man, no more than nineteen, carrying a copy of *A Portrait of the Artist as a Young Man,* hurried into the clinic and apologized for being late. There was not the slightest hint of embarrassment about him.

"It's almost on time for you," the receptionist said coolly. "Go on in."

Parks was still sitting in the chair in the reception room when the boy emerged. Parks eyed him with admiration. The fastest right hand in the Pepsi generation.

"Same time next week?" the student asked.

"Call first," the receptionist replied.

"Okay," he said, then tucked his copy of Joyce's burden to the Columbia freshman class under his arm and left.

The receptionist turned her attention to Parks.

"The doctor will see you now," she said.

Dr. Abraham Seahurst was an elderly man, bald, with soft eyes. Microscopes, test tubes, Bunsen burners, and other paraphernalia of a life given to research cluttered his office. He rose to greet Parks.

"Have a seat, please, while I read your file," Dr. Seahurst said, running his eyes down the questionnaire.

"You're not married," the doctor observed.

"No."

"Do you plan a vasectomy?"

"Not at present."

"At a future date?"

"Not really."

"Good. I don't recommend it for unmarrieds."

"I'd just like to make a deposit," Parks said. "For safekeeping."

"Always a good idea," the doctor said earnestly. "Tell me, have you been recommended to us?"

"Yes. By a friend who was, I believe, recommended by Adrian Reese."

The Doctor did not change expression. "Ah, yes," he said.

"You know him?"

"Mr. Reese? Not personally. He was one of the founding fathers of the clinic, but he was inactive by the time I came. Mr. Reese is a very generous man. From Philadelphia, I believe."

"I really don't know," Parks lied.

"Now," the doctor said, hurrying on. "Let me finish my questions. What kind of underwear do you wear?"

"Boxer, when I wear any at all."

"Do you take baths or showers?"

"Both."

"Hot? Warm?"

"Hot."

The doctor frowned. "You should take lukewarm showers if you are interested in fertility."

"What was that kid doing in here?" Parks asked, changing the subject. "He looked too young for worry."

"Quite right. He's one of our donors. Unfortunately, some of our tests come out negative and there's nothing we can do to help. In that case, if the wife is fertile, the couple may ask for artificial insemination. We try to match up the physical features of the husband to the donor."

"What does it take for a donor to qualify?"

"Good looks, good health, superior intelligence, and a high sperm count."

"You don't ask much."

"They are well paid for what they do," the doctor said, and smiled.

"When I was a kid, I did it for free."

Dr. Seahurst laughed. "Didn't we all. Now, it is time to collect a specimen." He handed Parks a small, wide-mouthed bottle. "Take the first room to your right. Room number two. If you care to watch a movie, just push the red button by the light switch."

As Parks was walking down the narrow hall to his cubicle, the business executive in the pinstripe suit emerged from one of the rooms carrying a glass vial discreetly in his hand, as if the contents were liquid gold. He seemed, at last, a bit embarrassed.

Parks entered the room marked "2," a small, windowless cubicle, bare except for a couch and an end table with a box of Kleenex on it. He closed the door, locked it, and took off his jacket. He searched for the red button and, finding it, pressed it and turned off the lights. Immediately, a Times Square special flickered on the wall. Parks took off his pants and folded them neatly on the arm of the couch, watching the movie out of the corner of his eye. At least the clinic went first class. He turned up his palms and looked down at his hands. Now, the really important decision: left hand or right?

The Central Park Zoo was teeming with small children and their mothers, East Side nannies pushing baby carriages, and businessmen in Burberry coats taking lunch-hour walks. The air smelled of roasted chestnuts.

Parks walked down the steps at 64th Street and Fifth Avenue that led to the front of the New York Arsenal building, a nineteenth-century red-brick structure built in the manner of a twin-towered medieval fortress. The ivy vines that covered the Arsenal and the brick walls surrounding the zoo had shed their leaves, and now looked bare and desolate. The green was gone from the edge of the stone walk that curved around the front of the Arsenal northward to the gorilla cages. Winter had finally come after an easy fall.

Charles Winston was already standing in front of the cages when Parks arrived. A weathered brown gorilla was pacing back and forth in one cage and an audience had gathered to watch him. The sign on the cage stated that while gorillas looked fierce and mean, they were really quite shy and gentle. The long-faced gorilla grunted and turned his raw backside to the people.

"Well?" Winston asked as they moved away from the crowd.

"It's a sperm bank, all right," Parks said. "Where the elite meet to beat."

"I gathered you read Stramm's report," the Director said dryly.

"Yes."

"What do you make of it?"

"Stramm was a damned good investigator. Did he have a photographic memory?"

"Close to it, I think. Very thorough, anyway. What do you think of Victory?"

"A collection of second-raters, fighting a foe they've never seen to defend a country whose history and purpose they've never understood." Parks paused. "Life's pathetic losers. But killers? I don't think so."

"Well, Henry Stramm is dead," Winston said, flatly.

"I know."

"And you don't think. . . ."

"I don't think that his murderer came out of the discussion groups. Not the shoe salesmen and the schoolteachers who sit around in living rooms and discuss the Red Menace. But the top of the organization . . . that's another matter."

"Like the President?"

"Adrian Reese? Not according to Stramm's diary. More like the Executive Secretary, whoever he is. He's the key."

"Do you think we ought to put Reese under surveillance?"

"Can't hurt." Parks put his hands in his pockets. "The diary didn't really say much about the Southern Region's part in the investigation."

"That's because we've worked rather independently, concentrating on different things," the Director said. "However, we keep each other well informed. Stramm was trying to infiltrate the national organization, find out who was behind it, what they were up to. That information was here in the East. Fleming concentrated on Victory's Southwestern activities. Most of the really big contributions came from there—Dallas, Houston, Orange County, Phoenix. Fleming thinks Victory is laundering money through Mexico and sending it abroad, but he can't prove it. Not yet, anyway."

Winston paused to pack his pipe with tobacco, then continued: "The two of you should get together to compare notes. I think you'll find him very satisfactory."

"I'm sure I will."

Winston took a long drag on his pipe. "I haven't told the Southern Director that Stramm is dead."

"I thought you kept each other well informed?"

"A small breach which I shall rectify very soon," Winston said. "I wanted to wait until you agreed to take over the assignment before I told him. I thought it would be easier." He shrugged. "But it won't."

They began to walk slowly toward the polar bear pa-
villion, down the path from the gorilla's cage. Nearby, a
wrinked old man hawked balloons. Children ran up and
down the path, their loud, happy voices screening the two
men's conversation.

"I'm coming around to agreeing with your assistant,"
Parks said, "that somebody squealed on Stramm."

Winston frowned. "What makes you think so?"

"Stramm," Parks said. "He was so fucking careful."

"Yes, but he was exposed."

"No more than ordinary," Parks said. "Unless there's
a leak. Who the hell even knows the Unit exists?"

"That's the puzzle," Winston said with concern. "But
still—"

"The leak didn't have to come from the Eastern Region,"
Parks pointed out. "I wouldn't rule anyone out. Not even
the FBI."

They reached the red brick arches that led to the giant
white polar bear's cage just as the bear plunged into the
cold water of his pond, then climbed back up to his concrete turf. The water rolled off his thick white fur. The
Director and Parks climbed the steep stairs to the left of the
cage and stood above the children gathered at the rail.

"John," Winston finally said, "endless speculation will
consume us if we let it. The main focus of this investigation ought to be Victory and the Executive Secretary.
That's what we've been asked to do."

"Don't you care about the leak?"

"Of course I care. But I'm still not convinced there is
one."

"Remember the name Mark Altman from Stramm's
diary?" Parks asked.

"He had an accident and died, as I recall. Fell in his
bathtub and drowned."

"He was murdered," Parks said.

"Really? I don't recall Stramm saying that."

"He didn't. He was suspicious, but he couldn't quite
put his finger on it. Altman was taking a shower when he
hit his head and knocked himself out."

"That's right. He fell down in the tub and drowned."
Winston shrugged. "Tragic, I agree. But not all that suspicious."

"Very suspicious, Director. There's no water in the tub when you take a shower."

A look of discovery passed over the Director's face.

"You don't plug the drain when you take a shower," Parks continued.

"If it had been any simpler, they'd have put it in the first grade reader. And Altman had an insurance policy made out to Victory."

"That's right. I suggest you check whether any other Victory members have died suspiciously under similar circumstances."

"It's a logical starting point," Winston said. "Then we'll know if Altman's death was a freak or if we have a case of mass murder. Now, what do you plan to do?"

"First, I'm going to check out something else in Stramm's diary. Remember the part where the Executive Secretary visited New York and an old woman threw a stone at him and called him a Nazi?"

"Yes, she called him an axe man."

"That's the way it was written. It could have been a nickname, the axe man, or it could have been his name . . . Axmann."

"Or," Winston cautioned, "it could have been a shopping bag lady. You've seen them standing on street corners, cursing the air. That's what it sounded like to me."

Parks agreed. "Perhaps, but it can't hurt to find out. After that, I'm going to Seaside. It's the last place where we know Stramm was alive."

The Director frowned. "We don't have much to go on, do we?"

"Enough."

Winston tapped out his pipe and put it in his pocket. "If you want to check out this axe man connection," he said, "I know just the man." He scribbled a name and address on the back of a card. "Tell him Otto Werner sent you. That was a code name I used when we worked together years ago. Also, tell him, when you see him in person, that the New York City Library was built in part by the Samuel J. Tilden Trust. Those words have a special meaning to him. He'll help you if he can. I helped him once when he was gathering facts for an extradition proceeding in South America. All very quietly, of course. The government wanted its name kept out of it."

"Did anything come of it?" Parks asked.

"Yes and no. They were trying to extradite a man from Paraguay. A man named Fritz Wagner, more commonly known to the inmates of Treblinka as the Black Angel. The proceedings got bogged down, as they always do in Paraguay, but then they became moot. Wagner was found floating facedown in the Paraná River, a bullet hole through his head."

"Suicide?"

"Maybe. That was the official verdict, anyway."

"Of course," Parks said, with a wry smile.

He reached into his coat pocket and retrieved the card with the numbers he had copied from Stramm's diary. "You remember these numbers?" Parks asked, handing the card to Winston. "They were at the end of Stramm's diary. He thought they might be a bank account or post office box."

Winston studied the card. "Yes, I remember. Too short for a bank account. Maybe a post office box."

"Can you find out?"

Winston sighed. "A needle in a haystack."

"Use some of your nefarious connections," Parks said, smiling. "I know you've got 'em."

The New York branch of the World Jewish Congress, preservationist and archivist for Jewish faith, culture, and tradition throughout the world, is housed in small, Spartan quarters on the third floor of 15 East 84th Street, a white limestone building owned by its more affluent affiliate, the American Jewish Congress. The World Jewish Congress is widely known for its scholarly research, particularly on the subjects of racism and anti-Semitism. But its importance to many lies in another kind of research: its documentation of the Holocaust. On the third floor, dedicated men and women spend their days poring over news clippings, photographs, letters, and affidavits, building cases against Nazi war criminals still at large. The World Jewish Congress serves as the arms, legs, and ears of some of the world's most famous Nazi hunters.

Parks entered the double doors and approached the receptionist sitting at the entrance to the great marble-and-stone center hall. At her back a pair of grand twin staircases lifted from the floor and wound through the core of the building.

Parks asked for Dr. Silverman. "Otto Werner asked me to call."

"Third floor. Take the elevator or the stairs," the receptionist said.

Parks took the stairs.

By the third floor the old building had lost the elegance of its grand lobby. The narrow landing was lined with tall, green steel file cabinets stacked high with thick folders neatly tied with red cords. The dim uncarpeted halls were painted a deep cream and the moldings and doors a glossy kelly green.

Parks found Dr. Silverman at his gray metal desk. There was no name on the door, only the stenciled number 308. It could easily have been the office of a lower-level government clerk instead of the workplace of a Talmudic scholar and former Haganah agent. The stark walls were painted a weak, flat green, the color of Army barracks and city health centers. The one small window in the room was bare and overlooked the rear walls of other buildings. Gray metal file cabinets lined one side of the room.

Dr. Max Silverman was a small man. His shoulders were rounded, as if he were continually bracing against the cold, and his skin was pale and speckled with brown spots. The years had not been kind to Max Silverman, but—perhaps in spite of it all—there was something proud and strong about him. His small brown eyes still held their fire.

He had been born in Vienna in 1904, where he lived until, in April 1938, Austria voted overwhelmingly for *Anschluss*, and Max Silverman, together with his mother and young wife, fled to England. Four years later Silverman slipped back into Europe to fight in the underground. He was captured in 1945, and in a strange twist of fate was not executed, but sent to Mauthausen, where he wore the yellow star alongside Simon Wiesenthal. When the Americans liberated the camp on May 5, 1945, Silverman returned to England, and later, with the consent of his wife (who was by then pregnant with their second child), became an unofficial agent of the Haganah, silently tracking down Nazi killers and dealing with them in unofficial ways. In 1956 he had come to work for the World Jewish Congress and opened the documentation center. With his campmate Simon Wiesenthal he continued to track down Nazi war criminals—now in a more official way.

"Please come in, Mr. Parks," Dr. Silverman said in a crisp, clear voice.

He extended his hand for a warm handshake. His fingers were scarred and bent, but his grip was firm. Silverman directed Parks to one of the plain wooden chairs in front of his desk.

"How is Mr. Werner?" Dr. Silverman asked, in a manner of friendly interrogation.

"Otto Werner is fine," Parks said. "I just left him thirty minutes ago, and he said to tell you that the New York City Library was built in part by the Samuel J. Tilden Trust."

Silverman smiled.

"He said that you would know what it means."

"It means, Mr. Parks, that you have come from Mr. Werner and that I will help in any way that I can." He leaned back in his chair and waited for Parks to speak.

"Dr. Silverman, I think we may have a war criminal living here in New York and I need your help to find him."

The Doctor nodded earnestly.

"You don't seem surprised by what I said."

"No," Silverman said sadly. "I am not surprised. I am only surprised that you think there is just one. There are many, in Yorkville, in Mineola, in Queens. They live among us as free men, as American citizens. And Mr. Parks, I tell you that the real disgrace is how much better they have survived than their victims."

The old scholar drew in his breath. Then, with a sigh: "It is no use going over old ground. Tell me, what do you have?"

"An old woman saw a man she recognized as a Nazi. She threw a rock at him and called out 'Axmann! Axmann! Nazi! Nazi!' Or the woman could have called 'axe man,' a nickname. That's all I have. A name or a nickname. The woman may have been crazy, we don't know. But we have to follow up on the accusation, for reasons which I can't disclose."

"Do not feel you have to," Silverman said. "But still, it is not much. Can the woman tell you more?"

"No. We don't even know who she is. We'll try to locate her, of course, but we don't even know her name."

Dr. Silverman leaned forward and smiled gently, as if to a discouraged son. "Do not despair yet, Mr. Parks. Successful investigations have been started on much less."

"Then you think—"

"I think we can try," Silverman said. "It is early in the day to feel hopeless. We haven't even made our first inquiry. At least we have a name—or a nickname. That is often the first stumbling block. The Nazis didn't always introduce themselves to their victims."

"Where will you start?" Parks asked.

Dr. Silverman looked at Parks with pride. Light danced in his brown eyes. "Why, right here, Mr. Parks. We start right here at the World Jewish Congress. It is part of our work. Let me tell you about it."

Silverman leaned back and folded his hands in his lap. "We are what they call a documentation center. Small, cramped, and overworked, as you can see. We collect testimony and documents that can be used in investigations of atrocities committed by the Nazis."

"How do you locate your witnesses?" Parks asked.

"Many ways, but mostly by advertising in the Jewish press, in New York, in Israel, wherever there is a large population of Jews. Sometimes we try to locate the survivors of the ghetto where the crime was committed. When the Germans and Austrians agreed to pay compensation to the Jews, committees were set up to administer the restitution. We sometimes locate survivors through their property settlements."

"Not exactly a piece of cake," Parks said, with admiration.

"No, it is hard, tedious work."

"Who asks you to collect the witnesses?" Parks asked.

"Sometimes the West Germans, sometimes the Immigration and Naturalization Service, anyplace where a Nazi is going on trial." The old man paused and smiled mischievously. "Sometimes they don't ask us—we just do it."

"Have you ever had a request to gather evidence on an Axmann?"

"Not that I remember, but we can check the files. Every time we receive a request, a letter, or an inquiry, it goes on an index card. Mrs. Feldman, our librarian, can find out for us. Come."

Dr. Silverman led the way down the dim hall. He took one step at a time, slowly, deliberately. His feet had not survived Mauthausen as well as his spirit.

The documents library was one long room, with a high ceiling and two tall windows at the far end. The walls were lined from floor to ceiling with industrial shelving and metal cabinets. On the steel shelves, wrapped in plain manila folders, were thousands of affidavits, letters, photographs, and documents that told the heartbreak of the Jewish people.

The folders were arranged on the shelves by location. The names lined up, a chronicle of horror: Auschwitz, Bergen-Belsen, Grossrosen, Landsberg, Sachsenhausen, Theresienstadt, Treblinka, Ravensbruck, Riga, Dachau, Chelmno, Breslau, Buchenwald, Belzec, Krakow, Sobibor, Mauthausen, Lwów, Maidanek.

The names of the villages, towns, and death camps were printed on rudimentary tags made from strips of index cards and colored paper; the history of six million dead, printed in pen and pencil and Magic Marker by the careful hand of Lilly Feldman and taped to the cold steel shelves with pieces of Scotch tape.

Lilly Feldman was sitting behind a desk by the window at the far end of the room. At her back was a Monet print of a field of red poppies. Lilly Feldman herself smelled of lilacs, and her short curly gray-blond hair, bright eyes, and quick smile gave her small round face the precious sweetness of honeysuckle in summer.

In the room where death lined the walls, life triumphed.

Dr. Silverman introduced Parks. "Mr. Parks has an inquiry," he informed her.

Mrs. Feldman nodded her head quickly, in three little jerks, and said "Good, good," in a thick Yiddish accent. Her soft warm voice filled the room.

"We have a name," Dr. Silverman said. "Axmann. Or, perhaps a title, the axe man. We are not sure."

Mrs. Feldman looked at the doctor, puzzled.

"That is all we have," he said and shrugged. "Do you remember such a name? It is important to Mr. Parks."

"No, but no matter." She shook her head as if it were a fault not to remember the contents of 5,000 white index cards. "There is so much, too much for me to remember anymore. I will look at the cards."

When she stood up, she was barely taller than she had appeared while sitting. She went to the alphabetical file, picked through the A's, paused, studied a white index card, then pulled it from the file.

"I have one," she said.

Dr. Silverman's face brightened. Parks took a step forward in anticipation.

"It is not much," she said, and handed Dr. Silverman the card.

"Do you remember anything?" he asked.

"Yes . . . now. It was a request from the Immigration Service, a long time ago."

Dr. Silverman gave the card to Parks. At the top, in Mrs. Feldman's large, elementary printing, was the word "AXMANN." At the bottom of the card was the date, December 20, 1964, the notation "INS—A. Riccio," and the explanation that a woman claimed that Axmann had killed her child in Poland in 1944.

"This could be what we are looking for," Dr. Silverman said. "Do you remember what we did with the request?"

She shrugged her shoulders in defeat. "We tried. We advertised in the *Forward,* and in *Lowyzaelka,* the Polish paper, but we got nothing."

Parks studied the index card. "The card says 'INS—A. Riccio.' INS is Immigration and Naturalization Service, of course. Who is Riccio?"

Lilly Feldman looked at Dr. Silverman for permission.

"It is all right," he said. "Mr. Parks is our friend. We can tell him."

Mr. Feldman smiled. "Tony Riccio, Antonio Riccio, is an investigator with the INS. He is the one who called. Mr. Riccio has done wonderful things for the Jewish people. That is why we went ahead, with so little information."

"Thank you, Mrs. Feldman," Parks said, and took her hand warmly in his.

The two men returned to Dr. Silverman's small, un-carpeted office.

"There, you see." Dr. Silverman lowered his body into the chair with difficulty. "You know much more now than when you first walked through my door. You know that the crime, if there was one, was committed in Poland in 1944. You know the woman called Mr. Riccio first, and if you call him, he may remember even more. Perhaps even her name." He looked down at his watch. "And," he said, "we are far from finished. I have one more call to make. Have you heard of the Vienna Documentation Center? It is run by Simon Wiesenthal."

Parks smiled. The Doctor intended to take his case to the top. "*Der Eichmann jäger*," Parks said.

"Yes, that is right. Simon Wiesenthal is an old friend. He will help us if he can."

"Dr. Silverman, you have been more than kind."

"Some years ago, Mr. Parks, Otto Werner was more than kind. There is a saying that when you light a candle to stop the darkness, the light will not die until there is sunshine. Otto Werner passed the light to me, I pass it to you."

The old man smiled warmly, remembering.

"Please tell Mr. Wiesenthal that I will cover all expenses," Parks said.

"I will tell him, Mr. Parks, and I am sure he will appreciate your offer. The Center runs on a very small budget. But the first thing he can do for us will cost him no more than a strain on his eyes. Wiesenthal has a master card file of over twenty-five thousand war criminals, most of them wanted for murder or mass murder. Also, he has a list of over fifteen thousand SS men, complete with rank, decorations, locations of service, and other remarks—a list prepared for Hitler's forty *Gauleiter*s in the occupied territories. Wiesenthal bought this list in 1960 from an old SS man who was down on his luck. It may be the only one still in existence.

"But if Simon Wiesenthal should fail us, we will try the West German State Attorney General's office in Ludwigsburg. They also have a list, a Wanted Book they call it, of more than 160,000 names." The old scholar's eyes were bright with excitement. The age had shaken from his shoulders. His voice was firm with purpose. "One way or the other, Mr. Parks, we will see this through."

"When will you call Mr. Wiesenthal?" Parks asked.

"It is too late now. I will call early tomorrow morning. Can you come back tomorrow?"

"I'll be here at nine."

"Good. By then I will have more."

Parks left the World Congress building with the tension of adventure in his shoulders. The hunt had begun. He called Winston and asked him to follow up on the INS lead, then went home and picked up *The Rise and Fall of the Third Reich* and started to read.

CHAPTER 6

Thursday, December 5, 1974

When Parks arrived at the World Jewish Congress, Dr. Silverman was seated at his gray metal desk, his notes spread out before him.

"I talked to Simon this morning," he began. "There were more than one hundred fifty Axmanns on the SS Service List, but none wanted for murder."

"Oh," Parks said, disappointed.

"It is not as bad as it seems, Mr. Parks. More than one hundred of them are dead. Some died on the Eastern Front, some in the last days of Berlin, some in their beds. The rest are old men now, working as watchmen, janitors, carpenters. Nothing spectacular in this group."

Silverman pointed an arthritic finger. "There is only one unaccounted for, a Walter Axmann. And he served with the SS in Poland—that goes along with the old woman's story. This is where Wiesenthal thinks you should concentrate your efforts, although, to tell the truth, he thinks you may be chasing a wild goose."

"Is Axmann in America?"

Dr. Silverman shrugged his thin shoulders.

"That we don't know. We only know the others are not. Walter Axmann disappeared after the war and was never heard from again."

"Are there any charges against him?"

"No, none. He is not wanted. He was just a little fish."

"If nobody cares about him, why did he disappear?"

"That was not so unusual after the war. Many SS men, even those accused of nothing, went underground, changed their names, and started their lives over again. They did not care to bear the shame of the SS."

Parks took a blue stenographer's notebook from his briefcase and, with a black felt-tip pen, he wrote the name Walter Axmann.

"Can you tell me more about him?" he asked Dr. Silverman.

"I can give you a little—what was on the Service List. He was born in Munich in 1909. He joined the Nazi Party in 1931 and the SS in 1932. Nazi Party number 2,123,332 and SS number 314,451. He was promoted to *Hauptsturmführer* in 1942. He served with the Lebensborn."

The Doctor paused and shook his head, and allowed himself a moment to reflect on the irony of the SS Service List.

"Now that is the Germans for you," he said. "Everyone with a number, everyone on a list—even in the middle of the storm. You have no idea how many men have denied they were in the SS only to have Wiesenthal pull out his Service List and say, 'What do you mean? There is your number.'"

Parks appreciated the irony. "Digging their own graves," he said. "I guess they really believed they would win. What was the Lebensborn?"

"An obscure department of the SS." Dr. Silverman spelled the word slowly for Parks so that he could write it in his notebook.

"It means Fount of Life," he explained. "It was an SS organization set up to promote the German race. About the only thing I know about it for sure is that it ran maternity homes for unmarried German girls."

Parks stopped writing and looked up. "Maternity homes?" he asked, remembering the scene from the Valley Forge Home in Stramm's diary.

"Yes, maternity homes," Silverman answered, attributing the look in the younger man's eyes to surprise. "You see, abortion was a crime under the Nazis."

"I see," Parks said, hand poised to continue writing.

Silverman continued: "Lebensborn was the propaganda arm of the Nazis' drive to increase the birthrate. It deified motherhood and campaigned against abortion. They distributed little booklets on pregnancy, health care, and fertility. Nothing particularly criminal, as you can see. No one in the Lebensborn was ever convicted of murder. A few got light sentences, but mostly because they were in the SS. Anything less than murder would now be covered by the statute of limitations that took effect in 1969. If Walter Axmann beat a prisoner half to death or sewed his fingers together to make a human duck, he is no longer a wanted man."

"But," Parks reminded him, "our accusation is one of murder."

"I know. That surprised Wiesenthal. After the war you heard a thousand rumors about Lebensborn, but never murder. Mrs. Feldman believes it ran human breeding farms where German women were forced to mate with good specimens of German men, like animals on a farm, to produce perfect Aryans. That was one of the rumors, never substantiated. My assistant, Benjamin Stein, says this is all in her head, that nothing was forced. Perhaps you should talk to him and hear what he knows."

The doctor chuckled to himself. "I will let you talk to him alone. Mr. Stein has a rather plain way of speaking. You and he will get along fine, I am sure. He is young and brash. Some of the old ones here think he is too brash. They complain that he spends half his time on the telephone talking to the girls. I admonish him sometimes, tell him the Congress is not a longshoremen's hall." He lowered his voice in confidence. "But I tell you the truth, I wouldn't change him."

True to his reputation, Benjamin Stein was on the telephone. Stein was tall and dark, with a full head of black curly hair with the texture of steel shavings, and a face that more than a mother could love.

Stein terminated his conversation with a line that only a teenager would buy, but he delivered it with conviction, then rose to shake Parks's hand. He was over six feet tall, with strong hands and a solid, well-proportioned body that moved with confidence.

"What can I do for you?" Stein asked, sitting back down and propping his foot on his desk.

"My name is John Parks. Dr. Silverman has been helping me learn something about a man named Walter Axmann, an ex-Nazi we think may be living in America."

Stein nodded. "Max told me about it this morning. He was in the Lebensborn, right?"

"That's right."

"I told him to forget it," Stein said.

"Why?"

"Because the only thing we can go after is murder or conspiracy to murder. A man in the Lebensborn might be guilty of crotch rot, but not murder."

"Why do you say that?"

Stein took his foot off the desk and sat up straight. "How much do you know about Lebensborn?" he asked.

"Not one hell of a lot. I just heard of it thirty minutes ago."

Stein laughed and leaned back in his chair.

"The rest of us don't know too much more than you do right now, Mr. Parks. But we do know a couple of things. Lebensborn set up homes for the *Frauleins* the SS knocked up behind the barn. All in the name of duty, you understand. The more Germans the better. When Germany went to war, any fool could see that it would need more sons. Lebensborn was put in charge of changing the psychology of the people. Abortion was discredited and childbirth was promoted. Legitimate or illegitimate, it didn't matter. Married and pregnant, great. We'll give you a bonus. Puffed up and not married, don't worry. We'll take care of you."

Parks laughed. "Nothing wrong with wanting children," he said. "Dr. Silverman believes the Lebensborn was dedicated to building the master race."

"That's true. At least an idealized master race. The modern Siegfried was supposed to be tall, blond, blue-eyed, built like Joe Namath, and hung like a mule. Completely opposite, you understand, to most of the powers in the Reich. Hitler was a short, dumpy Austrian missing a left nut. Himmler was fat and dark. Eichmann looked like pie dough, and Bormann was a peasant. Still, many of the day-to-day SS men were chosen for their looks and their swagger.

"Himmler wanted his SS men to breed, to procreate. It was their duty to fuel the master race, to fill Germany with blue-eyed giants. SS men were supposed to have at least four children. Himmler didn't care how they went about it.

Lebensborn was there to take care of your wife or girl friend, whichever, and to give them the best medical care possible. If your girl friend didn't want to keep the child, Lebensborn would place it with a good German family."

"Then Mrs. Feldman's breeding farm version is a bit of postwar fantasy," Parks said.

"Well, yes and no. Himmler was obsessed with the idea of the super Aryan. He surrounded himself with the proto-type. His personal bodyguards looked like the Manitowoc, Wisconsin, high school football team. He wanted the whole world to be blond. It was this obsession, together with one of the truly great creations of the Third Reich, that started all the rumors. Mrs. Feldman is giving you the animal-cage rumor. Stories went around that big, blond males and beautiful women were locked in cages and forced to mate, like in *Planet of the Apes*."

"Is there anything to support the stories?"

"No, nothing whatsoever. There is not one shred of evidence that Lebensborn ever made anyone do anything against her will."

"What was 'one of the truly great creations of the Third Reich'?"

"I was coming to that. A chain of SS fuck farms."

"You're kidding."

"No, it's the truth. Lebensborn set up some fuck farms where big SS studs were stationed to service willing *Frau*s and *Fräulein*s."

Parks laughed. "A whorehouse in reverse."

"Not bad work if you can get it," Stein said. "Stiff dicks for the state! It was the hottest franchise in Germany."

The two men laughed. Then Parks returned to the more serious side of the discussion. "But what was the point?"

"Expanding the Nordic race," Stein said seriously. "Women were virtually begged to have children during the war. For unmarried women or widows who wanted to have a child but didn't want to get involved, Lebensborn had the answer . . . a blond, blue-eyed SS stallion. It was all kept very secret. Not just any woman could go to the stud farm. Generally, only women in the Party administration or someone recommended by them. They went of their own accord, stayed the night, and left. Later, they would go to one of the maternity homes and have the child. A few of the women would keep their children, but most would let Lebensborn put them out for adoption. The point was to have the child, not to raise it."

"How long did this go on?" Parks asked.

"Not for long." Stein grinned mischievously. "The whole thing petered out—if you'll pardon the expression." Then he turned serious. "The extermination of the Jews became the overriding obsession of the SS and Gestapo, and they didn't have time to play games with Lebensborn anymore. The SS became concerned with death, not life."

"It doesn't sound like a war crime that an international tribunal would gave a damn about," Parks said.

"No," Stein agreed. "Your Mr. Axmann was very probably one of the SS studs. If that was ever a crime, it certainly isn't now. That's why I told Dr. Silverman to forget it. Nobody gives a damn about an old man who once dipped his wick for the state."

The telephone rang, and Ben Stein stretched out his long arm to answer it. Parks rose. Stein nodded and winked as he picked up the receiver.

Max Silverman was answering his mail, drafting his brief replies in his shaky, uneven handwriting for eventual retyping. He set aside his pen and looked up when Parks entered the small office.

"So, now that you have heard Mr. Stein's stories, what do you think?"

"Well," Parks said, "they were certainly juicy enough."

"And told in Mr. Stein's inimitable way, I'm sure."

"Yes."

"But they are still stories," Dr. Silverman said. "Is that what you are thinking?"

"That's exactly what I'm thinking. Good stories, but still stories. Not hard facts."

"I'm afraid there aren't many hard facts, Mr. Parks, except the ones I told you in the first place. At least that we know of. You see, there was never much reason for us to look any closer. Lebensborn did not touch our lives. The Jews were not to be a part of the master race."

Parks nodded. "I understand," he said. "In any event, it wouldn't have been too high on anyone's list. It was not the death camps."

"That's true. There has never been any suggestion that Lebensborn was an instrument of death." The old man paused to gather his thoughts. "You see, after the war, there was chaos. You had to set priorities. You couldn't go off chasing ghosts in the night that might turn out to be some old woman's laundry. Not when there were mass murderers to be caught. As it was, Eichmann, Bormann, Mengele, Roschmann, all slipped through our fingers at the time.

"But do not be discouraged, Mr. Parks. The mass extermination of the gypsies did not come to light until the fifties. We always knew, of course, that the Nazis considered them racially inferior, like the Jews, but the first real documentary evidence wasn't uncovered until nineteen fifty-four, when Simon Wiesenthal got a chance to read the Gestapo archives left behind in Bohemia-Moravia. It took Wiesenthal ten years to complete his research and send his files to Ludwigsburg."

Parks studied the old man. Silverman was telling him, in his own way, to go on, to continue the investigation.

"Then you don't agree with Mr. Wiesenthal that this is a wild goose chase, or with your assistant that I should drop the matter."

Silverman shook his head. "Indeed I do not. In the first place, Simon Wiesenthal said we *may* be on a wild goose chase. There has never been any evidence that Lebensborn was involved in war crimes. But still, we don't know. The Nazis were very good at keeping secrets. They kept secret the slaughter of a whole people, until it was discovered by accident.

"But, even if the Lebensborn was involved in war crimes, this Walter Axmann may turn out to be a *weisse Weste,* a white vest, an SS man who refused to murder. That, however, is less likely than you think. The SS Service list says that Axmann was decorated with the Iron Cross in 1944 for 'Secret Reich Matters.' That citation was often given to the commanders and guards of the death camps. But, of course, it could have been given for his service in the Lebensborn. That particular kind of service was kept a secret, too.

"As for dropping the matter, that is up to you. It is certainly a thankless road you will travel. The authorities

will give you the runaround. People will say you are opening old wounds. On the other hand, you may add another
piece to the puzzle of some of the world's blackest days."

"I don't intend to drop it," Parks said.

The old Talmudic scholar smiled. "I didn't think so," he
said, pleased. "I can tell you this. Already you have stirred
interest. You have made us focus on Lebensborn. Men
like Simon Wiesenthal and myself have dedicated our lives
to rooting out the truth about the Third Reich. We have
read many things never meant to be seen by eyes other
than those of the highest Nazis. We know things that would
frighten you, even today. Someday, at the right time, I will
tell you. But for now, you have enough. I've made an
appointment for you with Karl Frank, tomorrow at two,
at the West German Consulate General's office. He is one
of our main contacts with the Attorney General's office in
Bonn."

Parks rose from the hard wooden chair and extended his
hand. "One way or the other," he said, "we will see this
through."

Dr. Silverman took Parks's hard, firm hand and pressed
it warmly between his small, crooked fingers.

"I know, Mr. Parks, I know."

Parks smiled. The old rabbinical scholar understood
more than he let on.

"*Shalom aleichem*," Dr. Silverman said. "Peace go with
you."

The small, determined eyes of Dr. Silverman still in his
mind, Parks headed for Seaside. Like Stramm, Parks knew
that the truth about Victory lay not in New York, but in
that small New Jersey ocean town. It was there he would
have to establish his next base of operations.

Seaside was in its winter cocoon. The summer cottages
were boarded up, the pastry shops were closed, and drifts
of sand swept across the deserted streets.

Parks stopped at a Mobil station, checked the town's thin
Yellow Pages, and selected a real estate agent on a simple
basis: The name appealed to him.

The agent's office was at his home, a two-story, white
clapboard house with a yard of small white pebbles. Parks
knocked on the front door. The bitter wind cut his fingers

like razors. A short, bald man came to the door, beer can in hand. He looked at Parks curiously.

"Mr. Paccione?"

"The one and only."

"I'd like to find a place to rent for the next couple of weeks."

"What for?"

"Vacation," Parks said.

"You must be crazy." The agent shook his head. "I don't like this place in winter and I *live* here."

"Maybe I ought to try someplace else," Parks said. He wasn't getting any warmer talking philosophy in a wind-chill factor of ten below.

"Naw, don't do that," Paccione said, as Parks started to turn away. "Maybe I can get you a place. We don't have but one or two that are fit for the winter. Most people come here for the sun, you know. I'll see if they're rented."

Paccione started to close the door. Then, as an after-thought, he said, "Step inside. This place'll freeze your balls off."

He disappeared into the house, and returned a few minutes later with a look of satisfaction and a slip of paper in his hand. He gave the paper to Parks.

"Go see this woman," he said. "Name's Faith Henderson. She lives on the ocean. We call it the Gold Coast. I just talked to her and she'll rent her old servants' quarters. They're above the garage. Hundred dollars a week."

To Parks, Seaside's Gold Coast needed a little spit and polish.

Faith Henderson lived in a sprawling three-story house with a yard of white sand that sloped gently to the water's edge. It was covered with weathered gray shingles and capped with gables, facing the ocean with sturdy defiance. The double garage and converted servants' quarters were two hundred yards from the ocean house and parallel to it.

Parks got out of his maroon Mercedes and walked to the front of the house. The wind off the ocean cut through him and made him shiver. Faith Henderson greeted him before he had a chance to knock.

"Mrs. Henderson?"

"Miss Henderson."

"John Parks. I believe Mr. Paccione spoke to you."

"He certainly did," she said with enthusiasm. She took his arm. "Come inside, out of the wind. How about a cup of coffee?"

"If it wouldn't be any trouble."

"It's already made." She led him into her cavernous living room. From the bay windows the blue Atlantic was visible in all its insolence. The echo of money was in the room.

Faith Henderson was a small, bone-thin woman with a bright, definite face. She had large, round green eyes, a narrow, sharp nose, and the merest whisper of lips. Only the loose, wrinkled skin around her neck gave away her age. She wore a green shirtwaist dress with white polka dots, and low heels.

She returned to the living room, carrying the coffee and its complements on an ornate Victorian silver tray.

"Why on earth do you want to come here in the winter?" she asked, but without design. "Of course, you're as welcome as the flowers in May."

She served the coffee.

"Just for a break," Parks said. "I can't take the time to go too far. If something goes wrong in New York, I can always run back for the day and fix it. Then I can come back here. You can't do that if you're in St. Croix."

"Certainly makes sense," Faith Henderson said. "What's your line of business?"

"I'm an investment counselor. At least that's what they call us."

"You don't say! So was my father. An investment banker, anyway. But that was a long time ago. I'm sure things have changed."

"Not as much as you think," Parks said. "From the looks of your house, he must have been very successful."

"Oh, he was," she said with pride. "This was our summer house. I was raised in Manhattan."

"I should have known. Manhattan ladies never lose their charm."

Miss Henderson came close to blushing. Parks was good with women, young and old.

"How long do you plan to stay?" she asked, pleased.

"Two weeks. Maybe three. Does it matter?"

"Not in the least."

Parks took out his checkbook. "I'll give you two hundred for two weeks and decide about the third week later."

"Oh, you don't have to pay me now. Wait till you get here."

"Might as well," said Parks. "Then you'll know I'm credit worthy." He handed her the check.

"I have no doubt, Mr. Parks. Anyway, I don't need the money. You can see that. I rent for the company. It gets kind of lonely here."

"I imagine that it does."

"When do you expect to come?" she asked with transparent anticipation.

"Tomorrow or Saturday."

"I'll give you the keys," she said. "Then you can just move right in."

She went to the kitchen to fetch the keys. When she returned, she handed them to Parks and said: "It'll be nice to have a man around in the winter. I always liked that."

CHAPTER 7

Friday, December 6, 1974

Miss Jones greeted Parks's announcement of a winter holiday with a face of stone.

"You must be crazy," she said finally.

Miss Jones didn't believe in vacations in winter and in New Jersey in particular. To her, two weeks in New Jersey was equivalent to doing time in Sing Sing.

"That's the second time I've heard that in two days," Parks said.

"Take it as bad karma."

Parks could understand why the two hundred pounds of his secretary were the absolute terror of the steno pool. He had always suspected she was a Marine sergeant in drag.

"Just look after things," he said, trying to soothe her. "And don't let anyone bother me unless it's an absolute emergency. If you really need me, call Miss Faith Henderson in Seaside, New Jersey. She's in the book. But don't give anyone else her name or number. I want some peace and quiet."

"Take some long johns and a bottle of whisky," Miss Jones said. "You'll need them."

"You obviously haven't met the girls from New Jersey," Parks said, and returned to *The Wall Street Journal*.

The West German Consulate General's office was on the seventeenth floor of a rather plain, functional building of black marble and glass at 460 Park Avenue. The reception area was under heavy security. A solemn guard sat behind an enclosed booth to receive visitors to the floor, his shoulder holster and pistol butt in open view. In one corner were two plain modern chairs and a low, black Formica table with no magazines or reading material on it. The walls were painted a washed-out green and the floors were carpeted in no-nonsense gray. There were no flowers, no plants in the hall. No art from the homeland hung on the walls; only a simple sign that said, *"Generalkonsulat der Bundesrepublik Deutschland."* Nothing in the reception hall invited a visitor to feel at ease. Either he had business there or he did not. If he did not, he should leave.

The office of Karl Frank, First Deputy of the West German Consul General, was the office of a German bureaucrat. Like the reception hall, it was clean-lined, spare, and cold, with bare walls and windows and the same no-nonsense green walls and gray carpet.

Herr Frank, a tall, robust man in his fifties, with large hands and thick brown eyebrows, was clean-lined like his room, with a look of efficiency about him, as if he would never waste a paper clip. But his strong voice was warm and friendly.

"Dr. Silverman said you need some information," he began, inviting Parks to sit down.

"Yes, Mr. Frank, I do. I understand that you have helped Dr. Silverman in the past."

"My government has helped Dr. Silverman," Herr Frank corrected him. "Or rather, worked with him and his organization. I have been only the messenger. But I am familiar with his work."

"I take it you approve," Parks said.

"Yes, for the most part. Although I will be damn glad when all the old bastards die and we can forget about Hitler and his hoodlums. Now, what can I tell you?"

Karl Frank had done with preliminaries. He had had his say about history. Any further discussion off the immediate subject was for the *Rathskeller*.

"Have you ever heard of Lebensborn?" Parks asked directly.

"Yes," Frank said. "A Nazi thing. One of their better ones for a change, like the *Autobahn*. It was a maternity organization. You know how it is during a war. The men get ready to march off, the good-byes are hard. They stay in the field for months, or don't come back at all. Meanwhile the girls find they are, you know, *schwanger*." Herr Frank laughed and made a circle with his arms around his belly. "The Nazis set up maternity homes to help them out. Of course, you had to be a good German to get in. No Jews, no Slavs. But it took good care of the girls it let in, and their babies, too, for free."

"A charitable organization, then," Parks said.

Frank nodded. "Yes, that is the right word. It was what you call in the United States 'pro-life.' It campaigned against abortion and promoted motherhood. There were big posters all around with pictures of German women holding beautiful babies, with the slogan 'Every woman gives a child to the Führer.' It also built some homes, in Germany and other places, to take care of the war orphans."

"There has been talk," Parks said, "that Lebensborn ran SS stud farms, that it got into breeding people."

Frank frowned and waved away the suggestion.

"I know, I know," he said, impatiently. "After the war, there were many stories. I have heard them all—animal cages, beautiful girls kidnaped and made slaves in exotic brothels. After the Reich fell, you could hear anything. It all sounded as if it came out of a cheap tabloid. It probably did."

"Actually, I have had the same thought myself," Parks said. "I've a feeling I read those stories in *Stag* or *True* or some other of the men's pulp magazines when I was a kid. Late at night, you understand, with the door locked."

The two men laughed. The formality between them had been broken.

"I read them, too," Herr Frank said. "But they are stories. Just stories. Of course," he went on, "here and there, Lebensborn may have set up a brothel or two. I've heard that story and I believe it. There was supposed to be one in the Wienerwald and one in the Harz Mountains. But so what? The American Army did the same thing. It was wartime. The men were separated from their wives, their girl friends. Not much of a crime, if you ask me. If you convicted every man who ever procured for the state, half of Bonn—and Washington—would be in jail."

"If there's no truth to them," Parks asked, skeptical, "then how do you think the rumors started?"

"Because Lebensborn was associated with the SS," Frank said. "All these stories, Mr. Parks, say more about our own psychology than about the Nazis'. Why is it that we see good as soft and meek, and evil as tough and virile? You see a picture of a saint, he is painted pale and sweet, not a muscle to his body. But a Nazi? He is hard, strong; his pants bulge at the crotch; he swaggers when he walks. There is something wrong with that, Mr. Parks. Something very wrong."

"I know," Parks said, and shook his head. The German had spoken an unfortunate, universal truth.

"Is there anything more?" Herr Frank asked. He wanted to move the interview along, to keep it on its course.

"Do you know of a man named Walter Axmann?"

The First Deputy reflected a moment. "No," he said. "I don't think so."

"That's all I have," Parks said. "Thank you for taking the time."

Herr Frank nodded graciously and stood. "It was my pleasure," he said.

In the Christmas season, Rockefeller Center's massive Art Deco buildings dominate midtown Manhattan. The sunken plaza is flooded and turned into an ice-skating rink. Above the crowd of skaters flies golden Prometheus, clutching in his hands the bolts of fire stolen from the gods. And, high above Prometheus, a sixty-foot Christmas tree glitters with two thousand lights.

Up and down the mall leading from Fifth Avenue to the steps of the famous skating rink, Christmas shoppers come and go. Small children stand in awe, looking at the great Christmas tree, and tourists work their cameras overtime. Everywhere, the sounds of Christmas fill the air.

Charles Winston and Miriam Messinger waited near the entrance to the steps that led down to the sunken rink, out of the way of children and teenagers standing in an amorphous line for their turn to skate. Miss Messinger was dressed warmly in her new black ranch mink coat. This was the coat's inaugural exhibition, and she was more than

a little disappointed that it had become lost in the crowd
of other minks and silver foxes that strolled up and down
the center mall.

Miriam Messinger was a woman to whom time had been
kind. Tall and endowed with a matronly figure even when
she was young, she found at middle age that the other
women had caught up with her, and she now had as good a
figure as any of them. Her soft, fair skin, her large violet
eyes, and her sweet disposition now stood her apart from
most others. At fifty-two, Miss Messinger was in bloom.

Charles Winston spotted Parks walking down the long
mall toward the skating rink. Miss Messinger pulled her
mink coat tightly around her, turned, and started up the
mall toward Fifth Avenue. She passed within a few feet
of Parks without taking her eyes off St. Patrick's Cathedral.
She was a professional in every way.

The Director turned and began to circle the rink, walking toward the Avenue of the Americas.

"Beautiful day," Parks said as he caught up with him.
"Miss Messinger looks great."

"Yes, she does," Winston agreed. "I'm going to meet
her at Lord and Taylor when we finish to see the
window display."

"I've rented a place in Seaside for a week or two," Parks
said. "I thought it would be good for my soul."

"Why? Do you think it's purgatory?"

"No. According to my secretary, Baltimore is purgatory.
New Jersey is it—the final resting place. However, the
real estate man called it the Gold Coast. He and Miss
Jones don't see eye to eye."

"I thought the Gold Coast was in Chicago."

"In New Jersey, it's on Ocean Avenue. At least it was.
Maybe it moved to Chicago in the thirties. I'm renting
from an old woman named Faith Henderson. Number ten
Ocean Avenue. She's in the phone book. I've got the servants' quarters over the garage. No phone, of course, and
no servants. I'll have to be the one to keep in touch. In
an emergency, you can call Miss Henderson and tell her
it's the office."

"What name should I use?" the Director asked.

"Otto Werner?" Parks returned Winston's smile and
began reporting on his further conversations with Dr.

Silverman, Benjamin Stein, and Herr Frank as they walked to Radio City Music Hall, where *The Little Prince* and the high-stepping Rockettes were packing in the Christmas crowd. They turned left down the Avenue of the Americas.

"Interesting," Parks said, putting his hands in his pockets. "I could write a good story about it for *Screw,* but even if the Executive Secretary were really Walter Axmann, I couldn't even get the INS to deport him. The only crime they could charge him with is giving some girl the clap."

The Director frowned. "My talks with Immigration weren't much better."

"Did you find Tony Riccio?"

"Yes. He's still there. Riccio remembered the call quite well. He even went to see the woman. She lived in Greenpoint with her nephew and his wife."

"Anything come of it?"

"Nothing. She ran and hid when Riccio came to the door. Wouldn't even talk to him. Riccio spoke to the nephew, who apologized. It seems that the woman did live in Poland during the Occupation and she did have a child who died, but no one killed it. The baby was weak. Malnutrition. The conditions were intolerable in Poland, we all know that. It was a bad winter and the child died. The woman blamed the Nazis, which, the nephew agreed, she had a right to do.

"Riccio checked with the neighbors and they all said the woman was mad—wandered around Greenpoint at all hours of the day and night. If you spoke to her, she would run away. Sometimes she would get on the subway and disappear for several days until the police brought her home." Winston shook his head. "Not a very pretty story, is it? I guess the nephew would have put her away, but in Greenpoint you don't do that kind of thing. Anyway, there's not much in it for us."

"Maybe. I don't know. There are some funny parallels. The Lebensborn ran maternity homes, put children out for adoption. So does Victory. Both were against abortion."

They arrived at the corner of 42nd Street and Avenue of the Americas, crossed the intersection, and stood beneath the statue of José de Andrada, the patriarch of Brazil, at the entrance to Bryant Park.

"I still want to talk to the old woman in Greenpoint," Parks said. "Can you get her name?"

They climbed the steps to Bryant Park.

"I can get it, but there's no guarantee she'll talk to you."

"Let me try," Parks said. He stopped to light a Marlboro, cupping his hands against the wind that blew in gusts across the park. "I'd better let you get back to Miss Messinger. I have to go home and get organized. I'm driving to Seaside tonight, hell or high water."

A vagrant stumbled across the park, puffing on an imaginary cigarette.

"You think that's an omen?" Parks asked, half seriously.

"No, I don't. I think it's an undercover cop." The Director paused. "John . . . be careful. . . . Keep your eyes open."

"I will," Parks said.

It was well after dark when Parks arrived in Seaside.

The converted servants' quarters above the old garage were spare but pleasant. The plaster walls, cracked here and there, were painted a soft off-white, and the beige carpet in the small living room was frayed and worn in spots from many a summer's sand. The kitchen was more than adequate, at least for him. The bedroom was about the size of a double bed and dresser and not much else.

Parks unloaded the Mercedes and sorted his things. The refrigerator had a look of affluence for the first time since the end of summer, and the living room bore the clutter of emptied pockets. Unpacked to his satisfaction, Parks settled down to a Jack Daniel's on the rocks and a Nero Wolfe mystery, a steno pad at his side.

The wind howled off the ocean like a pack of grieving, hungry dogs.

CHAPTER 8

Saturday, December 7, 1974

Saturday morning came too early for Parks. The sun was pouring in and men were shouting beneath the window. He wiped the windowpane clean of frost and saw a tall, lean man standing by the open door of a white Ford, shouting toward the beach. Parks dressed quickly and went downstairs.

"It's really a damn shame," the man by the car said as Parks reached the bottom of the stairs. "It just don't seem right." He shook his head in disbelief, then walked toward Parks, extended his hand and said, "I'm Bob Fischer. Sheriff."

"John Parks. What's too bad?"

Fischer nodded toward the water's edge. Two of his deputies and a woman were huddled around a dark form on the beach.

The woman straightened up and turned toward Parks and the sheriff. Her long brown hair fell loosely around her face, which she hid behind large oval sunglasses. She looked as though she had dressed in a hurry, wearing a worn pair of trousers, sneakers, a gray trench coat, and no gloves.

Miss Henderson stood a few yards away, her small arms folded close to her body.

"The Rider girl washed up on the beach. Drowned, I guess." Fischer started to walk toward the water. "Come see, if you want."

The two men walked a few steps in silence. They walked slowly, Fischer compelled by duty, and Parks by that nagging curious force that begs us to look disaster in the face. *Rider*. The name leaped out at Parks from the pages of Stramm's diary.

"She was a strange one," Fischer said, flatly. "Suicide, maybe." He turned to Parks, his jaw set. "You ever seen a person who's been in the water for a while?"

"No."

"Well . . . it's ugly." Fischer's voice trailed off. That was as far as he was willing to go. He shrugged his narrow shoulders.

Miss Henderson hurried to Parks as he neared the beach. "Isn't it horrible?" she said.

"Not very nice."

"And on your first day here," she said gravely, her little sparrow's hand at her neck. "It's not much of a welcome."

The dead girl was lying rigid on the beach, her eyes bulging and fixed. Parks fought the urge to turn his head. The body was swollen and turning color. Miss Henderson stared across the water, unable to look directly at the corpse. She had seen it once. She had discovered it and called the police. She would not look again.

"Every morning I take a walk along the beach just after it's good and daylight," she said, her sweet, thin voice shaking. "Like my father used to do. But this morning I was greeted by tragedy. Why, I almost stumbled over her." She paused for a deep breath of ocean air. "In all my years, I have never had anything like this happen on my beach."

"You should get out of the wind," Parks said gently. "You'll get chilled from the ocean spray. Then I'd have to spend my whole vacation serving you chicken soup."

"I certainly wouldn't want that," she said, relieved to have a reason to leave. Suddenly her face showed her age. The tragedy on her beloved beach was almost too much for her. "I bet you can't even cook," she said, composing herself.

"Not at all," Parks said, "so you better get yourself inside and get warm. Don't worry, I'll take care of things here."

She put her small, veined hand on his arm. "I told you

it was nice to have a man around in the winter," she said with a soft smile.

Only the other woman continued to look directly at the dead girl. She stood at the feet of the corpse and stared into the glassy, horrible eyes, showing no revulsion.

"Things like this don't happen in the winter. Not around here anyway," Fischer said.

"No," the woman said, almost inaudible.

"People don't go near the water in December." Fischer scratched his head thoughtfully. "At least not without a wet suit."

"Nobody swims in the middle of the night," the woman said. There was an edge of anger in her voice.

"I guess not. Mary, I'm sorry as hell. That's about all I can say."

She shrugged. "What else is there to say?" She continued to stare at the lifeless form.

An ambulance arrived from Toms River Community Hospital, followed by the New Jersey State Police. Fischer ordered the dead girl covered and removed from the beach, then went to consult with the State Police. After a hurried conversation he returned to the side of the woman named Mary and put his arm around her shoulders.

"We have to take her to Community," Fischer said. "There's a lot of red tape . . . in a drowning."

Mary nodded.

"There have to be some determinations," Fischer said. "Like time of death, cause . . ."

"She drowned," Mary said. "What more do you need to know?"

"We have to notify the coroner, the Marine Police. It's the law."

Mary sighed in resignation.

Fischer turned to Parks. "You got a car?" he asked.

"Yes, I do," Parks said. "Can I help?"

Fischer tightened his grip on Mary's shoulder. "Mary, I'd like to go on over to Toms River, to the coroner's office. Maybe I can speed things up. I'm sure Mr. Parks would be glad to drive you home. It's best for now. I'll call you later."

She nodded her assent.

"Go on now," Fischer urged her.

The wind whipped her long brown hair around her cheeks. Parks took her arm and guided her away from the ocean. "Would you like a cup of coffee first, to shake off the chill?"

Mary nodded. "I could use some coffee. I could use a stiff drink, but it's too early in the day for my conscience."

"Mine too," Parks said. "I'm John Parks."

With the ocean at her back, the stiffness left her shoulders and she slumped badly. "I'm Mary Rider. Ellen, my sister, was the girl you just saw. We live—" She stopped and, with effort, corrected herself. "I live over by the bay. You don't live here, do you?"

"No. I'm renting for a couple of weeks."

"Oh," she said, and started up the stairs.

"I hope you don't mind instant," Parks said, as Mary sat down on the vinyl couch and began rummaging through her purse for a cigarette.

"Not at all," she said. "Black."

"Need a cigarette?"

"Please. I must have left mine back at the house."

Parks offered her a Marlboro, then put the kettle on. While the water was heating, he heard Mary crying softly and he decided to stay in the kitchen and let her cry. Some things were better suffered alone, at least for a while.

He returned with the coffee after the soft crying had abated. Mary had pulled her hair back, tied it with a rubber band, put on lipstick, and discarded the sunglasses. She wore a baggy gray sweater. The silver chain around her neck dipped behind the "V" in the sweater. Her jeans were loose and faded and rolled up at the bottoms. Still, there was something striking about her, and Parks realized for the first time just how very pretty she was, in just the right kind of way. She had passed the cheerleader and pom-pom years when the heart-shaped faces and pouty mouths fell apart, and entered the age when it took a strong face to be beautiful. She had it: high forehead, straight nose, large blue eyes, a certain grace to the mouth. No girl; in every way a woman. The kind of woman who could walk in heels.

"The cups and saucers don't match," Parks said. "Summer stock."

"We're used to it around here. They come out of king-size boxes of detergent." She took a sip of coffee, almost impervious to its steaming heat. "I'm sorry to put you through all this," she said.

"No bother."

"Now I guess you know why they call it the House of Usher."

"Call what?"

"The house. Miss Henderson's house. They call it the House of Usher. I guess your real estate agent left that one out."

"That he did. Why do they call it the House of Usher?"

Mary sighed. "Not because of Faith Henderson. She's a sweetheart. It's the house. One tragedy after another."

"And now your sister."

She looked down. "She was all I had," Mary said quietly. "Our parents came to this country when we were little. We were the only ones."

"No aunts or uncles to come help?"

"No, none. Our parents didn't keep in touch with their families . . . if they had any. I don't know. We don't have any here."

"Do you have any idea how it happened?"

"No," she said. "I don't know how it happened, but I guess I know why."

Parks waited for her to continue.

"Ellen got into trouble. At least that's what we used to call it. She decided to go to the maternity home near here, in Toms River. We were familiar with the Home. My father helped set it up. I worked there as a volunteer from time to time."

She asked for another cigarette. Her cup was half empty and the coffee was cold, but she drank it anyway.

"Ellen decided to keep her child. It was difficult for her. The Home was against it, and I was too. But she was firm. Then, the baby was born dead."

Her cigarette had gone out and she stopped to relight it.

"I was the one who had to tell her."

"Not a very pleasant task," Parks said with sympathy.

"Worse than you can imagine. Ellen didn't believe me. She said they had stolen her baby and begged me to find it. Later, the real hysteria came. She claimed the baby had been murdered."

Parks stiffened. The names and images from Henry Stramm's diary ran through his mind like a blinking neon sign coming on one word at a time.

"The Home. Was it the Valley Forge Maternal Care Home?" he asked cautiously.

"Yes. Do you know it?"

"No, not really," Parks lied. "I know someone whose daughter went there. I think it was there. He didn't talk about it much. Did Ellen recover?"

"Not immediately. For a while she was a madwoman, escaping from her room, running down the halls, confronting the hospital staff with accusations."

"Kind of tough," Parks said. Henry Stramm's words came back to him: *Do you call that mental illness? I call it grief.*

"The hospital shot her full of Valium to keep her under control. She finally quieted down enough for me to bring her home. But she wasn't really any better. Her eyes . . . they were sheets of ice."

Parks shook his head. It wasn't a very pretty story.

Mary continued. "The worst was yet to come. After I got her home, she wouldn't eat, couldn't sleep. She would just sit in the rocker by the window and hold an empty blanket and sing to it. Whenever she did fall asleep, she would wake up screaming, drenched in sweat, then cry herself back to sleep."

"Did it ever stop?" Parks asked.

"Yes, it finally did . . . at least I thought it had."

"The human mind is a strange thing," Parks said, trying to reach Mary. "We never know when our own is going, much less someone else's. You have to try not to blame yourself."

"Thank you for saying that," she said. "Oddly enough, I don't blame myself. It's hard to believe it was suicide."

"I know." Parks hesitated. "What were the marks on her arm?" he asked casually.

"She didn't have any." Mary rubbed the back of her neck and looked away.

"They were on her right arm. The blouse was torn and

you could see them. They seemed old, faded, but you could still see them."

"Maybe they were something she got on the boardwalk. It hardly matters now." She rose. "I had better go home. Fischer will be trying to get in touch with me, and I have to give instructions to the coroner's office. Can you drive me now?"

"Certainly. If I can be of any help, please get in touch."

"Thank you. But, I'm sure I can manage."

Parks knew that Ellen Rider fit into the Stramm-Victory puzzle, although he wasn't sure just how. He knew only that he could not afford to lose contact with Mary Rider.

He took her arm as they started down the stairs. "It wasn't an empty offer," he said. "I know a good deal about wills and probate. I have to. It's part of my job. There's no reason for you to go through all this alone."

Mary was genuinely appreciative. "That's very kind of you," she said. "I might have to take you up on it if it's not too much of a bother."

"No bother," Parks said gently. "I'd be more than glad to help. I've been on vacation less than twelve hours and already I don't know what to do with myself."

Mary smiled. "I don't think there was ever a man born who knew how to take a vacation."

When Mary Rider was finally at home alone, she walked to the small stretch of beach behind her house that bordered Barnegat Bay. The wind came off the bay, wet and cold, like bitter tears. She folded her arms around her and looked off across the water. A single gray-and-white herring gull cried and dove at the whitecaps. She was alone now, like the things around her. All her life, it seemed, she had taken care of others—her mother, her sister. Always, it seemed, her feelings had been those of others, and now they weren't there.

She stopped and looked down at her feet. A small piece of driftwood protruded from the sand. She bent down and stoked it, then pulled it loose and carried it to the house.

After he had driven Mary home, Parks spent the first part of the afternoon reconstructing the morning's events in his blue steno pad, trying to record the conversations verbatim. He didn't have complete recall like Henry Stramm. However, careful training had brought him close to it.

When the sun began to fade steadily to the west and day began to lower, Parks walked to the beach for a stroll. It was empty now; the smooth, white sand held no evidence of death. But the memory lingered. Miss Henderson had canceled her evening walk for the first time in many years.

The far north end of Miss Henderson's estate was guarded by a high wooden picket fence that ran almost to the water's edge. Sand and debris had collected against it and were beginning to form tall sand domes. On the adjacent beach, across the fence, a woman stood motionless, staring out over the ocean with such intensity that it seemed she might actually be able to follow the water all the way to Europe. She was a stocky woman, which made her appear shorter than she actually was, with gray hair and a blunt, square face. She was not dressed warmly, wearing only a light-blue sweater, open in the front, but she did not appear to be cold. As the sun fell far behind the horizon, day closed around the narrow island and the woman turned to go back to her house. When she saw Parks watching her, she turned her eyes away.

Parks waited until nine thirty, then drove to a phone booth just outside the Sea 'N Ski Laundromat on Central Avenue in Seaside and called the Director at his home in Brooklyn Heights.

"Good to hear from you," Winston said. "How are you?"

"Me? I'm fine. I'm about the only thing down here that is. Do you remember Stramm's visit to the Valley Forge Maternal Care Home? While he was there, a girl named Ellen Rider had a hysterical fit. This morning, she washed up on the beach, dead as a doornail. Mary Rider, her sister, doesn't think it was suicide."

"Very interesting," the Director said. "Anything else?"

"No. That's all from me. What about you?"

"I told the Southern Director."

"How'd he take it?"

"He was very upset, and ready, like the rest of us, to jump to the conclusion that Victory was the cause of Henry's death. He's also concerned for his own investigator, Peter Fleming—the man was really shaken. He and Stramm thought a great deal of each other."

"Did he have anything to report?"

"Just a tidbit. Victory has started transferring large blocks of money to Texas again."

"Where?"

"Austin."

"How does he know that?"

"Fleming is very resourceful. I imagine he has friends at the bank. Texans have their own kind of underground. I told the Southern Director that you and Fleming should try to get together soon."

"Good idea." Then, changing the subject: "What's Miss Messinger been doing lately?"

"Sitting at her desk reading a magazine."

"In her mink coat?"

"That was uncalled for," the Director said sharply.

"Not really," Parks said. "Do you pay her enough to buy a coat like that?"

"I don't know," Winston said, dodging the question. "Every person's finances are his own affair." He paused. "It would, however, seem a burden."

"Unless she got some extra income from another source." But Parks was not really prepared to believe it. Miss Messinger was not the type to take blood money.

"That would help," Winston admitted. "But if you suspect Miriam Messinger of being the informer, you'r driving your ducks to the wrong market."

"You're prejudiced. What magazine was she reading?"

"*Gotham Romances.* Not very characteristic. You usually find her reading something on the order of *Wuthering Heights.*"

"What issue was it?"

"Does it matter?"

"It might. Did you notice?"

"As a matter of fact, I did. It was the July issue. It was so unusual I made a point of noticing."

"Can you get me a copy?"

"You don't want to read that trash, do you?"

"A thrill a minute. Can you get me the July issue?"

"How shall I get it to you?" the Director asked in exasperation.

"Hold it in New York and I'll pick it up my next time through. And Charles—don't let Miss Messinger see it. Okay?"

"Certainly," Winston said, a bit annoyed. "Keep in touch."

CHAPTER 9

Tuesday, December 10, 1974

Ellen Rider was to be buried in Ocean County Memorial Cemetery in Toms River, three days after she washed up on Miss Henderson's Beach. Miss Henderson fretted until Parks suggested he accompany her to the funeral, which was to consist only of modest graveside rites. The suggestion calmed her immediately. "It's the least I can do," she said. "The very least." Although she had not known Ellen Rider at all in life, she felt she knew her intimately in death, for the single reason that the young girl had washed ashore on her property, barricading the direct path the old woman walked each morning as her father had walked before her.

The day began bright and crisp, but by two o'clock a thick blanket of gray-white clouds hid the sky. The smell of rain was in the air, and the wind was raw and sharp. Besides Parks, Miss Henderson, Mary Rider, and the minister, there were only two other mourners at the graveside services, two nurses from the Valley Forge Maternal Care Home. Mary Rider was dressed in appropriate black. The two nurses wept intermittently and audibly, and Miss Henderson wiped a tear upon the words "ashes to ashes." But Mary Rider was dry-eyed throughout. She was done with weeping.

At the conclusion of the service, she came over to Parks and took his arm. "It was sweet of you both to come." She smiled graciously to Miss Henderson. "I know how disturbing this must have been for you."

"Don't you even think about it," Miss Henderson said.

"Our prayers are with you. If there's anything I can do, you just pick up the phone."

"Thank you, so very much. I'm sure I'll be fine." Turning to Parks, she said: "John, do you think you could drop by this evening? I have some things I would like your advice on. I just don't understand all the talk about wills and trusts."

"I'd be happy to," Parks said. He tilted his head and looked at her, a bit surprised. "What time?"

She avoided his eyes. "Is eight too early?"

"Not at all. I'll be there at eight."

"You remember how to get there?"

"Of course."

As they walked toward the car, Miss Henderson patted his arm and said, "I told you it was nice to have a man around in the winter. And you probably thought I was too old to remember."

"I never thought that," Parks said, winking at the elfin old woman. "Not for a minute."

And it was true. He knew that Faith Henderson had never, never forgotten the days when she was young.

The driveway to the Rider house was half hidden by overgrown hedges and beach plum bushes. The house, a clapboard saltbox, was built in 1929, two months before the Great Crash. For five years it stood empty, but that was the last the house ever knew of hard times. From then on, all its misery was wrapped in silver.

Mary Rider was standing at the window when Parks pulled up in front of the house. "I'm glad you could come," she said, ushering him in and leading him to the dark, oak-paneled library at the rear of the house. She was dressed in a black velvet jumpsuit with a deep neckline and moved with the grace of a cat.

The library was lined with shelves filled with medical books, treatises, and dictionaries. A rolltop desk stood in one corner, closed and locked; in another, a large piece of driftwood. There were other pieces of driftwood on the tables and shelves. A weak fire burned in the hearth of the fireplace.

"What would you like to drink?" Mary asked.

"Jack Daniel's, if you have it."

"Done," Mary said.

"On the rocks."

Mary left the library. Parks added another log to the fire. He rearranged the wood with a poker and the flames began to gather strength.

"Was this your father's study?" he asked, when she returned with the drinks.

"Yes," she said. "It's mostly the way he left it, except for a few things."

They sat down on the dark leather chesterfield in front of the fire.

Parks nodded toward the large piece of driftwood sitting on the floor in the corner. "That is the ugliest piece of driftwood I have ever seen," he said.

Mary laughed. "I know. I think that's why I brought it home. Somebody has to love it, poor thing."

"Well, it's an unusual person who can find something to love in a dead piece of wood," Parks said, smiling. "Do you collect it?"

"Yes, I love it. I can spend hours walking along the shore looking for it. In winter, at the far end of Island Beach, there is almost no one. That's where you find it, washed up on shore, ready to travel again with the next strong tide."

"Each to his own," Parks said. "Give me a tree, or even a stingray."

"They won't last as long as a piece of driftwood," Mary said.

"No, but neither will I."

Mary laughed. "All right, next time I'm out, I'll buy you an octopus, something you can really get hold of! But first, I need some advice."

"What's the problem?" Parks asked, taking a drink.

"It's not the will," Mary confessed. "Ellen didn't have one. There were just the two of us, so everything passes to me, anyway." She paused. "It's something else. Do you remember that I told you that Ellen's baby was stillborn? In the maternity home in Toms River."

"Yes I do."

"There's no death certificate in the file," Mary said.

"Should there be?"

"Of course. If the baby was stillborn, Doc Webster should have filled out a death certificate."

"How do you know?" Parks asked.

"Because it's required."

"No, I mean how do you know there's no death certificate?"

"I checked the files."

"When?"

"Saturday night, after you brought me home."

"Was there a birth certificate?"

Mary looked startled.

"Why . . . no," she said. "There was nothing. It was as though there hadn't been any baby at all."

Parks leaned forward in thought, holding his empty glass with both hands. "Why did you check the files?"

"It was something I found," Mary said.

She pulled her feet up under her. "After you brought me home," she continued, "I went through Ellen's things to see if there was anything special . . . to bury her with. It sounds silly, I know." Mary breathed deeply to ease the pain of the memory, and touched her bare throat. "Anyway, I found an envelope . . . a letter . . . that Ellen had sent to a girl named Lila Hamilton. It was returned, address unknown."

"Anything special?" Parks asked.

"In the letter? No. But seeing it reminded me of the girl, Lila Hamilton. She was at the Home three years ago. I'd completely forgotten her."

"Let me guess. Lila Hamilton was blond, blue-eyed, and determined to keep her baby, only it was born dead."

Mary's eyes widened. "Yes, that's right. The baby was born dead, just like Ellen's. But there was something else. On the day she left the Home, I helped her pack. She told me when she was about to leave: 'I don't care what they say, Mary, my baby wasn't born dead. I heard it cry.'"

"Well, one thing is for sure," Parks said. "Dead babies don't cry. Did you believe her?"

"No, not then. But it's possible. She could have heard it cry. They don't always get the girls under before . . . Old Doc Webster runs a sloppy ship."

"Incompetent?"

"The only thing he is competent at is pouring a shot of Wild Turkey."

Mary lit a cigarette, then continued, her voice shaking. "One night, at the Home, after they had shot her full of Valium and she was falling asleep, Ellen said the same thing. She said she had heard her baby cry."

"Did you ever see the baby?" Parks asked.

"No," Mary said. "Davis offered to take care of everything so I could spend time with Ellen. It made sense . . . at the time."

"It still does," Parks said, offering what little comfort he could. "What do you think they did with the baby . . . if it was born alive?"

"I don't know," Mary said. "What do you think?"

"If I had three guesses, all three of them would be 'black market.' "

"You mean . . . ?"

"I mean just what I said. Your sister wanted to keep the baby and they wanted it for the black market, so they told her it was born dead and put it out to the highest bidder. It's not all that difficult if enough people are in on it. Have you told Fischer about this?"

"No." Mary hesitated. "I didn't know what to tell him," she finally said. "I can't prove anything. Not yet, anyway." Mary reached over and touched his arm. "John, I have to know. I have to know what happened to that baby."

"Don't you think maybe it's better to leave it alone, to let sleeping dogs lie?"

She shook her head. "No. I can't. You don't know how . . ." Her lower lip quivered. She was on the edge of tears. "These last few days, I thought I would break. I just . . ." She turned her face away and suppressed a cry.

Parks put his arm around her. "It's all right. We'll find out."

"Will you help me?" she asked. "I don't have . . ."

"I know," Parks said. He knew what it was like to be alone.

Mary wiped her eyes. "It seems like every time I'm around you, I'm crying. I'm really not a china doll."

"No, I don't think you are," Parks said, his thoughts going back to the afternoon services at the cemetery, when

Mary had stood alone, composed. She had seemed much stronger then.

"You were quite close to your sister, weren't you?" he finally asked.

"Yes, very," she said, bowing her head. Her voice grew soft as she remembered. "In some ways I was like a mother to her, although we weren't that much different in age. Mother was not in good health for the last few years before she died, and I guess I just took over, taking care of both of them."

She looked away. "It might have been different, living somewhere else. We were so alone here, so apart from everything, and we had no family. Ellen just stayed a child. First Mother's, then mine."

She fell silent, and Parks finished his drink, allowing her time for her memories. Then he asked, "How did your family get involved with the Valley Forge Home?"

"That's a bit of a story," Mary said, relieved to take her thoughts away from Ellen. "But first I need a fresh drink. How about you?"

"Good idea. But make it weak. I still have to drive back to my place tonight."

"Maybe I'll make it a double," Mary said, and smiled.

She returned with another Jack Daniel's on the rocks. It was anything but weak. Parks grinned. Fine. It was too cold to go home anyway.

"My father was Polish," Mary began. "In Poland, his name was Herman Gierek. After we came to America, he changed it to Rider. I don't know why."

Parks cut in. "Was he in Poland during the Occupation?"

"Yes . . . yes, he was. We all were." Her shoulders trembled, as if a cold wind had blown across the back of her neck. She paused, lit a cigarette, and continued with effort. "My sister and I were very young, of course. We lived just outside Krakow. My father taught at the medical school. At Jagiellonian. It was a terrible time to be a Pole. That's why we came here, to the United States."

"The concentration camps?"

"Yes. Everything. If the Nazis thought you were a partisan, they would shoot you on the spot. If the farmers didn't make their required contribution of food—the Germans called it *kontyngent*—they would beat them. Sometimes the women were sent off to work camps. Then came the rumors that the Germans were taking the children. Little ones . . . Polish children."

Parks set aside his drink, slowly. The Germans and children, again. "Was there any truth to the rumors?" he finally asked.

"I don't know," Mary said. "It was wartime. You could hear anything, I suppose. But when my father heard the stories, he decided we had to leave. After the children, the Germans would take the women, then the men."

Parks took a deep breath. His collar felt tight and he loosened it. "What do you think they wanted the children for?" Parks asked.

"I don't know," she said. "And I'm glad we didn't stay around to find out. In forty-four we escaped to New York. I can still remember the salt air and my parents' faces as we passed the Statue of Liberty. We came to Seaside, where my father set up his practice. In the late fifties he started the Home. He was its administrator, physician, parish visitor, social worker."

"Do you know why?" Parks asked.

"Oh, probably because of what he had seen in the old country. I don't know. After we came here, he refused to talk about the past."

Mary slumped against the back of the chesterfield, her face ashen and her body limp. She looked like a Raggedy Ann doll that had lost its stuffing. The light had gone from her light-blue eyes.

Parks put his arms around her, pulled her to him, and cradled her in his thick, hard arms. He kissed her gently.

Outside, the wind howled around the house.

Mary rubbed her eyes. "I'm sleepy," she said.

"So am I," Parks said, and he meant it. His eyelids felt like lead shades. "It must be the whiskey."

"Good. Then you can't drive back."

"I didn't intend to," he said, standing up. He felt a bit dizzy. *Damned whiskey*.

They undressed in the dark of the bedroom. Once under the warm covers, Parks felt himself drifting off to sleep and unable to stop it. It would have been embarrassing, except that Mary was already asleep.

CHAPTER 10

Wednesday, December 11, 1974

The sun came up the next morning bright and strong. The clouds had blown away, the wind had died down, and the ocean was as still as an old country pond.

Mary awoke first, huddled close to Parks. He was still in deep sleep, his chest barely rising and falling. She moved away. Parks pulled out of his sleep and reached over and took her hand.

"Did I miss anything?" he asked, feeling a bit groggy.

"No."

"Good," he said and pulled her back toward him.

She stiffened when he touched her and he raised up on one elbow to look at her. She turned her eyes away, but reached over to touch his bare chest, as if to say she would submit. It was then that he realized that she was a stranger to intimacy.

"It's not required, you know," Parks said softly.

"I know."

"Rather have breakfast?"

She nodded.

Mary prepared a simple breakfast of eggs and toast. Parks helped her set the table, then poured coffee. His mouth felt like cotton.

The Rider house backed up to Barnegat Bay. Herman Rider had renovated the bay house in 1958 and replaced the rear wall of the kitchen with a large expanse of glass, so that he could watch the sea gulls dive for food while he drank his morning coffee.

Parks sat down at the breakfast table by the window and studied the whitecaps.

"What happened to your family after your father died?" he finally asked.

"Well, we were pretty well off, I guess," Mary said. "He had set up trust funds."

Parks took a drink of coffee. "Who ran the Home after your father?" he asked.

"Percy Davis."

The image of the stiff, unbending director of the Valley Forge Home grimly staring out over his garden of peonies flashed in Parks's mind.

"Did they work together? Your father and Davis, I mean," he said.

"They never knew each other, thank God. Davis came to the Home after Dad died. The Trustees hired him. He was brought in from the outside."

"You don't like him?"

"He has ice water in his veins."

"Great guy," Parks said. "Were there many stillborns at the Home?"

Mary paused, considering. "I don't know. It's hard to say." She shook her head.

"Take a guess."

"Ten. Fifteen, maybe."

"A year?"

"Yes."

"Isn't that kind of high?"

"I never really thought about it. A lot of the girls come to the Home without receiving proper care." Mary looked down at the table. "That wasn't the case with Ellen, you understand," she finally said.

Parks reached across the table and took her hand. "I never thought it was," he said. "She had you."

Mary squeezed his hand. "I think I need to go to my private place," she said. "Will you come with me? It's down by the beach."

"Of course," Parks said.

"There's no wind," Mary said. "We won't need our coats. Just sweaters."

They walked along the shallow beach until they came

to the carcass of a shipwrecked boat buried in the sand. Only the massive wooden timbers in the bow protruded above the earth. The bow was filled with sand and rocks.

"This is it," Mary said, taking a seat on top of the compact sand that filled the rotting bow.

Parks joined her. To their left, in the distance, was Barnegat Light and the breakwaters to the Atlantic.

"They say this is part of the hull of a ship that broke up in a storm just beyond the lighthouse before the turn of the century." Mary said. "Most of it is buried, as you can see."

She stared off into the ocean. "This is where I came when I was small. When everything went wrong, I would come here." She paused. "I always feel I belong here."

A sea gull shrieked and dove for food.

"Last Saturday, after you brought me home, I came here and sat until the sun went down."

"Did it help?"

She nodded. "For a while."

Parks sorted a rock out of the sand and skipped it across the water.

"If we find Ellen's baby, will you take it and raise it?" Parks asked.

She turned to him. "I can't tell you how much I would like that."

"It won't bring Ellen back."

"I know," she said. "But it would help."

"Well, we won't make any progress sitting here," Parks said, rising and dusting the sand off his pants. He gave his hand to Mary and helped her up. "Have you asked Davis why the death certificate is missing?"

"No," Mary said. She rubbed the back of her neck, nervously. "I just couldn't . . . not yet."

"Would you like me to talk to him and see what I can find out?" Parks suggested. He wanted to talk to Davis. He felt there were answers at the Home—not only to the death of Ellen Rider, but also to the death of Henry Stramm.

They walked back along the beach.

"I could offer to make a contribution in Ellen's name," Parks said, thinking of Stramm's thousand-dollar contribution the previous May. "That ought to open him up."

Mary was hesitant. "John, I wouldn't want you . . ."

He put his arm around her shoulders. "Don't worry. I can afford it."

He moved close to her and they finished the walk in silence.

It was eleven thirty before Parks crossed the bay bridge and headed into Toms River to the Valley Forge Maternal Care Home.

The pinched-faced receptionist looked up from her magazine when he entered the Home, but did not rise to greet him. Parks introduced himself, but the woman still saw no need to speak.

"I'd like to see Mr. Davis."

"He's not here."

"Do you expect him to return?"

"Don't know."

"I wish to see him about a sizable contribution to the Home. I don't think Mr. Davis would like to see me go away mad."

The receptionist frowned and threw her magazine aside. "He hasn't come in yet."

"Has he called in?"

"I wouldn't know."

"Could you find out?"

"He hasn't. Why don't you try him at home if it's so important? He's in the telephone book," she said, and reached for her magazine.

Percy Davis lived on Old River Road in Toms River, a narrow asphalt lane that followed the course of the river as it wove its way through the town to the waters of the Atlantic. His river house was a massive single-story wooden structure with two odd-shaped wings flaring from either side. Notwithstanding its rambling irregularity, it had the charm of money.

Parks knocked on the thick oak door. No answer. The house was silent. He knocked again. Still no sign of life. He tried the door. It was unlocked. He opened it and called for Davis. Still no answer. He ran his eyes around the sun-lit living room. Then he saw it. A chill ran through him, as if the edge of an ice cube had been run down his spine.

From the front door, Parks could see the small, paneled den at the back of the house and two legs hanging in mid-air. He crossed the living room to the den. The wooden shutters on the six windows were closed and the room was dark and filled with the stench of death. Davis was hanging from an exposed rafter. His eyes were bulging slightly and his bowels had emptied upon strangulation and fouled the room. Parks pressed his thumbnail into the man's skin, making a deep dent. The depression was slow to recover. Davis had been dead for a while. It was time to talk to Sheriff Fischer.

"Good afternoon, Mr. Parks," Bob Fischer said, looking up from the papers on his desk.

Parks took a seat in a straight-back wooden chair facing Fischer's desk. "I just dropped by to see Percy Davis. Do you know him?"

"I know just about everybody who lives around here, and some who don't. Why?"

"He's dead. At least, there's a dead man in Davis's house. Having never met Davis, I can only assume."

Bob Fischer leaned forward. "How?"

"From hanging, it appears."

Fischer tapped a pencil against the edge of his desk.

"I thought you'd be interested," Parks said, flatly.

"I am." Fischer paused. "This ain't too good a week for this town, Mr. Parks. Davis makes three dead in less than five days."

"Who's the third?"

"Doc Webster. He was the obstetrician for the Home. Died in a fire."

Parks looked at Fischer curiously, wondering if the sheriff was having the same thoughts he was having. Three deaths. All connected with the Valley Forge Maternal Care Home.

"Do you mind telling me where you were last night, Mr. Parks?"

"At a friend's."

"For how long?"

"From about eight o'clock to about . . . let's just say, until very late. Will that cover me?"

"Depends on how late."

"Late enough."

Fischer did not intend to be put off. "Will she vouch for you?"

"How do you know it's a she?"

Fischer ignored him. "And you'll vouch for her?"

"Yes. Sorry, chief. I've got an airtight alibi."

"And now, so does she."

"Care to explain?"

"We found Mary Rider's cigarette lighter at the fire."

"What time was the fire?"

"About midnight, I'd say."

"Have you talked to Mary?"

Fischer nodded. "Saw her about eleven, a little after you left."

"What did she say?"

"Said she saw the doctor yesterday. Went to ask him some questions about her sister."

"You knew that Ellen had been in the Home? That he had delivered her baby?"

"Of course I knew. She wasn't in the Home two days until everybody knew."

"Small towns are the same everywhere."

"I guess. But this town is getting cluttered with dead bodies. Too many. I've got a rule of thumb. One means nothing, two may be coincidence, three is a trend."

"Rule of thumb for what?"

"Rule of thumb for anything. For life. Let's go check on Davis. What were you doing at his house anyway?"

Parks was fascinated by the small-town sheriff. "I don't suppose you'd believe I went there to make a contribution," he said with a smile.

"No. Want to try again?"

"I went there to ask him a few questions about Ellen Rider, at Mary's request. Ellen Rider believed her child had been born alive. Davis maintained that it had been born dead. I wanted to ask him personally. Sometimes you can tell if a person is lying if you can look him in the eye."

"Sometimes," Fischer said. "Not always."

Parks shrugged. "I don't know if there's anything to all this, but Mary thinks something's not right."

"Well, something was not right with Ellen Rider. I know that for sure," Fischer said.

"Always?"

"No, not always," Fischer said, gently. "I wouldn't want to be an old woman at a hen party. I knew Ellen Rider since she was a little girl." There was a soft quality to Fischer's voice as he reached back for memory. "She used to come to the hospital with her dad. Now that was a good man for you. Cared about people, not insurance forms." Fischer paused, reflecting. "She was always a child. How old was she? Twenty-five? Thirty? You could never tell. Somebody was always taking care of her. Not at all like her sister, Mary. She was the strong one, in a funny sort of way."

"Durable," Parks said. "Like a piece of driftwood."

"Yes, in a way," Fischer said. "The Riders were too old to be having two young girls. Mrs. Rider was nervous as a tic and sick half the time. I guess Mary had to take on a lot."

Fischer shook his head. "This is no place to raise kids, anyway. Too isolated, too damn cold. It's better to come here when you're old and don't have any more growing to do."

Then Bob Fischer came abruptly back to the present. "Well, let's go view the body."

On their way to the car, Fischer asked, "Did Mary tell you that Ellen was two months pregnant when she died?"

"No, she didn't. Do you know that for a fact?"

"Yes. The autopsy."

"Does Mary know?"

"Told her myself. Didn't want her to hear gossip."

"Did the girl have a problem?"

"You mean like keeping her legs closed?"

"Something like that."

"Seems like it, don't it. But no, she wasn't like that."

They reached Fischer's white sheriff's car.

"Hop in," the sheriff said. "We'll drive over together."

Davis's house was as undisturbed and quiet as when Parks had left it. Everything was in place, including the corpse.

"That's Davis all right," Fischer said.

He made the necessary calls to the Toms River County Coroner and the State Police. Death was as complicated in Toms River as in the rest of the world. Only the dying was easy.

"The County Coroner is gettin' tired of hearing my voice lately," Fischer said, as he began to inspect the house.

He found no apparent signs of foul play, but the suspicion was heavy in his old green eyes. After the medics completed their grisly chores, Fischer drove Parks back to his car. It was almost three o'clock and growing colder, as the sun tilted to the west.

John Parks drove straight to the Rider house on Bay Street. He knocked. No answer.

The image of feet hanging in midair swept over him and his heart began to pound. He tried the door. It was open. He called out: "Mary!" No answer. He went from room to room, running up the stairs, then down. *Where was she?*

Then, he remembered.

He walked out the back door and down to the beach and found her sitting on the sand-filled bow of the old boat, staring out over the bay. The mild breeze blew her hair away from her face.

She saw him walking toward her and held out her hand and beckoned him to come sit next to her. They sat in silence for a while, her eyes heavy with memories.

"I was thinking about Ellen," Mary finally said. "The way she used to be. Out here, I can think of her that way—happy, full of life. I never minded looking after her. It was a pleasure."

Tears came to the edge of her eyes.

"She had a green thumb. She could make anything grow." Mary picked up a handful of sand at her feet. "Except here, I guess."

"Where?"

"The sand we're sitting on," Mary said, letting the sand run loosely through her fingers. "They say nothing will grow in it, that it's dead. The legend has it that the ship belonged to a man who had been turned out of his home. He sailed these waters planning his return, but he was caught in the storm and died bitter and unavenged."

She looked down at her feet. "He's supposed to be buried under here, and that's why the sand is barren."

"Do you believe it?" Parks asked.

"It's just a story," Mary said. "But I really don't remember anything ever growing here."

"Maybe it just needs a different kind of seed," Parks said. "Try morning glories."

"Why?"

"They have the tenacity of a weed and the instincts of a wise man. In the dark, they sleep and conserve their strength, then awake in the morning and come to full bloom in the sunlight."

"That's a nice thought," Mary said, rising. "It's worth a try."

They started back along the beach.

"Doc Webster died last night. A fire at his house," Mary said.

"I know," Parks said. "Bob Fischer told me. There's one more you don't know about."

"One more? Somebody with Doc?"

"No. Percy Davis."

She looked at him without changing expression.

"He's dead," Parks continued. "Hanged. I found him about noon when I went to see him."

"Suicide?"

Parks shrugged his thick shoulders. "Certainly looks like it."

Mary fell silent. "I'm sorry to hear that," she finally said.

"You don't sound like it."

"Don't I? Well, I won't go to his funeral, if that's what you mean."

"No, I guess not," Parks said. "But his death has caused Fischer to become very interested in the Home. Fischer knows something is wrong. If we had evidence that the Home was dealing in the black market, I think he'd help."

"He's a decent man," Mary said.

"Are you still interested?" Parks asked. "We might be able to prove that the Home was working the black market, but we still might not be able to find Ellen's baby."

"What would happen if we proved it?"

"Every person who had anything to do with it would probably end up in jail. It'd be a major scandal."

"Then let's do it," Mary said firmly. "There have been other Ellens. There will be more if it goes on. How can we prove it?"

"Just like a corporate due-diligence investigation. We'll read the documents. Are there files?"

"What kind?"

"Files that tell us who adopted the babies."

"Sure. It's required by law. In Davis's office. I don't think they'll be all that happy to let us see them."

"Probably not," Parks said. "How did you get in to check the files for the death certificate?"

"I have keys. My father's master set. Davis never bothered to change the locks. I went over late and nobody saw me."

"Listen close. I want you to go back and get about twenty folders from those files. Get a random sample, that's all we can do, but don't overlook common names. Smith, Jones, Taylor. Those so-called common names aren't so common in the East."

"What good will it do us?" Mary asked, puzzled.

"I'll know better when I see the files. When can you get them?"

"I'll go tonight."

"What time?"

"Around eleven. It's easy to come and go then. The night watchman is asleep and the nurses are all at the nurses' station, gossiping."

"Good. I'll come back at twelve and take a look at them."

Parks returned to his garage apartment facing the Atlantic, made a pot of coffee, and settled down on the couch with his blue steno pad, ten sharp pencils, and a fresh pack of Marlboros. Painfully, meticulously, he recorded his day —what people said, how they said it, what they looked like when they said it. He concentrated on the small remark, the ordinary. In these, people revealed themselves, if they had anything to reveal. The big events took care of themselves. His visit to Davis's house took only six words.

At the end of his notes, he wrote in large, bold letters:

"One is nothing, two may be a coincidence, three is a trend."

The light in the small living room began to fail. Parks stood up and looked out his window to the white beach below. Faith Henderson had just begun her solitary walk along the beach, a lonely, sturdy reed of a woman bending defiantly into the wind as day began to fall. Parks grabbed his coat, stepped into his loafers, and rushed down the stairs to meet her on the beach.

"Mind some company?" he asked with a soft smile.

"As welcome as the flowers in May," she said, and looped her arm through his.

She was neatly dressed, as always, with her gray hair fashioned into a bun, pulling the skin tight over her cheeks. They walked in silence for a moment, their shadows falling long before them. A thin edge of light still hung over the ocean.

" 'The curfew tolls the knell of parting day,' " said Parks, looking off into the ocean, " 'The lowing herd wind slowly o'er the lea.' "

" 'The ploughman homeward plods his weary way, And leaves the world to darkness and to me,' " Faith Henderson finished. "I often think of those lines when I walk my property. It makes it even more lovely to share all this with someone who would think of them too. I told you it was nice to have a man around in the winter."

"Not just any man, I hope!" Parks said, teasing.

"Oh, no. A man like you, Mr. Parks. You wouldn't get away so easily if I were just a little younger," she said devilishly.

He put his arm around her shoulders as they reached the southern end of her property. They turned and headed along the shoreline toward her old, gabled house. The waves lapped at their feet, running thin and fading inches before the water reached their heels.

"How do you know I'd even try?"

"Oh, you'd try. I've lived long enough to know you'd try like the dickens."

"How many times have you walked your property anyway?"

Miss Henderson grinned like an elf. "Oh, no you don't.

If I told you that, you'd know how old I was. But you can just figure on many thousands of times."

"Well, I wouldn't be so impolite as to ask a lady her age."

"Wouldn't do you any good, anyway."

Parks spotted the short, blocky woman he had seen the evening before, standing near the water in a thin sweater. She paid them no attention, but kept her eyes fixed on the water.

"Who's your neighbor down there?" Parks asked.

"Her? That's Hilda Schaeffer. Isn't that just like her to stand out in this weather with hardly anything on. And getting her feet wet besides."

"You don't care for her, I take it."

Miss Henderson sniffed. "The day she moved in I took her a pot of vegetable soup. She cracked the door, took the soup, said, 'Thank you,' and that was it. Next morning I found the pot outside my door. No note, nothing. Now if that's a neighbor, I'm a cross-eyed mongoose. Her husband wasn't too bad. He'd stop to say hello and comment on the marigolds. But her—she's a funny one."

"Is her husband dead?" Parks asked.

"No, just sickly, I guess. I haven't seen him in a long time. He used to own the Seaside State Bank, but he's retired now." The day closed around them, and they finished their walk in darkness and silence.

"Have you had dinner yet?" Miss Henderson asked when they had reached the porch.

"No. Couldn't get up to it. I thought I'd drive over to Toms River. Will you join me?"

"There's no need to go all the way to Toms River. I just cooked the best pot roast you'll ever eat. I'd be proud to share it."

"I have never turned down an invitation from a good-looking woman in my life."

"On that, I'd bet my life, Mr. Parks."

Faith Henderson set the table with the family's Dresden china and Georgian silver, passed down through four generations of wealth and privilege. She hummed an old melody as she set about her tasks, her small, blue-veined hands steady and agile.

Parks went to the kitchen to offer help.

"I've set that table for twenty people before without any help, thank you," she said, as if correcting him.

On the coat rack by the side door of the kitchen were a raincoat and hat, a heavy navy jacket and red scarf, and a white smock spattered with paint. Parks indicated the rack with a nod of his head.

"You paint?" he asked.

"I dabble. That's about all. I have a little studio I fixed up on the next floor. You can see it after dinner if you like."

"I'd like," Parks said. "What do you paint?"

She smiled softly, preparing for the sweet indulgence granted to old ladies who take up painting in their twilight years. "Mostly the ocean, I guess. It's what I like best."

"I like the ocean, too," Parks admitted.

She nodded. "It's the closest comprehensible thing to immortality. It makes me realize my own insignificance."

"Why does it make you feel insignificant?"

"Oh, I don't know. Because it's so big. Because it just goes on and on, paying no mind to anyone or anything. But that's not the real reason I love it. I love it because it's mine. It belongs to no one and therefore it can belong to anyone, and not even God himself can take it away from me."

She stirred the green beans, added mushrooms, and started tearing the lettuce for the salad.

"Just let me heat the rolls and we'll be ready," she said. "And have I got a treat for dessert! You'll want seconds as soon as you see it."

They sat down to dinner with ceremony.

"How old is your house?" Parks asked her, beginning the dinner conversation.

"It was built around 1900, I think. My father bought it in 1910. For my mother. The doctors thought the salt air would help her. It did, for a while."

"You've been coming here since 1910?"

"Yes, but I won't tell you how old I was when I started coming, if that's what you're after."

Parks laughed. He enjoyed the spirit and the mettle of the old woman. "You must have had some wonderful times here," he said.

"Yes," she replied, softly. "Some good ones. Some bad ones. But mostly good." Her voice trailed off and Parks knew she was remembering some of the sixty-odd summers in the old house.

Faith Henderson was the second living child of Elijah and Sara Jane Henderson, born in 1898 in an elegant town house in New York's Murray Hill. Sara Jane Henderson, a North Carolinian by birth, was as frail and soft as Elijah Henderson was robust. Both of them had come from wealth, he from banking and she from cotton, and money and comfort were about the only things in life that did not ravage them. Their third and fourth born died in their cribs within a month of birth. Sara Jane's health began to fail after the death of her fourth child, a boy, in February 1910, and the elaborate ocean house was purchased sight unseen by Elijah within a week after the family physician suggested that the sea might restore her health. The summer of 1910 was a silver memory. Sara Jane's weak lungs began to respond to the fresh salt air. But in the winter she contracted pneumonia and, pale and weak and full of fever, she died.

In 1922 James Elijah, the older child and only son, drowned in a freak storm over Barnegat Bay and the family was reduced to two. For three years the old house stood boarded up. Finally, Elijah and Faith returned to the house of bittersweet memories with an understanding that they would bury the past, begin again, and live each day for itself without regret or sorrow for what had been or what might have been. For all the other things that came and went, the agreement remained unbroken all the way to Elijah Henderson's death in 1952 at the age of eighty-four.

"How long have you lived here year round?" Parks asked.

Miss Henderson awoke from her reverie.

"Since nineteen fifty," she said. "We sold the town house and moved here for good."

Miss Henderson cleared the table and took Parks's order for coffee. She reappeared from the kitchen with a steaming dessert plate piled high with deep-dish apple cobbler.

"How's that for fancy cooking?" she asked proudly.

She served the coffee.

"La petite fleur," Parks said, affectionately.

The gentle candlelight flickered in the room and illuminated her small face with its soft lines and bright green eyes.

"Oh, my goodness!" She smiled with pleasure. "What a sweet memory you have recalled. I haven't been called that in years."

"Who was it?" Parks asked. There was a shine in her eyes that told him that he would not be intruding to inquire.

"Bill Farley, my first and last fiancé, used to call me that."

Parks smiled. "What was he like?"

"Bill? He was a great hunk of a man, much like you. He had shoulders as big and thick as a stevedore's." She sighed and shook her head with pleasure. "He was just downright beautiful. But the thing I remember most was how he loved Vachel Lindsay."

"You're kidding," Parks said, rather astonished.

"Indeed, I am not. He was absolutely fanatical about the man."

"Where is Bill now?"

A large cloud passed over the moon, dimming the light that poured in through the bay windows. The dark cloud shattered into three parts as it passed the slice of silver, and the light became full again.

"The same place as Vachel Lindsay, I suppose," she said softly. "He was hit by shrapnel at the Battle of Château-Thierry. He's buried in France."

The loss of her great love, the love she had promised to wait for and was still waiting for, was still in her eyes.

"And I never met another man who really liked Vachel Lindsay," she said. "You'd have thought there would have been hundreds."

"No," said Parks gently. "I'd have thought there would have been only one."

She smiled softly. "They say there's another land where great hearts meet again. I can wait, Mr. Parks." She rose and blew out the candles. "Follow me, sir," she said, "and you shall see the real Faith Henderson."

* * *

The attic studio was as neat and orderly as the polka-dot dresses Miss Henderson wore each day. An easel with a half-finished canvas stood by a narrow east window, positioned to catch full light. A high-intensity gooseneck lamp perched over it to provide strong light by night. Long-stemmed brushes stood in jars beside a palette an arm's length away. There was not a careless drop of paint in the room.

On the wall hung the many moods and dressings of the majestic ocean she knew so well.

"I have more stacked in the room next door," Miss Henderson said. "But these are my favorites."

"They are quite good. Do you ever sell them?"

"Absolutely never," she said. "These belong to me. I give them away, but never, never sell them."

When the evening concluded with a final cup of coffee, Miss Henderson was still as fresh as morning rain and John Parks was filled with admiration and affection for her.

"Twelve o'clock," Mary said, after she had opened the door for Parks. "I could set my clock by you."

Parks yawned vigorously.

"I feel the same way." Mary said.

"Did you pull the folders?" Parks asked, taking off his jacket and handing it to Mary.

"Yes. I got more than you asked for. They're in the library."

"How many?"

"Forty. I thought if twenty would help, forty would be even better. They go back several years, but some are fairly recent."

"Good. Did anyone see you?"

"No. I was very careful, just as you told me to be. Hilda Schaeffer was leaving just as I got there, but she didn't see me."

"Why was she there?"

"I don't know. Why not? She's a Trustee of the Home."

"Oh."

The folders were neatly stacked on a table by the fireplace. Parks poked at the logs in the hearth, revitalizing the small fire that Mary had built, then sat down on the floor by the table and began to read the papers in the folders.

After a while Parks looked up at Mary. It was after one o'clock. "Everything seems very much in order," he said.

"Davis was very efficient."

Parks thought a moment. "We're going to have to visit some of the families listed in the file."

"Why?"

"To see if the baby in the files is actually with the parents in the files. It won't prove that babies were reported stillborn, then sold on the black market, but it will let us know what kind of operation we're up against."

"All right," Mary said. "When?"

"No time like the present. Let's do it tomorrow. I'll pick you up about nine. That won't give us much sleep, but—" Parks shrugged and rose.

Mary turned suddenly to face him. "Do you have to go?"

Parks reached for her hand and held it gently. "No, I don't have to. Not if you want me to stay."

She closed her eyes and nodded. He pulled her against him and kissed her softly. She yielded slowly, like a child afraid to be touched, but wanting to be touched with everything in its heart.

Slowly, carefully, he undressed her, and kissed the soft flesh that had buried all her memories of tenderness far beneath it. The flames from the hearth cast a pale light over their bodies, and outside the wind lowered to a whisper. When they were spent, she held him tight and whispered *"Tatuś, Tatuś."* Parks realized she was reaching back to the gentle love of another time and place, and he was glad to have taken her there, for he knew it had been a long, long time.

CHAPTER 11

Thursday, December 12, 1974

Parks rose at six, with Mary still asleep, and dressed in the cold house. Slowly, a weak light lifted the darkness. Then the sun rose over the ocean, spreading its golden light above the earth like a peacock fanning its tail.

He drove to the pay telephone on Central Avenue by the Sea 'N Ski Laundromat.

"Asleep?" Parks asked, as Winston came on the line.

The Director yawned.

"That answers it," Parks said. "Are you awake enough to talk?"

"I will be. What time is it?"

"Almost seven o'clock."

Winston ran his fingers through his gray hair and moved to his favorite high-backed leather chair, taking the long-corded special white telephone with him. The leather was cold. The temperature in the house was hovering around fifty.

"Is everything all right?" he asked.

"Depends on how you look at it," Parks said. "I want you to run a check on some people for me."

"All right. Who?"

"Dr. Herman Rider. Dr. Thomas Webster. Christian Schaeffer. Hilda Schaeffer. They are man and wife. I guess Stramm had already run a check on Percy Davis."

"Yes. Is that all?"

"For now. I don't know much about any of them."

The wind howled outside the glass telephone booth. Parks shivered, lit a cigarette, and continued.

"Rider and Webster lived in Seaside. Both are dead now. The Schaeffers are alive, if barely kicking. They live at twelve Ocean Avenue in a big, gray-shingled house."

"What do you want to know?" the Director asked.

"Ages, places of birth, where they've been and what they've been doing the past twenty years or so, whether they went by any other names, what their social, fraternal, and political affiliations were, and anything else you can find out."

Winston breathed in deeply and let out a low hum. He reached for his pipe. "Pretty tall order. How soon do you need it?"

"Yesterday."

The Director took a long draw on his pipe. "I figured as much. We'll see what we can do. Isn't there anything more you can tell me?"

"Not much. Herman Rider was Polish. From Krakow. In Poland his name was Herman Gierek. He was a doctor, lived there during part of the Occupation. He died in Seaside in 1968 of natural causes such as overwork and fatigue.

"Thomas Webster was a doctor who worked for the Valley Forge Maternal Care Home. He died last night—I guess it's now night before last—in a fire at his house.

"Percy Davis, the administrator of the Home, is dead, too. Died the same night as Webster. I found him swinging from the rafters. It looks like suicide, but my guess is that this is one book you better not judge by its cover."

"The bodies are beginning to litter," Winston said.

"I know." Parks hurried on. His feet were cold and his shoulders and calves ached with fatigue. "I don't have Christian Schaeffer's age. I've never seen the man. Apparently, he's been in poor health the last couple of years and rarely leaves his house. He was President of the Seaside State Bank. He retired a few years back. Hilda Schaeffer, his wife, is a bit of a recluse, and is a Trustee of the Valley Forge Maternal Care Home."

Parks cradled the telephone between his shoulder and head, and thrust his hands into his pockets. "That's all I know, except that it's cold enough here to freeze your ass off. What about you?"

"We followed up on your suggestion, checking for suspicious deaths among Victory members in the last year or so. It wasn't easy, but the Western and Southern Regions were very helpful."

"And?"

"Six in all, including Addie May Vernon. She fell down a flight of stairs and broke her neck. The others were in California, Texas, and Georgia. Some of them were old, some young, but they all had three things in common. They all died what appeared to be accidental deaths. They were all alone in the world, and they had each made Victory the sole beneficiary of their estate—which ranged from double indemnity life insurance policies to handsome portfolios. Victory realized about two million from the six. Addie May, for your information, was worth about a quarter of a million when she broke her neck."

"It just goes to show you how an ordinary, frugal American can build up a small fortune with the help of God and Xerox."

"That's one way of looking at it. But I'm afraid it's no joking matter. We only discovered six. There could have been twenty. Even at six, it's too parallel for coincidence. They could raise a fortune devouring their own."

"Yes, but why? All our information tells us that Victory is not hurting for money. Quite the opposite."

Winston sighed. "I know. It doesn't make sense. Well, at any rate, we can probably stop worrying about the Manhattan clinic. It appears to be legitimate."

"Why should we eliminate it?" Parks asked, curious.

"We checked out Dr. Seahurst. He has an outstanding reputation and is totally dedicated to infertility research. He's written about forty articles on the subject and one textbook.

"I also traced the numbers from Stramm's diary. They are the numbers to a post office box in Seaside in the name of Hilda Schaeffer."

Parks leaned against the cold glass of the booth. "Charles," he said slowly, "do you think that the Executive Secretary could be a woman? That Stramm was being led down the garden path by his buddy, Adrian Reese?"

"I certainly do," the Director said. "I'm going to tighten the surveillance around Reese."

"I'm coming to New York today," Parks said. "Will you be available?"

"Yes. I've asked Peter Fleming to come to New York. He should be in this afternoon, but if you miss him he can come to Seaside. I also have your copy of *Gotham Romances,* although God knows why you want it."

"I have a hard on just thinking about it," Parks said. "I'll see you tomorrow."

Miss Henderson was just ending her early-morning walk when Parks arrived back at his winter apartment. He joined her at the water's edge. She was wrapped in a thick sheepskin coat and wool tartan muffler. And, at the edge of her coat, there was the skirt of the green dress with white polka dots.

"Up early," she said. "I thought you were on vacation."

"I am, but I still like the morning," Parks said. "Does Hilda Schaeffer ever take a morning walk?"

"Never. Maybe that's what's wrong with her."

"When did she move here?"

"In May 1953. I remember it exactly. Mae Forman sold them the house and moved to Tupelo, Mississippi, to live with her daughter. She's probably been miserable ever since. Not that she wasn't before."

"Did you know that Hilda Schaeffer was a Trustee of the Valley Forge Maternal Care Home?"

"Is that supposed to make me change my opinion of her?" Miss Henderson asked tartly.

Parks laughed. "I thought it might at least make a favorable impression."

"Well, I didn't know it and it doesn't change my opinion. How does that suit you?"

"Anything you say," Parks said, taking hold of her arm.

"I'm not surprised, either. Her husband probably gave it a mortgage, then bought it back on default."

"You sound like a closet Democrat, Miss Henderson."

"I am," she retorted robustly.

"Oh, my God, another traitor to the class."

"And what about you, if I may ask?"

"You and I started out in different classes."

She moved closer to him, with the intimacy of old

friends. "Don't tell anybody in this town or I'll be run out of here on a rail."

"I'll never tell a soul. When was the last time you saw Christian Schaeffer?"

"A couple of months ago, I guess. He's not completely confined to the house, he just doesn't come out much. Whenever he does, he's always got his attendants with him. At least one of them."

"Attendants?"

"I guess that's what you call them. One of them is short and fat and kind of stupid-looking. His name is Spade. I don't see him around much. The other one—I don't remember his name—is younger. He swims in the ocean a lot in the summer, but he's not any friendlier than the rest of them. That Rider girl knew him."

"What?" Parks kept his voice even, disinterested, although it was no easy task. "Which one, Ellen or Mary?"

"The one who drowned. I saw her in the car with him one day. They pulled up in the driveway. He got out, but she stayed in the car."

Miss Henderson came to a stop in front of the long veranda of her ocean house.

"Anything else you'd like to know?" Miss Henderson asked, a bright gleam in her eye.

Parks laughed. "No, that's all. I'm going to Manhattan for a couple of days."

"Will you come back?" she asked, her green eyes searching his face for the truth.

"Of course," he reassured her.

She brightened. "Good. You might get a vacation yet."

Mary Rider, dressed in a tailored gray wool suit, was packed and ready at nine o'clock. She seemed eager to leave.

"First we're going to visit the John Smiths in Asbury Park," Parks told her. "I want you to call them from here. Tell them we're from the Home and that we have to come by and pay a personal visit. Tell them it's required by the State. They'll buy it, if they've got the child."

Parks was right. Mrs. John C. Smith invited them to come right over.

The John Smiths of Asbury Park lived in a small, white, mass-market colonial on a quarter-acre plot that crowded the neighbors. Mrs. Smith had decorated the house with large oval rugs, golden eagles, a replica of a spinning wheel, and heavy pine imitation Early American furniture. No house short of a Johnson's Wax commercial ever gleamed so bright. It was clear to Parks that upon receiving the call, Mrs. Smith had wiped the furniture with a lemon spray, dusted the polyurethaned floors, mopped the kitchen, tidied the bathroom, and changed her dress.

Enduring a cup of weak coffee and a slice of Sara Lee banana cake, Parks and Mary learned that Johnny Smith had started to crawl, that Mrs. Smith didn't believe in Pampers or Doctor Spock, and that Mr. Smith had already bought Johnny a football and a catcher's mitt.

In Edison it was the same story. Except that the name was Taylor and the baby was a girl named Debbie. While Parks and Mary visited with Mrs. Taylor, Debbie ate a cigarette, pulled a knob off the television set, and dropped her rag doll in the toilet. Mrs. Taylor believed in Pampers and sometimes Doctor Spock and hoped Debbie would grow up to be a nurse.

"Now what?" Mary asked, after they had refused Mrs. Taylor's offer of a second cup of coffee and said their good-byes.

"We'll drive to Manhattan. There are a couple of people in the city we can see."

It was one o'clock before they returned to the New Jersey Turnpike.

Mary rummaged in her purse. "May I have a cigarette, please?" she asked Parks. "I seem to have run out."

"Sure." He took a half-filled pack of Marlboros from his coat and handed it to her. "Light me one, too, will you?"

She lit the two cigarettes at the same time and handed him one.

"You know," she said, "I really don't know very much about you. Do you realize that?"

"All right," Parks said, watching the road as he talked. "I'll tell you. Take notes. I am approximately six feet two, with brown hair, blue eyes, and type O, Rh-negative blood.

I was born May 6, 1933, and am therefore forty-one and a Taurus. I hope our signs match."

"We were made for each other."

"I was born and raised in Stony Creek, Connecticut. My father's name is John Stuart Parks, Senior. My mother, Martha Parks, died of pneumonia in the winter of 1942 when I was nine. My father remarried two years later. My father and my stepmother, Ella, are still alive, still married. I love them both and don't see them half as much as I should. Ella raised me as her own, stayed up all night beside my bed when I had my appendix out, made every shirt I put on my back until I was eighteen, and yelled louder than the cheerleaders at football games."

"You're very lucky," Mary said sincerely.

"I know," Parks said, reflecting for a moment. Then he continued: "I graduated from Bramford High in 1950. I did not have a ducktail or a leather jacket. I had an old black Ford which I never polished, and kept a supply of Trojans under the floor mats. They generally dried up and turned yellow from old age."

Mary laughed. "It's getting juicy."

"You probably want to know about my first lay, but I'm not going to tell you."

"Why not?"

"Some things you just don't need to know."

"Was she special?"

"I hardly remember. She was in my history class. Now that's all. I threw the discus for Yale, being neither the best nor the worst, graduating in 1954. Are you remembering all this?"

"Every word."

"I went into the service for two years, then into business. End of story."

"What does your father do?"

"Right now? Nothing. He was a gardener for the large estates in Sachem Head and Ella took in sewing. I made them both retire in sixty-nine."

"They sound wonderful," Mary said.

"They are," Parks said with pride. "They're very special."

"And you never married?" she asked.

"No. Never."

"A special girl?"

Parks shrugged. "No." He winked. "Except you."

She laughed appreciatively. "You know what I mean."

"Yeah, I guess I do." His voice turned serious. "It's the time, I suppose. It just slips right by without much notice. There was a special girl once, but—"

Parks's mind fell back, just for a fleeting second, to another time and place, to Jane with the long, curly, sandy hair.

"We weren't much alike," he said. "She was like a piece of soap in the hands."

The Turnpike veered near the industrial complex of Elizabeth. They passed through the valley of rust-colored smokestacks spewing their waste into the air. Elizabeth, New Jersey, was the kind of town that could only be beautiful in a blizzard.

"She sounds as though she might have been very special," Mary said.

Parks turned to her with a gentle smile. "It was all a long time ago."

Just before Hoboken, the clutter of midtown Manhattan skyscrapers rose up before them. The tip of the Empire State Building was buried in clouds. The light over the city was a pale yellow, as if it were being filtered through a piece of gauze.

"Anyway," Parks said, "I wouldn't want you to get the idea that I was immune to marriage. It was just the time. It just kind of slipped by and was gone before I noticed."

They left the Turnpike, traveled through the Lincoln Tunnel, and emerged in midtown Manhattan.

"Where do you want to eat tonight?" Parks asked.

"Twenty-One," Mary said.

"Not on my money."

"Why?"

"I can't stand the food. How about Lutèce?"

"Is it shamefully expensive?"

"Conspicuous consumption at its most flagrant."

Robbie Davison stood at the entrance to Charles Winston's office in the brownstone on West 20th and waited to be invited in, but the Director was immersed in a report.

Finally, Davison cleared his throat and Winston looked up.

"Oh," he said, distracted. "I'm sorry. In a bit of a fog, I'm afraid."

Davison was apologetic. "I can come back later, if it's more convenient."

"Oh, no. Please come in." Winston waved him to the leather chair by his desk.

Davison sat down and nervously crossed his legs. The Director lit his pipe and the office filled with the aroma of sweet tobacco.

"I have a problem," Davison began, embarrassed.

The Director remained silent, waiting for his aide to continue, seeing no immediate way to ease his discomfort.

"I need an advance," Davison said, abruptly.

Winston took a long draw on his pipe.

"How much do you need?"

"Two thousand."

A look of mild surprise crossed Winston's face, and Davison looked away.

"I know," Davison said, shaking his head. "It's embarrassing, but—" He shrugged. "I just need some help at the moment."

"Do you mind if I inquire what the money is for?"

"Just some personal problems."

"Not gambling, I hope."

"No sir, the stock market is enough gambling for me."

"Well, we've all gotten into a bind at times. I can have the advance for you tomorrow. Is that soon enough?"

"That'll be fine," Davison said, relieved. He relaxed and rubbed his forehead with the back of his hand. "I can't thank you enough."

"There's no need," the Director said slowly. "No need at all."

Parks pulled up in front of the green awning on Mitchell Place in Manhattan. The doorman rose from the tall, wooden stool in the foyer, buttoned his coat against the cold, and greeted Parks at the curb. It was three o'clock. Parks asked the gold-braided doorman to take the luggage to his apartment, then tipped him a dollar.

"We're going across the street to the UN Towers," he told Mary. "To see the Norths."

The attendant at the lobby information desk had no record of a Mr. and Mrs. James North. The Hanovers lived in apartment 20Y, and had lived there for the last ten years. The guard offered to call the Hanovers for verification. Doing so, he learned that the Norths had sublet the Hanover apartment in July and August. Parks asked to speak directly to Mrs. Hanover, and the attendant reluctantly handed him the house phone.

"Mrs. Hanover? John Parks from Mitchell Place. I'd like to ask you a few questions about the Norths. May I come up?"

"I really don't know anything about them," Mrs. Hanover said bluntly. "We only sublet to them while we were in . . ." She hesitated. "While we were away."

Parks realized that it would take a court order to get admitted to the Hanover apartment. Mr. Hanover was probably still at his counting house on Wall Street, and Mrs. Hanover had no intention of allowing strangers to her door with him away.

"Do you recall where they were from?" Parks asked, resigned.

"Of course. Buenos Aires. They were in New York on business."

"What business? Do you know?"

"I really couldn't say." Her voice was cool, indifferent. The money was beginning to show. "Is something wrong?"

"A relative of Mrs. North is trying to locate her," Parks lied. "It has to do with probate."

"Oh," Mrs. Hanover said, relieved. A woman who lived in the glass-walled duplexes of the UN Towers knew the meaning of probate.

"Can you remember whether they had a small baby with them when they left?"

"I can't say. They paid the rent in advance and were gone by the time we returned. However, it seems unlikely. They were in their sixties."

"Thank you for your help," Parks said slowly.

"You're quite welcome."

Parks took Mary's arm and led her out of the red-carpeted lobby.

"What do you think?" she asked.

"Let's not jump to conclusions. We'll do one more

today." Parks checked his watch. "We'll drop in on the Fredstones in Queens. Unannounced."

The Fredstones lived in a large, red brick house in Forest Hills Village, with white shutters and dormers and a sunroom of wood and glass that formed an elegant left wing to the house. A nurse met them at the door. She was a big woman. Her body filled the doorway, almost touching from side to side.

The house was dark inside, its windows draped and shuttered.

"Are the Fredstones in?" Parks asked.

"Mr. Fredstone is. Mrs. Fredstone is not."

"May we speak with Mr. Fredstone?"

"I'm sorry, no," she said, courteously but firmly. "Mr. Fredstone is not receiving visitors."

"Is he ill?" Mary asked.

"Yes. Perhaps I can help you."

Parks came straight to the point. "Miss Rider and I are from the Valley Forge Maternal Care Home. Our records reflect that Mr. and Mrs. Fredstone adopted a baby boy from the Home last February and we are required by law to make at least one in-house visit. Just perfunctory. Perhaps it would be better to come back when Mrs. Fredstone is in."

"I'm afraid there's been some mistake," the nurse said. She narrowed her eyes and swelled to fill the doorway.

"Not according to our records," Parks said. "We'd better come back later."

The nurse shook her head adamantly and folded her arms across her huge body.

"I don't care what your records say, there's been some mistake. Mrs. Fredstone died ten years ago of cirrhosis of the liver. Nobody in their right mind would have let her have a child, even when she was alive. Mr. Fredstone has been an invalid for years. Parkinson's disease."

Parks looked at her curiously.

"Come see for yourself," the nurse finally said. "But don't say anything. Let me do the talking."

The nurse led them up the center hall stairs to a large corner bedroom on the second floor. Mr. Fredstone was sitting in a wheelchair by the east window. His head was slumped to one side and his tongue hung lazily out of his mouth. Saliva ran down his chin. The room was heavy with the scent of sweet aerosol spray, but still the stench of dying lingered.

"These are your old friends the Smiths," the nurse said sweetly. "They've come to say hello."

Edward Fredstone gave no sign of recognition. He continued to stare beyond them with dull, unfocused eyes. The big nurse gave a signal for them to leave, and they followed her down the stairs to the hall in silence.

"We're sorry to have been a bother," Parks said at the door.

"No bother, really," the nurse said. "You seemed to need convincing, that's all."

As they left the narrow, cobblestoned streets of Forest Hills Village and turned onto Queens Boulevard, Parks turned to Mary and said, "Now it's time to go off duty and play for a while."

The sky had lost its brightness. The streetlights were on and the cars had turned on their headlights.

"What would you think of seeing *Pippin*?" Parks asked. "I hear it's great."

"I'd love it."

"I have to go by my office and sign some papers before the theater. We'll go back to my place and change, then I'll go to the office and meet you at the theater."

While Mary was in the shower, Parks arranged to meet the Director on the first floor of the Metropolitan Museum, in the Egyptian section, and was told that Peter Fleming was in town. Then he called an influential friend and wangled two house seats for the evening performance of *Pippin*.

Winston was standing over the glass-encased mummy from the Pyramid of Howara when Parks arrived.

"A friend of yours?" Parks asked, easing unobtrusively to the Director's side.

"Never had the pleasure."

"Oh yes you have," Parks said. "He was on the train to Harrison last week. Hasn't even changed his gauze."

They left the Egyptian section and walked into the great center hall. The echo of heels crossing the marble floor made the two men inaudible to any but each other.

"I spent today investigating some of the families the Valley Forge Maternal Care Home listed as adopting some of its babies," Parks told Winston.

"How did you get the list?"

"Stole it."

"I should have guessed. What'd you find?"

"Two were legitimate, two were not."

"Tell me about the illegitimate ones."

"One couple was listed as living at the UN Towers. However, they were in their sixties and weren't even citizens. If they got a baby, they took it back with them to Argentina. The other couple was an out-and-out fraud. The woman died ten years ago from Gilbey's gin and her husband has been very ill for a long time. Parkinson's disease."

"So?" the Director asked, rubbing his chin.

"Black market," Parks said. "That's my guess."

"Why?"

"Big money. Especially in white babies."

"I'm sure," the Director said. "But why spend twenty years building up a secret, intricate organization just to sell babies?"

"I don't think it was organized for that purpose," Parks said. "Maybe they just saw a good thing and decided to take the money and run." He shook his head. "We're missing something, damn it! Somewhere we're not putting two and two together."

"Well, don't look to me for anything original." Winston seemed annoyed. "I don't even understand why it needs the money. Victory is supposed to be sitting on millions. That's why we're investigating it. Do you think organized crime is involved?"

"No," Parks said definitely. "I don't know why. I just don't." He nodded to his right. "Let's go to the Roman section. I still want to talk to that old woman in Greenpoint," he said. "Did you get her name?"

"Yes. Katherine Markowski. She lives with her nephew, Nicholas Kosinski, on Broome Street."

The Roman section was virtually empty. They walked to the stone chariot on a raised platform in the middle of the room.

"We have traced some of the names you gave us," Winston said. "Christian and Hilda Schaeffer come from Wisconsin. He opened the Seaside State Bank in 1954. Not a single black mark on their records. In fact no real records to speak of. They don't even cheat on their income taxes. The same is true for Davis and Webster. I brought their biographies with me. We'll keep checking, but don't expect much."

The Director handed Parks a manila envelope.

"That also contains your favorite issue of *Gotham Romances*," he said dryly.

Parks grinned. "I can't wait." He paused and checked his watch. "I have a date tonight. I better get going."

"Do you have time to meet Peter Fleming? He's down in the armory room."

The two men descended the stairs to the first floor.

The Director came to an abrupt halt before the bust of Constantine at the foot of the stairs. "My assistant, Robbie Davison, asked for an advance of two thousand dollars. Said he had personal problems."

"How much do you pay him?" Parks asked, digging his hands into his pockets.

"Twenty-two thousand a year. Enough for a single man to get by on, I should think."

Parks shrugged his thick shoulders. "It's hard to say. New York is an expensive town."

"It's more than the money. It's the money and—" Winston stopped to reflect. "And his overall state for the last couple of months. He's lost weight, maybe ten pounds. He seems distracted."

"Do you suspect him of being the informer?" Parks asked bluntly.

The Director frowned. "No, not really."

"You like him," Parks said with a sympathetic smile.

"Great affection," Winston said. "But I'm going to black him out on this investigation just the same."

Peter Fleming, a long-legged Texan from Fort Worth, was standing by the mounted tilting knights. He turned to greet the Director and Parks.

"Glad to meet you, John," he said in a slow drawl after Winston made the introductions.

Fleming had a firm, steady handshake. He was a tall

man with a strong, heavy frame that carried his two hundred pounds with grace. His face was large and friendly. Thick brown hair fell around his face and over his collar, and a band of freckles ran across his nose.

"I'd like to get together with you before I go back to Texas," Fleming said. "Some funny things are happening."

"Like what?" Parks asked, glancing at his watch.

"Victory's money keeps coming into Austin, from New York. Last week they bought some lake property, in the name of Adrian Reese, but that won't account for half of it."

"What are you going to do in New York?" Parks asked.

"With your Director's permission, I'm going to hook up our New York connection with our Texas connection so we can trace this goddamn money."

"When do you go back to Texas?"

"Wednesday."

"I'll drive back to the city on Tuesday and we can have dinner together."

"Now you're talking," Fleming said. He extended his hand. "You better get on out of here or you're not going to get dinner tonight—or anything else."

"You're right," Parks said. "See you Tuesday." He could tell that he and the Texan would get along just fine. They spoke almost the same language.

Mary was nervously pacing in the lobby of the Imperial Theatre on West 45th when Parks arrived in the yellow cab. It was two minutes to curtain. Parks picked up the tickets at the box office and they were seated just as the orchestra began the overture. Ben Vereen danced and sang his way to a standing ovation at final curtain, lifting the thin show about the wayward son of Charlemagne to a fine night at the theater. Afterward they dined at Lutèce on rack of lamb for a price tag of over one hundred dollars. By the time they returned to Mitchell Place, the hard day had been left behind.

"You only have one bed," Mary said, and smiled.

"Convenient, isn't it?" Parks held out his hand. "Will you stay?"

"Yes. I will stay."

CHAPTER 12

Friday, December 13, 1974

Mary Rider woke up violently. It was the way she awoke on many mornings, especially in the winter, when the mornings were dark and dull. She would come suddenly awake, shivering so hard her teeth chattered. For a brief, horrible second, she would be back in Poland in a dark, dank room, covered with a thin wool blanket, smothering a cry of terror, and longing desperately, but hopelessly, to hear and touch her mother. Then she would remember where she was and what day it was and the wailing hounds of Europe would recede—for a while.

Parks aroused at her sharp awakening. He reached out and touched her and the shivering subsided.

"Cold?" he asked, sleep still in his voice.

"I was," she said, and fell back into his arms.

Mary settled her bottom comfortably in his lap and the warmth of their bodies merged pleasantly.

He held her tight, wondering what or who it was that made her tremble so before she had even started the day. Whatever it was, he wanted to protect her from it. It was a new feeling for him.

She turned to him and laid her head against his chest. He kissed her tenderly and pulled her against him. They made love, slowly, gently. When it was over, he held her in his arms for a long time, his hands covering her breasts.

"Your hands are warm," she said. "And large. I wish we could stay like this forever."

"So do I," he said. "But we can't."

"I know."

* * *

Parks dressed and looked up Nicholas Kosinski in the Brooklyn directory.

The nephew answered the telephone.

"Mr. Kosinski, my name is John Parks. I'd like to talk to Mrs. Markowski."

"What for?" Kosinski asked. Suspicion edged his voice.

"Some years back, Mrs. Markowski called the Immigration and Naturalization Service and lodged a complaint. I've been asked to follow up."

"Mistake," Kosinski said. "She's sorry she did it. She don't want to talk to nobody."

Parks could almost see him begin to put the receiver back in its cradle.

"This is government business," Parks said sternly.

The working people of Greenpoint had a deep respect for institutions and authority. Kosinski was no exception.

"Look, Mr. Parks, we don't want no trouble."

"There isn't going to be any, but I have been asked to talk to her."

Kosinski grunted. "Look," he said, "I can explain. We don't want to be in trouble with the government. You gonna be in Greenpoint?"

"I'll be anywhere you say."

"The Polish and Slavic Center on Manhattan Avenue. Nine forty Manhattan Avenue. Twelve okay with you? I have to get off from work."

"Twelve is fine," Parks said. "I'll see you then."

He hung up the receiver.

Mary called from the kitchen.

"You can certainly tell a man lives in this apartment," she said.

"Why do you say that?" Parks asked, laughing and joining her in the kitchen.

"Because the entire contents of the refrigerator are one can of sardines, a loaf of stale bread, two cans of frozen orange juice, and half a six-pack of beer."

"Let's go out for breakfast. I'll buy, if you won't make any more remarks. Now get dressed. I have to be someplace at twelve for an hour or so."

"Can I go with you?"

"It'd bore you. Why don't you go shopping with the rest of humanity and get trampled in the street?"

"Maybe I will. Where can I meet you?"

"Meet me under the Christmas tree at Rockefeller Center, across from Saks, at two thirty."

By ten o'clock thick gray clouds covered the city and a light mist hung in the air. Although it was not freezing, the dampness and sharp wind made Robbie Davison cold to his feet. He ached all over. Davison buried his hands in the pockets of his London Fog and turned onto West 20th, a block from the CIU office.

The Director saved Davison the embarrassment of having to ask for his two-thousand-dollar advance. As soon as he entered the office, Winston handed him a check.

"I got this ready this morning," Winston said cheerfully, trying to put Davison at ease. "Consider it a long-term loan. We'll work out repayment terms later."

"I appreciate this, sir." Davison's gratitude was sincere.

"That's what directors—and friends—are for," Winston said.

"Yes sir."

"Robbie . . . is something wrong?"

"No, just the bill collectors."

Davison looked down at his hands. They were clenched. He relaxed them and shoved them into his pockets, but not before Winston noticed.

"I'll be all right," Davison said.

"I'm sure you will. I'm glad I could help."

"Thank you." Davison gave a weak smile. "Let me go deposit the check."

As Davison descended the steps of the brownstone, tears ran down his cheeks. He wiped them away and went to the Chase Manhattan Bank on West 23rd, deposited the check, and drew out six hundred in cash. Then he went to a pay phone, made a call, took a taxi to the corner of 44th and Fifth Avenue, and waited under the concrete awning of the Morgan Guaranty Trust Building until a chauffeur-driven black 1974 Cadillac Coupe de Ville drew up to the curb and the door was opened for him. He climbed into the backseat next to a handsome, silver-haired man in his late forties. The man instructed the chauffeur to drive up Sixth Avenue and on through Central Park.

The silver-haired man might have been the Chairman of the Board of AT&T, for all his calm elegance. He wore a three-piece navy-blue Savile Row suit. On his wrist was a Cartier electronic wristwatch that cost not a penny under a thousand dollars. His narrow face was smooth and lightly tanned, with bright, reflective blue eyes the color of cold springwater. Only his soft, pale hands gave him away. On the little finger of his left hand he wore a diamond pinky ring, a flourish to which no gentleman would succumb. For all his effort, he could not escape completely the trappings of his trade. The elegant man in the black limousine was a pusher.

"You have the money?" he asked Davison in a smooth, deep voice. He did not sound as if he cared one way or the other.

"Five hundred?" Davison asked. His voice was shaking.

"Yes."

Davison counted out five hundred dollars and handed it over. Without speaking, the man carefully recounted the money, then, satisfied, folded the bills, placed them neatly in his inner coat pocket, and handed Davison a small package wrapped in plain brown paper.

"The next time it will be six hundred. For the same amount."

"What if I can't pay?" Davison asked. There was fear in his voice.

"Then you can deal on Forty-second Street," the man said. It was not his concern.

"Six hundred, then," Davison said with resignation. He stuffed the package into the pocket of his overcoat.

The man instructed his chauffeur to pull over to the curb. "Until next time," he said.

Davison hailed a taxi to the East Side, to a tall, white brick apartment building at the corner of 64th and Third Avenue.

Kate Davenport was waiting behind the door when he rang. She opened the door quickly and hurried him in. There was panic in her eyes.

"I thought you weren't coming," she said, agitated.

"I started not to," Davison said, looking away from her. Her face was drawn and tight. Her hands shook.

"Do you have it?" she asked, anxious.

"What if I don't?"

Kate lunged at him, her fingers spread and arched. She aimed for his eyes. Davison grabbed her arms in midair, bringing the attack to an abrupt halt.

They stood silently, face to face, staring at each other.

"I have it," Davison said.

He retrieved the brown package from the pocket of his overcoat and held it up for inspection.

"But this is the last," he said.

"Yes, yes. The last. I promise. Just this." Kate was begging, reaching for the package.

"I'm not kidding, Kate. I've had to sell my soul to keep you in this stuff. I can't do it anymore."

"Do you want to kill me?" she shouted. She was on the verge of hysteria.

"You're killing yourself . . . and me."

"I will, I will. I will kill myself. Is that what you want?"

He handed her the package.

"I can't keep you alive, Kate. Not anymore."

But she wasn't listening. She was running to the bathroom, the package clutched tightly in her skinny white fingers. She slammed the bathroom door and locked it.

The apartment was dark. Davison opened the drapes and started to straighten the living room.

Poor Kate. She was as much a disease to him as the white powder was to her. He hated being with her almost as much as he feared leaving her alone. If she had been his woman, he would have walked out long ago. But this was the hold of blood. Kate Davenport was his sister.

"He went straight to the bank, to Chase on West 23rd, then to the corner of Forty-fourth and Fifth," Magda Hemmings reported.

Winston listened intently. Magda Hemmings was a woman to be respected.

In her mid-fifties, Magda was one of those rare women who combined beauty, wealth, authority, and a touch of the earth. She had a dramatic streak of white in the front of her short, dark-brown hair, and, as long as Winston had known her, she had always worn long, thin earrings which flapped about when she tossed her head with Latin pride. Born of upper-class Cuban parents, she had married an American heir to an import-export fortune and divided her early years between society watering holes in Key West and Havana. When her husband died, she joined the Cuban underground. She was imprisoned by Castro and released in 1971, weighing seventy pounds, crawling with lice, but absolutely unbroken. After she regained her health, she was recruited by the CIU Central Director in Washington to work on investigations that spilled over into Latin America, particularly drug-related matters. By all rights she should have been assigned to the Western Region, but she refused to live anywhere but New York City and there was no one who would take on the job of trying to convince her otherwise.

For the last year and a half she had worked closely with Winston, and he held her in high regard. She had connections from Maine to Chile, and her ability to gain the confidence of almost anyone was absolutely uncanny.

"Then what happened?" Winston asked.

"He waited for about five minutes until a black Cadillac pulled up to the curb and opened the door for him."

"How do you know the door was opened for him?"

"Because he got in," Magda said with a withering look. "From there he went to an apartment building at the corner of Sixty-fourth—the kind where all the stewardesses live."

"That's where his sister lives," Winston said.

"A Miss Davenport?"

"Yes, that's his sister. I see you still have your way with doormen."

Magda tossed her head and pulled her long black mink closer around her.

"Of course," she said. "After all, I am still a spy."

Davison awoke.

His throat tightened.

"Oh, my God," he shouted. "No, no, no."

The water was still running. He lunged for the bathroom door. It was locked.

"Kate! Katie!"

No sound. The water just kept running.

"Kate, open the door . . . please."

He was talking to himself. He knew it. God, why had he fallen asleep? Davison took two steps back and rammed the door with his shoulder. The cheap, hollow apartment door gave way. The last thing he wanted to do was look behind the shower curtain. He just wanted to run.

He parted the shower curtain.

"Katie," he said softly.

He turned off the water and felt her pulse. It was weak, but there was still a chance. He crossed to the living room and dialed 911.

"I've got a drug overdose." He gave the address and apartment number. "Get here quick," he pleaded.

He replaced the receiver and, after a fretful pause, dialed Charles Winston.

"Director?" Davison said when Winston came on the line. "I need your help."

Winston and Magda arrived just as the NYPD Emergency Unit was taking the cloth-draped stretcher from the apartment.

"She's dead," Davison said when he met them at the door. "An overdose."

Robbie Davison was dry-eyed. The fear he had lived with had come to pass. The time for crying was over.

"I'm sorry," Winston said.

"Yes, so am I. I wanted to help her live and I'm burying her instead."

"Let's go get some coffee," Magda said, taking Robbie's arm.

The Director was suddenly glad he had brought along his matronly spy. She had the touch of a grandmother, which, in fact, she was.

"We'll go to my apartment," she said with authority. "It is convenient."

"I think I should go with her," Davison said, resisting. "I wouldn't want . . ."

"It will wait," Magda said. "Unfortunately, I know."

Winston hailed a taxi.

Magda Hemmings lived in a ten-room coop on East 86th Street, two blocks from the Metropolitan Museum.

Magda took their coats and put on coffee.

Robbie Davison sat down wearily on Magda's long, yellow couch and slumped forward, staring at the white mohair carpet. The Director took a seat beside him.

"Your sister," Winston began. "She was . . . addicted?"

Davison nodded. "For a long time."

"But not you?" Winston asked, as delicately as he could.

Davison raised his eyes slowly. "No," he finally said.

"Please don't take offense," Winston said. "But—"

"You have to ask."

"Yes. And I have to ask you even more. Is that what you needed the money for?"

"Yes," Davison said. "I had to. I had to pay for it. Every bit. If I didn't, she would have been out on the street working for some pimp who'd shoot her up for thirty tricks a day. I couldn't let her. As terrible as it was, I just couldn't. She was my sister."

"I understand," Winston said with sympathy. "Sometimes it seems the things we love are always frail and weak, and the things we hate are strong and hard."

"I know," Davison agreed. "I did love her. She was my only sister. I would have done anything."

"I hope you didn't," Winston said tensely.

"Some of the things would disgust you," Davison said bitterly. "But nothing to compromise the Unit, if that's what you mean."

There was silence between them. Magda brought the coffee.

"I have to go," Davison said, after half a cup. "There's a lot to do."

"Let us help you," Magda offered.

Davison refused the offer. "I'd rather do this alone," he said.

Parks drove across the Williamsburg Bridge into the heart of Greenpoint, a neat, compact ethnic community that borders the East River. Narrow wooden two- and three-story homes lined the streets in long rows, some covered in asbestos siding, some in aluminum. Each was carefully maintained, the small yards trimmed, the fences painted. And yet a sense of style and affluence evaded them.

Greenpoint is a working-class neighborhood of Polish, Italians, and a few Irish. Blacks and Hispanics, for the most part, live in the surrounding areas of Williamsburg and Southside, and the people of Greenpoint prefer it that way. They are a tight group, conservative in their politics and habits, Catholic in their religion, and suspicious of "outsiders." They keep their streets neat and free of litter, their parks safe and green, and their shades drawn against the rest of the world.

Parks parked the Mercedes convertible on Greenpoint Avenue and turned the corner to Manhattan Avenue. Nick Kosinski was standing in front of the Polish and Slavic Center. He was a great burly man with a large face and an abundance of dark curly hair. He was dressed in a blue coverall and thick work boots.

"We can have lunch inside," Kosinski said. "A dollar fifty. Not bad."

The Polish and Slavic Center was in an old storefront, one long room with a concrete floor and rows of metal tables covered with white paper tablecloths.

The two men ordered lunch from a menu written in English and Polish.

Behind them sat a thin, weathered old man with two days' gray stubble on his face. He was hunched over a cup of steaming coffee, savoring its warmth. The man's eyes were faded, like an old shirt washed too many times. He was dressed in a frayed plaid wool shirt with two buttons missing, the gift of a friend or the bargain of a rummage sale.

"That's Edward Walenski," Kosinski said, pointing to the old man. "He was in Poland the same time as my aunt, but he didn't come out so crazy."

Parks got straight to the point. "Ten years ago, your aunt called the INS and said that she saw a man named Axmann. She said that this man had killed her child, when she lived in Poland."

"Mr. Parks, my aunt made that complaint through our neighbor. I don't know how she talked the neighbor into calling. Everyone knows what my aunt is like."

"What do you mean?" Parks asked.

"Didn't they tell you?"

"No."

Kosinski looked down at his rough, hairy hands.

"She's crazy," he said. "She don't know what she's doing most of the time."

"I'd still like to talk to her."

Kosinski shook his head. "It's no use. She'd just go away and hide, maybe leave the neighborhood, then we'd spend two days trying to find her."

A hard-faced waitress dressed in a stained white polyester uniform brought coffee. Kosinski took a pack of Camels from his pocket and lit one.

"Nobody killed her baby, Mr. Parks. It just died. It died of starvation. My mother got my aunt out of Poland in 1946, but it was too late. Her mind was gone. Not that you can blame her. Her husband was killed by the Nazis and she lost two children, a little boy and a baby girl in the winter of 1944. That is her story, Mr. Parks."

Kosinski paused and took a drag on the Camel. "She is old now," he said. "Crazy. Don't bother her. Give her a little peace."

Suddenly an old woman appeared at the door and stared at the two men. Her face was white and worn and wrinkled. Her eyes burned through Parks and Kosinski.

Nick Kosinski jerked, and raised up as she walked toward them, slowly, with purpose.

It was Katherine Markowski.

Her head was covered with a purple nylon scarf. She had put two large circles of rouge on her cheeks and pinned a plastic flower to her black coat. Today she would not be the hag who wandered the streets of Greenpoint and scared the children. No, not today.

"Please . . . go home," Kosinski said.

She replied to him sharply in Polish.

The nephew rose and went to her, took her arm, and led her to the table.

"She has come to see you," Kosinski said. "She has walked ten blocks in the cold."

Katherine Markowski took off her scarf and sighed wearily. Her hair was thin and white.

"Dolores told me," she said to her nephew, and completed her sentence in Polish.

"My wife told her about your call," Kosinski told Parks.

Katherine Markowski turned to Parks. Her gray eyes were pale and small. They lived in another time.

"I do not speak too good," she said. "Nickie will help me."

"You saw a man named Axmann," Parks said, measuring his words. "In New York."

Her eyes turned hard. She nodded slowly. "Nazi!" she said and spat.

"Where did he come from?"

"Polonia," Katherine Markowski said with certainty. "He was in Polonia. The Lebensborn, the Nazis that stole the children. They came to our village, to Rogozno, at night. They went from house to house, to take the children. They wanted my little boy. I screamed at them: 'Stupid Hitlerite!' That is when he did it, this Axmann. He pulled my little baby girl from my arms. . . ."

She hesitated. Her voice shook. "He threw her against the wall."

Her old eyes filled with tears. All the pain was still there.

"What a thing to do to a mother," she said. "She was two months . . . and still they took my little boy away. I never saw him again."

All at once her eyes were phantoms. She had gone back to Poland, to Rogozno. She was picking the shattered baby from the floor, cradling it in her arms, like a broken doll.

"Now you see, Mr. Parks," Nicholas Kosinski said. "We didn't want her to remember. That is why we didn't want her to talk to you, or the INS."

"Then it is true," Parks said.

"Yes, it is true."

"Do you really think she will ever forget?"

"No," he said.

Parks turned to Katherine Markowski to pull her away from her terrible memories, but she clung to them, her only possessions, now.

"You said he was in the Lebensborn," Parks said. "Are you sure?"

"I am sure," she said. "In the Lebensborn. The ones who took the children."

"Are you sure it was Axmann you saw in New York?"

"Do you think I would forget?" she asked. "He had a

scar." She pointed to her left cheek. "I will never forget."

"No, I guess you won't," Parks said.

"It was Christmastime," she said, speaking slowly in Polish as her nephew translated. "I remember . . . I didn't care to live. There was nothing more for me. I went down to the subway. I wanted the train to run over me. I got on the train, I don't know why. For two days I rode the train. Back and forth. I saw the people come and go . . . children . . . mothers . . . people with packages. Finally I got off. When I came to the top, it was the daytime. I walked. Then I saw him."

She hardened. "I hit him. Maybe I killed him. Maybe that is why you are here."

Parks could see the hope in the woman's eyes. The hope that she had killed her enemy with one small stone.

"He is dead," Parks said. "You killed him. But nobody is to know except you and me. Will you tell?"

"No," she said firmly. "I will tell just God. He will forgive me."

Katherine Markowski tied the purple scarf over her head and left. She had no more to say, perhaps to anyone.

Parks and Kosinski looked at their lunches. Neither man was hungry.

"Sometimes she is better than other times," Kosinski said. "Today she is better."

"Mr. Kosinski," Parks said, "if we had to live with her memories, we'd be mad too."

"I know," Kosinski said. "But we'll take care of her, the best we can. She's our aunt. We love her."

Kosinski shook Parks's hand, then turned and hurried down the street. He was a workingman for whom, day after constant day, sunrise came too early and sundown too late, and he had devoted all the time he could to the matter. He could not stop for grief. The world and the oil bills went on.

Parks started to his car, walking slowly, remembering the small, phantom eyes of Katherine Markowski. Suddenly he felt a chill on his neck, as if a shadow had fallen across it. He turned sharply, and standing behind him, two feet together like a cat, was the old man from the Polish center named Edward Walenski.

"Do you think she is crazy?" Walenski asked. His eyes were steady and burning.

"Who?" Parks asked.

"You know who. Katherine Markowski, the Hag of Greenpoint."

"Is that what they call her?"

"That, and other things. Do you think she is crazy?"

Parks shrugged. Did the man have something to tell? "Yes. A bit," he finally said.

"She is, a bit. But she still tells you the truth. I have been looking for my children for over thirty years."

"The Germans took them?" Parks asked.

"Yes, the Germans. The Lebensborn soldiers. They came to the village of Rydz and took my children. Do you want to know more?"

Parks nodded. "Would you like to sit in the car?"

Edward Walenski walked around to the passenger side and bent slowly at the knees to enter the low sports car. Settled, he turned to Parks. "Would you give me a cigarette, please?" he asked. "Whenever I talk about the Germans, it makes me smoke."

Parks handed him his pack of Marlboros. "Do you know anything about Lebensborn?" Parks asked.

The old man inhaled deeply on the cigarette like a workman at coffee break. "They took my children. Do I need to know more?"

"Well, I—"

"I know more," Walenski said, narrowing his small eyes. "I have spent half my life finding out about it. It was an obsession—knowing the monster that swallowed my children."

"Will you tell me?"

"Yes, of course. What do you know about it?"

Parks lit a cigarette and exhaled. "Not much. Every person I talked to had a different story. One person claimed that Lebensborn ran maternity homes. Another said it ran stud farms. You and Katherine Markowski say it took children from their parents."

"Stole children," Walenski said firmly.

"Facts are hard to come by," Parks said.

"Yes, they are, but if you spend a lifetime looking, you can find a few. It was one of the Nazis' best-kept secrets, and yet the Lebensborn organization was at the heart of the entire movement. Do you know what I mean?"

"Not really."

"Lebensborn was built on the belief that all good Germans were descendants of the ancient Teutons. Without this, there would have been no heart and soul to the great rallies in Nuremberg. Without the myth of the Aryan, the German people would never have allowed the Nazis to bleed the Rhineland and turn Europe to rubble."

Edward Walenski's cigarette had burned down to the filter. He rolled down the window and flicked it away. "Give me another cigarette and I will tell you the whole story."

Parks handed him the pack of cigarettes. He selected one, rolled it between his thin, arthritic fingers, lit it slowly, and settled back in the seat and told the story it had taken him a lifetime to piece together.

The Lebensborn organization was created in the early days of the Nazi movement and put under the jurisdiction of the SS Race and Resettlement Home Office, called RuSHA for short. Its original purpose was to spot those worthy of belonging to the Reich, when it came to pass. In 1931, the SS men were the uncrowned princes of the Third Reich, and every member was required to join Lebensborn. Lebensborn's early goals were to support genetically valuable families, to take care of unmarried pregnant women who could be expected to bear children who met the Nazi standards of superior blood, and to care for those children once they were born. After Hitler became Chancellor of Germany in 1933, the first SS maternity home was set up in Steinhöring, but only women corresponding to Nazi racial theories were allowed to enter. In 1935 RuSHA established the Lebensborn Registered Society to record the births of these children, so that they would not carry the stigma of illegitimacy. All RuSHA files were kept under lock and key in Munich, and access to the Lebensborn registry was severely limited.

However, the true importance of Lebensborn was in Hitler's plans to build a Reich that would last for a thousand years, and to people it with blond, blue-eyed giants. His goal was 120 million new Teutons by 1980. Himmler exhorted his SS men to have at least four healthy children.

Those who could not were expected to adopt racially valuable children selected by Lebensborn. But by 1939 it was clear that Lebensborn was falling short of its goal. The 115,650 SS men had produced an average of less than two children per family. The prudish Himmler then decided it was a high and honorable duty for German girls of good blood to bear children outside the bounds of marriage, particularly for soldiers going off to war, for men important to the Reich who could not marry, and for the SS men, whether married or not.

The day of the Lebensborn maternity homes had come. By the end of 1940 there were seven such homes, all deep in the German countryside, far from prying eyes: the original home at Steinhöring; others at Wernigerode, Klosterheide, Bad Polzin, Nordrach, Vienna, and Wiesbaden. As the Nazi juggernaut rolled across Europe, other homes were established in France, Poland, Norway, Belgium, and Holland. But never in Denmark. The resolute Danes refused to collaborate in any way.

The women came to the Lebensborn homes in secret. Many were from the German upper class or the Party administration, having been seduced by the theology of their time. Each woman was judged according to Aryan principles, and the father, if he was not in the SS or Gestapo, had to document his Aryan parentage. Those with Slavic or Mongolian features need not apply. The births were recorded with the Lebensborn Registered Society in Munich, and the local authorities were never notified.

The Lebensborn organization ran the maternity homes with true Teutonic efficiency. But the SS man were far less efficient in responding to Himmler's call to duty to the Fatherland. Thousands of children were born out of wedlock in the Lebensborn homes, but few were attributable to the dalliances of the SS. Apparently, the Black Order was not as spirited in bed as it was in the death camps.

Heinrich Himmler, however, was not a man to shrink from a task that involved the waste of human lives, and he decided to take the creation of 120 million new Aryans out of the hands of chance. Lebensborn adopted a new *Züchtungsziel,* "breeding objective," and took a turn to the tawdry—the establishment of Lebensborn "castles," a combination of SS bawdy houses and stud farms where women of good blood who wanted to bear a child for the Führer could come and have sex with SS men.

By 1945 there were eight Lebensborn castles spread across the German countryside. The SS men who came to the castles were mostly married. They would party late into the night, and consummate their lust with whomever they chose, and the women who conceived in the castles would deliver their children in the Lebensborn maternity homes. The children born in the Lebensborn homes were called the SS children, and were treated as small gods, which, indeed, they were intended to be. The SS children were to be the advance guard of the master race that would raise Europe from the ruins their fathers had turned it into. There were no christening ceremonies for the children. They were named and dedicated to the Führer in an afternoon ceremony held under the sign of the swastika and, after a year, put out for adoption with good Nordic families.

But by 1944 the SS had to abandon the maternity homes in all but Germany. In the final months of the war, all Lebensborn homes were closed except in Bavaria, where thousands of women and children were crowded into spaces meant for two or three hundred at the most.

By 1944, too, the stock of willing women for the Lebensborn castles had also dwindled. After Stalingrad, the SS men did not seem so invincible: The bright, victorious look was all but gone from their eyes. The SS then took to kidnapping Norwegian and Polish women for forced service at the castles. At the end of the war, even young German women were dragged to the castles and subjected to gang rapes.

"What about the SS children?" Parks asked, as Walenski paused in his explanation.

"At the end of the war?"

"Yes."

"Some of the women took them home," Walenski said. "But most were just left behind. They were later dispersed into France, England, and other places as war orphans." He paused and swallowed to ease his dry throat. "But we still haven't gotten to the worst part," he said.

"The kidnapings," Parks said.

"Yes, the kidnapings. It all began in 1941, when Himmler came upon the fanatical idea that any blond, blue-eyed child left in Europe without proper indoctrination was a mortal threat to the Reich. Poland was full of such children, so Himmler ordered them to be seized and taken to Germany. By winter the SS Central Office in Poland had finished their secret plans and was ready to implement them."

Walenski stopped for a moment, and pressed his lips together, as if to stop the pain from coming back through the years. Parks thought that he would not continue, but the thin, diminutive Pole was made of tempered steel. Walenski set his jaw and completed his story.

At first, Lebensborn took children only from orphanages and from the families of deported, liquidated, or banished partisans and other enemies of the Reich—abandoned children, children born in concentration and forced-labor camps, and children born to unmarried mothers, especially if the father was in the SS or Gestapo. Thus, the early repatriation of "good blood" to Germany caused little comment.

Reception centers were set up in Poznan, Pushkau, Brockau and Kalisz in Poland, at the Pommern home in Bad Polzin, and in the Gostynin area. The children were given German names as soon as they arrived at the reception centers, and all contact with Poland and the Polish language was broken. The day after arrival, the children who were old enough began to learn the German language and the Nazi ideology.

But, when the war turned against Germany in the winter of 1942–43, the systematic devastation of the children of Europe began. The Germans started to take the children by force. In the streets, in the playgrounds, at home and at school, blond, blue-eyed children became the victims of raids that no one could stop or oppose. Children were assembled in the square of a school yard, and after a summary selection taken in truckloads to transit camps where they were later examined and judged as to their value to the German stock.

From Poland, the kidnapings spread across Europe into France, the Ukraine, Russia, and the Balkans. A climate of terror prevailed. Children would scatter and run as soon as they saw the black uniforms of the SS. Parents withdrew their children from school and hid them. As resistance increased, the Lebensborn troops began arriving in the villages at night, catching the families unawares.

The children were taken to racial transit camps where they were poorly fed and ill treated. They were given little heat or warm clothing, and many were sick with hacking coughs for most of the cold weather. Those who wet the bed from the irritating chemicals in their food were sent to a windowless room with one thin blanket to cover them. In the harsh winter, the children often froze to death and had to be hacked apart the next morning before they could be buried. At the Potulice internment camps, in the district of the free port of Danzig, more than 5,000 children between the ages of one and fourteen died from starvation and abuse at the racial transit camp as they awaited examination. Thousands of Russian and Polish children kidnaped by the retreating *Wehrmacht* in 1945 died of neglect in the transit camp at the Moohren monastery in Unter-Thingen.

In its final days, Lebensborn, the fount of life, became Todesborn, the fount of death.

More than 200,000 Polish children were declared racially fit for Germanization. Hundreds of thousands more were rejected as racially unfit and gassed or worked to death. In France 40,000 children disappeared without a trace; 50,000 children were abducted in the Hungarian Ukraine and 500,000 more from the Balkans and Russia. Thousands more were taken from Norway, Belgium, and Holland. But virtually none were taken from Denmark, where the Danes protected their children with the same ferocity and resistance with which they had protected their Jewish countrymen.

Nearly eighty percent of the children kidnaped by Lebensborn were never returned to their rightful parents. They became Germans and were absorbed by the know-nothing masses who claimed they were ignorant of the Nazis and their atrocities.

Edward Walenski had finished his story, but not without feeling thirty years of anger and despair. His hands were

clenched into fists and thin beads of sweat lined his forehead. "It is almost too much to believe," Parks said
quietly.

"That is the way it is with the Nazis. Most people chose
not to, or to forget. But some of us, we cannot."

Parks offered him another cigarette, but he refused it.

"What did you do in Poland before the war?" Parks
asked, to break the intensity of the moment.

"You mean why do I speak so well and look so poor?"
Walenski said with a trace of bitterness.

"No, I—"

"It's all right, my young friend. I was an attorney. But
here—" He shrugged. "Well, not an attorney, anyway."

Walenski opened the door to leave, and Parks offered
him his hand. "Thank you," Parks said.

"You're welcome. I am glad I told it one last time. From
now on until the day I die, I am never going to say the
name Lebensborn again."

Parks reached Rockefeller Center at two twenty, and
waited for Mary at the foot of the giant Christmas tree.
She arrived empty-handed.

"Don't tell me you can actually walk down Fifth Avenue
and not even be tempted," Parks said.

"I had too good a time looking," Mary said. "It's beautiful."

Mary explained to him the lay of the land. Lord & Taylor's was littered with red paper roses. Saks Fifth Avenue
was hung knee deep in plastic silver icicles. Bergdorf
Goodman was subdued and elegant in blue and green
partridges in pear trees. And Gucci's was hardly decorated
at all.

"You should have dropped into Gucci's and bought
something so the salesman could have a chance to insult
you," Parks told Mary. "It's this sick game we play in
New York."

"I'll pass," Mary said.

"I have an idea," Parks said, taking her hand. "Let me
buy you a present. Something bright blue. Not to be
opened until Christmas."

"Blue?"

"Yes, like a morning glory."

He had never seen her in anything but grays, browns, and blacks, the colors of early winter mornings when the clouds roll in and cast a chill over the land. Somehow, it seemed important that his gift to her be bright and blue, like a morning glory, opening and spreading in a new sun.

"All right," Mary said, looking up at him, smiling. "Where shall we go?"

"Let's try Henri Bendel's. If you don't find something useful, you can at least find something expensive."

She moved closer to him. "What woman could pass up an offer like that?"

At Bendel's, Mary picked out a long red velvet skirt. Parks had it gift wrapped, and made her promise not to open it until Christmas morning. He bought her an ounce of Joy to tide her over.

It was almost dark before they were ready to leave for Seaside. On the way to the garage to pick up the Mercedes, Parks called Winston and was told about Kate Davenport.

"Well, if the need for money makes a suspect, Davison a prime candidate for Unit mole," Parks told him.

"I know," the Director said. "But I still don't believe "

"You don't believe anyone you know could have done ," Parks said, "but somebody did."

Winston grunted. "Did you go to Greenpoint?"

"Yes," Parks said, "and Lebensborn has taken a bad turn. That old woman is crazy. Mad is a better word. But I'll tell you this, I believe there was a man named Axmann and that he killed her child. Whether the Executive Secretary of Victory is Walter Axmann I'm not sure. She was half crazy when she threw the rock. A look-alike would have set her off."

"Mistaken identity?"

"It could have been."

"Do you still think the Executive Secretary could be Hilda Schaeffer?"

"I don't know. It could be Christian Schaeffer, and the post office box a cover-up."

"In that case, Walter Axmann and Lebensborn are not involved in this investigation," the Director said. "Did you read the biographies I gave you?"

"Yes."

"Then you know that Christian and Hilda Schaffer are native-born Americans. They have lived here all their lives."

"I know," Parks said, perplexed. "Every time we gain an inch, we lose a mile. Stop, go, stop, go, dead end. Nothing matches up. Nothing falls into place." Parks shook his head. "Goddamn it! I know Lebensborn fits into this."

"You don't know that, John," the Director cautioned. "Concentrate on Victory. The rest will follow."

In the late afternoon, Faith Henderson was cleaning her brushes when she heard a knock at the door. Thinking it might be Parks, she laid her brushes aside and hurried to the door and opened it.

Hilda Schaeffer stood at the doorway, a bundle wrapped in cloth napkins in her hand. Her eyes darted from side to side. "May I come in?" she asked, almost with apology.

"Why, of course," Faith said.

Hilda Schaeffer held out the neatly wrapped bundle. "I baked some bread—for you."

Faith Henderson took the bread. It was still warm. "How sweet," she said. "On a day like this, we can all use some warm bread. Will you stay for some? I have jam I made myself."

Hilda Schaeffer moved her shoulders nervously. "No, I cannot. I must pack."

"Going on a trip?"

"I am moving," Hilda said, looking down at her feet.

"Where, for God's sake?"

"Austin." Then Hilda Schaeffer stiffened. "Well, somewhere. I don't know." She turned to leave. "I have never forgotten that wonderful soup you made. I just wanted to say thank you."

"Why, you're quite welcome."

Hilda Schaeffer crossed the white sand yard with long strides. She looked up just once, and saw a face turn away from the window of her house. She pulled her arms close to her and quickened her step.

It was nightfall before Parks and Mary started back to Seaside. After emerging from the Lincoln Tunnel into New Jersey, they drove in silence along the Turnpike to

Woodbridge. At Woodbridge, they changed over to the Garden State Parkway and veered toward the shore points.

Finally, Parks broke the silence.

"Now that you know everything about me from my life's philosophy to the girl in my history class, tell me something about you."

"What do you want to know?"

"Oh, I don't know. How many times have you been in love?"

Mary rubbed the back of her neck. "You don't get many chances in Seaside." She looked out the window at the lights along the Parkway. "There was only one, I guess. He lived in the house next door. He was staying for the summer, to get the sun." The roar of waves rolling gently to the beach sounded in her ears as she reached back. "But it was a long time ago."

"What happened to him?" Parks asked.

"He died."

A hush fell over them and the hum of the wheels against the pavement filled the car.

"He died of cancer," Mary said. "In a way, he was already dead when I met him. But still—"

"Sweet memories?"

"Yes." Mary looked down at her hands. "The house will seem more empty, now that I've been away," she said finally.

"You're not going home," Parks said, with affection. "You're coming with me."

Mary smiled and touched his arm.

When they arrived at Parks's winter quarters above the two-car garage, a note from Miss Henderson awaited them. It was slipped just inside the door, on a folded piece of her blue stationery, sealed with an economical strip of Scotch tape. Parks turned on the lights and quickly read the note.

"Want to visit a friend?" he asked.

"Who?"

"Miss Henderson."

Mary was hesitant. "I think I'd rather not; I'm exhausted. Why don't I put on some coffee. Will you be long?"

"Not too long, I don't suppose. Why don't you come'
She'd enjoy having you."

"I really don't feel like talking to anyone right now,'
Mary said. "I'd rather just sit here and think about today.'

"It did turn out kind of nice, didn't it?"

"Yes, it did. I loved every minute of it."

She gave him an appreciative kiss.

Parks winked. "I'll make this quick," he said.

Faith Henderson was waiting in the alcove of the over
sized bay window of her parlor when he arrived. She wa
wearing her green dress with white polka dots, neat and
orderly to the last bobby pin. In her constancy, she was no
unlike the ocean which rolled out cruel and cold before
her.

"Keeping a check on me?" Parks asked when she let him
in.

The wind whistled at his back and she closed the door
quickly to preserve the delicate balance of heat in the
large house. He bent and kissed her on the cheek.

"No, just expecting you. I heard your car drive up."

"The woman of a thousand ears," he said, laughing.

"Well, yes and no," the old woman said in her light, high
voice. She offered him a chair by the fireplace. "I knew
you couldn't resist a message promising special news."

"You caught me," Parks said with a grin.

"I wish I'd done that about forty years ago."

"When you were eighteen?"

"Now don't start up with me," she said, her eye.
gleaming in the light of the fire.

"Okay, I give up. What's the news?"

"The Schaeffers have pulled up stakes and gone to
Texas."

Parks deliberately controlled the muscles in his face. He
was a long second before answering.

"Just like that?" he finally asked, his voice revealing no
great concern.

"Yes, just like that. Hilda Schaeffer came over to tell me
herself. Can you believe it? For twenty years she didn'
give a hoot, then today she comes over with a loaf o'
homemade bread, thanks me for the pot of soup I cooked
for her in nineteen fifty-three, and tells me she is leaving
this very day, never to return."

"Sounds a little strange."

"Hilda Schaeffer is a little strange."

"So you still dislike her."

"Did the tide come in this morning?"

Parks laughed. "Did she say where she was going?" he asked, looking into the fire.

"Austin. She didn't give an address."

Parks shrugged, trying to appear disinterested.

Miss Henderson laughed devilishly. "Perhaps we could work out an exchange," she said. "I'll tell you my age and you'll tell me what you're really up to."

"Who goes first?" Parks asked, grinning.

"Oh, posh," Miss Henderson said, with a wave of her hand. "Neither one because neither one would tell. But you're up to something."

"Have they gone yet?"

"That's right, don't let on to a thing. But I've got your number. Don't think I don't." She stopped for reflection. "They left just after sundown. I heard them from the kitchen. The house is all dark now."

She paused again, but this time her face was more studied. "She loved that old house, as ugly as it is."

"Do I detect some sympathy?" Parks asked, rising from his chair.

"Of course you do. I may not like her, but that doesn't mean I can't feel sorry for her."

Miss Henderson walked to the far end of the room and retrieved a large canvas leaning against the wall. It was a painting of the ocean and a stretch of white beach on a mild summer morning.

"This is one of my favorites," she said, returning to the fireplace. "I'd like you to have it, if you want."

"I'd be honored," Parks said, holding up the painting to admire.

Standing at the bay window, Faith Henderson watched Parks cross to his garage apartment. A good winter, she decided, although she knew it would end soon, because that was the way things were. She had come to accept that the great pleasures in life, like the cutting season for peonies, were of short duration.

The coffee was hot when Parks reached the apartment. While Mary was in the bathroom preparing for bed, he took a dark knit pullover, ski parka, and jeans into the living room and slid them under the couch. He would sleep in his underwear. Before going to bed, he set his mind to wake up at midnight.

Miss Henderson was going through her nightly eleven-o'clock ritual of turning out the lights, clearing the stove, and turning down the heat, when she heard a knock at the front door. Thinking it was Parks, she opened it.

"Why, Mr. Spade," she said, startled. "Is something wrong?"

Parks woke at five to midnight. Mary was in a deep sleep. He dressed quickly and left the apartment. The night was black and overcast. Not even the hint of a moon. He crossed the beach to Christian Schaeffer's large Victorian ocean house. The front porch creaked when he stepped onto it. He tried the door. It was locked. He retrieved a skeleton key from his pocket and the door unlocked easily. Inside, the house was dark and still. The furniture was draped in white sheets. It was like a funeral parlor after closing hours.

Slowly, Parks ascended the tall stairs. They groaned under his weight. He reached the second-floor landing, and pulled out his cigarette light to provide some light.

That was the last thing he remembered.

CHAPTER 13

Saturday, December 14, 1974

Consciousness seeped slowly back to Parks.

The back of his head felt as if it had been split open with a dull axe. The crushing pain racked his body and blurred his vision. His breath came tight and short.

Parks let out a deep, sick groan, and threw up violently, vomiting on one of the three men huddled around him.

"Goddamn! Shit!" Spade cursed, in the thick, lazy accent of the slums. "I'm covered in fuckin' puke."

"Go wipe it off," Christian Schaeffer instructed him. Schaeffer turned to Robinson. "Andy, get paper towels and clean this up."

The tall, slender Robinson turned and left the room quickly. He was glad to go.

As the voices talked over and above Parks's head, consciousness finally established itself. When it did, he stiffened. His butt was cold. Parks smothered a gasp. A deep chill ran through his body.

He was tied to a straight-back chair that had had its cane seat rudely ripped away for the occasion. The edges of the torn cane cut into his legs. There was little doubt in Parks's mind why the cane seat had been removed.

Parks was naked except for his socks, and he was straddling the chair backward. His hands were tied behind him at the wrists. His legs were spread apart and the chair's ladder back rose between his thighs like an evil wedge, so that it was impossible to close his knees and protect himself. Beneath the bottomless chair, he was exposed and vulnerable.

Robinson began to clean the vomit from the floor. Schaeffer and Spade waited in silence.

Parks surveyed his prison. He was in a second-floor sitting room which Schaeffer had apparently used as a study and office. It had two large cathedral windows that gave the room a breath of space and air, and the oak paneling had been painted a light cream. The room had been stripped of furniture, except for the straight-back chairs and Schaeffer's massive Victorian oak desk.

Christian Schaeffer paced the room with a gait of authority. He wore a three-piece blue pinstripe suit, a starched white shirt, and a red tie. Still, he did not have a banker's grace because he had a peasant's body. Schaeffer's neck was short and thick, sitting oddly on his huge ox's shoulders, and he was too small for his powerful build.

At last Schaeffer turned his full attention to Parks.

"Good evening, Mr. Parks. We have been expecting you."

It was said in the stilted, precise English common to the foreign-born. But it was not the voice that made Parks's spine stiffen; it was the long, faint scar on the man's left cheek.

"Of course, you were not expecting us," Schaeffer continued. "We apologize."

Betrayed. The word ran through Parks's mind. *Betrayed, just like Henry Stramm, but by whom?*

Schaeffer grinned, slyly. "We apologize for our little trick to get you here, but you will have to understand, it was tonight or never."

Faith Henderson!

"Let me make some introductions," Schaeffer said, with easy grace. "The gentleman on whom you so impolitely retched is Mr. Kirby. Mr. Kirby is usually called Spade. It is a nickname he thought up for himself because of all the graves he has caused to be dug. I am sure you understand. Grave . . . dirt . . . spade. Not very original, but he likes it."

The squatty gargoyle grunted in agreement.

Schaeffer continued. "A man such as you will find Spade a little stupid, and, I grant you, he may be. Nevertheless, he has some qualities lacking in most of us. He is as feeling as a dead fish, and that, Mr. Parks, should give you pause to think."

Schaeffer turned his attention to the younger one. "This is Andrew Robinson."

Robinson folded his arms across his chest and rocked on his heels in discomfort. He was handsome in an uncomplicated way, with thick blond hair and even, regular Anglo-Saxon features. But it was his eyes that set him apart from Schaeffer and Spade. They were still capable of more than one expression.

"Robinson is the apprentice of Spade," Schaeffer said. "They are quite good friends and one day he will do very well indeed. Right now he is not very polished, but he is very, very strong. That should complete my warning to you if you are half as intelligent as I believe you to be."

Schaeffer clasped his hands behind his back and took a rigid military stance. He stared directly into Parks's eyes. Neither man blinked. It was a draw.

Schaeffer broke the deadlock with a short laugh of admiration.

"Now, Mr. Parks, a few questions. The first, of course, is why are you here?"

"Vacation," answered Parks as casually as he could.

"What is your middle name? Quickly?"

"Stuart."

"Very good. You have been well trained."

"If you'll just give me my pants . . ."

"No. Besides, we checked your pockets very carefully. Your identification says you are John Stuart Parks and that you live at Mitchell Place in New York City."

"My doorman will identify me."

"I am sure," Schaeffer said. "Now, once more, why are you here . . . in this house."

"It has nothing to do with you," Parks said.

Spade grunted in ridicule. Parks wanted to cover himself with his hands so Spade would stop staring at him. It made his skin crawl.

"I am willing to listen," Schaeffer said. "Would you care to tell me about it?"

"I don't seem to have much choice."

"None."

Parks began slowly, fabricating his story.

"I'm the President of American Investing Corporation," he said. "A small money management company on Wall Street. Check it out. We're in the yellow pages. One Chase Manhattan Plaza. I came to Seaside for a rest. To get away."

Parks paused to draw his breath and collect his thoughts.

"Very interesting," Schaeffer interjected into the brief silence. "And very believable."

"One of my favorite pastimes is rummaging around these old, oversized houses when the owners are gone. It satisfies my criminal instinct suppressed since puberty. I heard you were gone, so . . ." Parks hesitated, then said with sincerity, "I didn't mean any harm."

Schaeffer folded his arms across his chest and glared at Parks. "It is a lie," he said coolly.

"I don't think you'll believe anything I tell you," Parks said calmly.

"I will believe the truth," Schaeffer said, his voice sharp and hard. He drew in a heavy breath, then continued: "There are a lot of ways to make a man speak the truth. Let me tell you some. We could break your arm at the elbow. Or we could pull your fingernails off one at a time. I saw that done to a man once—he screamed until blood ran from his throat. And, of course, we could improvise some electrodes. We could wire your penis to an extension cord and plug it in. What would you think of that, Mr. Parks?"

Parks remained silent. Only a thin line of sweat across his brow gave any hint of terror.

He shrugged, as if to admit defeat. "Okay, you win. I work for the government."

"Yes?"

"You are under a great deal of suspicion."

"Tell me more."

"The government doesn't think you pay your taxes—thousands of dollars in taxes. They aim to collect."

"You are with the Internal Revenue Service?"

"After a fashion."

"No, that is not quite the truth," Schaeffer said. "In fact, it has been tried on me before." He turned to Spade. "A little persuasion might help, don't you think?"

Spade moved slowly to the rear of Parks. His large, hard-tipped workman's boots thumped heavily on the floor. He stood behind Parks, breathing in short, excited gusts. The room was deathly silent. The ocean wind rattled the windows. Parks felt the muscles in his chest tighten.

Spade kicked with all his might.

Pain hit Parks in the gut and rolled to his chest. His head went light. He let out a muffled yell between his clenched teeth.

Spade kicked again. The steel tip of his boot landed dead center.

Sweat broke out on Parks's face. He started to black out. Quickly, Spade slapped him to consciousness, and Parks hung his head forward and retched in dry heaves.

"Enough!" Schaeffer commanded.

Spade withdrew.

Parks was weak and sick. Is this the way it was for Henry Stramm? Had they brutalized him until death was almost a reward?

"Now, Mr. Parks," Schaeffer said sternly. "Perhaps you will take us more seriously. I meant every word I said from the fingernails to the electrodes. For your own sake, I plead with you to tell the truth."

Parks's mouth was dry. He struggled to speak.

"Water . . . please."

"Yes, you may have water, but only after you agree to tell the truth."

"Water," Parks said again. Perhaps they would give him an easy death if he told.

"You haven't answered me," Schaeffer said angrily. "There are many more techniques, Mr. Parks, and Spade knows them all."

You bet, Parks thought with malice. And you've used every fucking one of them. God, why hadn't the Unit given him a fake tooth filled with cyanide?

"Spade has a particular favorite, but it gets quite nasty for men such as you, Mr. Parks, because it ties in with Spade's little perversion. On women, he uses the handle of a screwdriver, but on men . . ."

Schaeffer paused to let the terror set in.

"So there you are. You have a choice. You can talk or we can help you along."

Parks remained silent, even though his guts were screaming.

"Spade, an extension cord!" Schaeffer commanded.

It was an errand of pleasure for Spade. He returned with the cord curled around his fist. He severed the cord from the socket, and trimmed the rubber insulation from the wire. Parks watched the preparation. Sweat dripped from his face, but his eyes were steady.

Spade handed the shredded cord to Schaeffer, who swung the improvised electrode in front of Parks.

"Here it is, Mr. Parks."

Parks was rigid. He kept his eyes fixed on Schaeffer's face. If he looked at the bare wires on the cord, he knew he would tremble violently.

Schaeffer toyed with the cord.

"You are not even thinking about talking, are you, Mr. Parks? You are just preparing yourself to die."

Parks breathed deeply, irregularly, but did not speak.

"Don't worry, Mr. Parks. There is always something that will make a man confess. Sometimes it is not the threat of death, but the way of death. Do you know how Edward the Second of England died? They rammed a red-hot poker into his anus and burned out his bowels.

"It left not a single mark. They inserted the poker into the anus through a hollow bull's horn so it would not burn the skin . . . just inside. They say his screams were heard all the way from Berkeley Castle to the village below."

Schaeffer stopped pacing and glared at Parks. "Sweat is running down your face. Do you find it too hot in here?"

Parks did not respond.

"You see how it is," Schaeffer said in triumph. "How you die is sometimes more important than if you die." He paused, his malicious spirit soaring. "We could do that for you, Mr. Parks. Let you die like Edward the Second."

Parks took a deep breath. Yes, they could. They might. But he still would not talk. He would die, just like Henry Stramm, but he would not talk.

Schaeffer walked over to the oak desk under the arched window and dropped the extension cord into the top drawer.

"Very well, Mr. Parks. I accept what I cannot change. You have no intention of confessing, no matter what we do. Very unusual for a soldier of fortune." There was a trace of admiration in his voice.

Schaeffer waved his hand. "Enough of this." He shrugged in resignation. "I already know who you are and why you are here. I only wanted to hear it from you own lips. But I have not the time."

"Who am I?" Parks asked casually.

"You are John Stuart Parks, and you work for the Civilian Investigations Unit, otherwise known as the CIU."

Parks stiffened. Robbie Davison was right. The Unit had a leak and it certainly wasn't Faith Henderson.

"You want to know how I know, do you not?" Schaeffer asked slyly.

Parks shrugged as if he did not care.

"I paid for the information," Schaeffer said in triumph. "In America, it is possible to buy anything."

"Can I have my clothes now?" Parks asked.

"No."

"My ass is cold."

"It is the price you pay," Schaeffer said.

"Let me have a blanket. I don't like to give cheap thrills." Parks glared at Spade.

"I can understand that. Spade, get Mr. Parks a blanket."

"He is rather disgusting," Schaeffer said as Spade left the room reluctantly. "But Robinson does not seem to mind."

Parks looked over at Robinson, who turned away, embarrassed.

"Who are you, really?" Parks asked, looking directly into Schaeffer's eyes.

"I am Christian Schaeffer, the Executive Secretary of Victory."

The sick feeling in Parks' bowels was ebbing. He still had hope for escape, but he needed to find a trump card of his own to play.

"You are not Christian Schaeffer," Parks said.

Schaeffer stiffened. "No?" he said coldly.

"You are Walter Axmann."

Schaeffer did not react. He remained rigid, his eyes fixed in a stare. The pale light in the room cast long, grotesque shadows against his face.

Outside, the first snow of winter began to fall.

Schaeffer turned to Spade and Robinson. "Go finish the packing," he said abruptly.

Spade and Robinson left.

"We know everything about you," Parks said. He had to be careful. He was walking a fine line.

"I doubt that," Schaeffer said, finally.

"Let me tell you," Parks said slowly. "You were born in Munich. You joined the National Socialist Party in 1931 and the SS in 1932. You were in the Lebensborn, stationed in Poland, and you were decorated with the Iron Cross. Today, nobody knows where you are."

Schaeffer's face drained. The corner of his mouth began to twitch.

"Nobody cares where you are," Parks said. "They never will . . . unless you kill me."

"Do you think I have a choice, Mr. Parks?" Schaeffer asked. There was a tremor in his voice.

"Yes, you always have a choice."

Schaeffer stood silent. He was no longer the arrogant banker. Indecision had set in.

"You're going someplace. Leave me here, alive, and I'll let you get there. I will never say the name Walter Axmann again. I'm the only one who knows for sure. To the rest of the world you can stay Christian Schaeffer."

"We could take you with us," Schaeffer shot at him.

"You do just that. The CIU will track you to the ends of the earth."

"How will they know?" Schaeffer asked. He had returned to doubting.

"They know I'm here."

"Yes, I'm sure they do, but that will not help them for long."

"Long enough. Do we have a deal?"

"You are a man to be admired, Mr. Parks. You have a certain grace."

"Do we have a deal?"

Schaeffer smiled sardonically. He was a man used to dealing in lives. "How do I know I can trust you?" he asked.

"You don't," Parks said. The strength had returned to his body. "And you don't have to. If you kill me, the CIU will be after you by tomorrow. They know I'm here. If you let me live, they may not try. They may let it die. They don't want you, they want Victory."

"And what will *you* do, Mr. Parks?"

"I won't follow you, if we agree. We are equals. We can make agreements that bind us."

Schaeffer breathed deeply and eased his shoulders.

"We are equals," he said, almost inaudibly. *"Reichsführer,* in our own way."

"So? Do we have a deal?"

"Yes. A deal, as you say. I will let you live."

Schaeffer sat down in the red leather chair behind the oak desk.

Parks needed information. He had known other Schaeffers. Pride and arrogance were both their strength and their Achilles' heels. "I have heard a number of things about Lebensborn," he began.

"Yes," Schaeffer said with interest. His glory days in the Third Reich were still close to his heart.

"Brilliant," Parks said. "Absolutely brilliant."

"Really?" Schaeffer said cagily. "What do you know?"

"Everything," Parks said, careful to keep the disgust out of his voice. "The maternity homes, the castles, the children—everything."

"Then you know it was a good thing," Schaeffer said. He lit a black cigar and the room filled with the smell of the rich smoke. "We did nothing illegal, nothing for you to hunt us down for, Mr. Parks."

"No one is hunting you down for whatever you did in Lebensborn," Parks said. "The CIU cares about Victory, not Lebensborn."

Schaeffer waved his hand is dismissal. "What does it matter? I did no harm. First I worked in Brandenburg in a maternity home, then I was transferred to Poland. The only thing important that happened to me at either place was meeting Martin Bormann."

Schaeffer looked out the window into the night, slipping back into time, into the days when he had held his head like a prince and walked with the men who ruled half of Europe.

He could still remember the day that *Reichsleiter* Martin Bormann came to the transit camp at Kalisz. It was a bright cold day in March. Snow was on the ground. Bormann had arrived with *Reichsführer* Himmler and Hans Frank, the Governor General.

While Himmler and Frank were inspecting the camp, Bormann took him aside.

"The Führer is very pleased with your work here in Poland," Bormann said, placing his stubby, hairy hand on Axmann's shoulder. "It is very important to the Reich."

Axmann, the eager new *Hauptsturmführer,* was too overwhelmed to reply.

Then the Party Chairman said: "I would very much like you to tell me about your work here. Just a note, every month or so, about what Lebensborn is doing. In as much detail as you care to give."

"Shall *Reichsführer* Himmler sign the report?" he asked.

Bormann's eyes turned cold. "No," he said. "The *Reichsführer* has not been asked."

They stood in the cold, face to face, looking each other in the eyes. Their breath blew white and hung between them in the air.

Bormann waited silently for a reply.

Axmann understood perfectly well. Himmler was not to know. Bormann wanted the reports to be made in secret. This was how he had mastered the bureaucracy of the Third Reich and attained supremacy over all others.

Axmann hesitated. Himmler was a buffoon, but he was also brutal and ruthless. On the other hand, the Party Chairman was the genius and strength behind the Reich. It was Bormann who had the ear and heart of Hitler. Axmann made his decision. He would cast his lot with the Party Chairman.

"How shall I send the reports?" he asked, sealing the pact.

Before the year was out, Axmann had been recommended for the Iron Cross.

"That was my salvation, Mr. Parks," Schaeffer said, "when I met the *Reichsleiter*. Had it not been for Bormann, I would have ended up a corpse. The Russians would have slit my throat without even the sham of a trial. You do not know. They were vicious by the end of the war, spurred on by that reckless Communist, Stalin."

Schaeffer spat out the word "Stalin" as if it had lain bitter in his mouth.

"No doubt," Parks said easily. "But, of course, his son was killed in the war."

Schaeffer shrugged, as if the death of Stalin's son on the Polish front had been of no consequence to him or to history.

"Perhaps," Schaeffer said. "At any rate, it would not have been any better with the Americans. I was not in the right position. Unlike Reinhard Gehlen, I had no information to sell. And, besides, the Americans hated the SS. If not for Bormann, I would be dead."

"Bormann helped you escape?" Parks asked.

"Yes."

"Then you owe him a great debt."

"It can never be repaid."

"He must have been a clever man to have acted so fast," Parks said.

"The time was not so brief, Mr. Parks. This was the brilliance of Martin Bormann. By the end of 1942, Bormann knew the war was over and he began to prepare."

Axmann's voice filled with disappointment, and he looked ahead intently, narrowing his eyes to slits, as if he could still see the soldiers parading by, twenty abreast, to the triumphant thunder of a Wagnerian march. There was a long silence in the room. Schaeffer drew himself up in the chair and squared his shoulders. "By the end of the summer of 1945, most of us were out of Europe."

"Why do you need the children?" Parks asked, hoping that Schaeffer's reveries would make him reveal more.

But Schaeffer sighed, and came back to the present. He knocked the ashes from his cigar and crushed it in the ashtray. "The children? That you do not need to know. Let us just say I have an agenda."

He rose and turned to look out the large cathedral windows. The snow had stopped.

Parks stared at Schaeffer's back. Maybe Bormann was the key. He decided to try a different tack.

"Bormann didn't save your neck," he said. "You were too small a fish. You're just an old man, dreaming out a life. Bormann would have let you rot before he had anything to do with you!"

Schaeffer turned sharply and glared at Parks. "Little fish!" he said, his voice rising. "You have heard of Strasbourg? I was the Secretary! Our children will—" He stopped abruptly.

"We have been too long, I think," he said. "It is time that I go."

Schaeffer walked to the door. He paused and turned to face Parks.

"Good-bye, Mr. Parks," he said. "If it is of any consequence, you were a damn good soldier."

As soon as Schaeffer left the room, Parks began to work at the rope binding his hands. He knew that Schaeffer had no more intention of living up to his side of the bargain than he did. Schaeffer couldn't afford to let him live. The rope burned into his flesh, but it loosened only slightly.

Robinson came down the hall, walking with reluctance. He had been sent to stand guard while Schaeffer looked after the final details of the trip. As he entered the small room, Parks steadied his hands.

The sole light in the room, coming from the desk lamp, seemed to have grown weaker, deepening the shadows in the corners. Without speaking, Robinson pulled the leather swivel chair up to the old oak desk, retrieved a pack of cards, and began a game of solitaire.

"Mind if I join you?" Parks asked.

Robinson did not move his eyes away from the cards. "I don't see how you can," he said uneasily.

"I guess not."

Robinson would not confront Parks. He did not want to look the prey in the eye. It was a fatal weakness, and Parks knew it.

He worked at the ropes. They refused to give. If only there were a nail . . . It was no use. The ropes would have to be cut. Robinson was his last chance.

"You like it here?" he asked.

"Love it."

"There's more out there."

Robinson continued his game of solitaire. "Not from where I sit," he said without looking up.

"Wait till you see a little more."

"I've already seen enough."

"Let me guess," Parks said. "Worked weekends and summers in the packing factory. Got a basketball scholarship. Kicked out for shaving points, which was probably a frame. Couldn't go home so you hit the road. Made it to the Big Apple and hit the dope. Then Spade found you, peddling your ass in the Village, and brought you here. Here is just as good as anyplace else, so why not?"

Robinson scuttled his game of solitaire and looked at Parks for the first time.

"You should never have come here," he said, without malice.

"I can't very well help that now, can I?"

"No."

Parks decided to gamble. "But you can help me."

"No way, mister." Robinson shook his head. There was fear in his pale blue eyes. "No way."

The gamble had failed.

"You must like the action around here," Parks said, with insult.

"Make you sick?" Robinson shot back.

"Nothing makes me sick," Parks said dryly.

"Oh yes. Some things can make you sick. Spade can make you sick," Robinson said bitterly. "You want me to tell you about it so you can get the dry heaves again?"

"You can skip the details."

"Yeah, you bet, mister."

"What do you do? Pretend he's Ellen Rider?"

Robinson turned crimson. "What do you mean?" he said sharply.

"You know what I mean. I know a lot about you and Ellen Rider."

"Yeah?"

Schaeffer called from the hall. Robinson jerked to attention and went to the door.

"I am finished with packing," Schaeffer informed him. "Carry my bags to the car."

"Yes sir."

"You're going with them?" Parks asked.

Robinson turned to Parks, and shrugged. "Why not?"

Parks looked at him incredulously. "Why *not?*"

"Mister, I've been fucked over by everybody I've ever known except one person. I just don't give a damn."

* * *

Schaeffer was traveling light, having shipped most of his clothing and papers under a false name the week before. Robinson took the luggage to the black Mercedes. When he returned, Schaeffer was in the parlor completing his plans. He turned to Robinson.

"You are to stay here with our Mr. Parks," he said. "Two of my colleagues will arrive shortly after we are gone and take him off your hands. You can join us in Austin tomorrow."

"No," Spade said forcefully. "He ain't gonna do it."

"I'll decide that!" Schaeffer said sharply.

Robinson shrugged. "Well?"

Schaeffer bristled. "Take care of the matter and join us later," he said to Robinson.

"He'll screw it up," Spade said.

"There is no chance of that," Schaeffer said with finality. Slowly, he put on his gloves, then turned to Spade.

"I need you with me, Spade," he said softly. "Do as I say this one last time and then you and Andrew will have all the time in the world together."

Spade grunted pathetically.

"Are you afraid he won't come?" Schaeffer asked, coaxing. "You will come, won't you, Andrew?"

"I'll be there tomorrow," Robinson assured him.

Robinson walked to the rear of the house and, from the window, watched the black Mercedes drive away. Schaeffer's plans were well arranged. Spade would drive them to Washington, D.C., and they would take off from Dulles Airport on the five twenty Braniff flight to Dallas. The Mercedes would be picked up at the airport, stripped, and crushed beyond recognition and sold for scrap metal. It would never be located.

Satisfied they were well on their way, Robinson got the Smith and Wesson revolver that Spade had given him from his bedroom dresser, and went up to the second floor study where Parks was still struggling to free his hands from Spade's efficient knots.

"They've gone," he said.

Parks studied him. Robinson's eyes and voice were flat. They gave no indication what he was thinking.

"Both of them?"

"Yes. Some of their colleagues are coming to pick you up. They'll be here in thirty minutes. Until then, let's just play deaf and dumb. It'll be easier."

"For you, maybe."

Robinson shrugged and sat down at the desk.

"Think they're coming just for me, buddy?" Parks asked, almost mocking Robinson.

"What do you mean?"

"You don't catch much, do you? When those so-called colleagues get here, it's going to be for both of us."

"Good try, mister," Robinson said.

"What's the matter? Doesn't Spade let you go to the movies? It's all in the training. A spy's intuition is more important than his gun. Take you and Ellen Rider, for instance."

Robinson folded his arms, and stared at Parks.

"She had your baby. It was your child she had at the Home," Parks said.

"No!" Robinson said angrily.

"Yes! Then you drowned her."

"No, goddamn it! She killed herself." Robinson shrugged in a gesture of finality. "The baby was born dead," he said.

"The baby was born alive," Parks said forcefully.

"No."

"Yes, damn it. It was born alive and you know it."

Robinson began to break. His shoulders jerked violently. Finally, he tensed his whole body and pulled himself upright.

"They were going to ship him off to some old German couple," Robinson said quietly. His voice seemed far away, as if he were trying to reach someone beyond the small room. "When I found out, I tried to steal him. Davis caught me. Then he—" Robinson's voice cracked. He steadied himself against the desk with his hands. "Davis suffocated him with a pillow. Spade held my hands behind my back . . . and made me watch. . . ."

Robinson was panting, the pain was so deep. He had stopped fighting the tears, now. They filled his eyes and ran down his cheeks, making them shine in the dim light.

"He was so beautiful," Robinson said.

"Did you tell Ellen?" Parks asked.

"She knew the baby was born alive. She heard him cry. I told her the baby was sold on the black market."

"She believed you?"

"Sometimes. But sometimes she seemed to know the truth."

"Is that why she killed herself?"

"No," said Robinson, clenching his fists until they turned blood red. "I did it, I killed her."

"I don't believe you."

"No, you're wrong. You see, Ellen thought she knew a way out. She promised to give Schaeffer a child of his own if he'd let us just go away. She said she was a certified Aryan and Schaeffer knew it. Schaeffer agreed, provided he could choose the father."

"You agreed to the plan?" Parks asked.

"At first," said Robinson. "I thought I could get Schaeffer to let me be the father."

"You failed?"

"Schaeffer wasn't interested. Then your agent came along—"

"You knew he was an agent?"

"I didn't, but Schaeffer did."

Confirmed. The Unit was leaking like a sieve.

"So Henry Stramm was procured, then killed," Parks said.

"You got it," Robinson said. "It was later that I got cold feet. I told Ellen I didn't think I could marry her after she had another man's baby."

"What'd she say to that?"

"She asked me to leave," Robinson said.

"Was she distraught?"

"She didn't seem to be. Just sad."

"Did you leave?"

"Yes. But by morning, I had changed my mind. I was going to find her . . . but I didn't have to. The ocean brought her to me."

A long silence overcame them. The dead, swollen eyes of Ellen Rider lay between them. Andrew Robinson had only found one thing to care for, to fight for, in his whole life, and he had lost. The wind came off the ocean in gusts

and hurled itself against the old house and filled the room
with whispers.

Parks broke the silence.

"What about Davis?"

"I did it," Robinson said, quietly, firmly. "With my own
hands."

"And Doc Webster?"

"That flophouse medic?" Robinson shrugged, noncom-
mittal. "Not me."

It was obvious he was not going to tell. "Why do they
want the children?" Parks asked.

"For their business, whatever it is."

Outside, a car came to a halt and the doors opened and
slammed, ringing in the cold night. Two thick, burly men
headed for the house.

"If you want to live, Robinson, you damn well better
untie me. I know how to use that piece of steel you've got
in your hand, and you don't."

Robinson hesitated. He reached into his pocket and
pulled out his knife. Heavy footsteps thumped across the
weathered boards of the front porch.

"I could cut your throat with this," Robinson said, looking down at the knife.

"You can cut your dick off, too, but why don't you do
something intelligent for a change?"

Robinson took a step forward and began to saw franti-
cally at the ropes binding Parks's hands. The front door
of the house eased open. The men were in the living room.

The ropes around his hands free, Parks could feel the
blood rush back into his wrist and fingers. Robinson freed
the rope around his chest and Parks stood up for the first
time in three hours. His groin still ached from the tip of
Spade's boot, and his thighs were cramped.

"Give me the gun," he demanded.

Robinson handed the gun over.

The men began to ascend the stairs. Their footsteps
echoed through the dead house.

"Help me over to the door," Parks whispered.

Robinson took him by the arm. His legs were still
cramped. Sweat ran down his face. He paused at the door
and waited for the two men to reach the landing. He

swung the door open and fired point-blank at the two men.
One was thrown against the balcony, crashing to the living
room floor, a bullet in his head, his neck broken. The
other man was thrown back down the stairs from the force
of the gunfire.

Then the house was quiet again. Parks turned and
pointed the gun at Robinson.

"Oh, I see," Robinson said.

"No, you probably don't. Where are my clothes?"
Parks's strength was returning.

"In the double drawer . . . on the left," Robinson said,
nodding toward the oak desk.

"I'm going to get them," Parks said firmly. "If you try
to jump me, I'll kill you."

Parks took his clothes out of the desk drawer. They had
been wadded and stuffed carelessly into the desk. His bill-
fold and papers were loose and scattered on the bottom
of the drawer. He put on his underwear and jeans and ski
jacket. His knit pullover shirt he folded neatly and laid
on top of the desk. If he pulled on his shirt, his eyes would
be blinded just long enough for Robinson to charge him.
Whatever mistakes he'd made in the last three hours, he
wasn't going to make more.

After cleaning out the drawer and stuffing his belongings
into his pockets, Parks said: "You want to know something
else about Ellen Rider?"

"No thanks," Robinson answered firmly.

"She was already pregnant when Stramm came along,"
Parks said. "Almost two months. She was carrying your
second child. She used Henry Stramm as a dupe, to fool
Schaeffer. Ellen Rider never intended to have any child
but yours."

Robinson doubled over in pain and gasped for air, like
a man suffocating from emphysema. "I should have killed
you when I had the chance," he said bitterly.

"Good god, Robinson. Don't you know what that means?
It means she loved you. Doesn't that mean anything to
you?"

Robinson looked up at Parks and began to laugh un-
controllably. His whole face changed. There was no more
pain, no more freshness. His eyes were large and distant.

"Now you want to know something?" Robinson said.

He hurled his dagger with the malice of an ungrateful child. "Spade left you a present."

"What?"

"Under the sink, in the kitchen," Robinson said. "It's a dress . . . from next door."

Parks stiffened. It was a mistake. His weight shifted to his heels and Robinson uncoiled and struck with force, landing a blow to Parks's tender groin, slamming him to the floor.

Before Parks could react, Robinson hurled himself toward the door and raced down the stairs. Parks scrambled to his feet, but it was no contest. The blow had been directed with wisdom. Parks was forced to follow at half the speed of the frenetic Robinson.

Robinson bolted out the door and headed toward the water. He stumbled on the beach on a piece of protruding driftwood and fell forward. Quickly, with the grace and power of an athlete, he pushed off with his hands, came to his feet, and continued on. The motion was so fluid, it looked like Nijinsky in *Scheherazade*.

Parks reached the doorway and watched, puzzled, as Robinson loped with even strides toward the water's edge, reached the water, but did not stop. Suddenly Parks realized what was happening.

"Robinson! Come back!" he shouted. "Don't do it!"

But Robinson could not hear him. He kept on running. He thrust himself forward, his shoulders back, his chest out, his steps long and high, like a runner stretching for the finish tape. He stumbled and fell forward into the water. He got to his feet and continued. It became too deep to run. He slowed and walked, evenly, purposefully, without hesitation.

Parks watched him from the doorway without any hope that he could stop the tall, lean, washed-out young man who had been so ruthlessly appropriated by ruthless men in a ruthless world.

"There's no use living when you're already dead," Parks said, without contempt or malice.

At that moment, Robinson turned toward the house, and Parks thought at first that he was turning back; but no, he was simply steadying himself for the next wave. The cold, bitter water covered him, and rushed to the beach without a break in rhythm. Robinson did not emerge again.

The wind whistled off the water and Parks, noticing it for the first time, closed the door. He turned on a brass lamp by the doorway and headed for the kitchen. He was certain Robinson had told him about the dress under the sink to throw him off guard. It had worked as intended. Still . . . He flicked on the light and walked to the sink. The cabinet doors were closed. His hands trembled when he touched the cold porcelain knobs. The dread of uncertainty lay heavy in his stomach. He took a deep breath and jerked the doors open.

Parks stared at the rough cabinet floor.

Good god, no.

A green dress with white polka dots, ripped and soaked with blood.

Parks picked up the dress and held it in his hands. Why on earth? Because she knew where they were going. Christ! Why did Hilda Schaeffer have to say good-bye . . . after twenty years. To get *him*. They had used Faith Henderson to get him to the house, then . . .

Parks threw the ravaged dress to the floor and clenched his fists. His heart was pounding with anger. *Spade would die,* he swore it.

He began a thorough, rapid search of the house. He retrieved his knit sweater from the library and put it on; he located the Smith and Wesson and stuffed it in his belt. The rest of the house yielded nothing.

Outside, light snow began to fall again. The small flakes, driven by the wind, stung his face. Parks climbed the steps to Miss Henderson's veranda. The door was unlocked. He walked through the house carefully, like a cat on a ledge.

Halfway up the stairs, he found her. She had run, fighting for life, but she had been too slow. Spade had chased her down and caught her on the stairs.

Her eyes looked up at him. She looked like a sparrow that had fallen from a tree. Above her head, at the top of the stairs, was a painting of the Atlantic at midnight, tossed by a bad wind.

Parks picked up the frail body that had once held the great heart of Faith Henderson, carried her the rest of the way up the stairs, and laid her on her bed.

He would not leave her like this. No, he would dress her for the long night. He would leave her in peace.

He searched Faith Henderson's dresser and closet for a nightgown. There weren't any. Then it came to him.

Faith Henderson slept in the nude and only one man had ever known.

Parks pulled the covers up over her.

"They say there is another land where . . ."

He could not finish. He closed the bedroom door behind him and left as quietly as he had come.

"Mary, wake up!" Parks said, shaking her.

She woke suddenly, with a jerk. Terror flashed in her eyes.

"You scared me," she said, her voice trembling.

"I'm sorry. Now get dressed. Get your things together. I'm taking you home."

He was still reeling from the sight of Faith Henderson. The image of a dead sparrow hung in his mind. He threw his clothes and toiletries into a suitcase, and looked around the room to see if there was anything else he wanted to take. Then he saw it. The painting. Carefully, he carried it to the car.

As they pulled up in front of the dark Rider bay house, they saw the door. It was open.

"Did you—" Parks started.

"No," Mary cut in. "I locked it."

They stepped inside and turned on the lights. Mary gasped. Chairs were overturned, drawers emptied.

"You're coming with me to New York," Parks said tensely.

Mary rubbed the back of her neck.

"Where's the phone?" he asked.

"In the study."

Parks dialed the number of the brownstone in Brooklyn Heights. The telephone rang ten times before Charles Winston shook off his sleep and answered it.

"Yes?" Winston answered. It was late. He was apprehensive.

"This is Parks." It was past the time for protocol. "I'm coming in. Mary is with me. I need a reservation at the

Plaza. I'm going to put Mary in there. Make the reservation for both of us and get twenty-four-hour guard
service."

"I'll make the arrangements myself, in the name of
Mr. and Mrs. Herbert Jones." Winston was awake and
alert. "The guards will go by the name of Xavier Hum-
phrey Smith. They will change from time to time, but they
will always introduce themselves by that name, whether
male or female. Have you got that?"

"Yes."

"How long will you need the room?"

Parks reflected. "I don't know. Make it for two weeks."
He took a deep breath. "We have to meet. How about
five thirty at the Avalon Theater at Forty-fourth and
Broadway? Meet me in the front row. Admission is five
dollars."

The Director sighed.

"Sorry, Director. All the museums are closed."

"Are you sure the Avalon isn't?"

"Never closes. Can you get hold of Fleming?"

"Yes."

"Bring him."

Mary was waiting for Parks by the door, staring in disbelief at the ransacked room.

"Come on, let's go," he said. "And keep your eyes
open for cops. We're going to fly low."

It was five o'clock exactly when Parks pulled up to the
front of the green awning of the gilded Plaza Hotel. The
efficient Plaza staff had already prepared the Huntington
Suite for Mr. and Mrs. Herbert Jones.

Parks gave Mary her instructions. She was not to answer
the door for anyone other than the guard. She was not to
venture farther than two blocks from the hotel, and was
to eat all her meals downstairs in the Oak Room. Maid
and laundry service for the room had been suspended.

"I may be back this afternoon, this evening . . . I don't
know. Stay here until I get in touch with you, one way or
the other, and do everything I told you . . . even if it's for
a week. I'll get word to you somehow."

As Parks was about to leave, Mary started to cry.

"I'm afraid. I don't want to be here. . . ." She was unable to finish.

Parks took her in his arms. "You have to. It's too dangerous for you in Seaside right now."

"Please . . . don't go."

"I have to."

"No," she said. "Please . . . forget about Seaside."

"I can't, Mary," Parks said. "I can't explain now, but there's a lot more at stake than you know."

He kissed her good-bye.

Times Square is still asleep at five thirty in the morning. The prostitutes have retired from the streets and the pimps have hung up their leather boots for the night. The shopping bag ladies are curled up in the alleys and the winos have found safe harbor in the doorways.

At the Avalon Theater the clock keeps running, even though for the three old men who were still there at five thirty, time had already run out. Parks took a seat in the front row of the theater and was joined a few minutes later by Winston and Fleming.

Naked bodies flickered on the screen.

"What's this little epic called?" Fleming asked, settling his long frame into the seat.

Wild Pussy, Parks informed him.

"I see," Fleming said. "Do you think they sell popcorn?"

"Good grief," Winston said, looking up at the contorted copulation on the screen. "Let's get down to business."

"All right," Parks said. "Let me tell you about it. Christian Schaeffer is the Executive Secretary of Victory. He is also Walter Axmann, an old SS man."

Parks related the story of his capture.

"They've gone to Texas," he said in conclusion.

"Say—" Fleming started.

"I'm way ahead of you," Parks said. "The lakefront property. Where is it?"

"Austin. 331 Rocky Valley Road."

"How do you feel now, John?" the Director asked.

"I feel like a man who just had his balls kicked in with a steel boot. Other than that, just great."

"Do you need to see a doctor?"

"No, I'll be all right. Just a little bruised and sore. It quit hurting so much after I found the dress."

"Those bastards!" Fleming said, almost in a rage. "That sawed-off little Nazi pimp! Let's go get him and string him up."

On the silver screen, two couples entered into group sex, with all the energy and ability of a broken toy Slinky.

"I want the two of you to join forces," Winston said. "Go to Austin and get Schaeffer."

"First," Parks said, "I want to talk to Dr. Silverman. I want to know a little more about what we're chasing. Then we can go to Austin. Schaeffer will still be there."

"Then you had better call him early," the Director said. "By nine he'll be at the synagogue. He lives in Park Slope."

"It's almost six thirty," Parks said. "I'll call him at seven. What will the two of you do? Go eat or stay for the next feature?"

"What is it?" Fleming asked seriously.

"The marquee says *Rear Entry*."

"I'll buy breakfast," Winston said, "but I am not going to sit here another minute and watch this . . ."

The camera moved in for a closeup of one of the grubby studs erupting in a monumental climax.

"Let's get out of here!" the Director demanded.

Parks leaned against the door of the telephone booth. "I need to talk to you, Dr. Silverman." He did not try to hide the urgency in his voice. "Does the name Strasbourg mean anything to you?"

"The Strasbourg Conference," Dr. Silverman said, amazed. "I know it well."

"Walter Axmann was the Secretary," Parks said.

"Mr. Parks, I told you at our last meeting that I had read many things not meant to be seen by eyes such as mine. I think it is time I tell you about some of them. If you can come right over, I will cancel my plans for the morning and devote myself to you. My wife will make us breakfast."

The Silvermans lived in a renovated 1880's terrace house on Garfield Place, a tree-lined street in the Park Slope section of central Brooklyn.

Leah Silverman came to the tall foyer doors of mahogany and etched glass. She was a small, round woman with silver hair and the tender eyes of the first Leah from whose lineage came half the House of Israel. She led Parks up the stairs to the library on the second floor, then closed the double doors softly behind her.

Max Silverman was sitting at his desk by the window overlooking the garden. He was dressed comfortably in old gray pleated slacks and a blue wool cardigan sweater. He rose and greeted Parks warmly, then directed him to the overstuffed Victorian chairs in front of the fireplace.

One wall of the library was lined from floor to ceiling with books. There was a bookcase on either side of the fireplace, and another by Dr. Silverman's large walnut campaign desk. A low fire burned in the grate and filled the room with a soft warmth.

"So," Dr. Silverman said, "you found Axmann, and he turned out to be the Secretary of the Strasbourg."

"That's what he said."

The old scholar smiled. "For almost thirty years we have been trying to identify the man who recorded the minutes of that meeting. The man who wrote the memorandum of the final agenda of the Third Reich, and you have found him."

"What was the Strasbourg meeting?"

"It was a top-secret meeting of Germany's leading industrialists, the men who bankrolled Hitler to power. They were the first to fall in with Hitler—and the first to desert the sinking ship.

"From this meeting came the Nazis' postwar plans. Everything flows from this one meeting held at the Hotel Maison Rouge in Strasbourg in 1944. It was there that Odessa was born, that the seeds of the Brotherhood were sown."

"How did you find out about the meeting?" Parks asked.

"Quite by accident," Silverman said. "When Simon Wiesenthal was working with the OSS, an American Army officer brought him a thick, dark-blue file found at the SS internment camp near Bad Ischl. The file gave the details of the Strasbourg Conference, among other things."

Dr. Silverman paused. His old brown eyes glowed in the light of the fire. "Can you tell me what Axmann is doing in America?"

"Dr. Silverman . . ." Parks began, "Otto Werner and I . . . we work on very confidential matters."

"I understand," Dr. Silverman said, disappointed.

"But I will share what I have learned with you," Parks said. "I do not care if you repeat what I am about to tell you. I only ask that you never, in any way, identify the source."

"You have my word."

Parks told Dr. Silverman about Victory, the sperm bank, the maternity home, the theft of the children, the old woman in Greenpoint. He did not tell him about Henry Stramm or the CIU. When he had finished, Silverman sat back and reflected. He was slowly, methodically integrating the new information with the old.

"I don't know what all this means, but surely they don't believe in a Fourth Reich," Parks said.

Silverman shook his head. "You underestimate them, Mr. Parks. They may not believe in a Fourth Reich anymore, with swastikas and *Blitzkrieg,* but they still believe in *Der Tag,* the day they will return to power. The Nazis laid too many elaborate postwar plans to give up so easily. Many of these have been accomplished. By nineteen fifty they had already begun to work their way back into government in Bonn. Reinhard Gehlen, the Chief of Intelligence for the Nazis' German Foreign Armies East, used knowledge of Russian intelligence to go straight from Hitler's side to the payroll of the United States. He was appointed head of the West German Secret Service, a position he used in order to put hundreds of former SS and Gestapo members back to work in key positions. Little by little the men who ran and served in the notorious Reich Central Security Office have returned to duty in the German Army. They have been appointed to high positions in NATO, the courts, and government agencies. Others have come up through the ranks in the police and German industry.

"They have laid a solid foundation, Mr. Parks, but time and fortune have been their enemies. Still, old dreams die hard. They have probably not abandoned their dream, just changed it."

Parks nodded. "You may be right."

"When you find out Mr. Axmann's agenda, you will

know what *Der Tag* has finally come to mean," Silverman said. "Where is he now? Do you know?"

"On the run," Parks said, feeling he was not at complete liberty yet to reveal everything to the doctor. "But I hope to catch up with him."

"Then be very, very careful," Silverman said gravely. "He cannot afford to let you live."

Dr. Silverman rose and poked the logs in the fireplace to rekindle the fire. "As sure as I stand here, if I add another piece of wood, Leah will announce breakfast."

Parks laughed. "One thing confuses me," he said. "Axmann and his wife have lived in the United States since 1953 under the names Christian and Hilda Schaeffer. When a check was run, it showed the Schaeffers to be native-born Americans from a little farming community in Wisconsin."

"Very simple, Mr. Parks. The Axmanns must have exchanged places with them. Odessa probably offered them a great deal of money to sell their farm and live abroad under an assumed name. Today the real Schaeffers are probably buried under a coat of lime in a paupers' cemetery in Argentina."

Leah Silverman poked her head through the door. "Breakfast is ready," she said.

"We had better stop now," Silverman said and grunted. "She has cooked a twelve-course breakfast and if it gets cold, you won't have to worry about Axmann and his brothers."

The tiny Goliath knew how to pick his battles. The Nazis, yes. Leah Silverman, no.

"After breakfast," Silverman said, as they descended the stairs, "I will tell you the story of Strasbourg."

After a hearty breakfast, the two men returned to the library and, for the next hour, Max Silverman told Parks the history of the Strasbourg Conference and its legacy.

By 1942, while Adolf Eichmann was still throwing the resources of a bleeding Germany behind the Final Solution, *Reichsleiter* Martin Bormann was reading the handwriting on the wall. The German drive to conquer the East had ground to a halt. Two bitter Russian winters and endless Red Army columns had sent the *Wehrmacht* and the *Waffen SS* reeling. The Americans had entered the war.

But if 1942 was bad for the Nazis, 1943 was catastrophic. It started with the surrender of the German Army's eastern divisions at Stalingrad and went downhill after that.

The German industrialists of the AHSDI, the Adolf Hitler Fund of German Industry, who had put at Hitler's disposal in 1933 an untold fortune to build the Third Reich into a great war machine, were, by 1943, betting their money on Hitler's defeat. Men like Emil Kirdorf, the coal baron; Kurt von Schroeder, the Cologne banker; Fritz Thyssen, the steel magnate; Georg von Schnitzler of I.G. Farben, were ready to seek their profits elsewhere.

Martin Bormann began to meet secretly with the German industrialists to make plans for the postwar survival of the National Socialists. Bormann spoke to them with candor. The war, but not the cause, was lost. If the lessons of history held true, they could expect little sympathy and no justice from the victors. Some of them would go to jail. Some would escape, but must be prepared for a life of exile. Bormann proposed the liquidation of Nazi assets and their distribution to Zurich, Madrid, Lisbon, Buenos Aires, and other safe harbors. He also proposed the establishment of the Alpine Fortress in Bavaria, an area convenient to multiple escape routes through Italy and Switzerland.

The meetings held during the fall and winter of 1943 between Bormann and the Ruhr and Rhine barons climaxed in a top-secret conference held at the Hotel Maison Rouge in Strasbourg, France, on August 10, 1944.

Ostensibly, the meeting was called to discuss the dispatch of blueprints of new weapons and industrial secrets to sympathetic countries abroad. Representatives from Rochling, Siemens, I.G. Farben, the Goering Werke in Linz, and the oil and pharmaceutical industries were in attendance, as well as Dr. Boss of Albert Speer's Armaments Ministry, Willy Messerschmidt, the engineering genius who designed the great aircraft Me-109, top officials of the War Ministry, and, of course, the notorious Krupp. Bormann did not come to the meeting, but sent his emissary, Walter Axmann, to act as Secretary.

The men at the meeting knew the war was lost. The Eastern Front had exhausted Germany. The Western Allies

were approaching Paris. Willy Messerschmidt stated flatly
that anyone who believed that magic rockets would come
to the aid of Germany was living a dream.

It was agreed by the Conference that long-range prepara-
tions would have to be made to secure Nazi assets and to
salvage Germany's future. Plans were laid to fund a "technical network" that would ensure the prosperity of those
who went into exile, or spent time in Spandau Prison, or
were forced underground; and to seed the trust fund for
the Fourth Reich.

Corporations were set up abroad, all in secret and unknown to most leaders of the Reich except Martin Bormann—112 corporations in Spain; 214 in Switzerland; 98
in Argentina; the others in Turkey, Portugal, the Middle
East, and South America. At least 750, and possibly as
many as one thousand companies, were set up in all, and
funded with millions in German capital and assets, under
the guise of legitimate business deals. Secret bank accounts
were established in neutral and nonbelligerent countries.
Gold coins, precious stones, counterfeit dollars, and Bank
of England notes, as well as secret Nazi documents and
blueprints, were loaded into iron trunks and buried in the
Alpine Fortress in the Aussee region in Austria or dumped
into the Chiemsee, the Töplitzsee, and other lakes for safekeeping.

Operation Bernhard was instituted in the death camps
whereby perfect counterfeits of American dollars and
British pound notes were produced on a massive scale.
Discarded Allied weapons and transportation equipment
were sold through import-export agencies in Spain and the
Middle East. More than 100 million dollars in German
securities, issued in the 1930's and still valid and convertible thirty years later, were moved out of the country.
Art treasures and precious stones were hoarded in the Alpine Fortress. Gold fillings were extracted from the dead
and dying at Dachau and Auschwitz and melted into gold
bars.

At the war's end, a nest egg equal to more than 800
million American dollars had been moved out of Germany. It was destined to inflate into an incomparable fortune.

The "technical network" envisioned by the conferees was

the beginning of *Organisazion der SS-Angehörigen*, the notorious Odessa. The creation of Odessa was paramount to the success of the postwar maneuvers. It was Odessa that would set up the escape mechanisms, and collect and hold the money necessary to protect the fleeing Nazis at the end of the war and thereafter until they were no longer in peril. Hand in hand with Odessa was *Die Deutsch Gemeinschaft*, the Brotherhood, the black knights of the Odessa round table who kept no lists and never referred to one another by name, but whose one great purpose was to keep the spirit of Nazism alive.

In order to move Nazi assets and key Nazi leaders out of Germany, Odessa established the underground network known as *"Die Spinne"*—the Spider. It was a triumph of deception. Distribution routes were interrupted every fifty miles by way stations, generally inconspicuous inns, deserted hunting lodges, farm houses in the woods. The small staff at each way station knew only about the next station up or down the line. Only SS Colonel Franz Röstel and Bormann and their closest aides knew the complete layout of the great web of *Die Spinne*. Eventually, other escape organizations grew up under both Odessa and *Die Spinne*.

Formalizing and administering the various escape organizations presented no problem to Bormann; he already knew where he was going and how, and whom to contact when he got there. Long before the Thousand-Year Reich came to its violent end, Martin Bormann's genius for organizational detail had given him absolute control over the ways and means that loyal Nazi deputies and the great wealth of Odessa would leave Germany. On May 1, 1945, under cover of night, Martin Bormann left the ashes of the dead Führer's bunker in Berlin, taking with him the plans, the organization, and the money necessary to begin again once the storm had settled.

The early days of many of the exiled Nazis were not exactly a chronicle of success and comfort. Some were exposed and extradited from their safe havens. It was difficult for others to adjust. Odessa established well-guarded colonies for particularly vulnerable Nazis like Klaus Barbie, the Hangman of Lyons, Josef Mengele, and Hans Wagner, in the primitive state of Bolivia high in the Andes, in

Paraguay under Alfredo Stroessner, and in Argentina with the help of Juan and Eva Perón. It set up other Nazis, less vulnerable and more adventuresome, in business, opening restaurants, shops, export-import companies, and the like in Spain, the Middle East, and Germany. At last the displaced Nazis began to prosper, and Martin Bormann, perhaps the most tenacious plodder the world has ever known, began to draw his new plans for the postwar resurgence of the National Socialists.

"So, you see," Dr. Silverman said, drawing to a close, "we now know where they went, how they went, and what they took. Unfortunately, we do not know where the Nazi fortune is kept or what they plan to do with it. The next part of the puzzle you will bring to me."

"I'd be glad to," Parks said, stretching. The warm room was making him sleepy. "But I don't understand how I can."

"By finding Axmann," Silverman said. "The Secretary of the meeting, our Mr. Axmann, was instructed to prepare, with the help of Bormann, a statement of the sense of the body, and a memorandum of agreement that they would all sign, which outlined their goals and actions for the future.

"Unfortunately, the last page of the official minutes is missing and so is the memorandum. That is why we never knew the name of the Secretary of the meeting. If he signed the last page, it is gone now. Personally I think he failed to identify himself for other reasons. If the Gestapo had found out about the meeting, they would have all hanged. We do not know if the memorandum was ever written, but I think it was. That was the way Bormann was.

"When you find out why the Brotherhood wants the children, you will know what was in the Strasbourg memorandum. You will know the final agenda of the black knights of the Third Reich.

"You may also be able to discover the key to the Odessa treasury. The list of the people authorized to dispose of these funds is probably the most important unsolved secret of the Third Reich. Definitely, it is the best kept. There are said to be six such lists: two in the hands of certain Swiss banks, two buried at the bottom of the Töplitzsee, and two in the hands of the founders of Odessa.

"In all probability our Mr. Axmann is not important enough to have the list, but he probably knows who does. Can you imagine what it would mean if we could get that list?"

"Yes, I think I can," Parks said. *"Der Tag* would pass into history as the dream of washed-out old men."

"Exactly," Silverman said, excited. "If we find out who has control over the Odessa money, we will find the money. Without their billions, the nightmare would be over. It wouldn't matter what their agenda was, they couldn't accomplish it. They'd be too busy running for cover."

"Then let's hope I find Axmann," Parks said, rising. "I'm going to start looking tomorrow."

Parks returned to Mary at the Plaza. She ran to him, threw her arms around him, and started to cry. He held her close. He knew then that he loved her, no matter what happened later. He knew her secrets and his heart still longed for her.

That night, in bed, he told her that he loved her. She didn't answer, and he knew at last that she was slipping away from him like a cloud in a hot sun. Then he thought of the driftwood sitting in the corner of the library in the Rider bay house. It had been tossed from shore to shore, but it had survived. It had been cut, but its sap never ran. It had been smashed against the rocks and never bruised. Its strength lay in the fact that it was dead.

CHAPTER 14

Sunday, December 15, 1974

It was still dark Sunday morning when John Parks hailed a taxi to Kennedy Airport to catch American Flight 120 to Dallas. After announcing his destination, Parks fell asleep in the taxi and awoke as the bright-red mosaic spread across the American Airlines terminal came into view.

"You're five minutes late," Fleming announced when Parks took his seat in the coffee shop of the terminal. The broad-shouldered Texan was already starting on his second cup of coffee.

"Fire me," Parks said, and ordered coffee. He had barely taken a sip when a muffled female voice announced the boarding of Flight 120.

"Well," Fleming said, putting out his cigarette, "let's go do it."

The two men paid their checks, walked leisurely to the departure lounge, checked in, and took their seats in the first-class compartment.

Parks looked down at the airline employees maneuvering quickly and deftly under the wings of the plane. "Does it ever bother you," he asked, "when you realize just before takeoff that a bunch of clowns are still running around under the wing?"

Fleming shrugged. "Nothing bothers me unless I see the captain come on board wearing a beanie."

After the normal delay at Kennedy, the big plane moved down the runway, lifted itself gently up, and threw itself toward Texas.

As the plane began its slow descent 500 miles away from Dallas, Parks took a fresh cigarette from his pack, lit it, and lost himself in thought. Fleming, who had been sleeping lightly, struggled awake.

"Pete?" Parks asked.

Fleming yawned. "It sounds like I'm going to get interrogated and I'm not even awake."

"It's an old Chinese trick."

"I know. Spit it out."

"You know, I don't even know what you do for a living."

"I'm a legal beagle," Fleming said. "I have my own firm in Fort Worth. That's how I can get away and fight for God and country. How about you?"

"I own my own business . . . a brokerage house, more or less."

"Great. When this thing is over, I'll get some stock tips."

"You can have all the tips you want. No guarantees, of course." Parks paused. "Are you married?"

"Yes."

"Any children?"

"Two. A boy and a girl."

"And you stay in this game?"

Fleming seemed surprised. "Well, I'm here, aren't I?"

"Does your wife know about . . . all this?"

"Maggie? She knows enough. She keeps it from the kids. Maybe even from herself. Any special reason you ask?"

"Just interested. That's all."

"Thinking of becoming a family man?"

"Top secret."

"Have it your own way. I'm going back to sleep."

Fleming settled his lanky frame down into the oversize first-class seat. His feet were under the seat in front of him, and his upper body was twisted to fit into the available space.

Just as Fleming fell asleep, the seat-belt sign came on and the stewardess announced the plane's descent into Dallas.

"This is a plot!" Fleming said, sitting up straight and adjusting his seat belt. "A man needs his sleep!"

"Look alive," Parks said. "We've only got twenty minutes to make our connecting flight to Austin."

The two men disembarked from the plane in the pit of the color-drenched Dallas-Fort Worth Airport. The internal organization is so extended and confusing many Dallasites claim John Connally ordered it over the telephone during a fit. Nevertheless, they made their Texas International flight with five minutes to spare, and forty-five minutes later were in Austin, Texas.

The wind whipped their hair as they left the Texas International twin-engine jet and crossed the open asphalt to the terminal. The day was bright and clear.

As they left the airport, the city of 300,000 spread out before them on small hills. To their left was the state capitol, a massive domed building of granite. To their right was a tall, slender limestone needle, the University of Texas administration building and library, which dominated the distant skyline. On fall weekends the soaring tower was lighted orange to signify a football victory.

"See that building on your right?" asked Fleming. "Students here call it 'the tower.' One day back in nineteen sixty-six a guy named Whitman went up to the observation deck with a suitcase full of rifles and mowed down the students as they walked out of class."

They drove up Manor Road.

"Pull in at that building on your left," instructed Fleming.

"Why?"

"It's got great food."

"Good food at a place called Fritz's?"

"Best fried chicken in Texas."

Fritz's had a tavern motif with deer heads mounted on the walls and signs that flashed advertisements for Pearl and Lone Star beer. They ordered Southern fried chicken, mashed potatoes and gravy, and hot rolls.

"Yankees can't fry chicken," Fleming commented.

"They do it in wine."

"Do you think the waitress will know where Rocky Valley Road is?"

"Probably. Do you want to ask her?"

"I think it's safe."

When the waitress returned with the check, Fleming asked: "Is Rocky Valley Road anywhere around here?"

"Lord no," she replied. "It's on the other side of town. Up by Lake Austin."

"Now, just where is that little road?" Fleming asked solicitously.

"Well, if y'all will just follow this road to Lamar, turn left, then go up to Enfield to the low-water bridge and past the dam, you'll run into it."

"I think we can manage that. We thank you very much." They paid the check and left a generous tip.

Fleming got into the car, letting Parks drive, and lit a cigarette. "Cute little thing, wasn't she?" he said.

"I thought you were married," Parks said wryly. "Your bachelor side is showing."

"I should have asked her to come along," Fleming said, with mock regret.

"What would you have done with me?" Parks asked.

CIU investigators always shared the same room when on the road. Unit regulations.

"I'd have shared, of course," said Fleming.

"What a pal. Where are we going anyway?"

"Villa Capri," said Fleming.

The Villa Capri was a sprawling motor hotel at the edge of the Texas University campus. Its orange-and-white interior was becoming faded and a little worn, but its rooms were large and comfortable.

Parks and Fleming carried their own luggage to the room and left it there, still packed. It was time to take a look at Schaeffer's Texas redoubt while it was still daylight.

The two men followed their directions to Rocky Valley Road. Enfield Road was a wide, winding street lined with trees still in the fire of fall. Winter comes late and softly to Austin.

At last they reached the low-water bridge, and curved around the edge of a tall rock and onto Rocky Valley Road. The sides of the road were covered with thick undergrowth, almost hiding the narrow, rocky driveways that led deep into the bramble to large homes facing the smooth, blue waters of Lake Austin. Parks eyed the mailboxes mounted on cedar posts along the road. When he spotted the one marked 331, he slowed down and pointed it out to Fleming.

"I'm glad the rattlesnakes have gone to sleep for the winter," Fleming said. "I'd hate to work my way through that undergrowth when they've got their fangs out."

"Afraid of snakes?"

"Only when they don't crawl on the ground."

"In that case, you've got a couple just down that path you'll be meeting soon."

"Turn around and drive back by slowly. We've got to remember it at night," Fleming said.

"I won't forget."

It was a still, cloudless night. The sky was cluttered with stars, covering the Lake Austin region with a soft glow. Only the night creatures searching for food in the dry undergrowth disturbed the serenity.

They came up to 331 Rocky Valley Road.

"Go on up the road about half a block," Fleming instructed Parks. "We'll circle back from behind."

They parked the car and slipped behind a row of spreading water oaks lined up like sentinels along the road. Dressed in dark clothes and tennis shoes blackened with shoe polish, they became indistinguishable from the night. They worked back toward Schaeffer's lake house, negotiating the bramble and undergrowth like Sioux.

Parks drew his gun as the lights from the lake house became visible.

"Got your gun?" he whispered to Fleming.

"Yeah. And my knife."

Christian Schaeffer's new home was a two-story solar palace of glass, stone, and redwood, with a roof that sloped at a forty-five-degree angle toward the lake below. It was set well back from the road.

A new beige Lincoln Continental was parked in the driveway with its hood up.

Parks nodded toward the car. "That's Spade over by the car."

Spade was bent over the engine, cursing the car for all it was worth.

Fleming drew his knife. "I'll put Spade out for the evening. You get the house."

"Spade is my baby," Parks said.

"No dice. You want him too bad. You might mess it up."

Parks knew Fleming was right. "All right, but cover me quickly."

Parks started to circle the house. Hilda Schaeffer was in the kitchen, hovering near the wall oven. He dropped to the ground, crawled slowly to the kitchen door, and waited.

Out of Parks's sight, Fleming slipped up on Spade with the stealth and silence of a water moccasin. He drew his knife and plunged it deep between the shoulder blades. Spade jerked and gasped. The life went out of him. Fleming pulled out the knife, then slit the dead gargoyle's throat. He slit it again and again, until it was nothing but blood and shredded meat. Then, he carefully washed the blood from his hands under a faucet at the side of the house.

Parks opened the kitchen door slowly, his gun carefully aimed. Hilda Schaeffer's back was to him.

"No bread yet, Spade," she said in reprimand. "Soon enough, though."

"Sorry, not Spade," Parks said, and ran his eyes around the room. He backed into a corner so he could cover all the windows and doors to the kitchen.

Hilda Schaeffer turned around, slowly

"Just keep quiet," Parks instructed her.

She jerked, recognizing him immediately, then, stiffening, held her breath to check the terror. Her feet felt large and clumsy, and she could not have run if she had wanted to.

"Who else is in the house?"

"Spade . . . and me. That is all."

"Schaeffer?"

"Christian is gone. Just Spade and me."

Fleming came through the door in a crouch, his gun drawn.

"Check the rest of the house," Parks said, tightly. "She says it's just her and Spade." Fleming left for a tour of the house, his gun held tightly in his right hand, his shoulders tensed.

Hilda Schaeffer wiped a strand of gray hair from her forehead. Defeat showed in her eyes. Not the defeat of capture, but the defeat of life itself. Parks remembered the first time he had seen her, standing at the water's edge, staring beyond the horizon. She had been looking to her native land. Hilda Schaeffer, moved from country to country by men and beliefs she probably never understood, wanted nothing more than a home with a good kitchen, and she must have believed now that she would never have it.

"What do you want?" she finally asked.

"We want to talk. That's all. Then we'll leave," Parks said. "No harm will come to you."

"I will put on the coffee," she said, and rubbed her hands nervously against her skirt.

Fleming reentered the kitchen, his shoulders relaxed. "We're alone," he said.

"Good, then put the gun away. Mrs. Schaeffer is making coffee." Fleming replaced the gun in the shoulder holster.

Hilda Schaeffer turned from the white enamel stove where she had set the coffee to drip and smiled wearily. "The coffee will be ready in a minute," she said. "Take a chair at the table."

She was thankful they had found her in the kitchen, where she would always retain some authority. To a woman such as Hilda Schaeffer, even the ravages of death could not strip her of all her stern dignity if she met the shadowy horseman in her kitchen, among the copper pots and stainless steel and herbs and recipes.

Satisfied the coffee was made to perfection, she served it and joined the men at the table. The lines of her square matronly face had eased slightly.

"Where is Mr. Schaeffer?" Parks asked.

"Mexico," she answered simply.

"You have an address?" asked Fleming.

"No. Christian and I . . . I will not be able to see him again."

Her jaw tightened and for a moment it seemed that her face might break. She took a long drink of the steaming hot coffee. It burned her tongue and the pain eased the emotions rising in her.

"Has he left you?" Parks asked with sympathy.

"He has gone on to other things," she said, and looked down at her cup.

Suddenly Parks became painfully aware of the barrenness of her body. Her skin was dry and hard, as if it had suffered a long drought. Her hands were blunt and large at the knuckles, and lacked the tenderness of those that had rocked a cradle. Then Parks understood the defeat he had seen in the round curve of her shoulders that first day he saw her on the beach. The defeat which even now lay heavy in her eyes.

The muscles in his stomach began to cramp. The path to the information he needed was open to him, but it was brutal. He hesitated, but in the end knew he had no choice.

"He left you without a child to raise," Parks said finally.

She looked away.

"They have taken hundreds of children from the Home," Parks said. "Why not one for Hilda Schaeffer?"

"I was to have one, someday," she said, as if to redeem herself.

"But now you won't." He paused. His mouth went dry. He did not want to go on. "That's no way to live," he finally said. "No way to treat someone who has served so well. It's not fair."

Hilda Schaeffer tensed, then let the years of failure flood her body. Her eyes filled with tears. "No," she said. "It was not fair."

He had broken her. Now she would tell him what she knew.

"Who told you to come to America? Do you know?"

"No, I—"

"Was it the Brotherhood?" Parks asked.

Her eyes grew wide, as if a name had been spoken out loud which had been commanded always to silence.

"I do not know about such things," she said. There was a tremor in her voice.

"Of course you do," Parks said firmly.

"They were men, that is all I know. With money, with dreams, without names."

"Was Schaeffer one of them?" Parks asked.

Hilda Schaeffer was frightened. She had virtually admitted the existence of the Brotherhood. She twisted in her seat and beads of sweat broke out across her brow. She knew enough to fear the long arm of the Werewolf, the hangman of Odessa, who executed all who betrayed the secrets.

"I am in the kitchen," she finally said. "I am not political."

"You have nothing to fear," Parks said. "Not here. Not now. No one will ever know."

"You do not understand," she pleaded. "They have ears everywhere. They—"

"In that case, we will all be dead within a week," Parks said.

"Yes, we may," she said.

"They can't hurt you now," Parks said softly. "They can't hurt you any more than they already have. But you can help us. You can help the children."

She pulled herself upright and squared her shoulders. "Christian was one of them." Still she would not say the name. "They do not think I know. But I hear them. I understand everything."

"Yes," Parks said, coaxing her. "It is always wrong to underestimate the one who serves the coffee. More than just the walls have ears."

She smiled, flattered.

"Why did the Brotherhood start Victory in America?" Parks asked.

"It was the fifties, you know."

"The Cold War," Fleming added.

"Yes," Hilda agreed. "They thought that if they could make you fear the Communists enough, it would make you forgive them." She paused. "Everything seemed possible then."

"Do they still hope for a Fourth Reich?" Parks asked.

"Hope? No, not even hope. That dream died when they finally knew that Americans could have more than one enemy. The people, they didn't like the Russians, but they didn't like the Nazis either."

"Then why did they start cultivating children and shipping them to South America?" Parks asked.

She poured herself another coffee. "That started when

they still believed," she said. "But you see, time was not their friend. They were growing old, and a new Germany was not possible."

No, thought Parks, time and death never wait—not even for the knights of the Third Reich.

"So," Hilda Schaeffer continued, "they set up the Lebensborn in America to give them children to carry on. They made arrangements to save themselves for many years. You know—" Hilda Schaeffer hesitated, embarrassed. "To freeze—"

"I know about it," Parks said, saving her further embarrassment. Now he knew the purpose of the Manhattan clinic. It's vaults were filled with frozen Nazi sperm cells.

"Women were sometimes paid to have children," Hilda Schaeffer said. "You know, like a cow. When the children were born, they would take them to South America."

"Also, the homes for girls without husbands. That way, too, they got their children."

"But they still want children," Parks said.

"Yes," she said. "They want children, but not for the old dreams, for other things."

"Like what?" Parks asked.

"For nothing so bad," Hilda Schaeffer said. "For their business."

"Business?"

"Yes. For this, they raise the children."

Parks leaned forward.

"I don't understand," he said. "Can you tell me about it?"

"I don't know so much," she said hesitantly. "They hold meetings every November. In the early years they were in Bariloche. The first was in fifty-two."

"Who are 'they'?" Fleming asked.

"Bormann, Roschmann, Barbie, Eichmann, Mengele. Sometimes Skorzeny and Stangl, I think. Others. I can't remember them all. Christian was the Secretary of the meeting. Sometimes he would take me along, and I would make coffee, serve the meals, take care of them. They would meet in the library, around a long table, and talk and shout into the night. It was there at Bariloche they decided for Christian to come to America."

"Do they still hold the meetings?" Parks asked.

"Yes, early November. But after Eichmann was captured, they met in Paraguay. It is in these meetings that everything is decided. It is where they take care of their business."

"What kinds of business, do you know?" Parks asked.

"All kinds, I think. They are very rich, you know. They make big jokes, talk big, laugh about all the countries, the armies, and say they don't matter.

"They want the children to be their heirs, to run their business. They send the children to a special school in Paraguay where they are taught night and day everything about business." She paused and sighed. "It is not much of a way to raise a child, but still . . . Who knows, maybe they think someday they will buy the world."

Suddenly, like a pain from an old disease, the image of Señor Del Campo and his son came back to Parks. He could see the boy's cold blue eyes. They did not reflect the light. They were the eyes of an institutional child, raised without love or play. "It is only a teaching exercise," Del Campo had said. "You may make any assumptions you want. Unlimited money, hundreds of interlocking corporations . . ."

"Yes, maybe," Parks said, remembering the great German cartels of the thirties. He knew now that he was close to the final agenda of the Brotherhood. The agenda that had started in Strasbourg and was now being moved to completion from Paraguay.

"But this is useless talk," Hilda Schaeffer said, brushing aside a strand of gray hair that had fallen across her forehead. "All the men are old and dying. They have replaced one bad dream with another just to have something to live for. That is all. They just want something to live for. Someone to leave their money to."

Parks nodded. "Perhaps. No one wants to grow old alone."

Hilda Schaeffer looked away.

"Where is Schaeffer now?" he asked, repeating his earlier question.

"In Mexico, to open a clinic," she said. "For more children."

"Where in Mexico?"

She hesitated, then closed her eyes. Her defeat was final. "Monterrey. That is all I know."

Hilda Schaeffer fell silent. She had nothing more to tell.

Fleming stood up abruptly, hitting the table and sending his chair crashing to the floor. "What was that?" he demanded. His hand went to his gun.

Parks came to his feet. "What?"

"Somebody's out there."

"I didn't hear anything."

"I did."

"Maybe it's Spade," Hilda said, frightened. "Oh, my God. He's been listening." She touched Parks's arm. "He'll tell."

Parks drew his gun and started for the back door.

"It's not Spade," Fleming said.

Parks opened the back door and listened closely.

Nothing.

"We're getting jumpy."

"I guess," Fleming said, standing his chair upright and sitting down.

"The woods will do that to you," Hilda Schaeffer said. "It is not like the ocean."

She took a drink of coffee.

Suddenly, she screamed in agony and grabbed her throat. Her face turned hard and angry. She collapsed to the floor, her body twisted and jerking.

"What's happening?" Fleming shouted, stunned. Hilda Schaeffer looked like a rabid fox. She foamed at the mouth.

"Convulsions!" Parks said. "Come on. Let's get her to the car."

It was too late. Her death agony was horrible but brief. The convulsions stilled; the face eased.

Fleming picked up the cup from which the old woman had been drinking.

"In here," he said. "Poison."

Parks looked at the corpse. It was turning a violent pink. "Yeah," he said. "That's the way it looks, anyway."

"Wonder why she did it?" Fleming asked. He took the contaminated cup to the sink and rinsed it out.

Parks looked at Hilda Schaeffer again. The betrayal was spread across her face. "I don't know."

"Well," Fleming said. "Now let's burn this place."

"Are you crazy? We'll turn these hills into a bonfire."

"All right," Fleming said calmly. "Then let's get out of here. I'm getting the creeps."

"What about Spade?"

"Spade is dead," Fleming said flatly.

Parks stared at him. "All right. Let's go."

The road was deserted as they drove away from the house, weaving through the dry, brittle hills down to the low-water bridge, and back into the city of Austin.

"I'm going to go eat Mexican food," Fleming announced, when they reached the Villa Capri Motel. "Want to come?" His face was smooth, relaxed, and his eyes bright like hot coals.

Parks studied him for a moment before answering. There was no more regret about him than about a cat who had eaten a mockingbird. He had seen two people die—one horribly by her own hand; the other by his—and now he was ready for a meal. Fleming was indeed a man of his trade.

"No, I don't think so," Parks said finally. He was weary. The eyes of the dying Hilda Schaeffer burned in his mind. Perhaps he had been away from the CIU too long. Maybe he didn't have the necessary steel in the gut. "Anyway, I have to make some calls."

After Fleming had left for El Rancho to feast on tacos, nachos, enchiladas, guacamole salad, and steamed tortillas, Parks called Charles Winston in New York.

"Schaeffer is in Mexico," he said, after an exchange of greetings, then told the Director the story of the long night. "We'll leave for Monterrey tomorrow."

"Do you speak Spanish?" the Director asked.

"I speak better pig Latin."

"Then I'll send you help. Magda Hemmings. You've never met her, but she's very competent. A bit of a flair."

"Don't bother," Parks said. "Fleming has enough flair."

"You'll love her," Winston said. "Keep in touch."

Parks then called Max Silverman at his Brooklyn town house and told him of the meeting with Hilda Schaeffer.

"Someone will be at the house before midnight," Dr.

Silverman said, "and search it thoroughly. If the walls are hiding secrets, we will find them."

"Good," Parks said. "I guess we know the final evolution of the Strasbourg Conference. They have set aside rockets and guns for charts and graphs."

Silverman was silent a moment, then he spoke, his voice firm and bright as it traveled over the miles. "You will forgive me, Mr. Parks, if I take a moment to admire the absolute brilliance of Martin Bormann and his Brotherhood. They are without an army, a band of faithful, even a country. They have only their money, their corporations, and their genius for detail, and yet they have fashioned a perfectly believable way to return to power. They will ignore governments and world opinion. They will simply take over the heart of every nation—its business. If they do this, they will be stronger and more powerful than all the pharaohs.

"Now the list is more important than ever. We must know who controls their money."

"Well, I assume that if it is here in Austin, you will find it."

"You may depend on it," Silverman said firmly.

"I have only one problem," Parks said. "I can't bring Schaeffer back to the U.S. At least not alive."

There had never been question of Schaeffer returning to the United States under the Unit's jurisdiction. The publicity and resulting trial would expose the CIU cover.

"Will you give him to us, then?" Silverman asked.

"Yes, if it can be done discreetly."

"It can, and I will see that your wishes are adhered to. There will be no headlines, no trial in a glass booth. No one will know we have him."

"All right. How do you want me to do it?"

Silverman thought a moment before answering. "A man named Sol Perlman will contact you in Monterrey."

After his call to Silverman, Parks ordered a double bourbon from room service, and settled down in bed to record the events of the last two days in his notebook. He was barely into the exercise when he grew angry at himself. Bits of conversation eluded him and fragments of sentences kept occurring to him for no particular reason. He recorded all he could remember, even fragments which seemed to have no meaning. He would not part with his routine so easily again.

By eleven o'clock, John Parks was in a deep sleep.

While Parks slept, two Israeli agents flew in from Houston in a private four-engine plane and searched the Schaeffer lake house from roof to cellar. The men were experts in detection. They stripped woodwork, tore up floors, dismantled every piece of furniture, but it was all useless. The house yielded nothing. At four in the morning the two agents gave up the search and burned the house to the ground, with Hilda Schaeffer and Spade inside it. The Israeli agents were not as afraid of bonfires as they were of fingerprints.

The Israeli agents were not the only ones to work through the night. Max Silverman added two new logs to the fire and commanded his wife, Leah, to make a pot of coffee. Settled before his hearth, he set aside his talmudic studies and put on the shawl of the Haganah. Slowly, bit by bit, he put it all together, drawing on his vast knowledge of the Nazi philosophy, the tenacious brilliance of Martin Bormann, and the subtleties of the Strasbourg Conference which for so long had been misunderstood. The trail to Walter Axmann had led them to the final agenda of the Brotherhood.

The industrial giants at Strasbourg had never intended to compromise with defeat. And, indeed, they were never defeated. It was only the German army and Germany nation that had been defeated. The great factories of the Ruhr and the Rhine went on. The banking houses were needed more than ever to prevent another Weimar Republic where a loaf of bread had cost a barrel of Deutschmarks. The pharmaceutical and chemical monopolies were dismantled and separated, but the Boards of Directors were hardly changed at all.

All of which showed what the men at Strasbourg already knew: True power lay not among nations but among the world's great multinational corporations. It was easier to divide the world up into cartels than to fix national boundaries, and that was exactly what they intended to do. The Brotherhood, under the meticulous leadership of Martin Bormann, intended to create the cartels, then run them, and exercise control over the very necessities of life. Their power would be such that they could declare a famine or decree abundance by manipulating the world's food and water supplies. They could turn epidemics into pandemics by withholding petroleum, sulfur, and other ingredients of medicine from the market. They could destroy whole economies or grant prosperity. Their rule would be absolute. The countries of today would be the territories of tomorrow's business combines.

Children procured by the American Lebensborn were intended to create a brain trust of the world's most ruthless businessmen, who would divide the world into cartels of oil, copper, rubber, gold, and the like. They would have an unfathomable fortune at their disposal, and they would be taught how to combine their brilliance, power, and expertise rather than diminish it on the field of competition. And they would be raised with the single goal of creating the great monopolies. It would be their one purpose in life. They would know no other pastime.

The only roadblock to the Brotherhood's success was the wealth of nations, not the guns of war. But in that, the Brotherhood would have important allies, for men of wealth and power would try to join them, not fight them. A lust for profit is the common denominator among businessmen; it had made them rich and powerful in the first place. The very form of the corporation and conglomerate is but a paper monument to the greed of man. After the great families of wealth had been sucked in by the cartels, they would be stripped of their gold coats and spat back out as paupers.

The Brotherhood and its children would be supreme.

It was sunrise before Max Silverman separated the logs in the fireplace and climbed the stairs to his bedroom. His twisted fingers shook with the fear of his discovery. He almost wished he didn't know. The old dream was better. A Fourth Reich was the dream of weathered men, a thought for the beer hall, a joke in the cold light of day. And even if they could muster the men and guns, the world had already proved that a militia of men and steel was stoppable. But no one had yet proved that an economic juggernaut was anywhere so vulnerable. You cannot shoot a conspiracy. You cannot bomb a vertical trust.

Yes, Max Silverman liked the old dreams better. His best hope now was for John Parks to find the list that would lead to the hidden Nazi assets. But if Bormann ran true to form, it would not be so easy. No, not easy at all.

CHAPTER 15

Monday, December 16, 1974

By the time the morning coffee arrived, John Parks had dressed, smoked two cigarettes, and studied the road maps for south Texas and northern Mexico.

Fleming, a heavy sleeper, was undisturbed by the activity until Parks parted the curtains and let the bright Texas sunlight shock the room.

"What time is it?" Fleming asked, waking with a start.

"Eight thirty."

"To hell with it," Fleming said, and pulled the covers over his head.

"We're going to Monterrey," Parks informed him. "Today."

Fleming pulled the covers tighter. "I don't want to talk about it."

"We're going to drive."

"*I* am going to sleep."

"Look at it this way," Parks said. "If we drive, you can stop every hour and eat. We're certain to make it by Easter."

Fleming sat up in bed and threw back the covers in disgust. "What is this? A Chinese torture session?"

"You'll feel better after you eat. I'll explain everything over grits."

Parks and Fleming checked out of the Villa Capri and drove to Round Rock, a small slit in the earth just outside Austin whose only claim to fame was that Sam Bass had once robbed its bank. There they purchased a used 1972 green Mustang for cash. By noon, they were on their way.

They took Interstate Highway 35 past San Marcos, New Braunfels, and San Antonio. After San Antonio, the home of the Alamo, the land flattened and turned barren and sparse. The two-year-old Mustang held the road well at speeds of seventy and eighty, as they sped past the little towns of Pearsall and Cotulla, on their way to the Texas-Mexico border. By nightfall they were in Laredo, a frayed Texas border town overlooking the light-brown waters of the Rio Grande.

"Would you like to stop and eat, or do you want to drive on to Monterrey?" Parks asked Fleming.

"Eat."

"I knew it was a useless question. Any ideas?"

"You're damn right. The Cadillac Bar."

"You'd think I'd learn," Parks said. "Should we go through customs first?"

"No. It'll take hours this time of night, even if we bribe them."

Parks sighed in exasperation.

"I've got some ideas," Fleming said. "Let's stay on this side of the border tonight."

"Somehow, I've got an idea that your idea has nothing to do with this investigation."

"All depends on how you look at it. We can still be in Monterrey by midmorning."

Parks and Fleming checked into the Holiday Inn on Interstate 35, then took a taxi across the border and went straight to the Cadillac Bar, a landmark in the dusty, crowded Mexican city of Nuevo Laredo. The evening began with a round of Ramos gin fizzes, followed with *cabrito*. Fleming ate with relish, but Parks's appetite had vanished.

After dinner, they went to the Shamrock Bar for margaritas.

There was a happy edge to the Shamrock Bar. In the rear, an artificial waterfall fell over rocks behind a glass wall, providing light and distance and relief from the dirty streets and beggar children just outside. A mariachi band played music with a Latin beat, and beautiful black-haired women whirled on the small, raised dance floor.

Parks swallowed the last of his margarita. "How much do you believe of what Hilda Schaeffer told us?" he asked.

"Oh, come on, John. Stolen babies. Test tubes full of old men. Big business empires." Fleming frowned. "Wild dreams. Tits on a boar hog."

"Don't laugh it off so fast," Parks said. "Have you ever heard of I.G. Farben?"

Fleming shrugged. "I guess. They were Nazis, right?"

"It was a corporation which prospered very nicely under the Nazis. In the thirties it was a loose federation of German chemical firms which through some very skillful maneuvers managed to monopolize the dyestuff industry just before the First World War. During the war it produced the chlorine gas that crippled our soldiers."

"Nice guys," Fleming said, disgusted.

"Oh, it gets better," Parks said. "The Farben executives took a shine to the Nazis, all for good business reasons, you understand, and contributed hundreds of thousands of dollars to the effort to elect Hitler. Then it threw its technical brilliance behind the Reich to give Hitler the materials he needed to wage war. Without Farben, the Nazi war effort was impossible. Farben scientists discovered how to turn coal into gasoline and oil. They discovered how to make synthetic rubber for tires. They did this all for profits and power. There was not an ideologue among them.

"As the Nazis rolled across Europe, Farben followed close behind, confiscating the assets of the major industries of the conquered countries. By the end of the war, I.G. Farben controlled the chemical and pharmaceutical industries throughout all of Europe, except for England and Russia. It produced the poisonous gas for the death camps, the gasoline for the *Luftwaffe,* the aspirin for the Führer's headaches. It was as powerful as the Reich Chancellery. Hitler could not have dismantled it, even if he had wanted to."

Fleming grimaced. "Well, John Kennedy said that all businessmen were sons of bitches. No offense to present company intended."

"I'll bet," Parks said, and ordered another margarita. "But the history of I.G. Farben almost proves your case. After the war, many people wanted Farben burned to the ground, but somehow we just couldn't do it. Farben was dissolved and broken up into three companies, all of which survived and grew into giant corporations. Some people believe we were able to defeat Hitler but not I.G. Farben."

Parks paused for a moment to let the information sink in. "It is a perfectly plausible way for the Nazis to reassert their influence."

"If any are left," Fleming said and frowned.

"Well, we know perfectly well that there are some left, and Schaeffer is one of them."

"All right," Fleming said. "I won't laugh it off. It's a possibility. Anything is a possibility. Now, could we stop this serious shit and go play? I know a place near here that's got a live stage show and the best girls in Mexico."

Parks shook his head. "I don't think so. Not the whores."

"What's the matter? Don't like to pay for pussy?"

Parks laughed. "Is there anything you won't ask?"

"Not much," Fleming said, honestly. "Have you ever?"

"What? Paid for it?"

"Yes."

"When it suited me."

"Then come on. Let's go. This place I know, it's hot. You won't be one bit sorry."

"I thought you were married," Parks said, but not seriously.

Fleming frowned. "I am, but I'm not a monk." He looked down at the table. "Look . . . I've got to go. I can't explain why. It's just my head. And I don't want to go alone. I just don't—" He stopped, embarrassed, and turned his face away. "Look, I'm sorry. You go on back to the hotel. I'll join you later."

"I might get mugged," Parks said. "I better stick with you."

Fleming stood up. Relief swelled in his deep brown eyes.

"Thanks," he said, and extended his hand.

Fleming relaxed and led the way to the street. Parks studied him carefully. The Texan, in manner and body, had all the need and quiet desperation of a teenage boy trying to prove himself.

Fleming hailed a taxi and instructed the driver to Casa Rosa.

"It's the best place," Fleming told Parks again.

"If you say so," Parks said. He grabbed an armrest for support as the taxi ripped through the small, narrow, unlit streets.

"Learned about it," Fleming continued, "when I was at TCU and was supposed to be in prayer meeting."

"Come here often?"

"Well, not *that* often. It's just a diversion."

Fleming looked out the window, as if transfixed by the poverty lining the streets.

"You know," he finally said, "when those guys had you up in that room . . . in New Jersey . . . did they do anything to you?"

"They did a lot," Parks said.

"You know what I mean. That Spade . . . he was a goddamn queer."

"Was he?" Parks said.

Fleming shrugged. "He had to be . . . to act like that."

Casa Rosa was a white stucco bar deep in the heart of Nuevo Laredo's red-light district. Outside its doors, small, ragged, barefoot boys sold Chiclets for ten cents a package and promised their sisters for a little more. Inside, Casa Rosa was neat and clean, giving small relief to the tawdry streets of Boys Town and the damaged faces that walked them, barefoot.

The barroom opened into a large, open-air patio, strung with bright red, green, and white lights. In the center of the patio was a raised wooden platform, covered with blankets and a mattress. Lining the patio on three sides were the doors to the bedrooms.

Fleming led Parks to a small table in front of the raised platform.

"We can see all the action from here," he said, excited.

They were joined almost immediately by two dark-skinned Mexican girls whose bodies had not yet reached twenty, but whose eyes were already well past forty. They were dressed in white ruffled peasant blouses and bright skirts, with plastic flowers in their black hair. One of the two girls recognized Fleming and called him "Big Peter."

Parks laughed. "Is that your nickname or—"

"Both," Fleming said, wrinkled his freckled nose, and grinned.

"What's your name?" Parks asked the girl.

"Rosalita," she said and giggled.

Parks and Fleming ordered a round of margaritas. The waiter brought the men the drinks, and the two girls dark liquid in small jelly glasses.

Fleming nodded at the girls' drinks. "Tea," he informed Parks.

A crowd began to gather in the patio: high-school boys ready for initiation; college boys wearing their school colors; cowboys in dirty boots; middle-aged men in starched shirts and embarrassed faces; and old men in baggy pants.

A four-man ragtag band came to the edge of the wooden platform and began to play discordant music.

"Now for the big show," Fleming announced.

A Mexican girl of no more than fifteen, dressed in a dingy terry-cloth bathrobe, stepped onto the platform. The band played faster, but no better. The girl pranced around the platform for a while in her high heels, then slipped off the bathrobe and attempted a belly dance. After a few rounds, she gave up, lay down on the mattress, and plunged a Coke bottle between her legs.

The college boys gave a cry of delight.

A Mexican man jumped to the stage, shed his clothes, and received a burst of applause. Squat, slick-haired, he walked around the platform, exhibiting his only claim to fame. He retrieved the Coke bottle from the girl and mounted her. Two minutes later he withdrew, dropped his seed on the floor, and walked off.

The crowd booed in disgust.

The girls at the tables made their moves. Couples paired off and the doors around the patio began to slam and lock. Parks asked for Rosalita. Fleming winked and said to meet him afterward at the bar.

Rosalita led Parks across the patio to a small, musty room with a picture of the Madonna on the wall and rosary beads on a night stand.

"Fifteen dollars," she said, closing the door. "For the room. Okay?"

Parks handed her three fives. She stuffed them in the top drawer of the night stand and began to undress.

"Hold it," Parks said. "Let's talk."

"No talk," Rosalita said, shaking her head.

He handed her another five.

"You know Mr. Fleming?" Parks asked.

She looked at him blankly.

"Big Peter."

"Ah, *sí*," Rosalita said, her face brightening in recognition.

"Does he come often?"

She did not understand.

"Big Peter. *Vien aquí? Mucho?*"

She nodded. *"Sí."*

"When last time? *Cuándo . . . última vez?*"

"Dos. Dos mes."

"Two months?"

"Sí."

"Muchas gracias," Parks said, and started to leave.

Rosalita reached for his crotch. "No?" she asked, puzzled.

"No," Parks said, and left for the bar.

CHAPTER 16

Tuesday, December 17, 1974

They rose with the first weak light of morning. The sky was smooth and cloudless and the air was soft with an early chill. As the two men finished packing the car, the sky brightened. Slowly, the sun rose over the horizon, like an old man's gold watch carefully pulled from the pocket, and threw its brilliance over the desolate northern Mexican plains that led to Monterrey.

By eight thirty Parks and Fleming had purchased their Mexican insurance from Sanborn's. By nine thirty they had cleared Mexican customs with the help of a ten-dollar bribe and were roaring down the old, two-lane Pan American Highway to Monterrey. Fleming ignored the speed limits, whistling past the villages of Sabinas Hidalgo and Ciénega. By eleven thirty the peak of Saddle Mountain rose before them. By noon they were in the heart of Monterrey, Mexico's third-largest city, which, behind a façade of Spanish architecture and colonial plazas, harbored some of Latin America's largest factories.

Parks and Fleming pulled into the reception area of the Ancira Hotel on Hidalgo. From the car to the front desk to the hotel room, a succession of young Mexican boys dressed neatly in black and red passed the two men's luggage from hand to hand.

Finally, after Parks had distributed his last loose peso, he said, "If the service doesn't slow down, we'll be bankrupt."

"It's a national evil," Fleming said, unmoved. "Get used to it. Just don't be too generous."

"I can't," said Parks. "I don't have any more money."

They entered the lobby of the Ancira, an elegant mixture of mahogany, marble, and sunlight, with a grand staircase that spread its long run of steps into the lobby like an extended oriental fan. In the early 1900's Pancho Villa had commandeered the Ancira for the night, bedded down his horses in the lobby, and used the spindles of the great staircase as a hitching post.

"Now," Fleming said, "let's eat. I can't think on an empty stomach."

Fleming ordered lobster cardinal, and devoured it with relish. Parks ordered a salad, but barely touched it.

"Let's take a walk," Fleming said when he had finished.

"I guess so," Parks said. "Maybe a jog."

As they started down Calle Zaragoza, through Plaza de la República, and past the statue of Mariano Escobedo, the Mexican general who defeated Maximilian's generals at Querétaro, Parks was preoccupied with his thoughts. They turned into Benito Juarez Plaza.

Finally, Fleming broke the silence. "You still bugged by what that old German woman told you?"

"Not bugged exactly. Just thinking about it. You see, I believe—no, I *know*—the world is limited in its natural resources and someday there will be shortages on a massive scale. Now think about it." Parks paused. "Who, historically, has exploited shortages? Governments? Not really. Businessmen. Even the oil cartel acts more like a business combine than a League of Nations."

"Those kinds of things take money, power," said Fleming, as if he had laid the matter to rest.

"Precisely," said Parks, turning the tables. "A fortune in private hands, and Odessa has just that kind of fortune."

"It still takes more," said Fleming.

"Certainly. It takes the determination to do it, and the knowledge of *how* to do it."

"Which nobody has," said Fleming.

"Look at the robber barons of the eighteen hundreds. They were as strong as the American government. Just paint the Gilded Age on a greater canvas."

Fleming was silent, reflecting.

Parks continued: "Ever watch the women gymnasts from the Communist countries in the Olympics?"

"Yes."

"A perfect example of conditioning. The most agile are plucked from kindergarten at age five and drilled and shaped and motivated for the next ten years of their lives to win the gold medal."

"So?" said Fleming.

"Take the brightest, most savage children, teach them the intricacies of world economics by the time they are ten, the use of power by the age of fifteen, give them the greatest fortune amassed in private hands at twenty, and at twenty five they'll make a tender offer for Zurich."

Fleming gave a dubious grin. "I still think it's bullshit."

"No," Parks said, "it's not bullshit. It's not bullshit at all."

They continued their walk across the plaza.

"We have to take Christian Schaeffer alive," Parks said suddenly.

Fleming looked at Parks quizzically. "Who says?"

"I do. I've promised to turn him over to the Israelis."

Fleming frowned. "Look, buddy, don't get us involved in another Eichmann caper. You'll blow the Unit's cover to hell and back."

"It won't be like that," Parks assured him. "Schaeffer may have, or know who has, a very special list. A list of Nazi assets. If the Israelis get the list, the bank will be closed forever. I've promised to give them a crack at Schaeffer. But don't worry. Schaeffer's days are numbered. It will be a very private hanging. I've been assured of that."

Fleming lit a cigarette and inhaled deeply. "I still don't like it."

"I didn't think you would, but I've already made the commitment."

"All right. Then let's get started."

"We have to wait," Parks said. "The Director is sending us another investigator. A woman. She speaks fluent Spanish. He thought she would be helpful. She also knows the city."

At eight o'clock they walked across the street from the hotel to La Luisiane for dinner. La Luisiane is the most lavish restaurant in northern Mexico, with silver serving plates atop heavy starched white tablecloths and darkly handsome tuxedoed waiters. Turtle sherry consommé, duck à l'orange, Chateaubriand, and oysters with crabmeat are specialties of the house.

Parks and Fleming had almost finished with the restaurant's famous baked Alaska when they were approached by an expensively dressed woman in her late fifties. It was Magda Hemmings.

"Good evening, gentlemen," she said simply. "May I have a seat?"

She sat down at the table before the two men could respond.

"This is a disgrace," she said. "You come to Mexico and eat at a French restaurant. What is wrong with Santa Rosa?"

Parks knew without further documentation that this was Winston's "spy with a flair."

"I wanted to go for lunch, but they were closed," said Fleming, aggrieved at having missed a food stop. "Tomorrow night."

Magda was almost indignant. "I hope you do not plan an extended stay! I must be home no later than Saturday. I haven't done my Christmas shopping."

She gathered her shawl tighter. "Let's go for a walk. I do not care to carry out business in the presence of others." The matronly spy had not forgotten her days in the Cuban underground when Castro's G-2 men seemed to be everywhere. Her trust in appearances was thin. "Have you seen the cathedral? If not, I will show you."

Zaragoza Plaza, an authentic echo of Old Spain, stood in the heart of Monterrey, bordered on one side by the cathedral and on the other by the Palacio Municipal. The cathedral rose with authority over the Plaza, a reminder of harsher days in the industrial city. It was austere, the lack of ornamentation acknowledging the poverty of the city in the eighteenth century in the face of the great wealth of the mining districts of Mexico. Atop the simple carved stone façade, the Cathedral had only one lone, slender tower.

Parks, Fleming, and Magda took a seat on the low benches at the edge of Zaragoza Plaza and watched silently as young couples strolled by, arm in arm. On Thursday and Sunday nights, the young in age and heart would promenade around the old Plaza during the band concerts.

"Christian Schaeffer is in a suite on the top floor of the Ancira," Magda said, coming straight to the point.

"How do you know?" Fleming asked.

"I have my contacts. They can be trusted." She had no intention of revealing her sources. In Cuba, she had seen two of her correspondents executed by the secret police because of a loose tongue in the presence of an unsuspected double agent. "An old Mexican chauffeurs him around in a rented Cadillac," she went on, "but he spends most of his days in his room."

"Hates the natives," Fleming said.

"Certainly. A very arrogant man," Magda said. "Some days he travels to Chipinque to overlook the renovation of the old mansion he has bought for his home. Other days he goes to Villa Santiago, where he is building his clinic."

"Any particular time?" Parks asked. He resisted asking how she had discovered so much in so short a time. Flair, he thought, and gave her an admiring glance.

"Always after twelve o'clock, when the workers have gone home for lunch," Magda answered.

"Some things in Mexico never change," Fleming said, amused.

"I hope never," Magda said.

"Why do you suppose he came here to build his clinic?" Parks wondered aloud, looking across the ancient Plaza.

Magda thought for a moment. "Life is cheap here. It is convenient. There is land, industry, workmen. There are other Germans."

"Germans?" Fleming asked.

"Yes. Old families. From many years ago when the breweries were started."

"How long have they been working on the clinic?" Parks asked.

"I am not so sure. One month. Two." Magda broke off in a hacking cough. She waited until the attack had subsided. "It is better you see for yourself. It is up near Horsetail Falls. Beautiful."

"Excellent idea," said Parks, rising. "Feel like a ride?"

"Not me," Fleming said. "I'm going to have a drink and think this thing over."

"I'll go," said Magda. "I know the way."

"See you later." Fleming headed across the Plaza toward the lights of the Casino, a low modern building with stairs winding up to a grand entrance.

Parks watched the tall, lanky Texan walk slowly away, in search of freak shows and seedy women.

Parks and Magda drove out the Saltillo highway to the Chipinque Mesa, an area located in the mountains looming 2,500 feet above Monterrey, where the rich retreat in the hot summer months. Magda pointed out the house which Schaeffer had purchased. They got out of the car to take a closer look. The house reflected the traditional Spanish architecture of the mesa homes, with whitewashed adobe walls, a terra-cotta roof, and a colorfully tiled patio in the center. The renovation was almost complete.

The crisp night air overcame Magda and she broke into a severe cough.

"Are you all right?" Parks asked, concerned.

"I'm fine," she said, trying to catch her breath. "Sorry."

"You should see a doctor."

"A doctor?" She smiled wistfully. "If only there was one with such a skill."

"What's the matter, Magda?" Parks asked.

"The lungs, they are not good," she confided. "From my days in the prison."

Parks looked curiously at the graying investigator. She could tell he wished to know, so she took his arm as they walked back to the car and told him the story.

During the early days of the Castro regime, she was the CIA's society spy in Cuba. One of her jobs was to carry messages back and forth from Miami to Cuba. Because of her wealth and her early activity in the anti-Batista underground, she was allowed absolute freedom of movement. In October 1960, while she was conferring with the leaders of Brigade 2506, the CIA-trained invasion force, she was given an urgent letter to deliver to the chief of a large anti-Castro group in Havana who was also a high-ranking officer in Castro's G-2 military intelligence. The letter, which outlined the details of the coming Cuban invasion, was given to her in the presence of Ramon Parales, a CIA double agent. That afternoon she drove to Key West and boarded the auto ferry to Cuba. During the voyage, she noticed two men watching her. Acting on intuition, she went to the powder room, memorized the letter, then flushed it down the commode.

On arriving in Cuba, she was seized by the G-2 and ordered to turn over the letter. For two days they questioned her relentlessly. She yielded nothing. She was arrested, convicted on her silence, and sentenced to fifteen years in the Guanajay Penitentiary for Women. During her first year behind bars she was hit on the side of the head with a machine gun butt for refusing to eat the prison food and lost part of the hearing in her left ear. In her second year, she contracted pneumonia from the damp, ill-kept prison and almost died. She recovered with her lungs severely damaged. Because of her failing health, Castro released her in February 1971, and she came to America, stripped of her health, her Cuban possessions, and half her wealth.

"So you see," she said, "I do not hear so well or breathe so well, but I am still a spy."

"Very much so," said Parks. "Didn't you think about retiring?"

"I will retire when Ramon Parales is dead," said Magda, as they got into the car and headed for the little village of Villa Santiago.

"The double agent?"

"Triple agent." It was said in disgust. "He is now a rich man from his CIA connections. He is still at the game, but all the old players are dead. Everyone who was close to Ramon was shot upon returning to Cuba. It was Ramon who turned me over to the G-2." She looked out the window, far beyond the desolate plains. "Sometimes I think the CIA is a congress of fools."

Parks was interested. "How would you take care of a double agent?"

"Quickly," Magda said. "Very quickly."

Using the telephone in the lobby of the Ancira, Parks called the Plaza in New York. He was informed that Mr. and Mrs. Herbert Jones had checked out.

"When?" he asked.

"We're not permitted to give out that information," he was told, politely.

"No, I guess you're not."

Slowly, he replaced the receiver. Mary had gone home.

He could see her, walking slowly through the ransacked house, setting the chairs upright, picking up clothes thrown on the floor, putting things back the way they were. She would shrug her shoulders and make coffee. Then she would walk to the beach, her arms folded against her, her long brown hair whipping around her cheeks. She would stop at the rotting carcass of the old shipwreck and sit for a while atop the barren sand inside the hull where life would not grow. Off in the distance, children would run at sea gulls and squeal with glee; lovers would walk in silence, hand in hand. But she would neither hear nor see. Her heart was in another land, and try as she would, she could not reach it.

Parks crossed the grand Ancira lobby to the gilded elevator. A small, slim man with large black eyes and rimless glasses joined him in the elevator. The man watched him with the intensity of a coiled spring. When Parks stepped out of the elevator, the man followed.

Parks hesitated as the bright gold doors of the elevator closed. The man extended his hand. "I am Sol Perlman," he said firmly. "I understand you have a package for me."

"Not yet. Tomorrow."

"When?"

"In the afternoon, if we're lucky."

"Deliver it to the railroad station. My friends and I will be waiting in the southeast corner of the parking lot. It is quiet there."

Parks nodded. The two men had said all they needed to say to one another. They were not meeting for friendship. Perlman turned, walked down the hall to the door to the interior stairs, and disappeared.

Fleming had not returned when Parks reached the hotel room. He decided not to wait up for him. He could tell him the plans tomorrow. It was time for sleep now. Time for peace before facing tomorrow.

CHAPTER 17

Wednesday, December 18, 1974

John Parks slept in fits, waking up several times in a cold sweat. The face of the informer would come and go, then merge into another face. Sometimes there would be a blank face, a face that would start to cry. The last image he remembered was two half faces, each ravaged in its own way.

Finally, he could sleep no more. He was sure he knew who the informer was, but he felt uneasy. He had only his intuition, and that was a slender reed with which to hang a person.

He was glad when dawn came.

He dressed in the weak light, without turning on the lights, moving quietly, like a cat in a snowfall, careful not to wake Fleming. He need not have worried. Fleming slept like a rock.

He walked to Benito Juarez Plaza with the spiral stenographer's notebook that contained his careful observations of the Victory investigation.

He sat down on a bench in the deserted plaza and turned to the first page of the notebook. The day gathered strength and provided him with sufficient light to read. He read the notebook from beginning to end.

Finished, he stared off to Saddle Mountain. Its peak was covered in morning fog.

Yes, it was all there. Everything fit. It was still intuition, but he was now absolutely certain he knew the name of the informer.

Satisfied and resolved, he tucked the notebook under

his arm. At Hidalgo Plaza, where the vendors were setting up their stalls, he bought a silver cross for Mary. Then he called Magda Hemmings from the lobby of the Ancira, waking her up.

"I'm sorry to call so early," Parks explained, "but I've been to the marketplace."

"What did you buy?" Magda asked. "A chicken?"

"Some jewelry."

"Did you think they would run out?"

"I couldn't sleep."

"Neither can anyone else."

Satisfied that Magda would forgive him, Parks gave her the instructions for the day.

Fleming was still soundly asleep when he returned to the hotel room. At eight thirty Parks woke him and told him they would make their play for the fugitive German at noon.

"Magda said that Schaeffer often goes out to inspect the clinic when the workers go home for lunch and a siesta," Parks explained. "He'll be alone there, if he goes, except for his chauffeur."

"What if he doesn't go?" Fleming asked.

"Then we wait for tomorrow, or when he does go. Magda is keeping a lookout for us."

Fleming searched for a cigarette. He was out. "Got any smokes?"

"You want Marlboros or Mexican cigarettes?"

Fleming made a face. "Marlboro. I don't smoke rope except on Groundhog Day."

"Do you want breakfast?" Parks asked.

Fleming shook his head. "No. Don't feel like it. Just coffee."

They ordered coffee sent to the room, and packed. They took their luggage to the garage and had the young attendant put it in the car. Then they spent the rest of the morning waiting for Magda's call. Fleming paced and smoked. He started a game of solitaire, but couldn't concentrate. Parks stretched out on his bed and tried to read *Funeral in Berlin,* but it was a little like trying to take a shower and watch *Psycho.* Eventually, he gave it up and joined Fleming in pacing.

At ten after twelve, Magda called. Parks answered.

"He's going to the clinic," she announced.

"All right. We'll meet you in the lobby in five minutes."
Parks replaced the receiver and turned to Fleming.
"Let's go."

Parks called for the car. The two men gathered their
guns and shoulder holsters, attached the silencers, and put
on sports coats to conceal the marks of their trade. When
they joined Magda in front of the hotel, the Mustang was
waiting for them.

"You drive," Parks said to Magda. "We'll ride in back."
Parks tipped the garage attendant six pesos, and received
a flood of Spanish in gratitude.

"You gave him too much," Fleming said in reprimand.

Parks shrugged it off. "What the hell." After all, it
might be his last worldly gesture of generosity. "Maybe
he'll light a candle for me," he said, climbing into the
backseat.

Magda took the wheel of the green Mustang, cool and
confident, just as in the days when she drove her leather-
lined Ferrari down the streets of Havana with a 16mm film
cartridge concealed in her brassiere. Christian Schaeffer's
new Lebensborn clinic was twenty miles away.

On the outskirts of the city, Magda pointed out El
Tecnológico de Monterrey, the MIT of Mexico, a group
of modern school buildings much like any American university, complete with football stadium. Parks acknowl-
edged the landmark with a grunt. Fleming lit a cigarette
and remained silent. Neither was in the mood for sight-
seeing.

The land turned dry and barren. Small, ragged children
stood along the highway hawking straw hats, pottery, and
wilted flowers to the tourists who sped toward Horsetail
Falls. The children were dirty, with thin arms and legs
and necks, and protruding, bloated stomachs.

The black, hollow eyes of the children chilled the soul
of Magda Hemmings. They brought back memories of the
miserable poverty under Batista, when Cuba was a land of
the very rich and the very poor. That was why she had
joined the underground—for the children. Perhaps, she
had thought, with the wretched Batista gone, there would
be hope. But no, she had helped replace a man who had
ravaged the poor with a man who duped and used them.

And, from one to the other, still the children suffered, the pitiful victims of the games of men.

Magda lost her appetite for being a tour guide.

They drove the rest of the way in silence. Magda washed her mind of the children—those along the road and those in Cuba—and concentrated on the instructions Parks had given her.

Fleming set his jaw and watched the road ahead. Occasionally he checked his watch. It was twelve forty. He already knew what he would do when he found Christian Schaeffer. That had been determined a long time ago.

Parks stared out across the barren land. The long journey was coming to an end. For Schaeffer. For Victory. For Lebensborn. And, if he was right, for the CIU informer.

He prayed he was right. Never again would he take an assignment where he had to sit in judgment on his own colleagues. He had had to look too deep, too far:

The Director, growing old and a little bitter at his empty life.

Miss Messinger, lonely and alone and rudely abandoned by the CIU after thirteen years of service, half in love with Winston, a man too steeped in memories of his wife to notice.

Robbie Davison, driven to desperation by a junkie sister.

Magda Hemmings, with her singular hatred of Ramon Parales.

Fleming, with his ravaged manhood.

Mary, lovely Mary, with her transparent lies.

No. It was not good to have to know people so well.

They reached Villa Santiago at Junction K-166. High above them, four miles away, was Horsetail Falls, rolling its shreds of silver down the brown mountain.

Parks and Fleming made themselves invisible, a neat trick for two men over six feet tall in a small car. After trying several variations, Fleming folded down on the cramped floorboard and Parks lay down on the backseat.

Magda turned east on an unmarked dirt road. Christian Schaeffer's new Lebensborn home was six miles down the dirt road, standing in the middle of harsh flatlands graced with cactus and poverty. It was a two-story white adobe hacienda with double carved oak doors, undistinguished in either architecture or ornamentation, but elegant in comparison to the small windowless mud-and-grass houses they had passed on the way.

The renovation of the old hacienda was nearly complete. A new terra-cotta tile roof had been put on, new windows and window casings were being put in, and an east wing was about to be added. The forms had already been built and filled in. The wire mesh had been laid in preparation for pouring the concrete foundation.

It was one o'clock.

Except for the 1973 black Cadillac Coupe de Ville parked in front of the white adobe house, with its driver slumped behind the wheel, the place appeared deserted. The laborers had gone home for lunch and a siesta—some to Villa Santiago, others all the way back to Monterrey. They would not return until two o'clock.

As the Mustang approached, the chauffeur jerked his head at the unexpected sound, straightened, and stared intently at Magda behind the wheel.

Magda smiled in recognition but did not hurry to leave the car. Out of the sight of the chauffeur, she poured chloroform onto a napkin she had taken from her breakfast table at the Ancira, then replaced it neatly in her purse. She left her purse open for easy access.

She smiled at the chauffeur and waved, and the dark-eyed man smiled back. Though the years were starting to tell, Magda still had a way with men.

She eased out of the Mustang, letting her skirt ride above her knees, and walked slowly to the limousine. The chauffeur's quick Latin eye fastened on her legs. She hiked her dress higher. The chauffeur broke into a grin. He was thinking of a number of possibilities. Why, he could almost see her . . .

Magda was almost at the chauffeur's side. "I want to go to Horsetail Falls," she said in perfect Spanish. "Can you help me?"

The chauffeur's face fell. "You took a wrong turn," he said, disappointed.

Magda drew even with the car window. "Oh. And I am so tired . . . and hot."

She leaned against the car. Her skirt rose higher.

The chauffeur chuckled, and stretched his neck out the

window for a good look. His eyes fixed on her bare thighs.

In one fluid motion, Magda thrust her hand into her purse, grabbed the Smith and Wesson by the barrel, and delivered a crushing blow to the back of the chauffeur's head with the butt of the gun.

The man's head fell to one side, like that of a chicken with a broken neck. Magda applied the chloroform.

Parks and Fleming scrambled out of the backseat of the Mustang and rushed the double oak doors, their guns drawn. Magda was close behind.

The old hacienda smelled of new plaster and fresh paint.

Schaeffer called from the second floor, speaking slowly in Spanish with a German accent. He had been inspecting the renovation of the bedrooms when he heard a noise in the hallway.

"José! I'll be down in a minute. Wait in the car!"

The three CIU investigators climbed the winding wrought-iron staircase to the second floor.

"Gott im Himmel! José!" Schaeffer was irritated. He could not get used to his new life where he constantly had to repeat himself.

Schaeffer stormed out into the long second-floor hall, meeting Parks, Fleming, and Magda face to face. He stopped, abruptly, but made no attempt to run.

"So," he said, and rubbed his hands together, almost in satisfaction. The German gave no indication that he felt he was in immediate danger.

The three investigators faced Schaeffer with a wall of silence. They were lined up three abreast, their guns drawn and aimed, like a row of cannon in a forward brigade.

Still, Schaeffer showed no alarm. Instead of fear there was a chilling sneer of contempt. Parks had an overwhelming urge to turn around to see if they were being covered from behind.

"We meet again, Mr. Parks."

Silence.

Finally, Schaeffer began to show the discomfort of uncertainty.

"I suppose you think you have caught me off guard. For an intelligent man, you don't seem to see—"

The muffled fire of a silenced gun pierced the air. Steel ripped through the German, spinning him around and throwing him against the wall. Schaeffer collapsed on the tile floor, his gray pinstripe suit soaked in blood.

Parks turned sharply and with the swiftness of a black-snake cracked the butt of his gun across Fleming's wrist. Fleming's gun flew from his hand and skidded across the tile floor.

"I said to take him alive," Parks said.

Fleming's face was blank. His eyes were wide and dull. "Did you?"

Parks pointed his gun at Fleming's stomach. "You know I did." *One is nothing, two may be a coincidence, three is a trend.* The knowledge that had been at the tip of his mind for days came over him. "I guess you just couldn't afford to."

Fleming held his wrist. It was red and swelling. "No," he said, "I guess I couldn't."

Magda watched the two men in silence as they stood apart, facing each other, the pain making their bodies as rigid as flagpoles.

"Peter, was it you?" Magda finally asked. Disbelief hung in her voice.

Fleming remained silent.

Parks looked him in the eye. "It was all there for me to see," he said. "I guess I just didn't want to. Was it for money, Pete? Is that what it was?"

"I didn't talk for money. There was something else."

"What else is there?" Parks asked. For the first time, the contempt came through.

"You really want to know?" Fleming said bitterly. "All right, you got it. Yes, there was money. They gave me money. But it didn't start there." Fleming cleared the catch in his throat. "I was working with Stramm, as you know. I was tracing the Victory money leaving Texas for Mexico. It led me here to Monterrey. I was onto this clinic two months ago."

His voice began to tremble. "Schaeffer and his goons caught me. I guess, all told, I'm not much of a spy." He frowned in deprecation, then continued. "They tried to get me to talk. Spade worked me over, knocked me punchy.

I passed out. I puked in his face. But I wouldn't even tell them my middle name." He paused. "I hope you believe that."

"I do," Parks said.

"Well, at least that's something," Fleming said quietly. "I was hard . . . tough. Just like they teach you in training. . . . I wasn't afraid to die.

"Then they went into their little act. They made me take off my clothes . . . bare-ass naked."

"I've been there," Parks said. Just remembering made him shake.

"Yes, so you have. For a bit of it." Fleming bent his head, his face flushed with embarrassment.

"Let's talk about it later," said Parks.

"There is no later. . . . Schaeffer turned me over to Spade and left. Now the good part. The part you missed. Spade tied me down to the bed, spread-eagle. Facedown. Do you get the picture?" His face contorted with shame and agony. "I'm sure you don't need the details. When Spade had his fill, he made the kid take over, and when the kid begged to stop he used a broom handle."

Parks went sour in the stomach.

Tears were streaming down Fleming's face. "It was worse than dying."

Fleming broke completely, bending over with the pain of heavy sobs. He gasped for breath and continued. "I wanted to die." He shouted at the top of his lungs so that the heavens would hear. *"I prayed to die."*

There was a chilling echo in the long hall.

Fleming continued in a monotone. "I was torn up, hemorrhaging, out of my fucking mind. . . . I told them everything."

"Peter . . ." Magda began.

"Yes. I told them everything. I would have told them anything—I just wanted them to stop!"

"But you are alive, Peter," Magda said quietly. "You should have told us."

Fleming shrugged. "They brought in some quack, a greaser, to stop the bleeding. Then——" He laughed with scorn. "They gave me two hundred thousand dollars. Can you believe it? My ass for two hundred thousand dollars.

They didn't kill me because they knew I'd never turn them in. Not after what—"

"Pete . . ." Parks began, but Fleming stopped him with his fury.

"They ripped me up, gutted me." Then he spat it out. "A queer!" His face contorted with self-loathing. "A fucking queer."

"No, Peter," Magda said, trying to ease his shame.

"You don't know!" Fleming shouted in anguish.

"I do, yes," Magda said, and she did. At Guanajay Penitentiary in Cuba she had been brutally raped by two guards while their fellow workers watched and laughed.

"I didn't know they would kill Stramm, John. Not that it matters. I would have done anything just to—" He drew a deep breath, fighting back tears. "They gave me another twenty thousand later for information about you. Twenty thousand and a promise that Spade would never touch me again . . . never . . . so long as I told them what they wanted to know."

Parks thought he would vomit.

"Do it now, John," said Fleming. "Please . . ."

Magda took a step forward. "No, you can't!"

Fleming ignored her. "Don't make me beg, buddy. Do it now. Quick. While I'm ready."

"No," said Parks. "You don't know . . . It's not all your fault."

Fleming's face twisted into madness. He let out a high shrieking animal scream of distress and hurled his body at Parks.

Parks fired. His aim was perfect, gouging the devastated heart of Peter Fleming, a man who, by his own account, had really died some time ago.

Parks slumped against the whitewashed wall while Magda stepped to Fleming, crumpled on the floor. She raised his arm. The life was gone. The body had followed the soul.

Suddenly, the silence of the old hacienda was too much for both of them to bear.

Magda began to cough. "Let's go," she said.

"No. Not yet." Parks rubbed his head to clear the fog. "We have to clean up."

Slowly, as in a fading dream, Parks and Magda descended the stairs and walked out into the sunlight. Without further words they methodically set about their work. Magda gave the chauffeur an extra dose of chloroform, then went back inside to wipe the walls and floors clean of splattered blood. Parks carried the bodies of the two men down to the construction site and buried them in shallow graves under the wire mesh. By nightfall, the Nazi and the Texan would be sealed forever in their Mexican tomb.

It was almost two. The workmen would be returning to work soon.

"Can you drive that Cadillac?" Parks asked Magda.

She was almost insulted. "Of course!"

"Good. Then follow me."

They abandoned the Cadillac and its anesthetized driver by the side of the Saltillo highway near the Garcia Caves.

"When will he wake up?" Parks asked, when Magda rejoined him in the green Mustang.

"Oh I don't know. After dark."

"Are you sure?"

"Positive."

Magda had also worked as a doctor's aide in the underground.

"Where are your things?" Parks asked.

"My suitcases? In a locker at the railroad station."

"Let's pick them up and hit the road. I have some people to meet there anyway."

They drove to the Monterrey rail station near Cuauhtemoc Park, where Magda retrieved her two Louis Vuitton suitcases, and Parks told Sol Perlman that Walter Axmann, alias Christian Schaeffer, was dead. Perlman sighed, stamped out his cigarette, and turned and walked away. His disappointment was too great for him to bother with amenities.

Parks and Magda ditched the Mustang at Sabinas Hidalgo and took the five-thirty Transportes del Norte bus to Laredo, where they caught an Air Southwest flight to Dallas. Upon arrival, Parks called the Director from his hotel room in the Adolphus.

"As far as I know, they haven't discovered the bodies," Winston informed him.

"Well, if they do, don't fly him home. Pete's wife . . ."

"It could get complicated."

"Breathing is complicated," Parks said flatly, "but I still do it."

"We'll take care of it," Winston promised. "We found out something else yesterday. Dr. Seahurst at the Manhattan clinic has been experimenting with artificial reproduction. He has apparently discovered how to mate a cell and an egg outside the body, freeze it for sixty days, then plant it in a womb."

Suddenly Parks knew the purpose of the Monterrey clinic. "Life is cheap here," Magda had said of Mexico.

"Can he be stopped?" Parks asked.

"No, there's nothing illegal."

"Maybe not. I'll talk to you tomorrow."

Parks took Magda to Ports-of-Call for a late-night dinner, but neither one had an appetite, so they got drunk instead.

When Parks got back to his hotel room in the Adolphus, he retched until he got the dry heaves.

CHAPTER 18

Thursday, December 19, 1974

By two o'clock the next day, Parks was at his desk, easing back into his position as President and Chairman of the Board of American Investing Corporation. He felt empty and alone, and showed it.

Miss Jones greeted his arrival with a question meant to be a reprimand. "I thought you were going to get some rest?"

"I did," said Parks. "Don't I look it?"

Even Parks didn't like to set off the stern-eyed Miss Jones, whose great bulk took up two lanes when she stormed down the hall.

"No. You look terrible."

She handed him a stack of mail.

"These are the important ones," she informed him. "Arranged in order of importance. I took care of the rest myself." She put her chubby hand on her hip. "Any questions?"

"No. Bring me some coffee and I'll get down to work."

"Right away," Miss Jones said happily. She was glad to have Parks back at his desk, even as ragged as he looked.

As for Parks, it hardly seemed he had been away, or that it mattered one way or the other. The Dow-Jones average was down, but it would go up. Interest rates were up but they would go down. Treasury certificates were a good investment, common stocks a bad one. Next week it would be the reverse. Wall Street was like the great Atlantic. It ebbed and flowed, but there was an undercurrent of constancy, mostly because it was always there.

Parks called Miss Jones on the intercom. "Get Michael DeFalco for me."

Miss Jones rang back. "He's on the commodities trading floor. Apparently coffee futures are going through the roof. Do you want me to call him off the floor?"

"No," Parks said. "I'll go over."

The New York Commodities Exchange Center is housed in a modern building of black steel and glass at 4 World Trade Center. The trading floor is a large cavernous room, three stories high. Its walls are painted a fresh gray. It is carpeted from one end to the other in gray. All around the walls are thirty-foot-high black scoreboards labeled, in large white letters, Coffee, Sugar, Cocoa, Cotton, Soybeans, Bellies, Wheat, Corn, Copper, Gold, Silver, and Platinum, which, in changing digital numbers, keep track of the bids for the world's commodities, for the next twelve months. Here, in this room of gray and black and white, men barter the world's food supply with all the dignity and subtlety of barkers at a street fair.

When Parks walked onto the floor, the Exchange was swarming like an anthill under attack. Runners in gray jackets raced from phone booths to the pits with the latest bid or offer. Traders crowded around octagonal counters in the heart of the pit, trying to outshout each other with higher bids.

Michael DeFalco was standing near the coffee pit watching two hundred men elbowing and pushing ruthlessly to get a chance to join the auction. Every time someone shouted a jubilant "Deal!" the consumer suffered a setback.

"They're going crazy," DeFalco said, half shouting. "I'm going to cut down on coffee."

Parks looked at the sugar board. "Looks like you better quit putting sugar in it too," Parks said.

The frantic shouting at the pits made it difficult to hear.

"Make jokes," DeFalco said. "We were long in coffee. We just lost some of your best friends and customers about two hundred thousand dollars."

"We'll turn it around tomorrow," Parks said dryly.

The noise level at the coffee pit became impossible.

"Let's go outside," Parks said. They left the floor and went to the lobby.

"How far have you gotten with your memorandum for Señor Del Campo?" he asked.

"Half finished," DeFalco said.

"Don't do any more," Parks said. "Destroy everything you've already done."

"Why?"

"Because we're not going to do it."

"Any reason?"

"It's too damn strange. I don't trust him." Parks wished he could tell DeFalco the real reason. Maybe someday he could. DeFalco would be a good man for the Unit.

"They'll just go somewhere else," DeFalco said.

"Let them."

"Has Harry Rylander told you about the funny request he got?" DeFalco asked.

"No."

"Boy, this is the season for weirds. An international investment company has asked us to act as their broker in buying farmland in the South. A lot of the family farms are going bankrupt down there, with no end in sight. It's just going to get worse. Fertilizers are going up, the weather's been bad and getting worse, grain prices are dropping. If they were in coffee, sugar, or toilet paper, they might survive."

"Where's the company headquartered?" Parks asked.

"Munich. Owned by some Germans and Austrians, with Swiss and Spanish clients. They say they want to cash in on our commercial development, if you can believe that. I told Harry he should tell them to roll their proposal in a tube and give them a few suggestions."

Parks looked off into the madness of the commodities floor. Was this the beginning? Is this how the cartels would start?

"What do you think?" DeFalco asked.

"The same as you do. Wouldn't touch it with a ten-foot pole. I'm going to tell Rylander to report it."

"Anything else?" DeFalco asked. "I want to get back to the floor and see whether the proletariat is going to starve this winter."

"Go on back," Parks said, and laughed. "Go back and make up that two hundred thousand dollars we lost, or it'll come out of your Christmas bonus for the next ten years."

"Yessa, bossman."

* * *

The five-fifty-nine express from Grand Central to Harrison, keeping a timetable known but to God and the New Haven Railroad, arrived at six fifty. The blue-suit-and-briefcase crowd, the life supports of American capitalism, marched off the train. They had done with merging giant into greater giant, refinancing General Motors, creating paper empires, and directing arbitrage transactions with a ruthlessness that would chill the soul of Lucrezia Borgia. It was time for a drink.

The lights along the depot cast circles of brightness over the Harrison station and adjoining parking lots, creating, at the same time, pockets of darkness. Parks waited near the edge of the platform, just outside the light.

When he was finally alone, he walked uphill to the small, manicured park overlooking the asphalt lot. Charles Winston was already there, as planned, sitting on one of the metal seats. Parks spotted him. They were alone in the park, hidden by the shadows of the tall trees.

The Director rose and extended his hand. "A job well done," he said.

"Thanks." Suddenly, to Parks, the night seemed dark and hateful. "I'll brief you on the details," Parks said.

"Please."

The Director tapped out his pipe, repacked it, lit it, and leaned back as Parks accounted for his days since he last met with Winston near dawn at the Avalon Theater on West 44th Street. He recounted some conversations verbatim; other he summarized. He left out very little. It took Parks a full forty-five minutes to tell his story.

"I'm sorry for Max Silverman that we didn't take Schaeffer alive," Winston said. He took a long drag on his pipe and reflected. "But there was no way to know about Fleming."

"Actually, there was. An old sheriff in New Jersey taught me a rule. It uses quantity as a guideline. One is nothing, two may be a coincidence, three is a trend. Unfortunately, I ignored it. I ignored all the clues."

"What were the clues?" Winston asked. He was relaxed and eager for the discussion.

"The first one he dropped at the Avalon Theater. He called Schaeffer a sawed-off Nazi. I never said whether

Christian Schaeffer was small, medium, or large, merely that he was an old SS man. The common image of an SS man is blond, lean, and tall. Fleming's accurate description of Schaeffer went against the grain of a universal stereotype.

"Second, he poisoned Hilda Schaeffer. Hilda Schaeffer had no intention of dying. She had already been through too much to bother killing herself."

"Why do you think he killed her?"

"Probably because he was afraid she might remember having heard his name. The lady had very big ears and she was learning to have a mouth."

"What was the third clue?"

"It was a little more cumulative," Parks said. "He killed Spade. That didn't seem to register at the time, but we really hadn't discussed finishing Spade off. Not then, anyway. We might have needed him for information about Schaeffer. But I think I was so glad that someone else had killed Spade for me, I wanted to ignore it.

"Then, in Nuevo Laredo, he called Spade a queer. I never said Spade was gay. I said he was sadistic."

"No, you didn't actually say so," Winston said. "Was he?"

"As a matter of fact, yes, which was not a difficult conclusion to draw. But there was something else. Fleming seemed to know more about Spade. Now, of course, we know what."

"Why do you suppose they let Fleming live but not Henry Stramm?" Winston asked, looking off toward a string of neon lights across the street.

"Because they broke Fleming. I don't imagine they broke Stramm. But Fleming would never have told anybody about them. He was too ashamed—ashamed of what they had done to him, ashamed that he had talked. They would have let him live only as long as he was useful to them, and as long as he was still afraid of them and what they could do to him. Eventually they would have killed him, too."

Parks looked down at the ground. "Not all of this will be in the report, of course," he said.

"No, I guess not," the Director said.

"I couldn't. Not about Pete. Not all that."

"No."

"I don't want some bureaucrat to find out that he received any large sums of money. They'd just dun his wife for taxes."

The Director was not so harsh. "I don't think so," he said.

"Well, just in case."

"Yes. Just in case."

"What did they tell his wife?"

"They told her he had been working on a secret project for the government and that he was in a boating accident. She now presumes him dead."

"Not too far off," Parks said. "He drowned, just not at sea." Parks shuffled his feet. The night seemed oppressively heavy. "Actually, I had already gone through a process of elimination and had decided on another informer."

He lit a cigarette, then continued.

"By the time I got to Monterrey, I had already eliminated Miss Messinger and Robbie Davison. Each of them knew about Stramm and me, but there were good reasons to think neither one was the informer."

"What were they?"

"Robbie Davison just isn't the type. He's an overgrown Boy Scout. Loyal, true, helps old ladies across the street. Even a junkie sister wasn't enough."

"And Miss Messinger?"

"Miss Messinger was mostly suspect because of her new mink coat. Once I found out how she got the money to pay for it, I eliminated her."

"How did she get the money?"

"She sold a story to *Gotham Romances*. It was in the July issue under a pseudonym. It was about this secretary and her boss, both two decades past being spring chickens when . . . You probably know the rest. The details were so similar I did a little digging, and found out the author's real name."

The Director was silent, thinking of that Christmas Eve in 1973.

"After eliminating Miss Messinger and Robbie, that left Fleming and you."

Parks rose and thrust his hands into his overcoat.

The Director looked down at the ground. "And since you didn't suspect Fleming—"

"It makes it easy when you devise a rule and everything fits into place." Parks gripped the gun in his pocket. "Unfortunately," he said, tightly, "things don't always come in threes. Sometimes you just have to use your intuition."

Charles Winston rose to face him. "Surely you don't still think it was me."

Parks didn't answer the question. He didn't want to hear the denial. "The one loose end in this whole affair was how Victory found out about Peter Fleming. Before the chicken comes the egg. . . . There was only one way. You told them."

"You always did hate loose ends," Winston said quietly.

"Yes. Always."

Winston met him eye to eye. "You have your hand on your gun."

"Yes."

"There isn't any need."

Charles Winston sat down heavily in the metal seat. He leaned forward, his shoulders sagging. "No one was supposed to have been hurt," Winston said, but it was not a plea of mercy.

"They never are," Parks said. There was a hard edge to his voice.

"Bea was dying of cancer." Winston's voice cut into the night. "The medical bills were almost more than I could handle. Then she asked to go to France. It was the one thing she wanted before she died, and I—" The voice broke. "I didn't have the money. So I contacted Victory and told them they were being investigated by the IRS. I had no idea I was dealing with an international ring of murderers and fanatics."

"Didn't you?"

"No. I swear it."

"Did you tell them who you were?"

"No. I didn't tell them about me. I didn't tell them about the Unit. I didn't tell them about Fleming. I just told them they were being investigated by the IRS."

"Whom did you tell? Schaeffer?"

"No, I didn't know any more about the Executive Secretary than Stramm did. I had only his monthly reports, so

I knew only about Adrian Reese in Philadelphia. I arranged the whole thing through Reese."

"How much did he pay you?"

"Twenty-five."

"Thousand?"

"Yes."

"You sold out cheap."

Winston stood up. "I think you missed my point."

"Not really," said Parks, but without malice. "There's only one thing I want to know. You could have stopped the investigation at any time. Why didn't you?"

"I wanted to avenge Stramm. Is that so hard to believe?"

"No, it's not."

"Thank you," Winston said. "I appreciate that."

"Didn't you think I would find out?"

"No. Particularly not you."

Parks frowned. "If it's any consolation, I tried not to."

"I know. The psychological profile in your file said you only had one weakness. When loyalties were involved, you tended to overlook the obvious and keep your loyalties intact. Not a bad trait for a government man."

There was silence for a moment between them.

"What will you do now?" Winston finally asked.

"I've asked myself that question a thousand times. I didn't know the answer until just a minute ago."

Charles Winston waited in silence for Parks's next sentence.

Finally, Parks said: "I'm not going to do anything. Not a damn thing. I've got enough blood on my hands. You'll have to let your own conscience tell you what to do."

The train for New York City was coming down the track from Rye. Its distant roar filled the night.

"Then it's up to me," Winston said.

"Yes. It's up to you."

Parks turned and walked toward the station.

CHAPTER 19

Saturday, December 21, 1974

Parks left early for Seaside.

It was true, he had always hated loose ends, unfinished business. He had to find the final answers to the Lebensborn puzzle. He wondered what Mary would say when she saw him. He had not called to tell her he was coming.

The day was mild for December, almost as if Christmas had been postponed for another week. He found Mary on the beach, sitting on the sand inside the rotting hull of the old shipwreck, dressed in dull olive fatigues from the Army surplus store and a thin jacket.

She was looking off into the bay, her arms folded against her, when he called her name. She jerked. "Oh . . . hello," she said, almost as if they were speaking for the first time.

He climbed to the top of the protruding hull and sat beside her. They sat together for a long time without speaking.

"Mary, why did you leave the Plaza?" he finally asked.

She continued to stare across the bay. "I didn't think you were coming back," she said, her voice falling.

"Well, here I am, and you don't seem exactly thrilled to see me."

"John, please . . ."

He reached into his goose-down parka, retrieved a small box, and handed it to her. "I bought you this in Monterrey," he said.

She opened it slowly. It was the silver cross.

"The first time we met you were wearing a chain around

your neck," he said. "I couldn't see what was on the other end because it was covered by your sweater."

"You have a good memory," she said, touching the cross.

"You never wore the chain again," he continued. "You buried Ellen with it."

She nodded. "It was my mother's. The only thing . . ." She hesitated. "I wanted Ellen to have it."

"Let's go back to the house," he said.

They started back along the beach. Barnegat Light glistened in the distance.

Parks paused to light a Marlboro. "Schaeffer is dead," he said.

"Good."

"I thought you'd say that."

They reached the bay house.

"Would you like coffee?"

"No."

There was a chill in the house. They went to the library and sat on the leather chesterfield.

"Now," he said, "let's play a game. It's called truth. You ask me a question and I'll tell you the truth. Then I'll ask you one and you tell me the truth. You first."

"All right," she said. "Why are you *really* here?"

"You mean right now or in the first place?"

"In the first place."

"I'm a government agent," Parks said. "I was sent here to get Schaeffer."

"I see."

"No, you probably don't. But now it's my turn. Why did you want Schaeffer dead?"

"I didn't."

"Is that why you were so grief stricken over his death?"

She rubbed the back of her neck, nervously, and turned away.

Parks looked at her for a moment before he spoke. "Whenever we talk about Schaeffer or Poland, or you're afraid, you always rub the back of your neck."

"It's just a nervous habit," she said.

"It's where the numbers are," he said. "Just like the numbers on your sister's arm."

He took hold of her shoulders and lifted the hair from

the back of her neck. She offered no resistance. Faded numbers, barely visible, were engraved into the flesh.

"They're from a Lebensborn camp. You were one of the Lebensborn children. In Poland."

She looked up at him, frightened. "How long have you known?"

"I don't know . . . for a while."

She took a deep breath. "I think you'd better go, now."

"No, damn it, I won't. Mary, what are you hiding? It's all over now."

"Can you wipe these numbers off my neck?" she asked bitterly.

"I can't wipe them off your neck, but I can wipe them out of your mind."

For the first time, she smiled. "Thank you," she said softly. "You can't, but thank you."

Parks straightened up.

"Will you let me try?" he asked.

"I can't."

"Why not? It wouldn't be the worst thing you've ever done. Don't you think I know that? The first night we spent together, you drugged me so you could have an alibi while you and Robinson took care of Davis and Webster."

"I didn't have anything to do with Davis."

"No?"

"Robinson did it. My job was Webster. I walked to his house. He was already dead drunk. I smothered him with a pillow."

"Just as they did Ellen's baby."

"Yes. Then Robinson set fire to the house."

"Why did you get me involved? Did you know I worked for the government?"

"No, I didn't know those kinds of things. At first I only wanted to cover myself so Sheriff Fischer wouldn't suspect me. He was too smart to believe that Davis's and Webster's deaths on the same night were just a coincidence. We— Robinson and I—intended to get Schaeffer later. Davis would never have killed Ellen's baby unless Schaeffer had told him to." She paused. "You seemed willing to help. I didn't know why. I didn't really care. I was just glad to have it. I wanted Schaeffer destroyed . . . dead."

"Well, now he is."

"I know," she said, flatly, as if the victory had been an empty one.

"Herman Rider wasn't your father, was he?" Parks asked.

She shook her head.

"Tell me," he asked.

"No. You don't need to know."

For the first time, Parks grew angry. "Don't need to know! I've had my tail kicked in, I've come two inches from having my head blown off, I've been lied to, I've been betrayed, but I don't need to know!"

Mary looked away. "I didn't do anything to you. I didn't ask you for anything."

"Mary, for God's sake, have some compassion. I *do* need to know. You can't just leave me like this!"

She stiffened. "All right. He was a doctor in the Lebensborn. He looked after us after we were taken from our village, from Rydz."

The color left her lips. "It was in the summer. The Germans came in the middle of the night. Two big SS men burst into our bedroom. I could hear my mother screaming, but then a Nazi hit her and knocked her to the floor and smashed his boot into her face."

Mary fell silent for a moment.

"They crammed us into an open trailer, like cattle. There were so many of us, I was pushed against the rail. Then, I saw my mother coming toward us. I called to her: 'Mama! Mama!' There was a shot, my mama fell to the ground . . . then the truck pulled away. . . ."

Parks reached out and touched her. "Mary . . ."

She shook her head, straightened up, and pulled herself together.

"No, let me finish. They took us to a children's camp near Auschwitz. They gave us soup with chemicals that swelled our stomachs and made us sick. If you cried, they would beat you.

"Herman Rider was the doctor that certified us as Aryans. He tried to adopt us, but they told him no. They told him he could raise us, but he couldn't adopt us. When we were older, they were going to give us shots to make us mature early, so we would bear children at twelve or thirteen. As soon as we could have children, they were going to mate us with pure Aryans. We would have three or four children, then disappear.

"That is why I have numbers on my neck . . . why Ellen . . . We were marked for the breeding farms.

"It was too much for Herman Rider and his wife. The horrors of the Nazis came home to them. He took us home with him that night and the four of us escaped from Poland."

Her face began to swell with pain, and she covered it with her hands. All that she had tried to forget, to cover and bury with a life filled with gray, was coming back to her, seeping back through her skin. Her stomach twisted and she breathed deep to fight back the rising nausea.

"He was a good man, Herman Rider," she finally said. "But I don't think I ever forgave him. At least I pitied him. The Nazis tracked him down and blackmailed him into starting the Home. From the day they found him, he was dead."

"Did you know Schaeffer's real name?" Parks asked.

"No," she said. "I never knew if his name was really Schaeffer or not, but he always frightened me. Sometimes when I looked at him, I would start to cry. There was something about his face . . . They tried to keep me away from him."

"His name was Axmann," Parks said. "Walter Axmann."

Mary closed her eyes. The breath went out of her. She started to shake. It was night again, in Rydz, and a voice was calling "Axmann! Axmann!" From the boxcar, she could hear her daddy, her sweet *tatuś*, shouting, but the crush of the other children in the boxcar kept her away from the door. Then the train pulled out for Kalisz.

There was silence for a moment, as the wind from Barnegat Bay flung itself against the windows.

"It didn't end with the death of Herman Rider, did it?" Parks asked. He could almost guess the rest.

"No, there was no end to it. Schaeffer was a cruel man. He tried to get my mother to work in the Home, but she couldn't take it. I agreed to take her place. Then, when I found out that Ellen was pregnant, I thought I had a perfect way out. Schaeffer had always wanted a child, so I offered him Ellen's baby in exchange for our peace."

"He agreed?" Parks asked.

"Without hesitation."

"Did you tell Ellen?"

"Not at first. I convinced her to go to the Home and give her child up for adoption. But when she got to the Home, she changed her mind and wanted to keep it." She paused and looked down. "I did tell her later . . . after she came home. I told her that I had made the offer, but the baby was born dead."

"What did she say?"

"She said I should have told her, that she would have agreed to it. She said that if one baby could have bought our freedom, and Andy's, she would have done it gladly."

"Did you believe her?"

"Yes. There wasn't much guile in her. But because I didn't tell anybody, everything failed."

"It wasn't your fault."

"Yes, it was. You see, I didn't know who the father was. Ellen wouldn't tell. You know why, of course. Robinson found out about the arrangement and tried to take the baby from the Home. Schaeffer had the baby killed out of spite."

"Robinson told you about it?" Parks asked.

"Yes. The night after Ellen washed up on the beach, after you brought me home. So you see, Ellen is dead, the baby is dead, Andy is dead. And I am dead."

"No, Mary. It's all over now. Now the living begins." She was silent, crying.

"Mary," Parks said, "come back with me to New York. . . . Marry me."

She hesitated. "I can't." Suddenly, her veins were all glass, and she felt as if she would break.

"Why not?" He tried to jest. "I'm not too old, I'm rich, in good health, and I don't snore, as you know. What more can you ask for?"

"John . . . please. I'm like the sand in that old shipwreck on the beach. I always wondered why I felt I belonged there. Now, I know. We are both barren. Underneath that sand lies an old sea captain who died with a bitter heart. I'm just going to die without one. It's in Poland. I know that now."

"No, Mary . . ."

"John, please listen to me. Do you think I didn't want to love someone? Someone who would give me . . ." She shook her head. "Please . . . don't make it so hard."

Parks buttoned his coat, pulled on his gloves, and walked to the door. At the door, he said: "Mary, if you have second thoughts, call me. I'm past the age for pride."

Before he pulled away, he turned to look at the old bay house once more. Mary was at the window. She was watching him go, her neck bowed in defeat.

As Parks turned onto the highway, he thought about the lives that had been crushed under the heel of Lebensborn. There was Faith Henderson, who, he hoped, in that other land, was together again with the man who loved Vachel Lindsay. There was Peter Fleming, who could stand against steel but not against shame. And, there were Ellen Rider, Andrew Robinson, Hilda Schaeffer, and Henry Stramm. But the most pathetic victim of all was Mary Rider, because she had been condemned to be dead among the living.

Long after the gates of the Nazi hell had closed, Lebensborn still devoured the children.

EPILOGUE

The United States government acted swiftly to extinguish the American roots of the Lebensborn movement. The State of New Jersey was ordered to take over the Valley Forge Maternal Care Home until it could find an appropriate sponsor, and to tighten up its adoption procedures. The Manhattan Medical Services Corporation was closed down until the Surgeon General could decide whether a bunch of frozen Nazi sperm cells could do anyone any harm. In the end, he decided they couldn't. The clinic was reopened under closer supervision, for, as the Surgeon General said, it did fulfill a certain need. The CIA, which was still not speaking to the FBI, took over the building in Villa Santiago, which was to have served as Lebensborn-South, completed it with Agency funds, and turned it into a Latin American command post.

In the spring of 1975 Charles Winston resigned as Director of the Eastern Region of the CIU and married Miss Messinger. They retired to Arizona where, three months later, Winston suffered a heart attack and died. John Parks kept his word and allowed Winston to carry his secret to his grave.

Robbie Davison was appointed Director of the Eastern Region without ever knowing of Winston's treason, and Magda Hemmings became his closest and most trusted advisor.

After much thought, John Parks filed his report on the Lebensborn investigation. He recommended no action against Victory as it was now nothing more than a harmless band of eccentrics after the purge of its Nazi stench. He did, however, recommend a further investigation of the

Lebensborn children. He urged the CIU to heed the lesson of OPEC, and take steps to block the cartels while they were still only a dream in the aging Germans' hearts. Parks pressed his belief that the cartels were possible and that it was not unreasonable that the next great war would be fought with economic charts and graphs rather than tanks and guns.

Parks's report was passed from the CIU Steering Committee to the Secretary of State. The Secretary of State was too busy to read it so he gave it to his Undersecretary of State for Latin American Affairs, who thought the report was ridiculous and had it shredded.

John Parks had been astute enough, however, to give Max Silverman a copy of his report. The old scholar was not as unimaginative as the State Department, and used and shared the information to hunt for the list which would unlock the Nazi treasury and put an end to *Der Tag* once and for all. The list has not been found, but the hunt continues—as do time and the Nazi fortunes.

In November, the high command of the Brotherhood assembled in the impoverished country of Paraguay for the annual conclave. It was spring in Paraguay, and the air was warm and dry. The long flat plains had been turned and planted with coffee, cotton, and *yerba mate*. The singsong chants of barefoot Indian peasants filled the air.

The meeting had been set at the Hotel Tyrol near the old German settlement of Hohenau in eastern Paraguay. It was safe there. Interpol had no authority in Paraguay, and President Alfredo Stroessner, the German brewer's son, made certain that Israeli secret agents would not pull another Eichmann.

One by one, the men arrived at the hotel, under the cover of night:

Martin Bormann, traveling under the name Adolf Brunner. He was seventy-five now, and completely bald. The skin hung in wrinkles around his neck and his shoulders had lost their powerful sway, but his small eyes were as shifty and hard as in the days when he covertly ruled the Third Reich.

Dr. Josef Mengele, traveling under the name José Schwartz, came from his protected home in the military zone of Puerto San Vincente on the Paraná River. He was

escorted by two members of Stroessner's goose-stepping
state police, for he was a hunted man, high on Simon
Wiesenthal's Wanted List. Mengele had been the head of
the "medical research" department at Auschwitz, where he
tried to produce blue-eyed Aryans from dark-eyed Jewish
and Gypsy children. Mengele had sent thousands of children to horrible deaths.

Klaus Barbie, traveling under the name of Señor Alt-
mann, came from his home in La Paz, Bolivia. As a
Gestapo chief in France, Barbie had tortured to death
some of France's great resistance fighters and had emptied
the orphanages of Lyons into the gas chambers. Tall and
thick, he was as arrogant as ever.

Eduard Roschmann, the "Butcher of Riga," traveling
under the name Fritz Wegener, came from his stately
mansion in Bariloche in the heart of the lake district of the
Andes. He was still tall and thin. His pale blond hair had
turned to yellowed gray, but his sadistic blue eyes were as
cold and unrelenting as during the years when he worked
so tirelessly to make Latvia *Judenrein.*

Rolf Günther, Eichmann's first deputy in Bureau ivA, 4b,
came from Buenos Aires. Dull and single-minded, he had
helped carry out the Final Solution with the dedicated,
plodding attention that a lowly clerk gives to a column of
numbers. Günther would replace Walter Axmann as Secretary of the Brotherhood.

Alfons Sassen, still hiding from a death sentence handed
down by the Dutch courts, came from his estate in Ecua-
dor. He was the Treasurer of the Brotherhood, and the
head of Odessa's sprawling business enterprises that were
set in motion at the Strasbourg Conference.

It was a bright, clear night. The old white stucco hotel
glistened in the moonlight. A rumba band played gaily in
the dining hall. The lobby and grounds around the hotel
had been secured by Odessa agents against any intrusion.
The men took the gilt lobby elevator to the penthouse
suite, which was guarded by strong, fair-haired young men
with walkie-talkies to provide ground contact.

Bormann called the meeting to order with a rap of his
knuckles against the table. The men had long ago dispensed
with the salute of "Heil Hitler."

"As you know, our American Lebensborn operations

are at an end," Bormann said. "They have been dismantled. Herr Axmann is missing and must be presumed dead. There will be no more children."

"I was to have a son," Klaus Barbie said.

"There will be no more children," Bormann repeated firmly. He was still not to be crossed, not even by Klaus Barbie, the "Hangman of Lyons."

Barbie put his face in his hands. He took a deep breath, rubbed his eyes, and said, "Excuse me, Herr Bormann. There is so much dust in the air in November. It affects my eyes."

There was a long silence in the room. Suddenly, the men felt the press of time. Eichmann and Axmann were dead. Franz Stangl had been extradited and was dying in prison. Roschmann was sick most of the time with a hacking cough. Someone said Skorzeny had cancer.

Finally, Mengele said: "Is there nothing we can do about it?"

"Nothing," Bormann said. "We will have to go with what we have."

"We have enough," Roschmann said, suppressing a cough. "We have all agreed that the eighties are our last chance to act. That much has not changed. Let us get on with it."

With that, the men set to work to lay the foundation for the great business trusts that would allow National Socialism and its loyal deputies to rise from the ashes.

AUTHOR'S NOTE

While this book is a work of fiction and the events described in it are imaginary, and the characters (with the exception of persons of historical note referred to by their true names) are also imaginary and not intended to represent or resemble any specific living person, there is nevertheless a great deal of historically true information contained herein. The Lebensborn Society was a real department of the SS, and its atrocities, just now being brought to light, are well documented in *Of Pure Blood* by Marc Hillel and Clarissa Henry (McGraw-Hill, 1977).

Simon Wiesenthal, a great and dedicated man, has devoted his life to tracking down Nazi war criminals, often with striking success. His research uncovered the details of the Strasbourg Conference and the reader is referred to his memoirs, *The Murderers Among Us* (Bantam, 1973), edited by Joseph Wechsberg, not only for details about the Strasbourg Conference and the notorious Nazi organization Odessa, but for the details of the life of a most unusual man.

For those who doubt the single-minded preparation of Martin Bormann and other high-ranking Nazis for leaving a sinking ship long before the fall of Germany, or the vast fortune now under the control of fugitive Nazis around the world, the reader is referred to *The Bormann Brotherhood* by William Stevenson (Harcourt Brace Jovanovich, 1973).

Sometimes fact is more terrible than fiction and less believable. Certainly it is always harder to understand.

Dell Bestsellers